STRANGE LOVE

REMASTERED TALES

CARA McKENNA

Second Edition

Ruin Me, Dirty Thirty, Brazen, and *Ready and Willing* originally published 2010; *Don't Call Her Angel* originally published 2011

Edited by Jaynie Ritchie, Kelli Collins and Jana Armstrong

Cover design by Cara McKenna

ISBN 978-0-9977834-9-0

RUIN ME

CHAPTER ONE

WHEN JAY PROPOSED, I immediately began to cry.

And these weren't tears of joy, mind you. These were frustrated tears because I really, really wanted to toss my arms around his neck and say yes, but I couldn't.

I bet Jay wasn't surprised. I bet if I *had* tossed my arms joyously around his neck and screamed my affirmation the euphoria would've lasted a day or a week, but soon enough the giant asterisk that hovers above our relationship would've popped the happy bubble.

I'll say right off that the problem isn't Jay. Jay is awesome. He's my age—thirty-three—and he's funny and smart and patient and I'm definitely attracted to him. My name is Robin. Jay and Robin. I mean, that's so obnoxious it just has to be right.

Jay's the only guy I've ever suspected I might want a child with, which is huge, since I'd always assumed I'd take a pass on that. He'd be a great dad. A stay-at-home dad, since he works out of our little house, writing reviews and articles about techie stuff. I like that he gets free smart phones and gaming systems before they're released and he plays with them for a few days and types up his verdict in his hilarious, trademark style. I like it even more that as soon as the clock hits five thirty he tosses aside whatever toy he's playing with and starts dinner. I like that he runs or swims every morning and that there's one of those Bowflex contraptions in his office, and he actually uses it, three days a week. He doesn't look *quite* like one of the guys from the ads, but he's not far off. For a guy you might run into at the drugstore in our little town in Vermont, he's a total babe.

What I'm saying is, I love Jay. The trouble isn't him, so process of elimination points a big fat finger at me. I'm not afraid of commitment and I sowed my wild oats enough to know if I'm missing out on anything, and I'm not. Jay's even better at sex than he is at fixing things, and that's saying a lot.

When Jay proposed, he didn't get down on one knee. We were sitting on the couch watching *Dumb and Dumber*, which is what we watched on our very first date four years ago. We watch it every six months or so because Jay can't get enough of how I start convulsing when Jeff Daniels whacks Jim Carrey in the back of the knees with a walking stick. This time when I caught my breath again and opened my streaming eyes, I found Jay turned toward me, holding a little polished wood box. I stared at it for a while and when he opened it, I started crying for real. Eventually he closed it and I'm pretty sure I ruined that movie for us forever.

The way Jay puts it, our problem is "that asshole".

Personally, I don't think the guy's an asshole. I can't, because he may have saved my life. I call our problem "the Patrick issue". Patrick is the name you'd see typed in fine print next to that hovering asterisk I mentioned earlier.

Yesterday, the day after Jay proposed, he made us breakfast as usual before I left to go to work. We've always been good at keeping our disagreements out in the open and not stewing over things, but we hadn't talked about the proposal since it happened. Twelve hours is about our limit, elephant-in-the-room-wise, and Jay cracked first.

"You want to talk about what happened?" he asked, buttering toast.

I shrugged.

He put the knife down and made an exasperated noise. "You showed me which ring to get."

"I know."

"Is this ever going to go away?" he asked. "I mean, are you *ever* going to be able to say yes to me?"

I pushed my chair out from the dining room table and walked over and squeezed him. He smelled nice, like always. I wondered what was wrong with me that this wonderful man wasn't enough.

"I want to say yes," I mumbled into his shoulder.

"We've got to figure this out soon."

"It's my problem," I said.

I felt him stroke my hair, heard him swallow. "Maybe we should move," he said. "So we just don't run into him anymore."

I pulled away. "I don't want to move. I love this town. And my store and our neighbors. We'll never find another neighborhood in this country and this century where people still drop by to borrow things. I like lending things to people."

Jay shook his head. "I can't keep going like this." He looked older in an instant, his hazel eyes framed by fine lines, those half dozen gray sideburn hairs stark against their brown cohorts. "If you won't move," he said, "then I don't know what else there is we can do. Except, maybe…"

I gave him a puzzled look because I sure as hell had no clue what else we could do.

"Maybe you should… Maybe," he said again through a huge sigh, "you should just go ahead and sleep with him."

I felt my face go numb and I snaked my arms across my chest, as if I were naked and trying to hide my breasts. "No way."

"We both know you want to."

I shook my head. "I don't *want* to want to though."

It's no secret I'm attracted to Patrick Whelan.

It goes beyond a lack of girlfriendly diplomacy to what I can only describe as an allergic sexual reaction. I can't control or conceal it. When I see him, I start sweating, my whole body starts buzzing and I can't *not* look at him.

For the first few years I thought I was having flashbacks—panic reactions to the memory of the guy who held a knife to my throat in the parking lot of Dereham, Vermont's only bar, before Patrick Whelan spotted us and kicked the living shit out of him.

That was the only time I've ever touched Patrick. I'd been shaking uncontrollably and before anyone even called the police about the man still lying on the asphalt, twitching and bleeding from his mouth and scalp, Patrick held me. He pulled me down to sit beside him on the hood of my old Saab, and he wrapped his big arms around me and rocked me until I could breathe properly again. Then he told me to go inside and phone the cops.

Twenty minutes later Patrick and I got taken to the station to file a report, and the man who attacked me was taken to the emergency room. He spent a couple nights in the hospital and was released without charges in time to get back to Dartmouth for Monday classes.

Seven months after that, Patrick got released from prison, where he served an aggravated assault sentence for having the misfortune of beating the holy hell out of the sheriff's step-nephew.

This happened more than a year before I met Jay, but despite Patrick and me both being single and becoming friends when I drove up and visited him in prison once a week, we never got together. After he was released, when we'd run into each other at the diner or the bar or a store, we'd just wave politely. I'd work hard to hide the somersaults my stomach was doing, the ones I thought for ages were some kind of PTSD from the attack. It took me a long time to admit I just plain wanted to fuck Patrick's brains out.

"I can't sleep with him," I said to Jay, then bit my lip. "I love *you*. Plus I really like the idea of monogamy."

"We'll never move forward if this doesn't get resolved. I can live through you sleeping with another man, Robin."

I blinked a few times, feeling slapped. "Can you?"

"Well, I'm pretty fucking sure it'll suck worse than anything I've ever gone through, but…I know you'd never do it behind my back. You don't want to hurt me."

I shook my head vigorously.

"I want to be with you and that might just be a price I'm willing to pay to get us there," Jay said.

I was crying again and the sobs blended into tiny laughs. "Sometimes I can't figure out if you're the most rational person I've ever met or a complete sociopath."

He smiled and hugged me and sent me back to the table with some toast and scrambled eggs.

"Well, I'm *your* sociopath. Think about it for a few days. I don't want to go anywhere, but you need to figure out a way to move forward. So *we* can move forward."

He said that yesterday, and when I kissed him goodbye to head out to open my shop, I thought it was the worst idea ever. Now…

Now I'm not so sure.

CHAPTER TWO

I KNOW WHERE PATRICK WHELAN LIVES. Everybody in our little town knows where everybody else lives and for how long and with whom.

Patrick lives alone toward the end of a long dirt road that winds into the woods, just on our side of the town line between Dereham and Riverdale. I've never been to his house but I find it easily.

There's a bank of mailboxes at the foot of the road and the one labeled fourteen says Whelan on the side. I take a right at the long, anonymous drive just after the one marked twelve, my old navy hatchback bucking in the dry potholes.

My heart starts to hammer when I spot Patrick's ancient pickup in the driveway. It's Sunday morning and I wish I were religious so I could remember I'm supposed to be at church like a good person and get the hell out of here. Instead I park my car behind his truck and slam the door as loud as I can—a warning. I trot up a path of slate flagstones to the door of his small red house and I push the bell, contorting my face into an imitation of casual cool.

But Patrick doesn't come to the door. He appears around the side of the house with an axe in one gloved hand. This deviates from my script and I falter.

"Hi!" I call, way too perky, and wave like a moron.

"Robin."

Goddamn, he's so tall. I always manage to make him shorter in my mind's eye. He doesn't smile but that's not surprising. Patrick Whelan's not a smiley guy.

"Can I interest you in the word of Our Lord, Jesus Christ?" I ask and grin.

He grins back, cautious. That's what I always used to say to him when I'd sit down at the table in the correctional facility's visiting room. It freaked him out the first time but broke the ice once he realized I was kidding. Then it became our greeting. This is the first time I've said it since he got released, over five years ago now.

He leans his axe against the side of the house and crosses his arms over his chest. I should mention Patrick's an honest-to-God lumberjack. That's probably not his actual job title, but he spends four months of the year in northern New Hampshire, logging. It must pay well because it's exceedingly dangerous. The rest of the year he works at a lumberyard here in Dereham. I think he does some contract carpentry too, because every once in a while I'll see his truck in some random driveway, its bed full of two-by-fours. A couple times I've been tempted to call him up to do some carpentry for me, but I can never think up a project. Not one that Jay couldn't probably do a decent job of, anyway. God, there's a metaphor if I ever heard one.

"Can I help you with something, Robin?"

"Maybe." Being close to him makes me shake, as always. "Can I talk to you for a few minutes?"

He thinks a second and nods. "You talk, I chop," he says and grabs his axe and heads around the house again.

I follow, watching his ass. You would too, if you were here.

There's a mountain of firewood at the edge of his backyard. He must have just had a couple cords delivered.

"Don't mind me," he says and starts splitting logs at a stump. "You just do your talking."

I don't want to launch into the meat of the matter right off, not after we haven't had a real conversation in half a decade. I toy with the fringe at the end of my scarf. "How have you been?"

"All right." His brown eyes meet mine. He's got several days' worth of stubble and is a couple months overdue for a haircut. I want to run my palms over his face and neck and devour him.

I clear my throat and point to the wood. "Why do you do this by hand?"

"Relaxes me." He splits a log down the middle with a whack then adds another to the stump. It's so unselfconsciously manly I have to stifle an urge to tear my clothes off and tackle him.

Instead I ask, "How's your mom?"

He shrugs. "'Bout the same."

Despite all those visits, I don't know a ton about Patrick, but I know his mom lives a few towns away and she's some kind of compulsive hoarder. I think about Patrick whenever I see a show about people with that problem. I know he worries about her and that she drives him up the wall. Or she would, if you could get to her walls through all the stacks of moldy old catalogs and magazines Patrick said she's got herself barricaded behind.

"I don't suppose you could invite me in for a coffee?" I ask. "It's not really a wood-chopping conversation I've come here to have with you."

He thwacks the blade into the stump and mops his brow. Snow starts to drift down, the first of the season. The flakes linger in his dark hair for a second before dissolving. He nods and I follow him to the side door.

His house is small and as soon as I step inside I'm struck by how cool it is. He's got tons of recessed shelving built into the walls and a handsome granite counter running along one side of his kitchen. Everything feels Spartan and organized—a poorly veiled filial rebellion.

We don't talk and soon a kettle's whistling. He puts grounds into a little metal basket and steeps me a cup of coffee.

"Milk?" he asks.

"Please. And sugar if you have it."

He hands me the mug, royal blue with the logo of his lumber company. I take a sip even though it's way too hot and pretend it doesn't hurt, and he sits down opposite me at his scrubbed pine table, looking patient. He's got way more grays than Jay, mostly in his temples and his not-quite-a-beard. I think he turned thirty-eight or -nine last January.

"So," I finally begin. "I want to apologize in advance, about this. It's really weird, what I have to say. You're going to think I'm crazy."

His gaze darts around the kitchen—scouting for escape routes, I suspect—then settles back on my face. "Okay."

"I, um… I was wondering if maybe, sometime…if I might possibly…kiss you," I mumble. "Maybe not just kiss. Maybe more. I'm not sure. And not today, just sometime."

His mouth twitches behind his stubble. His dark eyes widen, which is a strange look for him because normally they're sort of squinty. He's got hooded eyes, I think they're called. They make him look a bit Slavic, like a moody Russian exile from Romanov times, with an Irish name. I realize I'm staring when I should be elucidating.

"So that's why I'm here," I say lamely.

Patrick clears his throat. "No offense, if you're a feminist or whatever, but aren't you Jay Fleury's woman?"

I nod. "Yeah."

"He seems like a good man," Patrick says, cautious and clearly confused.

I nod again. "He's wonderful."

His fingers wrestle with themselves, as though he wishes he had a mug, too, to keep them busy. "Well, I'll be honest with you. Even if he was a world-class shit, I wouldn't ever mess with another man's woman."

"It was his idea," I say and watch Patrick's hands go perfectly still.

"That sounds a bit fucked up. No offense, Robin."

"It's a lot simpler than I'm making it seem," I say, wondering if it might not be the opposite. "Would you consider it? It's important. To him. To both of us."

"Why do you need to…do whatever you need to? With me?"

I think I catch his ears go a bit pink then wonder if they've been like that all along from the cold.

"I have some feelings for you, and they won't go away," I say. "I don't think I can move on with Jay until I—" I pause, dogged by my own flagrant selfishness. "Oh my God, I'm sorry. This is the most psychotic thing I've ever done. I can't believe I came here and said this to you. I'm so sorry."

I get up and abandon my still-steaming coffee on the cutting board by the sink, stuff my arms into my coat sleeves and head toward the door. I hear Patrick's chair scrape behind me.

"Don't just dump that on me and run off," he says.

I stop. I turn and look at him and my face must be as red as my scarf.

"It sounds really horrible when I say it out loud." I look at his feet. "Like I'm propositioning you. And I guess I am."

"I gotta say, I don't get it."

"Me neither," I say and I laugh, wanting to die.

"I'll think about it."

His words knock the sense clear out of my brain. I blink a few times. "Will you?"

He nods. "Send your man over this afternoon. I want to hear him explain it."

"But you'd…you'd think about it? You'd be okay with kissing me, or more?" I blush so hard I feel sunburned.

"I'm not okay with anything 'til I talk to him," Patrick says, walking over. "You tell him two o'clock." He pulls the door open for me. "Drive safe now."

* * *

IT'S A QUARTER AFTER FIVE.

When Jay left to go to Patrick's three hours ago, he'd looked pale and understandably freaked out. I don't know what I'd have felt if I was him—how I'd feel toward Patrick Whelan. I'd be scared, I bet, because Jay is a slender five-foot-eleven and Patrick's probably four or five inches taller and he's pretty jacked, if his arms are any indication. There's no reason Patrick should have a beef with Jay but that's bound to be intimidating.

I'd also be super pissed, I think, because if I was Jay I'd have been on my way to talk to the man my long-term girlfriend—who I'm super-awesome to—admits to being obsessed with.

Obsessed in a joyless kind of way, I should add. I don't like having feelings for Patrick. I never think about him when I'm having sex with Jay…at least I never mean to. Sometimes I slip up but I'm always careful to come staring right into Jay's eyes if we're face-to-face. Sometimes my brain gets itself in trouble if he's taking me from behind.

You can probably tell that I fret a lot. It's one of my dearest hobbies, one that drove my dad nuts while I was growing up. I wish I could call him now and ask his artless, sage advice. He makes everything sound so obvious. If I could somehow explain my problem without creeping both of us out, he'd probably say, "So, Jay's upset because you want to bang this lumberjack guy? Well, of course he is. Haven't you ever heard of monogamy? Christ, Robin, it's not rocket science."

I jump when I hear the car door slam in the driveway. I run downstairs to the living room like a puppy and watch through the picture window as Jay walks up the side steps. He does a little dance, a shuffly mashed-potato dance on the doormat, cleaning off his shoes before he comes in. It seems obscenely normal in light of what's going on.

"So?" I ask, nearly falling as I slide across the kitchen floor in my socks.

He kicks his sneakers off and tosses them in the bin by the closet, just like normal. When he looks at me, I can't read him. He holds his hands up, showing me a pair of red, blistered palms. I notice little bits of wood stuck to his hat.

"Oh my God, he made you chop wood with him? For how long?"

"Three. Fucking. Hours."

"He didn't give you gloves?"

"This *is* with gloves. Look." Jay raises his arms up like a zombie, not quite to the shoulder. "That's as far as they'll go, now."

"Yikes."

"Can you take my hat off for me?"

I do and he walks to the table and slumps into a seat, looking wrecked. I sit across from him and clasp my hands, pretending to be patient, dying of curiosity.

"So what happened?"

"I tried to explain it to him, and I think I made as much sense as I could've hoped to."

"What did he say?"

Jay purses his lips. "He said he likes you. That way. He said he's always liked you."

"Really?" My heart doesn't flutter, I promise you. It sinks straight down into my feet.

He nods. "But he never thought you felt that way about him. Because you always seemed to avoid him, after he was released. And, he said, because every time he runs into you, you always look worried he might headbutt you or something."

"Oh." That was never my fear. As threatening as Patrick Whelan arguably looks, I've always been more afraid of what *I'm* capable of when I'm within ten feet of him.

"I think he's like half in love with you, Robin."

"Do you think that'll make things more complicated?"

"Probably." Jay sighs and finally makes solid eye contact. "But I think he'll do it. Are you... Do you think you're in love with him?" There's a cold fear hiding behind those words.

I shake my head. "I don't really know him that well. It's just sexual. Or whatever primal kind of thing you feel when somebody rescues you. I love *you*," I add emphatically. "And whatever I feel about him, it's nothing like that. Like us."

He nods, solemn but steady. "Well, if I had to guess, I think he'll do it."

I marvel that we can even be having a calm discussion like this.

"Although he kept squinting at me, like I was trying to trick him or something," Jay says.

I smile to cut the tension. "Do you still think he's an asshole?"

He sighs again, so theatrical I assume it's a joke. "Jury's still out... I guess he's okay. He gave us some wood," he adds. "But I don't think I'll be able to get it out of the car for a few days. I could barely turn the key in the ignition."

I stand and give Jay's shoulder a squeeze.

"Ow."

"Sorry." I pat his head instead. "Go find some football to watch or something. I'll bring you a beer and start dinner."

CHAPTER THREE

THREE DAYS LATER I'm meeting Patrick at the bar. I dropped by his house again on Monday evening to ask if he'd like to come out for a drink this week and see what happens, or to talk more. He said sure, and now I'm sitting in one of the booths by the window, just before eight o'clock, eyes on the parking lot, heart jack-hammering my ribs. I'm afraid he won't show and even more afraid he will.

I wasn't sure what to wear. Jay was around when I was changing and I hope he noticed me putting on my crappiest underwear, so he'll know I'm not planning on going hog-wild tonight.

I'm trying really hard not to appear too eager. Actually, I think I'm overdoing it a bit, acting as if this whole situation pains me greatly. If there's a tightrope for people walking the line between "selfish harlot" and "dewy-eyed martyr", it's *very* narrow, and the chasm is so deep I couldn't tell you if there's a net or not.

Jay's gone from disbelief to acceptance in the past few days and is now treating the whole thing like a project. He bought a copy of this book called *The Myth of Monogamy* and seems to be tackling the situation sociologically. Typical, rational Jay. Pragmatism is his Prozac.

From my seat in the booth I can almost see the spot where I got threatened at knifepoint back when I was twenty-seven. Our town is small and the Tap is its only bar. I decided I liked beer enough to get over my bad memories a long time ago.

I hear a door slam out in the dark and then Patrick Whelan's walking toward the entrance. I look away. I don't want him to see me watching if he glances at the window, which is so stupid.

He spots me when he enters and heads right to the booth and sits down across from me, looking tall and solid.

"Hey, Robin."

"Hey." I glance around, feeling as if everyone must know exactly why we're here.

"You have a good day?" he asks, chattier than I've ever seen him. I realize he must be as terrified as me and I relax.

"It was all right," I lie. I was useless and jumpy at work all day, counting down the seconds to this very moment. "Can I get you a beer?"

"Sure." He taps my plastic pint glass. "What's that?"

"Sam."

He pulls out a battered old leather wallet and hands me a twenty. "Get us a pitcher. We'll probably need it."

I laugh, relieved beyond words. He smiles at me. I haven't seen him smile like that in years—not since our visits.

I deliver our pitcher and Patrick's change. We say cheers and clack our glasses together.

"So," I say. "Jay can almost lift his arms again. After all that chopping."

He nods. "I didn't think he'd keep going for that long."

"Why'd you make him chop wood?" I ask.

"I figured it might get his aggression out so he wouldn't snap and try to kill me."

I laugh. "So you gave him an axe?"

"I'm not really an expert about stuff like this."

I nod and smile and look down into my beer, turn the glass around and around on its coaster. *More Than a Feeling* comes on the jukebox and I tap my fingers along to it. "So. Jay said you said you feel…something? For me?"

He nods, casual, as if I'd asked if he's ever been to Montreal.

I take a deep drink. "I don't really know what I'm after," I admit and meet his eyes.

"He said you guys are happy. But you…"

"I'm obsessed with you," I offer, voice low and private. "Or my body is."

I catch his eyebrows contract. "Because of what happened?"

"Maybe. Probably." I didn't know Patrick before the attack but I'd seen him around town. He never really made an impression before that night. I touch my neck, the spot where my slim cut faded into nothingness years ago.

Patrick watches my fingers. "And you think if we, if you and me, do something…then you'll get over it?"

"That's the idea. I don't know if it would work or make things worse, to be honest."

"I don't want to be responsible for breaking up anybody's home," he says. "I'm here because your man said maybe it would help you guys. And because I like you. Not just *like* you, I mean. Because I'm attracted to you." He huffs out a breath, looking as if he just spoke fluent Esperanto and blew his own mind.

Seeing Patrick this way—sitting across the table from me looking so lost—reminds me of visiting hours. I do something I'd always wanted to do then but wasn't allowed to. I reach out and put my hand on his wrist and smile at him.

He stares at my fingers for a moment then pulls his arm back and covers my hand in his big one. Then he seems to remember where we are and takes it away, eyes darting toward the bar.

"Jay said he thinks maybe you…like me. A lot," I say.

He nods, giving me nothing to work with.

"I'm a little worried I might end up jerking you around. God, that sounds really egomaniacal. Plus I'm probably jerking you around already."

Patrick shrugs. "I think you both did your best to explain it. I know the score." He takes a couple swallows of his beer. "Look," he says. "We can talk this to death for the next five hours, or I can lay it out for you."

"Okay."

"I like you," he says, eyes watching his fingers drumming the tabletop. "As a person. And I'd genuinely like to see your relationship work out." He clears his throat and continues, quieter. "But I'd also like to sleep with you, or however far you want to take it. I also think this idea's nuts and I wouldn't be surprised if it wrecks things with you and your man and I wind up in the middle of it."

"Oh."

"But I also think that you and me, we're not close or anything. Not for a long while. No offense, but there's not a ton at stake here. You know, friendship-wise? There's not a lot at stake for *me*. So sure, I'll go along with whatever you guys agree on."

"Wow, okay. Thanks. That actually made everything seem a lot clearer."

"But listen." He rubs a palm over his eyes. "I don't want this to end up like *Springer*. I don't want your man calling me or showing up at my house with a shotgun or hassling me at work or any of that. Or worse, taking it out on you. If you think he might get that way, do everybody a favor and call it off now."

"I follow. I don't think any of that will happen. He's known I have feelings for you for four years. Since before I even knew what they were all about. He knows it's just part of the package with me. And he's not a jealous guy."

"Yeah, I guess not... This whole letting-you-be-with-another-guy thing," Patrick says. "Would you do the same for him?"

I grin, guilty. "Not in a million years."

He nods. "Anyhow, that's all I've got to say about it. Count me in."

"Wow. Just like that?"

He smiles. "Just like that."

I feel my body relax. I realize I've been hunched forward, shoulders tight, elbows on the table, and now I lean back into the booth's vinyl padding and push out a long breath. I stare at Patrick, like *really stare*, because I feel like I finally can, now that everyone knows where everyone stands. I move my foot under the table and press my ankle against his. He presses back. It's just legs, not even the sexy parts of legs, but I feel energy, electricity zapping through two pairs of jeans and shooting right up my bones into my hair and fingernails. I lose my mind a little. Patrick sips his beer, looking dutifully neutral, scanning the activity around the bar.

Moondance comes on. I push my shoe off and run my stocking foot up the inside of Patrick's leg. His eyes glaze over. I'm not trying to tease or torture him. I just want to turn him on, plain and simple. I want proof that he wants me back and that I have the power and also the permission to fuck with our boundaries, shamelessly. I rub the ball of my foot up the inseam along his big thigh, stopping an inch or two from where I guess his crotch is.

He clears his throat and refills his glass.

"So," I say, foot still nestled between his legs. "Are you free later this week at all? Maybe you could invite me over for dinner."

"I'm a pretty lousy cook."

"Well, I'll bring something then."

He nods. "Okay."

"Friday? Seven?"

"Sure."

I smile. Friday is perfect. Firstly because I don't think I can wait more than two days, and secondly because I don't want this ridiculousness to eat into my weekend time with Jay. I feel as though it's something I should be fitting in, like a doctor's appointment.

We sit, sipping our beer, listening to Van Morrison, not saying anything. I study Patrick, and he seems to study me back. I take my foot away as we drain our glasses.

"Well, I better get home soon," I say finally.

"You good to drive?"

I nod. "Walk me to my car?"

"I can't stand up yet," Patrick says. "Why don't you go use the ladies' or something and let me cool off?"

I have to bite my lip to keep from grinning, so outrageously pleased that I've managed to arouse this man.

I take our empty glasses and pitcher and leave them on the bar on my way to the bathroom.

Patrick's standing beneath the keno monitor when I emerge and I stare at the numbers to keep my eyes from drifting to his crotch. He pulls the door open and follows me out into the parking lot. I walk to my car and hear him behind me.

I turn and smile up at him. "Thanks for meeting me tonight."

He nods. He looks around us, maybe avoiding my eyes, maybe on the alert for knife-wielding Dartmouth poli-sci majors.

"Can I kiss you good-night?" I ask, more nervous than I've been around the opposite sex since eighth grade.

"Sure. Maybe we should go behind my truck though." He nods to where he's parked, farther from potential prying eyes.

I put my hand in his and it's warm and big. He leads me to the edge of the lot and we stand behind his cab, mostly hidden. The parking lot's got a streetlight at every corner—it didn't used to, trust me—and I stare at Patrick in the pinky-orange glow and watch the steam of his breath form and disappear in the cold breeze. I watch his lips.

"You're sure about this?" he asks.

I nod, still focused on his mouth.

When he leans in and kisses me... Shit, I don't know. People talk about melting and that's how it feels, honest to God. My bones go soft and my body warms and if I wasn't held in place between a truck and a solid wall of man, I bet I'd fall over.

I feel those big, rough palms on my jaw and he angles his head and kisses me deep, filling me with his tongue and his heat and his noises. And he can *kiss*. My hands flap around, unsure of where to go until I settle them flat against his chest on his black fleece jacket. I feel and hear him groan when I kiss back and it triggers something in me. I pull his zipper down and run my palms over his work shirt, so tempted to rip it open and scatter his buttons all over the asphalt.

He tastes like beer and impatience. His fingers tangle in my hair, hands covering my ears so it sounds as if we're underwater. I stand on my tiptoes and press myself against him and he's warm and sturdy and goddamn if he's not hard for me.

I slide a palm down between us, pausing at his belt, needing some natural disaster to stop me from groping him.

Instead there's a flare of music as someone exits the bar. We both freeze then pull away as an engine starts a few cars down. Patrick releases my head and pushes me back a pace by the shoulders before cramming his hands in his pockets. I meet his eyes and they look as wild as I feel. I move away a little more and the car swings out, washing us in its headlight beams.

I clear my throat. "Friday at seven?"

He nods. He puts his hand on my back between my shoulder blades and steers me to my car. He watches me climb inside. He waves at me as I reverse and I wave back.

I wonder if sexual frustration exacerbates blood-alcohol level. It sure feels that way. If I get pulled over on the short drive between here and my house I'll have to say, "I only had two beers in two hours, officer, but then I made out with a lumberjack. You know how it is."

I don't get pulled over, though, and after a minute or two I feel perfectly sober if a bit suddenly exhausted.

One thing that both surprises and relieves me when I get home is how I feel about Jay. There he is, sitting on the couch with a copy of *Wired* on a pillow in his lap, TV tuned to a basketball game. And I'm attracted to him, just like always.

Nothing about it feels diminished. Not cheapened, not weaker compared to what I felt with Patrick. It feels the same, except now there's a deep vein of gratitude running through it.

He stands and I dump my coat and bag and walk over and hug him—hard. He's wearing my favorite sweater of his, soft merino wool that smells musty in the best way.

He strokes my hair. "How did it go?"

I sigh and sit back on the cushions and he mutes the television.

"It went pretty well."

"Did anything happen?"

I nod. "Not a lot. Do you want to hear about it, or should I just keep it to myself?"

"No, I want to know," Jay says. "This is part of our sex life, I think. I want to feel like there's a place in it for me."

I feel my brows rise; impressed or skeptical, I'm not sure which. Sometimes his reasoning is like magic to me.

"Okay," I say. "Well, we split a pitcher and sort of flirted and then I kissed him. In the parking lot. We made out. It was pretty nice," I admit, and smile, sheepish.

He nods. "How do you feel now?"

"I feel calmer. And satisfied."

"Do you think that's all you needed?"

I look around the living room with an ugly, selfish pang of anger. I hate the feeling and I tramp it down. I don't have any right to feel as though Jay's out to spoil my fun.

"I couldn't tell you yet," I say. "But right now I feel pretty…sated." That word sounds stupid in my ears, as if it was never meant to be used in conversation.

Jay pats my knee, looking thoughtful. "Okay."

"How do you feel?"

"I feel all right," he says. "It was hard, when you were gone. Not knowing what was happening. But I lived through it and that feels all right."

I laugh, a goofy, dorky laugh. "You are so level-headed it, like, breaks my brain."

"I'm trying, anyhow."

"We decided to meet up on Friday," I say, plunging onward. "Is that cool?"

Jay blinks and nods and his face is impossible to read. It kills me that the thing I want so badly is hurting him. Not enough to give it up, though, I hear you saying.

"We should set some ground rules," I offer. "Or you should. About what you're comfortable with happening."

"Everything but," he says, clearly having given this some thought already. "Just not sex. Intercourse, I mean. I want that to be for us, only."

"Fine with me." As if I'm in a position to be anything aside from grateful.

He nods, relieved, I think. Then his brows bunch and a breath sputters through his lips.

"What?"

"This is going to sound really weird," he says.

I laugh. "The bar's been set pretty high lately, but go on, what's weird?"

"When you were gone, and I was trying not to think about what you were doing…"

"Yeah?"

"It sort of…"

Made you die a little inside? Made you go shopping for guns online? Made you hate me, since it probably should?

"It sort of turned my crank," Jay says.

"Oh." My mouth freezes in its little round shape.

He laughs, instantly relaxed. "Yeah, it kind of turned me on."

"Wow. I wasn't expecting that."

"Me neither," he says.

"What about it?"

"I dunno… The idea of you with some other guy. Some guy wanting you and having to come to me to get permission."

"Well, that's a zillion times better than you feeling left out or insecure," I say.

"Yeah. I bet that makes me some kind of Neanderthal pimp-wannabe sexist man-pig."

"Beats cuckold," I offer.

"Yeah."

We sit for a while not saying anything, contemplating Jay's revelation as we watch the Pistons play the Clippers with no sound.

I finally turn to him. "Do you want to have sex?"

"God, yeah."

I grin. I'd been worried about that, afraid the next time we'd have sex it'd be a disaster, Jay understandably paranoid that I wasn't thinking about him.

He tosses aside his magazine and pillow and pulls me onto his lap. I straddle him and we kiss, hard and ferocious. His hands cup my ass, tugging me close and I lock my thighs around his hips, feeling his excitement. I peel my sweater and shirt off, feel his hands on my breasts, squeezing and kneading. I unhook my bra and he wrestles it away, mouth hungry.

"Jay."

His hips pump, stroking his arousal against mine. I can feel in his touch that he wants to be in charge. He gets this way sometimes and it's fine by me. I like when he's all possessive and rough. It usually means I'm naked and he's dressed, as if I'm the vulnerable one being taken advantage of.

"Get your clothes off," he mutters against my neck.

I slide off his lap and drop my pants and my strategically homeliest underwear, and kick them away. He's got his pajama bottoms on so he just pushes them down to free his erection and he strokes himself, studying me. I wait for permission, eyes on his hand.

He nods, slow and thoughtful, approving. "Fuck me."

I straddle him again, running my lips up and down his cock a few times.

"Yeah." His hands guide my hips, making the thrusts aggressive.

"I want it," I say.

"What do you want?"

"Your cock." I stare him dead in the eyes. I love when he looks this way, all flushed and mean. His lips are parted and his hazel eyes look green tonight and a little crazy. Horny Jay is worlds different from regular Jay. He's like a secret only I get to enjoy. I know—my hypocrisy is staggering.

I angle my hips back as he reaches down and guides his head to my pussy. I sink down, slow, and his moan is harsh, giving me a happy chill.

His hands clamp to my waist. "God, fuck me."

There's no one in my mind except Jay. I'm short and he's fairly tall and I love how big he feels when I'm in his lap getting ordered around. I find my angles, giving him long pulls, ones that rub his shaft against my clit as I ride him.

"That's right. Nice and rough." He pretends this is all about him, but I know better.

I fuck him, hard and steady, hands on the back of the couch, smelling that wool sweater smell, that Jay smell, loving everything familiar and wonderful about this. He wants this to be about power so I keep my romantic feelings to myself.

"Good," he says. He always knows when I'm close from the way I move—short, greedy strokes, building all that heat and tension in my clit plus whatever intimate clues my pussy is giving him.

"Fuck my cock, Robin."

I start to moan.

"Tell me how I feel."

"You're big," I say. "Your cock's so thick and hard."

"That's right."

Technically I suspect Jay's about average, but damn if I'll let him think that when the flattery gets him so insanely hot.

"You're so big." I say it again and again, right against his ear, an incantation guaranteed to make Jay lose his mind. I whisper it over and over until the friction drives me crazy and I surrender, riding him slow and deep as the climax rips through my body. He comes too, pushing all the way in and holding there, groaning into my neck as he shoots.

I'm allowed to hold him now. I wrap my arms around his neck and bury my face against his skin. He makes a happy, dirty sound and I laugh.

Knowing I haven't managed to break us is the sweetest relief imaginable. I give him a last squeeze and kiss his temple and get up. When I come back from the bathroom Jay's got the sound turned back up on the TV. I tug my pants and shirt on and flop down next to him.

"What's the score?" I ask.

"We're up, seventy-one to sixty-five."

"Nice."

"I love you, Robin."

I lean against him, glad he can't see how broad my grin is. "I love you more, Jay Fleury."

CHAPTER FOUR

ALL THROUGH WORK on Friday, I'm useless.

I own and manage a shop in Dereham's town center, selling stationery and bookbinding supplies and photo albums, upscale paper and calligraphy pens, those sorts of things. It's called Roche Paper & Scissors, as my last name's Roche, and if you've taken grade-school French you know what a terrible pun that is. I paid a local artist to paint the store's name on the windows in an arch in gold and black, old-timey style. I'm here whenever it's open, which is ten to six weekdays and noon to four Saturdays. On Fridays I do inventory and it takes me about ten times longer than usual today because I can't keep any of the figures in my head for longer than a second.

Carrie, my only full-time employee, can tell something's up. For a twenty-year-old who's going to develop carpal tunnel from her incessant texting, she's exceedingly perceptive.

"You want me to do any of that?" she asks.

I'm staring blankly at spools of book cloth, clipboard and pen frozen in my hands as if I'm posing for a statue. *The Catatonic Paper Merchant.*

"No, I'm cool."

There's a giggle in Carrie's tone. "You aren't high, are you?"

I walk over and set the board on the counter. "No, just distracted."

"Clearly. What are you up to tonight?"

"Oh, just meeting an old friend for dinner," I say. "I can't figure out what to wear."

"Are you going anywhere fancy?" she asks.

"No, just to their place."

"Just wear what you are now," she says. "Friends don't care."

I look down at my boring black pants, gray sweater, salt-bleached Chuck Taylors.

"I want to look a bit more impressive than this," I say.

"Ohhh," Carrie says. She's insanely blonde, eyebrows so pale they're translucent. One of them floats up, intrigued. "It's not a guy, is it? Is it an ex?"

I am literally saved by the bell. The door jingles open and I lavish more attention on the browsing woman who enters than is probably good for business.

Two hours later, standing before my closet, I'm still baffled about what to wear. It's tough because I want to look sexy, but I don't want to make too much effort lest I hurt Jay's feelings.

He wanders into the room. "What are you going to wear?"

"Hell if I know," I say, tossing my hands up.

"He's a guy. He won't really notice."

I pout at him. "Tell me what to wear."

"A chastity belt," Jay says. I study him carefully and he cracks a smile. "What about that polka-dot dress you have?"

"Don't you think a dress is too dressy?"

"I think you should look smoking hot," he says.

"Really?"

Jay nods and starts flipping through the hangers. "I mean, the whole point of tonight is sex, right?"

"Well, not actual sex."

"You should look sexy," he says again and pulls out a couple dresses.

"Are you sure?"

He tosses the candidates across the bed and turns to me, puts his hands on my shoulders. "You know what I said the other night, about this turning my crank?"

"Yeah."

"Well, it still does. We've decided to go through with this, so if you're going to do it, do it right. You want my Neanderthal reasoning?"

I nod.

He rubs his thumbs over my collarbone. "I want you to look insanely hot. Then, in a year or whenever, I want to invite that asshole to our wedding so he has to watch you marry me. And I want him to go nuts with jealousy, knowing what I get and he doesn't." Jay smiles, pure evil.

"Patrick's not an asshole," I remind him.

"Trust me, Robin—he's agreed to screw around with my girlfriend. He's an asshole."

"You said you think he's an okay guy."

"He is, but he's an asshole too." Jay kisses my forehead. "Now get dressed and go drive that douchebag out of his mind."

* * *

JAY'S ENTHUSIASM ASIDE, I don't go so far as to make dinner for myself and Patrick. It didn't feel right, using our groceries and kitchen to accessorize my infidelity, just as I wouldn't have gone out and bought a new outfit for the occasion. Instead I drive to an upscale deli and buy some rotisserie chicken and Thanksgiving-type sides and grab a six-pack from the plaza's liquor store.

I get to Patrick's place ten minutes early. I ring the bell, a paper bag of good-smelling food in each hand.

He opens the door and smiles. "Hey, Robin."

"Heya."

He lets me in and I'm glad to be inside since it's November and I'm wearing a dress and no stockings. My Mary Janes are stiff from the cold, their leather cutting into the backs of my heels. I set the bags on his kitchen table.

"I have beer in the car too."

I catch Patrick blushing. "I bought wine. I didn't know what you'd want this to be like."

I try not to smile but it's no use. "This can be however we want it to be. And I'd love some wine. I'd love a lot of wine, actually. I'm a little terrified."

While I take my coat off Patrick goes to a cabinet and pulls out a bottle, a middle-shelf Australian red with a penguin on the label.

"That'll be nearly enough for me," I say, pointing at it. "What are you drinking?"

He looks over his shoulder as he winds the corkscrew in. "You really that scared?"

"I'm mostly teasing. But I *am* pretty nervous."

He tugs the cork out with a *foomp*. "Sorry if this'll kill the mood, but how's your man dealing with all this?" He finds two tumblers and pours us each a healthy glass, hands me one.

"Thanks." I follow him to his living room and look around before I answer his question.

He's remarkably tidy but not quite so much that I worry about his mental health. Patrick's got lots of bookshelves and lots of books, which surprises me for some reason. Not that he doesn't seem smart or anything. I've just only ever pictured him doing manly, active tasks in his spare time, like refinishing floors or fucking the living daylights out of me.

I sit down on the couch, an old, comfy, mauve monstrosity half-hidden by a colorful afghan. Patrick goes to the hearth and assembles a fire. I know that sounds romantic but I'm almost positive that it's his primary heating method. He's got a woodstove in his kitchen too. He's such a lumbercrat.

"Well," I finally say, watching his back as he gets the flames lapping. "Jay seems to be taking it pretty well, actually."

He pulls the wire screen over the fireplace and comes to sit on the couch, a couple feet between us as a buffer. He takes a deep drink and clears his throat. "Seems to be?"

"Yeah, but like legitimately well."

"I gotta say, I'm impressed."

"Me too. Oh, he said we have permission to do everything but. You know, intercourse."

"All right."

"He's sort of into it, now, actually," I add, wondering immediately if I just shared too much private info about Jay. Then again, he's sharing me. That's pretty private.

"Into it, like…"

"Like it turns him on," I say. "He likes that I'm over here torturing you, I guess."

"Oh."

I laugh and take a drink. "Like he's got some super-amazing car he'll let you test-drive, but only because he knows you'll never actually own one yourself and he wants to lord it over you."

Patrick laughs too. "Kinky."

"How do you want to do this?"

"Tonight?" he asks. "I was figuring we'd treat it like a date. But if that's too romantic, we don't have to." His gaze drops to my outfit, first-date fare if ever you saw it.

"Maybe more like friends to start out," I say. "I know I'm sort of over-dressed. That was Jay's idea. This is like him waxing his super-amazing car."

Patrick smiles, looking happily puzzled. "You're a weird couple."

"So I'm realizing."

"But sure, friends is fine."

"Thanks." I look at the clock. "In that case, can we watch channel five?"

It takes Patrick a second to realize I'm serious then he gets up and switches his late-model television on. We catch most of the first round of *Jeopardy!* and we drink our wine and shout answers at Alex Trebek. During the ads and the boring part where Alex talks to the contestants we go into the kitchen and dole out the food.

I like being Patrick Whelan's friend again, sitting on his squishy old couch, watching *Jeopardy!*, eating Thanksgiving-y food and drinking wine with him. Knowing what dessert's going to be.

We eat fast and while the contestants are deliberating over Final Jeopardy, Patrick heads to the kitchen and comes back with the bottle. He guessed the answer right and I didn't, so I clink my refilled glass against his.

He looks over at me, shifty.

"What?" I ask, knowing damn well what.

He takes my wine and sets it on the coffee table beside our dirty plates and clicks off the TV. The room smells like New England winter and I hear the wood popping in the fireplace. He scoots over a cushion and puts his hands to my face.

Patrick tastes of red wine and gravy tonight. He kisses me deep, just as he did in the parking lot, his mouth rough and urgent and dominating. I hold on to his shoulders, hard and strong behind his sweater.

For the first time, I worry that I won't be able to keep my promise to Jay and stop at third base. Patrick's been kissing me for thirty seconds and I'm already feeling crazed.

I push my shoes off onto the floor and break away from him long enough to half recline. He takes my hint, getting one knee between mine and wedging the other in the crease of the couch.

He lowers and I feel all that weight on me. He's the biggest man I've ever been with by far and it's sinful, his size. I want him to rip me apart like one of those bears with a taste for human meat.

"God," I mutter against his mouth. "You're fucking huge."

He pulls away an inch. "That good or bad?"

"It's phenomenal," I say and yank his face back.

He settles closer each minute, his chest grazing mine then his stomach then his hips. His thick thigh pushes the dress up my legs until the skirt's gathered at my waist. Through his kisses I hear Patrick's sounds—hungry little grunts and pants. They warm my skin and vibrate my nerve endings. The room felt cold before but now it's sweltering.

"Take this off," I say, tugging at his sweater.

He leans back on his haunches and tugs his sweater and shirt up and over his head. His body is even hotter than I'd let myself hope. He's broad but lean, raw-looking like a wild animal.

"Can I touch you?" I ask, probably looking possessed.

He grabs my wrists and presses my palms against his skin. I feel his stomach, his hips, his arms. This is my new territory, his shapes and smells, the soft hair of his chest, the noises I'm coaxing from him. He puts his hands on mine and rubs them up and down his hard body. I can see him getting hot, the ridge of his cock growing behind his jeans. My mind wills him to force my hands onto it but he keeps them above his waist. I want him to unbuckle his belt and open his fly, take his cock out and make me see it and stroke it and suck it. I want his voice mean and loud, bossing me around.

He gets both his knees between mine and lowers again, pushing his erection between my thighs.

"Patrick."

"You gotta tell me to stop if I go too far," he says in a scratchy voice I don't recognize but adore.

"If you stop I'll kill you," I say.

He starts to thrust and I can't tell you what's hotter—how hard his cock is, how fierce his arms look or how deep the growl is, rising from his throat. Or maybe it's the look on his face and those heavy-lidded eyes trained on me, predatory.

My pussy's hot and wet and after a couple minutes the friction of his fly against my panties is too much. Gosh, what a shame.

"Take your pants off."

Patrick leans back again and I revise my command. I reach out and grasp his belt for him, jerking the buckle open and fumbling with the button of his fly. I lower the zipper over his erection. He pushes his jeans down his hard thighs and I touch him.

I stroke his heavy cock through his straining underwear. "Patrick."

"Touch me." His head rolls back as he gives himself over to the pleasure. His hips thrust into my hands. I cup his swollen balls and give his cock slow pulls through the cotton. "Oh God, that feels so fucking good."

"You have no clue how much I've fantasized about this," I say, in awe of him.

His head comes back up and he watches me, mouth open, cheeks pink. "I think about you when I jerk."

"About what?"

"About this." He moans, eyes glued to my hands. "Sometimes I think about the day I got released. I think about finding you waiting for me when I got home that day, in my bed."

"Jesus, I wish I'd had the balls to. Back then."

If only I *had* done that. I know the day Patrick got released he came home to a cold, empty house, one that had been pretty badly vandalized while he was away. I want to make all that up to him tonight.

"I need to see you," I say.

He moans and pushes the waistband of his shorts down, showing me an impressive measure of mouthwatering, rock-hard cock. I stroke him, tight and slow. When his slit starts to weep I rub the pre-come up and down his length, making him slick.

"Let me watch you," I beg.

"Lemme watch you then," he says.

"Whatever you want."

He stands and gets his jeans and shorts all the way off and I yank my stretchy dress over my head. I don't own any crazy-sexy underwear, like lacy thongs or push-up bras or any of that. My undies match, at least—blue with white stars. I feel silly in my cutesy get-up until I see the wicked gleam in Patrick's eye.

"You allowed in my bed?" he asks, standing over me, staring down, chest rising and falling fast.

I nod. He takes my hand and leads me to the next room. He clicks on a dim reading lamp beside his bed. I can smell him here. I sit on the worn goose down comforter and breathe him in. I stretch out on his mattress and he kneels between my legs again.

"Still wanna watch?" he asks.

I nod vigorously, eyes on his dick. He reaches down and tugs at my panties and I bring my legs to my chest and let him slide them all the way off. His dark eyes take me in as I spread my thighs beside his knees. He swallows. One of his hands wraps around his cock and the other inches slowly up my inner thigh, giving me plenty of time to tell him no.

Fat fucking chance.

He runs his knuckles over my lips and our moans blend together. "You're so wet."

He dips his fingertips inside me and heat boils up through my cunt, tensing every muscle in my body. He gives me more, two big fingers, and he thrusts in time with his strokes, driving both of us insane for a few minutes.

"You feel tight," he mutters.

I don't doubt it. My pussy's never been this hungry for anyone before and his cock's so goddamn close. My palms are on his hips, on the dent where his thighs meet his ass. I tug at him. "Let me feel you. Just a taste."

He lowers, bracing himself on one strong arm. His other hand angles his cock and I feel the smooth, slick skin of his head slide up my lips and over my clit.

I groan and my fingers curl, clawing his ribs.

"God, Robin." He traces my entrance, slow and cruel.

Shit, it'd be so easy for him to just push in, fill me up, reclaim all the chances I wasted back when I could've had this.

"Do you want me?" he asks, almost a whisper. There's a cruel glint in his eye.

I'm too ashamed to say the word so I just nod, teeth clenched.

"Too bad." His head slides up and down, up and down.

"Patrick."

"Wish I could," he says, taunting. Affected or not, his calm is impressive.

"Patrick."

He pulls away. "Touch yourself." He watches my fingers take over where his cock left off. He strokes himself, looking mean, just as I always fantasized.

"Play with your clit," he says. I do and he slips two fingers back inside me. "Think about me fucking you."

"I am." I watch his cock, dark and heavy in his fist, I feel his fingers, slipping in and out, rough and deep. But not deep enough.

"What did you think about?" he asks. "Back when we were close?"

He means back when I visited him. Christ, what didn't I think about? It was tough then, back before I understood that fearful feeling his body gave me. It never stopped me from fantasizing about him though.

"It's sort of fucked up," I say, eyes still glued to his dick.

"Tell me."

"I used to imagine that night." Saying it leaves my throat tight and I try to swallow the anxiety. "I thought about—after you beat the shit out of that guy—I thought about sucking you in the parking lot. Like, while he was still on the ground." I feel my face color as I admit this. "I'd think about how you comforted me, and I'd imagine that while you were hugging me, I'd reach down and open your jeans and get you hard. And then I'd get on my knees on the asphalt while you sat on my hood, and I'd suck you off."

Patrick doesn't reply, just keeps fucking me with his fingers, stroking his cock.

"Say something or I'll feel like a pervert," I tell him.

His words come out hoarse. "I wanna fuck you so bad, Robin."

Relief and arousal course through me, the heat and tightness flaring in my cunt. I watch his cock, dying to taste him. My lips feel swollen, aching to slide over his head and suck him and feel his hot come stream over my tongue.

The pleasure tightens into a ball, humming, mounting each time his fingers drive into me. I can smell his perspiration and his sex and the room feels surreal around us, a dream.

"God, Patrick."

"You gonna come?"

"Yes." I tease my clit and watch the rough pulls he's giving his dick, watch his stomach clenching with his thrusts, shining with sweat. I imagine him alone on his back, shooting his come right there across those gorgeous muscles. All the strings of my composure snap in quick succession and I'm there, climaxing around his curled fingers.

"Oh, good girl."

I say his name, how many times I don't know. I go limp as the spasms fade, but he's still in thrall. His fingers slip out of me and he tastes them, brown eyes staring me down for a long moment.

"Spit in your hands," he says.

"What?"

"Make your hands wet." He's begging now, desperate, all his earlier composure crumbled to dust.

I get both my trembling hands slick and he wraps them around his cock, holding them still. He pumps his hips, fucking my fists, and I understand what he wants. I make them tight, as tight as I guess my pussy would be. He shuts his eyes and braces his arms beside my ribs, strong body above me.

"Yeah."

"Patrick."

"Fuck. Say my name."

I say it again. I lift my hips, hug my thighs to his waist as if we're fucking.

"Robin. Robin."

My eyes are wide, unseen by his closed ones. I watch him, his chest and stomach and arms, watch what he'd look like if we were allowed to screw. I feel him faltering above me. His breaths come in harsh gasps, punctuating each thrust. His cock pumps fast and hard and I feel his balls smack the backs of my fingers. We need more spit, but I'm afraid to interrupt him and shatter the illusion.

"Fuck me, Patrick."

"I am. I am."

"You're so big. Give me your big cock, Patrick."

He's falling apart—before my eyes, in my hands, all around me.

"Oh God. Here I come, Robin."

"Give me what I want, Patrick. Give it to me."

His voice becomes a deep, mean groan. His hips clench and I feel his cock shudder, watch the hot cream lashing my belly until he's empty.

CHAPTER FIVE

FOR A LONG TIME Patrick and I lie on his bed, staring at the ceiling, catching our breath. I worry he might do the manly thing and fall asleep, leaving me in an awkward position where I'll have to sneak out, stressed about Jay stuck waiting at home, chewing his fingers off, dying for me to get back.

But Patrick gets up first, alleviating my worries. He tosses me a hand towel to clean myself up and I watch him wander into the living room.

A clear and precise pang of guilt stabs me. It's weird, in light of what we've just done, but I feel really shitty that I watched *Jeopardy!* with him. I watch it with Jay most nights.

I push the feeling away as Patrick comes back in, dressed.

I sit up and smile at him as he buckles his belt. "Thanks."

He nods. "That scratch your itch?"

"I couldn't tell you for sure just yet, but I feel pretty fantastic right now."

He sits on the edge of the bed, making me slump against him as the mattress tilts. He presses his lips to my temple. "When's your man expecting you home?"

"No particular time. But I should head out soon." I feel him nod. "Thanks for having me over."

Patrick stands and I follow suit, suddenly shy. I find my panties then pad into the living room to get my dress and shoes back on.

"You should keep the leftovers," I say to him when he passes me to stoke the fire. "Practice for Thanksgiving."

He doesn't reply. He finishes with the hearth and crosses the room, stopping right in front of me. He's troubled in some way I can't pinpoint. I start to say thanks again but his mouth shuts me up, covering mine, the kiss brief but deep.

"I hope I wasn't too rough or anything," Patrick says when he steps back. "Earlier, I mean."

"You were exactly how I'd hoped you'd be." And more, I amend to myself, picturing his bare body.

He smiles. "You talk a lot dirtier than I expected."

I offer a guilty grin and shrug.

He slides his hands into his pockets. "You think this is the end of all this?"

I can suddenly read his expression—that uncertain end-of-the-first-date look.

"That's up to Jay." I decide to tell Patrick something I'm not ready to admit to the man I've got waiting at home. I put my hands on his chest, running them over his sweater, studying the little white flecks in the gray wool. "I'm probably never going to stop wanting you."

One of his black eyebrows twitches. "Oh."

"Either Jay's going to put a stop to all this or you are," I say. "I think you're both insane for agreeing to it in the first place, so no hard feelings when one of you finally comes to your senses." Weird, I think, how the two men I'm most attracted to are bossy in bed but do my irrational bidding so willingly while everyone's clothes are still on.

"Well," Patrick says, "I enjoyed tonight. If your man stays nuts, I'd be happy to see you again this way."

"Deal."

"And tell him not to worry, I know you're never gonna leave him or anything like that. I still know my role."

"Thanks. I'll let you know how he takes it. Maybe—oh wait, Thanksgiving is next week." I scowl to myself, thinking how quick holidays sneak up when you're busy orchestrating your inaugural infidelity. "Are you going to your mom's?"

"Dear God, no."

"Oh right."

He shakes his head. "I told her I'm not setting foot inside her house until she gets it cleaned up. Which'll be never. But I'm driving up there on Thursday and we're going to my aunt's for dinner."

"That'll be nice."

"It'll be hell," he says. "She gets all bent out of shape when she's away from her junk, now. She's convinced somebody's going to break in and steal things."

"That sounds rough," I say.

"I'm used to it. What about you?"

"We're going to Michigan to see Jay's parents and sister on Wednesday. Should be fun. I guess I'll see you after next weekend, sometime."

He nods and while he takes the dishes and wine bottle into the kitchen, I get my coat and scarf on. We meet at the front door.

"Is it weird if I kiss you again?" he asks.

"Probably. Well, wait, no. I mean, I'm here with permission to act on my feelings for you," I say. "So I guess that's fine."

I catch his tongue flick to the corner of his mouth as he thinks. "These your rules or your man's?"

I shrug and smile, dopey. "Hell if I know."

"You're a strange girl, Robin."

I shrug again.

Patrick leans down and kisses me, slow and sensual but no tongue. I sneak a peek, curious if his eyes are closed. They are. If he hadn't made me come fifteen minutes ago I'd probably faint. As it is I feel my legs buckle a little but I keep it together. He pulls away and I watch his lips purse.

I fish my keys out of my coat pocket. "I'll let you know what he says."

"Can I ask you something?"

"Sure."

"Why would you want to be with some shithead who'd sleep with some other man's woman?" he asks, squinting at me.

I bunch my scarf in my fist, trying to find a poetic justification and failing. I think about how Jay might answer. "I don't feel like I have any choice," I say. "But you're the one I need, so I guess I'm just lucky you're enough of a shithead to go there with me."

Patrick laughs. I can't remember the last time I heard him laugh like that. Five years at least, if ever.

I pull the door open. "I'll see you in a week or two, shithead."

"Drive safe, Robin. Enjoy your holiday."

* * *

I GUESS JAY WASN'T TOO FRANTIC while I was gone. I close the door behind me at nine o'clock exactly, and he's asleep on the couch with a book on his chest. His eyes open as I sit down by his feet. I see a couple beer bottles on the side table.

"Hey," he says, cute and bleary.

"Hey, you. What'd I miss?"

"You're looking at it," he says. "Me and my Friday night shenanigans." He swings his legs to the floor and sits up. "You wanna tell me about it?"

"Let me pee first."

When I get back, Jay's in the kitchen watching a bag of popcorn spinning in the microwave. I hug him from behind and wonder if he can smell the enemy on me.

"You're awful squishy," he says. "Have a good time?"

I talk into his shirt, muffled. "I did. Thank you." I realize with a start that I've just cheated on someone, properly and thoroughly, for the first time in my life. I'm not sure having permission excuses it all that much.

The feeling reminds me of the first time I was in a fender-bender, one that I caused. Before then I'd never expected I'd be at fault for such a thing and I remember grieving that day as a hunk of my potential for being a perfect person crumbled away. If I'd known about all this back then, I'd have been a lot easier on myself about denting somebody's stupid bumper.

The microwave beeps and Jay dumps the popcorn in a mixing bowl. I follow him back to the couch where he clicks on the television but keeps the volume down. It's what we do sometimes if we need to have a fight, or what constitutes a fight in our hyper-functional relationship. Neither of us actively watches the TV but it gives us something to focus on while we attempt to articulate whatever emotional gristle we're gnawing through.

Jay stares at the images flashing by on the screen. "So. Tell me what happened."

"You still want to hear about it?"

"Yeah. Tell me all the horny details," he says, and tucks into the popcorn.

"Okay, but don't ask me to compare you guys or anything, all right?"

"I won't."

"Good. Well…" I sputter out a breath. "I picked up some food at the deli and went over there. And we had wine… I watched *Jeopardy!* with him," I say, cringing. "I'm sorry. I wish I hadn't."

Jay meets my eyes. "Why not?"

"Isn't that, like, our thing?"

"*Jeopardy!*'s as ubiquitous as saying you guys drank wine. Don't worry about it."

"Oh, good."

His gaze returns to the TV. "What else happened?"

"Well, he made a fire, and we ate dinner and drank wine and kissed and messed around on his couch."

"Was it romantic?" he asks.

"No, it was more like friends, actually. Even though there was a fire and wine, it didn't feel like he was seducing me or anything. We just ate dinner and screwed around." I leave out the part where Patrick kissed me goodnight.

Jay sets the bowl down and grabs a paper towel, wiping his fingers. He turns to face me. His salty lips sting my own, still savaged from Patrick. We make out for a couple minutes and it's as much a relief as it is a turn-on. His mouth slides to my neck.

"Tell me exactly what you did." He sounds horny as all get-out. Awesome.

"We kissed, first, and then he got on top of me."

I feel Jay's breath flare hot on my throat. "What else?"

"We kind of dry-humped for a while, and he took his shirt off and I touched him. Above the belt."

Jay cups my breast as his teeth graze my skin.

"And my dress was up around my waist and he rubbed against me, through his pants."

"Did you like it?"

"Yeah. It was pretty fucking hot."

Jay sits back and yanks me into his lap just like the other night. "Then what?" He pulls me close so I can feel how excited he is. Dear God, who is this man?

"I told him I wanted to see it, so he let me. And I touched him."

Jay pulls the V of my dress down and kisses the tops of my breasts. "Is he big?"

"Yeah, he's real big." I hold my breath.

"What did you want to do to him?"

"Everything. I wanted to suck him, really bad. But we didn't do any of that. I just stroked him."

"What else?" he asks.

"We went to his bedroom and got our clothes off. Except my bra."

"Did you want him?"

"Yeah," I breathe. Jay's lips take my ear in a way that always makes me go feral. "I told him I wanted to watch him. You know, touch himself. So I lay down and he got between my legs—"

I'm distracted as Jay scoots me back a few inches, undoes his pants and takes his cock out. I study his face, the familiar, glazed look I know and love so well.

"Keep going," he says.

"I touched him, and he touched me. And he asked me what I used to think about, back when I visited him. Before you," I add, probably too quickly.

"What did you say?"

"I told him I used to think about sucking him off in the parking lot, that night he saved me." I blush, still not entirely comfortable with that fantasy.

"Yeah?"

"I didn't want it that night, of course. But I used to think about it."

"What did he say?" Jay asks.

"Well, he told me about how he used to fantasize about getting home after he was released and finding me there, waiting for him."

"Did he want you, tonight?"

I nod. "But he never asked me to. He knows you're calling the shots."

"Fucking right," Jay says and his hand speeds up.

"Then I played with my clit and he fingered me, and I came."

"Did you jerk him off?" he asks.

"He touched himself, first. Then after I came he made me hold my hands like this." I wrap both my hands around Jay, thumbs on top. "And he sort of fucked my fists, with his eyes closed, like he was imagining we were doing it." I run my hands up and down Jay's shaft.

"Did he come?"

"Yeah, he did."

"Did you wish you were allowed to screw him?" Jay asks.

"Yes. But I wouldn't have." I think I hide my lack of confidence in this statement pretty well.

"I bet he wanted to fuck you," he says. "I bet he was dying to, after he felt how tight and wet you are."

"Only you get to do that, Jay."

He takes my bait. He pushes me back on the couch and shoves my dress up my legs and yanks the crotch of my panties aside. He sinks in deep, my pussy wet from thoughts of both men.

"God, yeah. This is what he wants." Jay pumps me fast and greedy. I bet he'd pay for Patrick to have to watch this.

"Take your shirt off," I say.

He pauses to lean back and indulge me and I grin at him. Jay's got such a nice body. He's got hardly any chest hair and he's pretty muscular, though far smaller than Patrick. He looks different than you'd expect with his clothes off. He used to swim competitively when we started dating. He never won but I always loved going to his meets because he looks damn fine in a Speedo and I wanted all the women in the stands to see who he kissed when the competition was over.

Patrick Whelan, on the other hand, looks exactly how you'd guess, if you have a greedy, idealistic imagination.

I watch Jay's chest and abdomen as he fucks me. He's sleek and smooth and commanding. A zillion women would prefer him to Patrick and probably want me stoned for thinking I need more than this.

I watch Jay, but I imagine Patrick. He had that same mean look in his eye as Jay does now. When he fucked my hands he'd been out of his mind, wild and frantic. I liked that. I like that I have the power to make a man that big and self-possessed into a desperate animal. I like that Jay should be the desperate, insecure one, but here he is, banging my brains out as if he hasn't got a doubt in the world.

I think any woman who says men are predictable should try fucking an ex-con lumberjack and a cuckolded technology journalist in the same day and see if they don't just have a change of heart on the matter.

CHAPTER SIX

"HEY. ROBIN."

Carrie gets my attention from the counter and I look up from pricing sealing wax.

"What's up? Is it time for your break?"

"Nearly. But that guy is across the road. That Patrick guy?" she elaborates, brows raised.

"Oh." I walk over, casual, and look past the window display to where Patrick is indeed locking up his truck on the other side of Main Street. My pulse hums.

"My dad said he saved your life," Carrie says, watching him. "Is that true?"

"I don't know if I'd go that far, but yeah, he did help me when a guy had a knife to my throat in the Tap's parking lot. A long time ago."

Carrie's blue eyes go big and round. "Oh my God, that's scary."

"So yeah, that's my hero, right there." I point to where Patrick's waiting for a break in traffic to cross the street. I wonder if Carrie can hear my heart pounding.

"God, I'd be afraid *he'd* be the one lurking in a parking lot," she says.

"Don't say that. Patrick Whelan's a very nice man."

"Yeah, but he looks like a psychopath. And I heard he was in prison."

"Only because he beat the tar out of the guy with the knife," I say, sounding defensive.

"Wow, really?"

"Yeah. He's as nice as they come."

"Well, he looks super-scary."

"You're twenty." God, twenty. That's probably how old the kid with the knife was. I make my voice breathy and patronizing. "When you hit your sexual peak you'll be all over guys who look like Patrick Whelan."

"No way, Robin."

"Call me in ten years and we'll see who's right. And anyhow, don't let anyone tell you he's a psycho. He's my friend."

I watch Patrick jog across Main and head straight for our door. My body tingles, just like always. Like always, I love it and hate it in equal measures. "Why don't you take your lunch break?"

Carrie hurries out from behind the counter, presumably so she won't have to greet the psychopath pushing the door in. Patrick watches Carrie jog through the store and up the half-flight of steps to the stationery section then through the door to the back room.

He turns to me. "Hey, Robin."

"Hey, yourself. What can I do for you?"

"I've never actually been in here before," he says. "Nice place." He's got on a black knit cap and gray Carhartt pants, looking like a working-class wet dream. He approaches the counter and as soon as I look in his eyes I remember everything from three nights ago.

"Thanks. You saying hello, or can I help you patronize me?"

"Mostly hello. I just did at job on Brewster Street so I thought I'd stop in. This isn't weird, is it?"

I pause, about to speak, and we both straighten up on opposite sides of the counter as Carrie reappears in her coat and heads for the front door. "See you at two," she says.

I turn back to Patrick as the door jingles shut. "No, it's not weird. I'd ask you if you want to go get some lunch, but I've got to watch the shop."

"Are you hungry?" he asks. "I could grab you something."

I think a moment. "Yeah, okay. I was going to get a bowl of soup from next door."

Patrick nods and walks away before I can give him any cash. He returns in five minutes with a deli tub and a brown bag. He takes his hat off and tucks it in a pocket.

"Butternut squash," he says, and hands me a plastic soup spoon and a napkin.

I peel the lid off the tub and take a deep whiff. "God, I love fall."

Patrick pulls out a sandwich wrapped in waxed paper.

"Eat over here," I say, patting the side of the counter away from the register. "In case I actually get a customer."

"Business slow?"

"It's not bad, considering. It's just that everyone's traveling or at the grocery store. The card companies haven't made Thanksgiving into a stationery holiday yet. People don't think about me much until December."

Patrick nods, looking me over. "You have glitter in your hair."

"I'm sure." I shake my head and a few red flecks float down to the floor. "I was digging through the Christmas window display stuff this morning. I'll be coming in on Sunday to holiday the hell out of this place."

Patrick takes a few bites of his roast beef sandwich, glancing around the store. His eyes look complex in the daylight coming in through the front windows, deep brown, but with that striated iris texture to them. Everything looks complex just now.

I lean in and eat my soup, elbows on the counter just like how Patrick's standing on the other side. There's something familiar and conspiratorial about being close to him, knowing him the way I do now. I get a nervous thrill, thinking how caught I'd feel if someone did come into the shop and saw me eating lunch with this man who isn't my live-in boyfriend.

"So," I say. "Jay's still taking it pretty well."

He nods. "Maybe we can hang out after the weekend?"

I want this man now, now, now, but I'm driving to Michigan tomorrow at the ass-crack of dawn with Jay. Jay will drive, and I will spend most of the journey thinking about fucking Patrick Whelan. I always think about sex during long rides, for whatever reason—automotive vibrations maybe or plain old boredom. Jay probably does too because by now I've surely programmed him to expect to get laid as soon as socially possible once we reach our destination.

Patrick clears his throat and makes a project of flattening the waxed paper on top of the brown bag. "I'm glad he's taking it well."

"Yeah, he's really shockingly okay with it," I say.

"I'm glad." Patrick finally looks up. "But I don't know if I'm taking it quite so well."

"Oh." I feel the blood drain from my face and chemicals invade my pulse. Fear messes with my physiology, blurring and blunting reality.

I calmly grab a piece of paper from the printer and calmly write *Back in 15 minutes* on it in marker. I tape it to the door and twist the deadbolt. I touch Patrick's arm as I pass him and he follows me up the steps to the back room. I close the door behind us and sit on the edge of the break table.

"What aren't you taking well?" I ask.

He holds my eyes with his then looks away as he speaks. "What we're doing."

"The cheating?"

"No. The being with you but not actually being with you."

"The no-sex rule?" I ask.

He pushes a frustrated noise through his nose. "No. The you belonging to someone else thing."

I look down at his boots. "Do you have feelings for me?" The store phone rings, making us both jump. "I'm sorry. I have to get that."

He nods as I reach for the cordless. "Roche's Paper."

"Hey, lady." Jay.

"Hey. Can I call you back? I'm right in the middle of something."

"Just wanted to see if you could pick up some olive oil on the way home."

"Consider it done. See you tonight." I wait for his goodbye and hang up the phone. "Sorry."

"That was him?" Patrick asks.

I nod. I watch him take a deep breath.

"So, you have feelings for me?" I prompt. "Because of what we did?"

"I've always had feelings for you."

"Oh. Since that night?"

"Since before that," he says.

"I didn't think we'd even talked before then."

"We hadn't."

I frown. I don't feel creeped out, exactly, just confused. "For how long, then?"

"Since maybe two years before that night. It was after your store opened but probably that same year."

I would have been about twenty-five. That was when my grandmother died and I inherited the money that helped me move to Dereham from Montpelier and open this store and put a down payment on the little condo I owned before Jay and I moved in together.

Patrick licks his lips, looking nervous. "I don't know if I'm in love with you or anything," he says. "But I've liked you for a long time."

"Why?" I'm cute enough, I guess, but I'm not infatuation-worthy gorgeous or crazy-charismatic or intriguing. Just a short brunette with a paper shop and a rusty hatchback.

"I was across the street one day," Patrick says. "At the hardware store. You came running out of your store with a broom and started whaling on these two kids for throwing rocks at birds."

I haven't thought about that in years, but as soon as Patrick says it my blood starts pumping, hot with the adrenaline I felt that afternoon.

These two teenage boys had tried to rush at the pigeons on the sidewalk and stomp on them and, failing that, they decided to whip rocks at the awning that runs above my store, and the ones to either side of it, where the birds roost. It was right around the time the shop opened, when my grandma's death was still an open wound. My grandma had loved birds and I completely flipped out. I was young and easily wound up then, plus the store was new and stressful and I felt vulnerable when I was there.

"It was a mop," I say. I remember seeing red and grabbing it from beside the door and stalking outside and screaming at them. I hit one of the boys hard in the ear and left a big wet sponge print on the other's tee shirt. I probably looked totally insane, swinging a mop at those idiot kids and shrieking about animal cruelty.

"That's when you decided you liked me?" I ask. "When I was assaulting junior high schoolers? I've probably never been such a spaz in my entire life."

"I always thought that was really cool, that you did that."

I shrug. "I think they only took off because they thought I'd call the cops. Not because of my bad-ass samurai-janitor skills."

"They called you a crazy bitch." Patrick smiles deeply and it gives him little squinchy rolls beneath his eyes.

"Well, that was pretty accurate. I'm lucky their parents didn't sue me."

"You know that night, in the parking lot," he says. "That wasn't just luck. That I found you."

I feel another buzz in my pulse, another sip of a stiff brain-chemical cocktail. "No?"

He shakes his head. "I'd been wanting to talk to you all night. Well, I'd been wanting to talk to you for two years, but that night I told myself I finally would. I was going to offer to buy you a drink the next time you dropped your glass off at the bar but then you left. And I was drunk enough to follow you and drunk enough to not think trying to talk to you for the first time in a dark parking lot wasn't totally sketchy. So I went after you, and you know how all that turned out."

"I'm sure glad you did," I say. "Well, actually, I wish I'd still been thirsty. Then I guess we would have just talked, without me getting traumatized or you spending half a year in prison."

"You would've let me buy you a beer?"

"Sure." I probably would have felt intimidated by Patrick though, and I don't know if my attraction would have ever bloomed the way it did if things had gone down how he'd envisioned. I probably would have flirted politely with him and gone home alone, and he'd have ended up a tiny footnote. *April 14, went to the Tap, got hit on by a bona fide lumberjack.* Instead he's got his own chapter in the book of my life. More than that. For the first time in the years Jay and I have spent trying to ignore how the living ghost of Patrick Whelan haunts our relationship, I feel uncertain about how I honestly want all this to play out.

"I want my relationship to work," I say quietly, trying to remember that it's true.

Patrick nods and I catch his eyes dart to the clock on the wall. We have a few minutes before Carrie is due back. He steps close to where I'm sitting on the table and against anybody's better judgment I let him nudge my thighs apart with his. I put my hands on his waist, on his soft, old, flannel work shirt. I feel his lips touch my forehead then my temple. Then he kisses me, once gently with his lips closed then deeper. My body rouses when his tongue slides against mine and my skin prickles as I feel the hum of his moan.

This time though, more than I want to fuck him, I want to cry. I want to slap him for making this complicated or for yanking open a curtain and shining the harsh light of reality over how complicated it's been all along. I want to hurt him for how good he makes me feel, but I hate that I have the power to hurt him if I want to.

I push him away after an excruciating minute and slide off the table.

"I have to unlock the store," I say and wipe my lips with the back of my wrist.

Patrick doesn't reply, just follows me when I open the door and head back to the front. I take the sign down and flip the bolt and find him pulling his hat on, dropping his half-eaten sandwich in its sack.

"I'm sorry if this was a mistake," he says evenly.

"You probably shouldn't come by here again for a while. Why don't you let me come to you after I have some time to think?" I ask.

He nods and heads for the door. "You have a nice holiday, Robin."

I listen to the bell tinkle, watch him cross the street and climb into his truck and drive off. I glance back down at my unfinished soup and the smell of squash and ginger suddenly makes my stomach turn. I snap its lid back on and toss it in the trash.

* * *

IT'S DARK AND DAMP AND COLD OUT when I lock the shop door behind me, five minutes early. During the drive across town, I make a mental list of pros and cons for leaving Jay to be with Patrick.

Con: Jay is wonderful. I think I might want children with Jay.

Pro: Patrick sets me on fire in a way I don't think I ever want to live without.

Con: Patrick spends a third of the year in New Hampshire.

Pro: Patrick would kill a man to defend me.

Con: I'd be a hugely self-serving bitch.

Pro: Patrick built his own house, so that's the mortgage taken care of.

Con: what the fuck is wrong with me?

I knock on Patrick's door at six ten. When he appears I don't even give him a chance to say hello. "I need to talk about what we started talking about."

But we don't talk.

He lets me in and when I get my coat off, I don't stop there. He watches, wide-eyed, as I strip down to my underwear in his kitchen. He doesn't say a word. I catch his dark eyes roam from my head to my toes and back in a breath, and then he's on me.

I feel every pound of muscle as that huge man lunges, pushing me against the refrigerator. I feel the fridge slide back an inch across the tile then two strong hands grasp my thighs and wrap them around his waist, holding me up with a hand under each ass cheek. Patrick's belt buckle jabs my pubic bone but the pain feels so fucking perfect. I've never been screwed against a wall, never thought it really happened outside well-choreographed late-night movies, but feeling this man in control of my body, I know Patrick Whelan could do it.

His mouth is rough, borderline violent. I run my hands through his messy hair, wanting to pull him so close and hard against me that our bodies fuse into one despicable whole.

His hips push into mine, thrusting, and I hear magnets clatter to the floor and papers crumpling behind my back. Something on top of the fridge teeters and topples and rolls away. Patrick's tongue is hot and aggressive, filling my mouth exactly how I want his cock to fill my pussy. Between my legs, he's rock hard.

I find a break in the kissing, enough to kiss him back, slide my tongue between his lips and take the lead for a few glorious seconds. A moan rises from his throat, hot and sharp like electricity. He tears his mouth from mine.

"Why did you come here?" His voice is new, that baritone I thought I knew sounding deeper and darker and full of pain.

"I thought I wanted to talk."

"This ain't talking." He pushes his hips into me a little harder, emphasizing exactly how far this is from talking.

"I can't stay away from you," I say, truly accepting it myself for the first time.

Patrick buries his face against my neck, sort of kissing, sort of just breathing, mainly suffering in some complex male way I'll never fully understand. After a minute he pulls away and lowers me until I'm standing.

"He doesn't know you're here, does he?" Patrick asks.

I shake my head.

"What do you want, Robin?" He doesn't meet my eyes when he asks this—he stares at the sliver of tile between our two pairs of feet, looking hypnotized.

Be a horrible person with me, I think. *So I don't have to be horrible alone.*

"Let's go to the living room," I say.

He holds his ground so I slip away from him sideways and walk into the next room. It's cold in his house and my body's showing it—not just ooh-sexy taut nipples, but less attractive evidence too, like the goose bumps and tiny hairs rising all over my chilly, mottled skin. I don't feel sexy either, but it doesn't matter. I feel something else, something stronger and totally removed from my ego.

Patrick follows eventually, slowly, as if each step is another chance to change his mind. By the time he reaches where I'm sitting on his couch his expression's changed. The pain has turned to hunger, the guilt to wickedness. Each button he undoes on his shirt is another increment of time, another squandered opportunity to stop. He drops it off his obscenely strong shoulders and peels his undershirt up and over his head, giving me a front row view of that chest, that stomach. I watch his hands undo his belt, wishing he'd use it to bind my wrists together, to tie me up and make me a victim so when he fucks me, it's not my fault. But he doesn't. His jeans slip to the ground and he kicks them away along with his socks and stands before me in gray shorts, that delicious bulge filling them.

Certain things make sense in this moment, such as pheromones, and the fact that humans are animals, and the idea of mating as a form of biological insanity.

"Come here," I say.

He gets onto the couch, knees between mine, and suddenly we're teenagers—frantic, graceless near-naked bodies, groping and rubbing and grasping and panting. His cock feels sinful, pressing between my legs. I want him to rip through our two pairs of underwear and be inside me, pumping. I don't even care if I come—I just want this bestial version of Patrick to fuck me senseless. I want bruises tomorrow. I want scratches and sprains and bite marks, enough to make Jay leave me and absolve me of my hard decisions and the power I don't deserve to have over either of these men.

I shove Patrick's shoulders, force his body away enough that I can cup him. He's already swollen and hot and heavy, growing even harder as I fondle him.

He leans back on his haunches, watching. "I can't stop thinking about you."

"About what?" I ask, making the strokes tight and long.

"All the stuff we did on Friday. And everything we're not allowed to."

I nod. "I've thought about it too. About how you looked when you fucked my fists in your bed." I see that look now, in his face and those heavy-lidded eyes, in the strained muscles of his body. I feel it in the pulse of his dick against my palm. "Let me suck you, Patrick. Please."

His voice turns scratchy and shallow. "God, I want you so bad."

"How do you want me?" I ask, pulling his shorts down to expose every decadent inch. I grip his cock, running my fist up and down, up and down. I push at his hard stomach until he takes the hint and lies back at the other end of the couch, letting me kneel between his spread thighs.

He watches my hand. "Rough, from behind," he finally says, flooding my overheated brain with every guilty mental image I entertain when Jay fucks me that way.

I lean in and reward his answer with a lap across his slit. I taste his sex as his groan fills my ears, licking until he's rock-hard, throbbing in my hand. "Tell me more."

"I'll go down on you first, 'til you're sopping wet," he promises.

I feel his palm, hot on my cheek. I slip his head between my lips, sucking as I swirl my tongue over the smooth skin. I taste his excitement, that salty, sinful sex flavor coming in little bursts as his cock tells me how ready he is. His fingers tangle and twitch in my hair, wanting to force me closer but resisting the impulse. I slide him out and meet his eyes.

"I love your cock."

His lips part and his cheeks flush, his eyes narrow and a darkness passes over his face. "I need to fuck you, Robin. I feel like I'm going crazy."

I take half his length into my mouth, luxuriating, memorizing, torturing. I cup and squeeze his balls as the other hand strokes him. Part of me wants to make him so insane that he pushes me back onto the couch and takes me, no permission requested or tendered, too fast and too forceful to allow a protest. Then, us. Patrick's body pushing mine into the cushions, this gorgeous dick taking what it needs. That deep voice, wild and mean, all that damp skin and hard muscle pressed against my bare body.

There's a cloud in my skull, making everything hazy, the way it feels when you stand up too quick from a hot bath. I realize I'm moaning with his cock in my mouth.

"Suck it," he says. "Suck me, Robin."

I stroke him harder, moan louder.

"Suck me like you wanted to that night."

I do. Just thinking about it makes me feel ferocious—fierce and worshipful, needy and thirsty and utterly animalistic.

Patrick's hands feel insistent, palms cupping the back of my head, not forcing but urging. Begging. I take him as deep as I comfortably can, making up the rest with my fist, now slick with spit.

"God, yeah." His fingers are trembling in my hair, arms tugging, matching the thrusts I'm offering. "Suck me, Robin."

I slip him from my lips again and catch his eyes. "You're so big, Patrick."

He groans when my mouth returns. "Is that what you've been needing, Robin? A big cock?"

"No," I say, and lap at him. "It's you. I need you."

"I wanna know everything you've been dying to do with me."

His hands leave my head and suddenly he's pushing me away, back to my end of the couch. I recline and Patrick gets on his knees on the floor, yanking my panties down my thighs and calves, slinging one of my legs over his shoulder and propping the other against the back cushions, spreading me wide.

He brings his face close, so close I feel his breath on my pussy when he speaks. "Tell me everything you think about." His tongue laps, slow and deep, and the sensation zings through me, making my legs jerk.

"Oh, fuck."

"Tell me," he whispers again.

"I think about you when he fucks me from behind."

Patrick's tongue flicks my clit, sharpening my shame with a flash of pleasure.

"I think about you and I tell him harder and faster and I have to bite the pillow sometimes, to keep from screaming your name."

"You think I'll be hard and fast?" he asks between licks.

"Yeah. I need you to be rough. You're so big—your body is. I want to feel like you're...like you're owning me."

His fingertips tease my lips, sliding up and down my slit, threatening.

"God, Patrick."

"You belong to someone else," he whispers. "But you fantasize that it's me that owns you." His fingers penetrate, shallow.

"Yes."

I feel more—three fingers now, to the second knuckle. "Tell me how I take you in your fantasies."

"Rough," I say again. "And so deep."

His fingers drive into me as his lips suckle my clit.

"And I imagine you being greedy and fast and mean. And that your hands are on my hips when you take me from behind or if I'm on top and you force my thrusts." God, I love that idea—being controlled by a man so much stronger than me. "I want you to use me. And I want to see it when you come. I want you to make me watch when you shoot, or make me taste it."

Patrick makes dirty noises in time with his fucking fingers, grunts and hums and growls. His tongue sets a flickering rhythm against my clit, one that dissolves the muscles in my legs and makes my hands twitch and grasp at his hair. In my mind this man is usually selfish. I hardly ever imagined him doing this, and I'm shocked by how amazing he is at it.

"You're so good, Patrick."

His face seems angelic from this vantage, eyes obscured by his dark lashes as if he were sleeping or praying. I admire the angle of his eyebrows and the shapes of his ears amid his chaotic, wavy black hair. The collection of grays at his temples makes him seem so…experienced. Intelligent. Something like that. Like someone who should know better but is here nonetheless, making terrible mistakes with me.

His fingers fuck harder still and his tongue leaves me a moment. "Pretend it's my cock," he says.

I close my eyes and focus on the impact of his hand as his fingers pound me. He makes it rough and frantic, makes me hear his skin slapping mine.

"Patrick." I imagine that dick, hammering me. "Fill me up, Patrick. Nice and deep. Make me feel how big and thick you are."

"I'll give it all to you," he whispers. "Think about it. What does it feel like?"

"Huge. Like you're splitting me open. Like you're punishing me."

"I want it so bad," he says. "I want you to come on my cock and milk it with your pussy." Dear God, where did he learn to talk like this?

"I want that too."

Patrick abandons his verbal torture to focus on my clit. I can feel my climax building. Usually when I come I'm edging myself forward, trying to keep up the momentum until I get myself over the edge. This time it's as if I'm being pushed. No coaxing, just me grasping and struggling to make it last longer and failing. Patrick's tongue laps with a steady, firm stroke, every lick driving me closer to the precipice. There's no mental image in my head to help things as normal. Everything I could ever want to fantasize about is right there. That face, that strong, coarse hand on my thigh, those half-closed eyes, that voice. And when I come, I stammer his name.

Patrick laps at me as my legs twitch and relax. His fingers start to thrust again, deep. His eyes are on me, on whatever cruel invitation is spread out before him like a flapping red bullfighter's cape.

I tug at his hard shoulders, desperate. "Let me make you come."

Obediently he stands and ditches his shorts and joins me on the couch, hips settling between my thighs. I see his hand trembling when he guides his cock to my pussy and sweeps his head over my lips. The guttural sounds he makes intoxicate me all over again. He runs it up and down, over and over, and not just gentle strokes. Dangerous ones.

His head is thick and shining from me, sliding and stroking and teasing and threatening. His abs clench in time with the motions, giving me a glimpse of how he'd look, really fucking me. Then his eyes meet mine and the gleam in them feels a hundred times more forbidden than what's going on between our bodies.

"Tell me to and I'll do it." His voice is gruff and tight and he means it.

"I can't."

"Why'd you come here tonight?" That question again, impossible to answer. The expression on his face is wounded and scared. It breaks my heart. He never wanted to be the kind of man who'd ever sleep with someone else's girl, but I'm making him that way. I'm making him want that so hard it must ache. He pushes against me, just a little. Not quite penetrating, but showing me how it might feel if he did.

"I don't know why I came here," I say. "I just had to." I stare at his body, awed. It's hard to explain, but when I look at him everything feels right. Everything feels like *enough*.

"It's terrible that I'm here," I add, grasping at a little scrap of sanity. "We shouldn't have sex…but let me suck you off. I'm allowed to do that." In theory, anyhow. Not that I think Jay would be so keen right now, considering he's surely pacing the kitchen, reaching my voicemail, wondering or worrying what's happened to me while our dinner grows cold.

Patrick stops teasing my pussy and settles back on his knees, stroking himself. "How do you want me?"

Part of me wants to be on my knees, him in charge. But no. "Can we go to your room?"

He stands and I follow him to his bed.

"Lie on your side," I say, and he does. I lie down the other way, face at his waist, thighs by his head, knees on the pillows. I want as much of our bodies touching as possible when I do this, all the contact I can get. His breathing's heavy and I feel his stomach swelling and contracting against my breasts, and I think I can even feel his heart beating against my belly. I push one hand beneath his hip and take his cock in the other. He tastes like me when I slip him into my mouth.

"Robin." He forces an arm under my body so he can hold my ass with both hands. I hadn't intended it but I certainly don't protest when he drapes my leg over his shoulder and I feel his tongue on my pussy again. It isn't like before—he's not trying to get me off. This is for him, a complement to what I'm doing to his body. I feel his nose against my lips as he suckles my clit and he makes loud, hungry noises. He breaks away to say, "Suck me, Robin. Suck me. Make me come."

His cock is heavy and intimidating and wonderful, the first couple inches filling my mouth. I fondle his balls, gently squeezing and pulling. I free my mouth to say, "Tell me what you need, Patrick."

"Just suck me. Hard."

I leave his balls to wrap my hand firmly around his base. I slip his head in my mouth and take him, aggressive.

"Fuck, yeah." His hands clamp tight to my flesh. "Just like that." His tongue laps me in long strokes and I know it's about him tasting me, not about my next orgasm. I love that thought, that he wants this for his own pleasure and I shiver, imagining him as a ravenous, greedy beast.

I feel when he's close. His hips move—tiny, involuntary jerks that beg me for more. I keep stroking and sucking and do my best to take what he gives me when he starts to thrust. His mouth abandons my pussy and he fills the room with his moans and pleas.

"Don't stop. Don't stop."

I wouldn't dream of it. I taste more of his pre-come and on a primal level it's the most addictive flavor I've ever experienced. His smells are all around me, his energy, these intimate parts of him right here in front of me.

"Oh yeah," he groans. "Yeah. Don't stop. Please. Robin."

His hips thrust and freeze a moment and I taste the first spurt. Another thrust, another taste, again and again until he's empty. I swallow everything he gives me and lave his cock as his body relaxes.

"God, Robin." He sounds delirious and I feel giddy. I extract myself from his grasp and flip around to lie against him, chest to chest. He grabs me around the waist and pulls me on top of him, knocking out my breath. We kiss for a minute or two—light, fond kisses.

As the euphoria wears off it feels obscene, reveling in this post-sex haze with him. I glance at his bedside clock—five minutes of seven. I'm usually home by six fifteen, plenty of time to hang out with Jay while he finishes the dinner prep. "I need to go soon."

I feel very cold again, very suddenly.

I roll gracelessly off Patrick and pad to the bathroom. It's odd, his bathroom. Really clean, so bare and white it's nearly like a hotel. A razor and shaving cream, toothbrush and paste on the sink, a bar of soap and a bottle of shampoo in his shower stall. A stick of deodorant and a nearly empty prescription bottle in the medicine cabinet. I glance at the label—nothing scandalous, just scrip-strength pain reliever. *Patrick J. Whelan, 14 Fencroft Drive, Dereham, Vermont. Take up to four times daily for muscle aches.*

I quit my snooping and stalling and get myself tidied up. I walk through the living room past where Patrick is finishing dressing, tugging on his socks. I feel his eyes on me through the kitchen threshold as I get my clothes on. When I finish he comes over to me, puts his hands on my shoulders and stares me straight in the eyes.

"I know you're not supposed to be here."

I shake my head.

"If you get home and all hell breaks loose, you can always come back here to stay. But if he takes it okay, I think maybe we shouldn't talk until we've both had a week or more away from each other."

"That's probably wise," I say.

"I shouldn't have come by your work, just like you shouldn't have come here. So let's not talk until at least next weekend. Why don't you call me if you see fit? Or don't call if you think that's better."

I nod. He lets me give him a quick hug and a kiss on his stubbly jaw. He walks me to the door and holds it open.

"Have a nice holiday," he says.

"You too. Happy Thanksgiving."

CHAPTER SEVEN

I FEEL NEAR TO VOMITING as I turn the knob to the side door of the house. I don't fear Jay's anger, but I'm shaking, petrified of the pain I might see on his face. I checked my phone in the car before I left Patrick's and he'd called three times. Two messages.

"Hey, lady. It's six forty. Did you go to Italy to get that olive oil?" Shit. I forgot about that.

Then, "It's almost seven. Give me a call so I know everything's okay."

I push the door in and there he is. Jay. Jeans and a button-up sweater. Jay's one of those rare, slender, modern men who can make a cardigan seem hip. He's stirring pasta sauce in a pan by the stove, looking as though it's all he's done in the last hour. He must have heard the car when I pulled in. The fact that he doesn't stop stirring to hug me says he came to the right conclusion about my whereabouts.

"Hey, you." Still stirring. "Where have you been?"

I had the whole drive to think up a lie and I think it's some meager sign of redemption that I didn't. I meet his eyes. "I'm sorry. I stopped by Patrick's on the way home." "Stopped by" in this case meaning I drove clear to the far side of town.

Jay's expression goes blank. "Oh," he says, and keeps on stirring.

I shrug my coat off, sure that I'm sending a huge cloud of enemy-male scent wafting in his direction.

"I'm sorry," I say. "I should have called. And I forgot the oil."

His hazel eyes look grayish-yellow tonight and distrustful. "I see."

I'm not sure what else I can say. I'm very good at admitting when I'm wrong but this isn't like stranding Jay with inadequate toilet paper or shrinking his sweater. There's nothing I can offer that will fully express how far off the deep end of wrong I've plunged.

"Did you guys..." He trails off.

I shake my head. "Nothing you said we couldn't." If barely. "But I should have called to ask. I don't know what to say. I did it without thinking."

"You knew I'd be here, waiting and making dinner. Expecting you."

"I know."

He looks down, at my knees or something behind me. "That's pretty shitty, Robin. I'm pretty fucking pissed."

You have to really know Jay to spot the signs that back this statement up. I know all of them. His ears are pink and there are tight lines beside his lips. His voice sounds flat. His eyes look dull and they won't meet mine anymore.

"Would you like me to leave or go in a different room?" I realize I'm wringing my hands and will them to be still.

"Dinner's ready," he says. "Why don't you eat in here and I'll take mine in and watch the game."

"Okay."

"I don't really want to talk to you right now, but I'll let you know when I do."

"What do you think about tomorrow? Should we still go?"

Suddenly, Jay laughs. Not a big laugh, but a genuine one. "I'm not going to break up with you, Robin. We're still getting up at five and driving to Michigan. If I'm still pissed, it could be a long-ass thirteen hours."

"Okay." I want to hug him so badly. It's strange how only a half-hour ago Patrick felt like the entire world. Now that I'm here, Jay is the only man I can imagine. "I'll be in here then."

"If I don't speak to you before I head up," he says, "you should still come to bed. Just don't talk to me, if you can help it."

I nod. I dawdle in taking off my shoes and scarf, creating plenty of time for Jay to get his dinner and leave the room. I walk to the stove. Marinara sauce with big slices of chicken sausage. The linguine look sticky and gluey, overcooked and in need of oil. I hope dinner tastes so bad that I can't eat it since I probably deserve to go hungry. But I will eat, because not eating would be a willful display of self-punishment and Jay hates theatrics. He meant what he said. He doesn't want to talk to me right now. Everything else can go on like normal.

Like normal.

I stare at the pans a long time. I know I'm going to do the dishes like normal after dinner, but I bet I'll do a better job than I ever have before in my entire life.

* * *

JAY DID TALK TO ME before we went to bed that night. We didn't have a discussion, but when he came into the kitchen to drop his dish in the sink, he stopped behind where I was sitting at the table and put his hands on my shoulders.

"I always knew this idea was crazy," he said softly. "But tonight was the first time when I couldn't recognize you during all this."

I held my tongue, feeling his fingers gently squeezing and releasing as he thought. "I've been really good about what you need."

"Yes," I said. "You've been amazing."

"You really let me down tonight. I would have said it was okay, if you'd just asked me. It really fucking hurts that you didn't."

I nodded.

"Am I losing you, Robin?"

Maybe. "No."

Jay sighed, long and mournful. "I don't really want to talk about it anymore," he said. "Let's sweep it under the rug and get on with everything."

"I'll never do that again," I promised him. "And I don't think I've ever felt so horrible in my whole life. I'm so, so sorry I hurt you."

God, I was. I still am. There's a danger when you're with someone who loves you enough to forgive you and you know that about them. I'd never exploited that aspect of our relationship before—never did something bad because I knew Jay would eventually forgive me. And I didn't mean to do that, Tuesday night with Patrick. I went there as if under a spell. I feel utterly humbled, having accidentally abused my power. Over both of them.

Thanksgiving went as it always does. We had a couple lovely meals and played board games and took long walks with Jay's parents and his younger sister. Jay treated me as he always does, both in their company and when we were alone. The only thing different was that we didn't have sex.

Penitent or not, I thought about Patrick a lot when we were in Michigan. I thought about how lonely I suspect he is. I thought about him pulling up to his mom's house and seeing piles of stuff looming behind the garage windows, or whatever evidence of her hoarding might be visible. I imagined him sitting in his truck with the engine running, refusing to go inside. I pictured him having a frustrating holiday and then driving back to Dereham to his cold house all alone, sleeping in his cold bed. A couple times I pictured him lying on that bed, jerking off, thinking of me, but I caught myself and pushed the image from my brain.

Presently I look up from my crossword at the smell of burning ginger.

"Fuck!"

I run across the kitchen and yank a sheet of blackened cookies from the oven.

It's Sunday afternoon and Jay wanders in from his office holding the business section of the paper.

"Everything okay? Smells smoky in here."

"I burned the first batch," I say. "It's okay, there's plenty more dough."

Then the smoke detector blares, those hateful, mind-splitting beeps assaulting my ears. Loud noises terrify me—I fear the smoke detector more than an actual fire.

I run through the next room and up the stairs. The shrieking stops shortly and I know Jay's climbed onto a chair and disabled the battery. I go back down to the kitchen as he's opening windows, letting the freezing outside air drift in to fix my mistake.

"Thanks." I'm jangled, nerves buzzing like wasps. Tears come to make up for all the ones I've been blocking since Tuesday.

Jay hugs me while I sob into that favorite, good-smelling sweater of his. I feel his palm running up and down my back, feel the cold air on my hands and face, smell the scalded sugar. I step away when I'm calm.

"Thanks," I say again, and wipe my cheeks on my sleeve. I go back to the counter to roll out a fresh ball of dough. Jay stands beside me and watches. I hand him the male gingerbread person cutter. The other one has a skirt and before you decorate the cookies they look like bathroom door icons. We cut out the shapes, doing our best to make them tight like tessellations and not waste the dough. I'm going to ice them when they're cool and leave a heaping plate of them on the counter at the shop tomorrow. I did the holiday decorating there this morning and aside from the crying and the recent drama, I'm feeling very sparkly and yuletide-y. Christmas is like Bailey's to me. It's so sweet you don't notice yourself getting drunk on it until you wake up with a hangover on December twenty-sixth.

Jay slides the sheet into the oven and I muster the good sense to set the timer.

"Thanks," I say for the third time.

"I think we should have that asshole over for dinner," Jay says, the words like a baseball flying out of the clear blue sky to hit me in the teeth.

"What?"

"I think you should ask Whelan over for dinner."

"Dear God," I say. "Why?"

"Because he's a part of our lives now, like it or not." He's leaving something out of this answer, I can sense it.

"I sort of… I sort of assumed you'd forbid me from seeing him anymore. After what happened on Tuesday."

"The longer he stays a taboo, the longer you'll want him," Jay says. "See if he's free some night this week." He turns away to move dishes from the drying rack to the cupboards. "Tell him to bring a bottle of something."

I blink at his back. "You aren't planning on murdering him, are you?"

Jay laughs. "Just ask him. He might say no."

I feel uncomfortable. Not suspicious, just…scared. About talking to Patrick. About hearing him say he doesn't want to ever see me again. I'm positive he's decided that's best in the few days since I made him an accomplice to infidelity.

After the dishes are put away Jay wanders back into his office. I stand stock-still in the middle of the kitchen floor, staring at the motion of the curtains as the breeze pushes them in. I shriek when the oven timer buzzes.

* * *

THE GINGERBREAD MEN are going over well. I missed out on Black Friday, keeping the store closed through Thanksgiving weekend, but the first few days of shopping are mall days, when people want to hit a dozen stores all in one trip. People think about cards and crafts more after the initial big-picture items are purchased. Business is bustling today, Monday. The locally made stockings are selling especially well.

I get Carrie's attention when the lunch-hour rush begins to lag. "I have to run an errand in a bit," I say. "Will you be okay for a half-hour?"

"Sure thing."

At one fifteen I get into my car in the little employee parking lot behind Main Street. I drive ten minutes to the edge of town to Mullaney Lumber, a long, spruce-colored building like an airplane hangar. Rows of fresh-cut Christmas trees are lined up out front.

It smells good inside, like a new house. Paint and sawdust and potential. I head to the nearest apron-clad employee, a chubby man wearing a Santa hat and a down-home friendly smile.

"Afternoon, miss. Can I help you?"

I grin and try to look as un-sordid as possible. "I'm trying to find Patrick Whelan."

"Whelan'll be out back." He motions for me to follow him and takes me down the fixtures aisle and through a heavy door into a cold warehouse. We walk to where some guys are unloading a pallet of boards off a forklift. I recognize Patrick by his height.

"Whelan!" the friendly man shouts.

Patrick turns and I catch his eyebrows bob up above his clear safety glasses. He leaves the project to walk over. He's wearing a forest green hard hat and thick gloves and a work shirt with his last name embroidered above the pocket.

"Thanks," I say to the friendly man, who does as I hope and leaves us alone.

Patrick glances around then leads me out through a back door, into the bright sunshine and the cold and the privacy.

"I wasn't expecting to see you so soon," he says.

"How was your Thanksgiving?"

"Aggravating," he says, making a face to match. "Why are you here?"

"You're invited to dinner," I blurt.

His brows jerk up again and stay there. "Am I?"

"Jay wants you to come over. And he said he's not planning to murder you. You can think about it first, of course. But he said pick a day this week and bring something to drink."

Patrick's dark eyes roam all over the lumberyard. He takes his gloves and hard hat off and runs a hand through his matted hair. It looks as if he got a trim for the holiday but it's still pretty messy, just how I like it. I breathe him in while he ponders and marvel again at how his proximity makes me flush.

"Um," he says, putting his hat back on. "Thursday?"

"Sure, whatever you want."

"Do you know what this is all about?" he asks.

"Not really. I think he wants to clear the air. Or demystify you. I think he thinks if I see you somewhere boring, like my house, you won't seem so…exotic. Or irresistible." I feel my cheeks color.

Patrick shakes his head. "You are one fucked-up couple, Robin." This time when he says it, he doesn't smile.

I'm tempted to defend us but he's right. "So, Thursday? Feel free to change your mind, just let me know ahead of time if possible. I'll let you get back to work."

He nods and motions with his hand after he tugs his gloves on. "Go around the side so you don't get clocked by something."

I head toward the corner of the building, looking at him over my shoulder. "I'll see you Thursday. At seven!"

CHAPTER EIGHT

BY SIX THIRTY-FIVE on Thursday night, I still don't know what Jay's
up to.

I watch him open the oven and reach in to peel the foil off the top
of the casserole dish so the cheese on top of the lasagna will brown
just right. He makes a kick-ass lasagna and he knows it. I wonder if
he's trying to impress Patrick or shame him by showcasing what a
perfect husband he'd make. Maybe he just felt like Italian tonight.

I wander around the first floor of our little house, puttering. Not
cleaning, just doing things no one will ever notice—squaring up the
angles of the photo frames on the mantle and pounding the couch
cushions until they're fluffy.

I'm painfully aware of my own house right now. It's a cute place
with decent furniture and neat accent pieces. It looks decorated,
unlike Patrick's, and it's bigger than his house. I wonder for a
moment if he'll feel poorly because of these facts, but then I realize

two things. Firstly, Patrick built his own house, with his own hands. He surely made it the exact size he wanted. Secondly, he probably makes more money than Jay and I combined, so it's not as if he couldn't own nice things if he wanted to. These thoughts flip-flop my worries, making me feel shallow and materialistic.

The doorbell rings and I abandon my self-analysis.

I open the door to find it's started snowing again. Patrick has on his black knit cap and fat flakes are sticking to it. I see his truck parked in the driveway behind my Saab. Surreal.

"Hey there." I step aside to let him in.

"Hey. Smells good." He hands me a wine bottle shrouded in a paper bag. He glances at the carpet and my stocking-feet and pushes his boots off and leaves them on the front step.

And then suddenly, Patrick Whelan is in my home, standing in his gray wool socks in my living room. In Jay's living room.

"Come on through," I say.

He follows me into the kitchen and I set the wine on the table. Jay puts the lasagna on the stovetop and takes off the oven mitts. He turns around and looks between us.

I've only seen Jay and Patrick interact a handful of times. Usually it's at the Tap, where Jay's always made a point of offering to buy Patrick a beer, an unspoken debt for him possibly saving my life all those years ago. Except for that day Jay went to Patrick's to talk about this arrangement, I don't think they've ever exchanged more than a dozen polite words on a given occasion.

"Hey." Jay steps forward with perfect confidence to shake Patrick's hand. "You can hang your coat by the door."

Soon enough, I'm pouring three glasses of wine as Patrick takes a seat at the table. Jay sets down three plates and the parmesan cheese shaker, two big forks and one small one, a roll of paper towels. He sits across the table from Patrick, me parked between them, apropos of farce.

Patrick looks to each of us as I serve myself.

"So," he says. "Robin said you aren't planning to murder me."

Jay smiles down at his empty plate a moment. "No. Although the idea has some appeal."

"I don't see why I'm here," Patrick says, stripping the veneer of sociability right off the entire evening.

Jay shrugs. "Just a bit of a summit. Thought we could all use a little air-clearing."

"Am I here to have the law laid down about how you think this is going to work?" Patrick asks, looking openly impatient as he dishes out his food.

"I don't know how this is going to work. If you think this is fucked up," Jay says, waving around the serving spoon Patrick hands him, "try being on my side of it."

"I wouldn't let my woman mess with some other man if I was you," Patrick says, damn cold.

My eyes volley between them and I gulp nearly all my wine before they've even touched theirs. Amid the squeaks of forks against plates, they continue their manly caucus.

Jay nods at me. "I love her, and I'm going to marry her. You saved her life and now she wants you—she needs you—to fuck her brains out. For whatever reason. She seriously can't control it. And I love her more than I love the idea of her being faithful to me, so I'm going to have to let you." Jay digs into his food, having said what he needed to.

Patrick eats too, brow furrowed. I suspect he's wondering the same thing I am. Does Jay mean Patrick should fuck my brains out *tonight?*

"Pass the paper towels," I say.

Patrick does and he says to Jay, "Then what? What happens after me and her…" He trails off.

Jay shrugs. "I don't want to share her, trust me. We've been happy for four years. I'm hoping the more she gets to know you, the less she'll need you. I think she'll get bored with you and maybe realize how good she has it at home."

"I know how good I have it," I say quietly, ignored.

"But she's mine," Jay reiterates. "And if you want her, and she wants you, I'm going to be a part of it."

"What do you mean?" I ask, mouth full.

"I get to watch," Jay says after a pause. "And you have to watch us," he adds to Patrick.

Patrick's normally hooded eyes go wide, so wide you can see white all around his brown irises for a second. There's a pouch of food in his cheek where he froze in mid-chew, and he swallows and sets down his fork. I wait for him to push his chair back and storm out of the house, but he reaches for his wine instead, downing half of it.

"When?" he asks.

I wouldn't be more shocked if he'd challenged Jay to pistols at dawn.

"Tonight," Jay says.

I think something insanely banal, just then. I think, *Thank goodness my period's not due for a couple days.*

Patrick nods. "Fine. Where?"

"Here," Jay says. His territory, I think.

"Fine," Patrick says again.

The men tuck into their food, me vibrating with adrenaline between them. My intuition is tugging frantically at my sleeve, demanding my attention, but I kick it away. The rest of the hurried meal passes in silence and Jay stands up first, taking his plate to the sink. When he comes back he pulls me to standing by the arm. I can sense Patrick's hackles rise, perceptible as a dog growling.

Jay takes hold of my shoulders, his eyes darting over my face. They look green tonight. His hands slide up to my neck and he kisses me.

Regular kisses at first then deeper. Cinematic kisses—deep and smooth and meant for Patrick as much as they are for either of us. It takes me a few seconds to relax into it but when I do, I melt like butter.

A chair squeaks against the floor and Jay breaks away from me as Patrick steps close. I see Patrick's brown eyes staring into Jay's hazel ones, posing a question. Jay glances to me then puts a palm on my back, gently urging me toward Patrick. If being literally passed back and forth between these two men wasn't so incredibly hot I'd be insulted by their pushiness.

I catch Patrick's eyes for a second before his face lowers. He tastes just like Jay—same wine, same tomato sauce, acidic and salty. He tastes different too. Feels different. He's just plain bigger, a bigger jaw under my fingers, bigger hands tangling in my hair. I want to see Jay's face, to check that this is actually turning his crank as it did in theory. I don't though. I surrender to Patrick's mouth. His tongue delves deep and explicit, stroking mine, multiplying all the heat Jay roused in me.

He breaks away. He keeps his head close, whispers something Jay's not meant to hear. "Is this what you want?"

I breathe my answer against his cheek. "Yes." *Maybe.*

I hear him swallow before he replies, nearly too quiet even for me. "I'd never share you."

I lick my lips and stall a moment before I look at Jay. There's a gleam in his eye, honest to God—there's an actual brightness there, like fire. It's either anger or arousal or a hybrid of the two. He curls his finger to beckon me over.

He puts his mouth to my ear. "Go to the bedroom and put on something sexy."

I nod, nervous, and cast a glance back at both of them as I leave the dining room.

As I climb the stairs I wonder what they're talking about. I bet Jay will be laying down some ground rules for Patrick. I push the dimmer switch up until the bedroom lights are barely on and I stare at our pillows and covers, unable to fathom that Patrick's about to be here with us. Unable to fathom that Jay is inviting his sexual rival here to desanctify our bed with another man's memory. Then I realize something incredibly obvious. I'm about to finally have sex with Patrick Whelan.

And all at once, I know why Jay's doing this. He's not letting Patrick be a part of our sex life—Jay's making sure he's an inextricable part of my soon-to-be sex life with Patrick. He's going to make sure that whatever happens after tonight, if there should ever be a me-and-Patrick, it'll be haunted by Jay, just like he's had to put up with Patrick haunting our twosome from the very beginning.

I bet Jay trusts me exactly as much as I trust myself. Clever boy.

The sexiest underwear I own is a matching silk bra and panties set, plum-colored. I look at myself in the full-length mirror when I'm changed and marvel that this is the woman who's managed to corrupt and compromise the two intelligent and attractive grown men currently circling each other in her kitchen. This must be how pretenders to the throne feel. Powerful and paranoid.

I hear footsteps on the uncarpeted stairs. Jay enters carrying one of the dining room chairs. He sets it by the dresser, a stadium for a one-man audience with a perfect view of the action. Tomorrow morning one of us will probably eat breakfast sitting on that chair.

"You look good," Jay says, nodding at my underwear.

I shiver and rub my palms together, though it's perfectly warm in here. "Thanks. Are you sure about this?"

"Yeah."

"Do you think we'll regret it?" I ask.

Jay walks over and we sit together on the edge of the mattress. "Strong relationships survive way worse things than threesomes," he says, running a blissfully familiar hand up and down my arm. "If you and I are supposed to stay together, we'll get through this."

If we're supposed to stay together…

"I'd never do this for you," I whisper. "With another woman, I mean. No chance in hell."

"I know," he says and kisses my temple. "I love that about you."

"That I'm a hypocrite?"

"No, just that you're honest about how horrible you are." He grins at me, bumps my shoulder with his. "I know how your brain works, Robin. You're probably psychoanalyzing this sixty levels deeper than me or that asshole downstairs ever will."

"Probably. And don't call him an asshole."

"I know you," Jay says. "And that's why I'm not worried about what's going to happen after tonight."

I wish I were as confident as Jay.

I pray to God Patrick Whelan is lousy in bed. That might make everything way simpler.

More footsteps mount the stairs and Patrick appears at the door. I stare at his silhouette framed in the threshold, lit by the glow leaking up from the den. The fact that he's here makes me realize I don't know him that well. I wouldn't have guessed he'd agree to this. I wonder if that makes him more horny than honorable or just more desperate to be with me than I ever imagined.

"Take a seat," Jay says.

Patrick sits on my other side on the bed. I succumb to a moment of female insecurity and glance down to check how unflattering this posture is to my belly. I feel Patrick scrutinizing my body too, but without any criticism. A broad, warm, half-familiar hand drifts up to cup one of my breasts, sucking the air from my lungs. Patrick leans in and kisses me again, softer than before. I feel Jay's hand on my shoulder, urging me to lie down. I recline on my side, head on the pillow, and Patrick lies down to face me. Jay slides up behind me, warm mouth on the nape of my neck, palms on my waist. Smooth palms, way different from the coarse ones Patrick explores me with.

"You can touch him," Jay says, voice low just behind my ear. Then his fingers reach around to settle on my mound over the silk, knuckles surely touching Patrick's stomach. He strokes my clit, light and teasing as I take the invitation.

Patrick seems brand-new tonight, surrounded by so many familiar things. The bed feels predictable beneath me, as does Jay's body behind me and his fingers between my legs. Patrick feels foreign. His smell stands out, and his voice when he clears his throat. I rub my hand over his chest, his arm, his neck.

"Get him hot," Jay whispers. "Then he can watch us."

My hand slides lower, passing by Jay's, passing over Patrick's thick belt, finding him already hard behind his jeans. He groans faintly at the contact. His hands slide from my belly to my collarbone and back, weighing my breasts with each pass. There's a magic to Patrick when he's turned-on, a teenage-boy quality that contradicts his steady façade. I cup my palm over the ridge of his erection and angle my head to kiss him, deep. He grunts against my mouth as our tongues tease and explore, igniting me.

Between my legs, Jay strokes my clit with perfect mastery. We know each other so well, he's better than I am at getting me off. I can feel him too, his hard cock pressed to my butt. The heat builds like a drug, changing everything. The room grows warm, as hot as the two male bodies against mine. Jay's hand slips inside my panties, multiplying the pleasure threefold. He makes a happy noise behind my ear. "She's already wet."

I hear Patrick suck in a breath through his nose. His tongue plunges deeper, sweeping against mine, making my hand tighten around his cock. His mouth leaves mine to whisper, "I want you so much."

Jay takes his hand away. "Go sit on that chair, Whelan."

Patrick gets up, walks obediently to the chair by the dresser and waits.

"Sit on the edge of the bed," Jay tells me.

I do.

He sits behind me, both of us facing Patrick. "Spread your legs," he orders.

I do.

His hands stroke up and down my thighs, slow and rough, his short-nailed fingers curled into harmless claws. I gasp as his hand comes back to my center, stroking my lips through the silk. Patrick and I share a private, awkward dance, both our pairs of eyes meeting then moving to each other's crotches, meeting again, fleeing again.

Beneath the pleasure Jay's giving me there's a wide river of *wrong* running through this. Not just societal wrong, but intuitive, *this-ain't-right* wrong. Part of me wants to tell Jay to stop, but it's vetoed by the bossier parts that are throbbing against his fingers.

"Take these off," he says, thumbs tugging at my waistband. I stand for a second and push my panties to the floor. I sit and Jay resumes. Five feet in front of me, Patrick's nostrils flare. His lips part when Jay slides two fingers inside me and the flush in his skin is ten times hotter than the penetration.

"Take it out," Jay says to Patrick. "Let her see."

As always, Patrick pauses before he acts but he eventually obeys, opening his belt and his fly and pushing down his shorts. He wraps a hand around his erection.

"He's big," Jay whispers, right in my ear. "Is that what you fantasize about?"

I nod, intoxicated by the guilt of the lie. As I told Patrick, my infatuation is with him, elementally, not merely his body.

"Did you suck him yet?"

I nod again. Patrick's hand starts moving up and down his length.

"You make him come?"

"Yeah."

"Did you swallow?" Jay asks.

Patrick breaks his silence to speak for me. "Yeah, she swallowed. She drank it right up."

I freeze, feeling Jay's fingers do the same on my clit. I've never heard Patrick talk this way—dirty, sure, but not with an intent to incite. I hold my breath and wait for Jay to explode. Instead he puts his mouth to my temple and says, "Tell me about it, Robin."

I take a breath. "I begged him to let me. On his couch. I got him as big and hard as I could, and teased him while he told me how he wanted to fuck me."

"You want to fuck my girl?" Jay asks.

Patrick's eyes jump from my cunt to my shoulder—to Jay's face. "It's all I can think about."

"Did he eat you?" Jay asks me, fingertips circling my clit.

"Yeah," I say.

"Come over here," he says to Patrick. "I want to see you get on your knees and make her come."

Patrick tucks his cock back behind his shorts, slides off the chair and walks forward on his knees, settling between my thighs. I hold my breath. Jay's fingers tease me, dipping inside, taunting Patrick.

"She's so wet already," Jay says.

I feel his slick fingertips stroke my lips, and the look in Patrick's dark eyes deepens all the longing. Jay takes his hands away as Patrick brings his face close. Jay cups my breasts, tweaks my nipples through the fabric to spread heat through my chest. Patrick's tongue flicks my clit and my thighs jerk. His strong hands hold them steady. He laps at me for a long minute, flicking his wet tongue against my lips before he pushes the tip inside. I whimper at the sensation and close my eyes, the sight of his face all at once too intense.

"Taste her," Jay says.

Patrick makes a hungry noise, plunging his tongue deep. The pleasure is tearing me apart, so hot, so massively screwed up—this big man's mouth on my pussy, Jay's palms coaxing pleasure from my breasts as his breath steams against my neck. Two men. Jay's fingers move to the front clasp of my bra, exposing my breasts, fondling them.

"I get to fuck her bare," Jay says. "I should have fucked her first and made you eat all my come out of her."

I gasp and my eyes pop open, unsure if what he said is utterly, insanely hot or completely fucked. But only Jay gets to decide what's hot or fucked tonight. Patrick doesn't protest the idea, just keeps doing what he's been ordered to, fucking my pussy with his mouth.

Jay lets one of my breasts go, reaching down to my mound. He makes a V with his fingers on either side of my lips, pulling the skin a bit tighter, exposing my clit more to Patrick. I know Jay must feel Patrick's tongue and Patrick must be licking Jay's fingers and the idea that they're sharing the barest of sexual contact sends a crackling bolt of selfish pleasure through me.

I think something evil as their hands and Patrick's mouth pleasure me—about Jay's ultimate revenge, making Patrick suck him. I don't think there's any chance of that happening but the thought makes me so hot I feel the climax reach boiling, the heat in my toes and the muscles of my legs, gathering and whirling in my pussy and breasts and my skin and my shaking hands.

"She's coming," Jay says. "Don't stop fucking her 'til I say."

Patrick obeys. His licks and sucks grow rougher as I lose myself, turning the orgasm from exquisite to excruciating.

"Keep going," Jay orders.

I wriggle and jerk between them, my clit dying for a respite, but Jay knows how I work. There's a peak to the torturous sensitivity and once they get me over it the second climax rips through, twice as hard as the first.

"Drink it up," Jay says.

I feel utterly wrung out and I know Patrick must be drowning in my come. His tongue laps, lips suck, and I feel his fingers coaxing all my juice out so he can swallow it.

Jay speaks close to my ear, the shallowness of his voice giving away his arousal. "You happy now, Robin?"

"Yes." The tiny word comes out polysyllabic from my hitching breath.

"Is two men enough for you?" Jay asks.

"Yeah."

"You want us both at once?"

I don't know exactly what he means, and I hesitate, falling back to earth with an unceremonious plop. Jay knows anal skeeves me out and I look over my shoulder at him, nervous.

"Maybe he can fuck you from behind while you suck my cock."

I don't have a chance to decide if this idea is brilliance or sadism because Patrick suddenly stands, zipping his jeans over his erection and buckling his belt, looking ten feet tall.

"I can't do this," he announces. And that's all he says.

He turns and leaves the room, heavy footsteps thumping down the stairs. I stare wide-eyed at Jay and he nods to the door to say I should go after him.

With my bra still flapping around my shoulders I grab my bathrobe from the hook by the dresser and nearly break my neck, yanking it on and stumbling down into the den. The front door's open and Patrick's tugging his second boot on. I rush to him but realize I have no clue what to say.

He straightens up. "I'm sorry. I can't do this." He walks to his truck and I follow.

"No, I'm sorry," I say. "I didn't know this was what he had in mind. If I'd had time to think about it, I might've realized it's fucked up."

He looks down and shakes his head. "You have no clue how bad I want you… But I can't share you. Not like that. You guys'll have to work this out without me. I'll see you around."

I think I've earned a far harsher ear-bashing than this, considering how massively Patrick's been getting dicked around for the supposed benefit of my relationship.

I hug my robe closed as he climbs into his driver's seat and slams his door. He rolls his window down and leans out on his elbow, eyes trained on my bare feet in the snow. "Go inside, Robin. Go back up to your man."

His engine starts and his lights flick on, making the white numbers on my license plate flare before he swings his truck out onto the street. I watch him drive away then I watch the empty road, snowflakes passing under the streetlights. After a minute or two Jay comes out and leads me inside on my prickling feet.

I tie my robe closed and wander into the kitchen and clear the table. Jay stands in the threshold, quiet for a long time.

"Robin."

I dole the leftover lasagna into a Tupperware, thinking Jay better finish it because there's no way I'll be able to.

"Robin?"

I look over my shoulder and I don't recognize the man standing there, dressed in my boyfriend's clothes. Whatever person Jay became tonight… Well, I'm largely to blame for the change. But I hate him for letting it happen. He's supposed to be the rational one.

"I'm sorry," he says.

I turn on the tap and fill the casserole dish to soak. I want to grab the open bottle of wine by its neck and whip it against the tiles at Jay's feet, but I recork it instead and set it beside the toaster, turning it neatly label-side-out.

"Robin—"

"I don't want to talk about it." I toss all the utensils into the casserole dish and dry my hands on a rag. I walk past Jay to head upstairs but he grabs my arm and turns me around.

"Let go of me."

"I'm sorry." He doesn't let go, but he's not hurting me.

I feel a big ball of something thick in my throat just before the tears come. When I cry Jay's hand loosens and I yank my arm away and march upstairs to try to shower off the creepy awfulness I'm feeling.

His pillow's gone when I go to change into my pajamas and I know he's exiled himself to the couch. I wish I'd beat him to it because I want him to be the one lying in the dark, surrounded by the memories of everything royally fucked that just happened in here.

I lie awake so long I end up going to the bathroom and swallowing a couple NyQuil capsules. They gives me restless, disturbing dreams, but it sure as hell beats consciousness.

CHAPTER NINE

A WEEK ISN'T REMOTELY LONG ENOUGH to mourn someone you've been with for four years.

Actually, I think I'm mourning us both, collectively, Jay-and-Robin, and how we were up until last Thursday. We made sense before then. I miss making sense. And I miss Jay too, more than I'm pissed at him. Strange how he managed to be the one who took things too far.

He left on Friday while I was at the shop. He propped a note on the dining room table, right where the parmesan cheese had been sitting the evening before.

Robin, I'm going away for a couple weeks to give us both time to think about what we want. Let's not call each other until next weekend unless there's an emergency. Love, Jay.

"Away" means Michigan, I assume. Jay's got plenty of old college friends there he could crash with. Someone must have given him a lift to the bus station or the airport, as there were fresh tire treads in the snowy driveway when I got home that night. I wonder what he told them. His stuff is still in the house, minus his laptop and some clothes. I guess you might say we're having a separation. I smile grimly to myself, imagining explaining that to my dad.

"Dad, I have some sad news. Jay and I are separating."

"Separating? You're not even married. You modern kids. You make everything into a goddamn hippie drum-banging therapy retreat."

I miss my dad. Today's Thursday. Maybe I'll drive up to Maine and visit him this weekend and cook him a belated, mini-Thanksgiving dinner and pick his brain about how to know who you're supposed to be with…though he's probably not the one to ask. I think he only ever loved my mom, and after she died he never tried dating anybody new, as far as I know.

It's been deadly cold this week. Dog walkers pass in front of the shop windows and they yank their leashes with a new impatience, more interested in getting back indoors than indulging their pets' olfactory curiosities.

I slit a shipping box open on the floor of the stationery section and unload stacks of colorful cover stock, and Carrie helps me price and deposit them in the appropriate cubbies. She acclimated to my emotional vacancy by Tuesday and has stopped asking if everything's okay. She must know Jay and I are on the outs, since he usually calls once or twice a day to say hello or ask a favor. He hasn't called since requesting the olive oil. Which I still haven't picked up. I've been using an old bottle of canola oil instead and it's foul.

Carrie's a nice girl and I know she cares that I'm upset. I also know she's got a bit of a crush on Jay, and how could she not—he's easily the hippest guy in Dereham. She's bright and she was raised in the gossip-centric atmosphere of a small town with long, boring winters. She's hardwired to not miss the fact that Jay and I split up within a stone's throw of Patrick visiting me at work. Her sympathy is like a cupcake with a rusty nail in it, a big old biteful of tetanus lurking beneath cheerful pink icing.

The end of the day comes after an eternity of anticipation. I want to see Patrick tonight. I've waited so I can tell myself I'm not running into his arms too soon after Jay left me, and now I need desperately to talk to him. About what, I don't know, but logic hasn't ever gotten itself much of a foothold in my dealings with Patrick.

I go home and heat up some soup for dinner then leave for his house just after eight. His driveway's empty and as I aim myself toward to the Tap I worry maybe he's gone nuts and skipped town in the last week. But there's his old truck. I park beside him and my jitters kick in as I slam my door. I run to the entrance, just as I used to run from the neighbors' house back to mine after dark when I was a kid, breakneck speed in case goblins tried to grab my ankles as I flew past the hedges.

I see Patrick the second I push the door in. He's at the bar talking to old Hank Grenier, who owns the hardware store. I watch them for a minute, guessing at their conversation. Probably something manly about lathes or table saws or contemptible, modern women.

I gulp a deep breath and round the bar to where they're sitting, taking a seat next to Patrick. He's still talking and doesn't see me.

"But the manufacturing's all gone overseas," he's saying to Hank.

Hank smiles past Patrick at me. His big ears are weighed down by his even bigger bifocals. "Ahoy there, Robin. How's business your side of Main?"

Patrick's eyes are round as he swivels to face me. "Hey, Robin."

I address them both but look only at Patrick. "Hey, guys. Business is fine, thanks, Hank. How about you?"

There are two ways the men in Dereham handle gossip. Typically they ignore it, figuring it's too frivolous to bother with. Hank, however, is a seasoned practitioner of the second approach—

innocent, tactless, male nosiness. "Heard you and Jay Fleury split up."

"Sort of," I say. "We're taking a break." My eyes jog to Patrick's face for an instant, which is all it takes to catch his mouth fall open.

"Always thought he was a decent guy," Hank says, shaking his head.

"Yes, he's lovely," I say. "But you know how relationships can be. We were at that juncture. You know, get married or call it quits."

Hank laughs and I can see in his hugely magnified eyes that he's a bit drunk. "This new crop of kids with their internet lifestyle—these young bucks don't know how to commit anymore," he says, bundling himself in the earned wisdom of his roughly seventy years. "Probably doesn't know how good he had it with you."

I let Hank get it all wrong, not to protect my own reputation but because telling him I'm the gun-shy one would prompt a conversation I'm not willing to have. It would start out fatherly in timbre and wind up with an awkward, generationally disturbing flirtation. Pass.

"Hey, Patrick," I say. "How's lumber?"

"'Bout the same as always. How's paper?"

"Bit pulpier than lumber."

I order a beer and Patrick and I begin a long and mind-numbingly dull conversation. By the fifth minute, still on the topic of paper, we inspire Hank to slide off his stool to go in search of more thrilling company.

"How are you?" Patrick asks, voice low.

"I'm sort of a wreck and sort of relieved."

"So, are you two…" His eyes dart away and he trails off, just as John Mellencamp starts crooning from the speakers.

"He left, but he hasn't gotten his stuff out or talked to me about the mortgage or anything. We're separated, I guess. It's up in the air."

"I'm real sorry I was a part of it."

I laugh. "I'll bet."

"No, sorry for you guys—"

"I know, I'm just teasing. And I'm the one who should be sorry. Sorry for you."

He shrugs and takes a sip of his beer. "I could've said no."

"And you did. Just a couple weeks later than maybe you should have." I smile at him, apologetic.

Our heads are close, scandalously close by Dereham's low standards. "It's like Jay said, though—if he and I are supposed to survive this situation, we will. Maybe we're not. I don't know yet." I suspect I do, though, if only I'd let my intuition get a word in edgewise.

Patrick nods.

"I'll understand if you want me to leave you alone," I go on. "Last week was royally fucked up. I totally get if you want me to back off—"

Patrick gets to his feet and I don't know how it happens but somehow, suddenly, he's kissing me. Right here in the bright, ugly light of the too-many beer signs. He's standing, I'm sitting, and he's bent over, lips on mine, hands on the back of my head. The music fades to a dull hum as Patrick eclipses my world. A long, low whistle from the bartender cuts through the dark then I'm lost again.

Patrick lets me come up for air after ten seconds or ten minutes—I couldn't tell you which. I hear *Jack and Diane* just ending so I guess it was somewhere in the middle.

I glance around and about twenty pairs of eyes are on us. A couple townies laugh and a couple more make teasing, flirtatious noises. Someone claps. I feel my face color and take a deep drink of my beer.

Patrick's still standing. He empties his glass and makes a throaty noise after he swallows, wiping his mouth with the back of his hand.

"You wanna come home with me?" There's more to this question than just its boldness. Patrick's eyes are loaded with fear and hope and held breath, their jumpiness telling me that he really, truly likes me. A lot.

I nod. Patrick pulls a ten from his wallet and tosses it on the bar for the both of us. I swing my legs to the side and slide off my stool, tighten my dangling scarf around my neck as we walk to the door. Patrick's hand envelops mine under the keno monitor. The door eases shut to cut off another lascivious whistle from the peanut gallery and he leads me across the crunchy, salted asphalt to his truck.

"You want to follow me?" he asks, letting my hand go to find his keys.

"Yeah. That's probably easiest. For tomorrow."

He nods and I watch his Adam's apple jump. He gives me a last look and climbs into his truck. I get in my car and we flip our lights on together and I follow him out of the lot and onto the dark road.

The world looks crisp, as if it's under the influence of some drug I've never tried. Everything's sharp and clear and I watch the occasional red bursts of Patrick's brake lights as I tail him to the edge of town. I bet I don't blink once before I pull into his driveway and flip my engine off. We slam our doors nearly simultaneously and his outside lights come on, leaving me blind for a few seconds as we walk to the front steps.

I hear the key in the lock, the creak of a hinge, the flip of a switch as he illuminates the kitchen. I close the door behind me and look up at him, blinking away the blobs in my vision. He seems very real. I don't know how else to say it.

I glance at his fridge, wondering if things'll be like that time I came over without permission. Rough and frantic.

When he steps to me and leans in close, I know it'll be nothing like that. I wrap my arms around him, feeling the pilled fleece of his jacket with the cold still clinging to it, breathing in that wintery, lumbery Patrick Whelan scent from his neck.

"He's about to leave you," he says, "and it's still not enough to keep you away from here."

I shake my head.

"What does that mean, Robin?"

"That I'm lousy at learning my lessons?" I offer, knowing it's too trite a reply to the question he's really asking.

"Is this only about sex?" He steps even closer, stubbing the toe of my shoe with his boot.

"Is it only about sex for you?" I ask.

"Of course not. You think I'd fuck around with somebody else's relationship just over sex?"

"That's sort of how you packaged your offer," I say.

He comes so close I have to step back, back, until I'm against the wall. Patrick braces a hand beside each of my shoulders and leans in. "Things've never been simple between us, have they?"

I shake my head again, looking into his eyes, remembering all those hours I stared into them from across the visitation room table. Definitely not simple, no. Though it could have been.

"I really thought we'd give something a try, after I got out," he says.

"I was too afraid of how I feel when I'm around you."

"You feeling it now?"

I nod, and his breath flares against my temple.

"I seem to have a real knack for complicating your life when you're only trying to help me," I whisper.

He pulls back, face so close I can't bring his features into focus.

"I don't regret that night," he says. "In the parking lot."

I frown. "You lost seven months of your life because of that."

"Even if you'd never visited me in prison, that night would've still been worth it, because I got to spend those couple hours with you at the sheriff's office. But then I ended up getting to see you every week, just you and me. I'd do it again in a heartbeat."

I put my fingers on his stubbly jaw as I ponder this. "Do you think you're in love with me?"

He nods.

I laugh softly. "Do you wish you weren't?"

He shakes his head. "Nope."

I press my mouth to his, a long, shallow kiss while my hands explore his face.

He licks his lips as we separate. "I've been real good about not badmouthing your man this whole time. But I'd like to make a case for myself. Or at least try and explain how I see things."

"Okay."

"He wants you so much, he'd let you be with another man if that's what he needed to do to keep you."

I nod.

"I want you so much that if I was him, I'd kill that other man."

My eyes dart between Patrick's as I try to guess if this is poetry or hyperbole or the honest-to-God truth.

"And I'd spend another fifty years in prison," he says, "and it'd still be worth it."

I blink a few more times.

"Me and your man," Patrick says, "we're both fucked-in-the-head crazy in love with you. You need to figure out which kind of crazy you want to be with and cut one or both of us loose."

I nod, slow and long, studying his zipper pull before I look up. "I think I know which kind of crazy I want."

I bring my lips to his neck and kiss his cold skin from his collar to his ear. His big fingers tangle in my hair and I feel his moan as much as I hear it.

He pulls away. "You think you might ever love me?"

"I think I might already… But I'm not sure. I know what I've felt for Jay is love, but with you, it doesn't feel anything like that."

"What's it like, then?"

"With Jay, it was always comforting, like a warm glow or whatever. With you, I look at you, and I feel…itchy. Like I'm going to claw my skin off, I want you so much. I don't know if I know you well enough to say if I love you yet."

Patrick's eyebrows bob up. "You know me better than anybody."

"Oh." I try to comprehend the loneliness of this statement. "Really? I feel like I hardly know anything about you."

He shrugs. "There's not that many layers to me."

I bet he's wrong. I picture him as a tree, with all those rings. He probably only sees the bark or the leaves, not the inside parts, the ones that reveal his violent and self-sacrificing layer, the helpless, sexual, passionate layer, the boy in the center who grew up amid the clutter and misery of his mother's beloved squalor. I want to cut in deep and see the different layers of Patrick Whelan and get my hands sticky with sap from all the unpleasant bits.

I unzip his jacket and put my hands against his work shirt, tracing the thread spelling out his last name with my fingertip.

"Make love to me," I say.

Patrick kisses me, first. Sweet and thorough.

He pulls away and takes my hand and we walk to his room. He switches on the light. "Hang on," he says and leaves me.

I hear him starting a fire in the living room and I notice how cold it is.

I unwind my scarf, taking in his room for the first time. His walls are wood-paneled, stained a dark oak color. He has a couple framed photographs on his walls and I wander over to one. It's black and white, a picture of pigeons on a busy urban street. I'm still staring at it when Patrick comes back in.

"Did you take this?" I ask him.

He shakes his head. "I bought it because it reminded me of you, actually." He blushes, visible even by the dim reading lamp's glow. "I always think about you when I see pigeons."

I walk over to him and walk my nails up his arms in a creepy manner. "All those mites and ticks and diseases."

"You know why," he says, quiet.

"What does it mean that our common character flaw is whaling on idiots who are ten years younger than us?"

"I don't care what stuff means," Patrick says, still quiet.

I let him hold my jaw and tilt my face up to meet his. His kisses come slow, perhaps a celebration that I don't have to leave tonight after we're done using each other's bodies. He covers my mouth with his, slips his tongue between my lips, just enough to taunt. He lets my face go as I push the sleeves of his jacket down his strong arms. Our clothes fall away—shirts and pants and socks and underwear—until we're standing in the warming room, naked, studying each other.

Patrick's the first man I've seen who looks sexy with his clothes off. Not that naked men aren't sexy to me if I'm in the mood, but usually they seem a bit dopey with all their stuff just dangling how it does. Not Patrick though. Everything about him seems right, as if he were designed without clothes in mind. I smirk by mistake.

"What?"

"Sorry. You just look so damn good naked."

He doesn't seem to know what to do with this compliment so I go ahead and kiss him again, pressing my body right up against his. He moves close as he did in the kitchen, pushing me into the wall. He has to crouch to keep us kissing since he's over a foot taller than me. I feel his cock growing hard against my hip as our mouths wrestle.

"Can you do what you did, that time against your fridge?" I ask. "Can you hold me up against the wall?"

He reaches down and grabs me behind the knees, lifting me so I can wrap my legs around his waist, pinning his erection between my pussy and his stomach.

"Is this how you want to do it?" he asks, not sounding at all as if he's burdened by a hundred and thirty pounds of woman.

I shake my head, smiling at him. "Not tonight, anyhow. I just like that we could, if we wanted to. I'm just objectifying you."

Patrick's eyes narrow until they're nearly closed and he laughs—a throaty, sweet, manly chuckle. "You get weirder and weirder, the more I get to know you."

"Want to go to your bed?"

"Sure." He carries me over there and lets me tumble onto his comforter and the anxious grappling begins in earnest. He climbs on top of me, that big body casting mine in its shadow. I hear him through the kissing, delicious wet grunts full of hunger.

"Do you have condoms?" I ask.

"Someplace."

"You better get them."

Patrick leaves me to disappear into the bathroom and return with a box, frowning. He pulls out a plastic square.

"What's wrong?"

"How expired can a condom safely be?" he asks, squinting at the wrapper.

"Golly, I don't know. A year, maybe?"

"We're cutting it close."

I remember that scene from *Grease* in the back of Kenickie's car, glad I'm not at risk of repeating its cautionary tale. "I'm on birth control," I offer. "And I'm clean. You know, in case it like disintegrates on us."

"Me too. I don't get around much," Patrick says and we both glance at the boxful of corroboration he's holding. I scan his body again and all I can think is, *Damn, what a waste.*

"I'm sure it'll be fine." I pat the covers beside my hip.

He tosses the box on his nightstand and joins me on the bed again. I push his shoulder so he lies on his back and I touch him. I love the way his eyes fly to my hand as I grip his shaft, how they go a bit vacant as I make his cock heavy and hard and big.

"Robin."

I keep all my attention on him, running my fist up and down, torturously slow. He covers my hand in one of his and tightens it, making the strokes rough. His voice is sexier than any other gorgeous, obscenely masculine part of him, that deep bass moaning and grunting and telling me just how badly he wants this.

"I thought about this a lot," he says.

"About me touching you?"

He nods. "Yeah. You've got really soft hands." He watches a few moments longer and swallows, deep. He looks me in the eyes.

"What?"

"Do you think this'll ever happen again? After tonight?"

"Yeah. Why?"

He swallows again. "I'm pretty sure I'm going to be really lousy. I promise I'm usually better than I will be tonight."

I pause with my hand still wrapped around him and lower my chest to his, burying my face against his neck, and I laugh. Patrick laughs too, his ribs jumping beneath me.

"Just a disclaimer," he says and I hear a wide smile in his words.

I push myself back up and straddle his hips, settling my pussy on the underside of his cock. I slide up and down, slowly to start. He watches, breathing labored. Then his hands grasp my hips and he speeds the friction.

"God, Robin."

"You feel...awesome." Literally. I am full of awe from how wonderful he feels beneath me. I lean down and suck in two brimming lungs' worth of Patrick Whelan. He probably showered after work but it's all there, his smell.

Patrick flips us onto my back and I feel his hips take over for mine. There's a force behind his thrusts, a strength that intimidates me as much as it turns me on. For a gorgeous minute he rubs his cock over my wet lips then my impatience comes to a head.

"I want you."

"I want you too."

"No, I really, really want you." I tug at his hips to tell him it's an order, not a sweet-nothing. "I need you. Now."

His breathing halts. He gets a condom open, rolls it on, angles his head to my entrance.

"Now," I say, tugging on his hips. "Now, Patrick."

Nearly six years, my body's been screaming for this.

He puts his weight behind his cock and though my pussy's probably wetter than it's ever been before in my entire life, it's not a perfect moment. I suck in a breath as he starts to penetrate.

"Okay?" he asks.

"Just stay right there for a minute." I ooze out a long exhalation, ordering my body to relax. "Okay, go a little deeper."

Another couple inches and he feels wonderful, now. Patrick pulls out all the way then drives back to that depth.

"Wow," I say, staring between our bodies.

He doesn't say anything, looking as though he's in deep concentration. He gives me another inch, starting to pump faster. I want all of him, deep, deep, deep until our hips touch.

"More. Please, Patrick."

He pushes into me, hard, and I yelp at the sharp cramp he triggers. He pulls out halfway, looking down with wide eyes, half concerned, half out-of-his-mind horny.

"Sorry," he says. "Use your fist. Gimme a couple more inches." He guides my hand to his cock and wraps my fingers around him. He starts to fuck again, and I love the feeling of his skin sliding through my hand, his balls hitting me when he pushes deep. There's something sweet and so elementally *us* about the fact that we don't fit. We're wrong together, right down to our anatomy. I smile so hard I can't even bite it back.

Patrick looks insane in the best way imaginable—eyes wild, muscles clenched. I watch with wonder as his shaft drives in and out between our bodies. I never knew a cock could get so stiff and swollen. I never would have guessed the man attached to it could be so attached to *me*. Amazing.

He sucks shallow breaths through his gritted teeth, rabid. "God, Robin."

His strokes are pure sexual heat, blazing hot but not enough to make me come. The fingers I have wrapped around him are in the way of me getting what I need.

"Patrick."

"Yeah?"

"I really want to come. Can you go shallower for a minute?"

He nods like a madman—as if he's drowning and I asked him to hold his breath just a little longer, please. He leans back on his haunches, thrusts going from animal to machine for me, giving half his length so I can play with my clit. He puts his hands on my knees and closes his eyes.

The pleasure mounts fast. I rub myself, watching Patrick. "God, you feel incredible."

He inhales sharply, closes his eyes tighter. "Please don't say anything. I'm trying really, *really* hard not to come."

I keep my mouth shut, letting Patrick concentrate on whatever's holding him back from the edge. As much as I need my fingers, I need him too. I need to hear him, moaning. I need to look in his eyes, if only they'd open.

"Patrick—"

He groans, frustrated by my inability to respect his wishes.

"I don't care if you come," I say. "Just please, Patrick, open your eyes."

Those heavy lids lift as his lips part. His hands tighten over my knees and I tease myself, frantic, knowing it's a race now.

His sounds return, gasoline on my fire. I can sense how violently his body wants to intensify this, the muscles of his stomach and hips fluttering, struggling to stay in control of the pace and the depth.

"Fuck, Robin." He lowers, hands beside my ribs. His cock is calling the shots and within seconds he goes too deep, shocking me with another cramp and making me gasp.

"Fuck. Sorry." He pulls out, turns me onto my side, spoons his body behind mine. He guides himself to my pussy, the position keeping him from ramming too deep.

I prop a leg up and stroke my clit, insane with the pleasure and the contact—his firm muscle against my soft backside, the aggression of his thrusts and his noises.

"God, Robin."

He's gone. For a dozen beats his dick hammers me, graceless and unspeakably hot, then he pushes deep and holds as he shoots. I come just after him, the spasms clenching me tight around that still sinfully hard cock.

I hear his voice, soft now, urging me. "Yes, yes, yes." A warm, broad palm kneads my hip until I'm still. He strips the condom away and we lie this way a long time and it feels right, his big, damp body wrapped around mine, possessive.

The wake of the sex is like the days following a hurricane. Things are askew, scattered, altered, and my sense of safety and normality is battered. There's cleanup to do and adjustments that need to be made but I'm not ready for all that. I want to rest here in our smoking rubble for a long time and appreciate the force of the storm.

We lie still, surrounded by the triumphant smell of our bodies, our breathing calming in tandem. After maybe thirty minutes I shift my legs and yawn.

I discover Patrick's been lying in wait, his silence more patient than sleepy. He climbs on top of me, staring down. He smiles, the gesture subtle and warm and familiar.

I smile back. "Hey."

"Are you tired?"

"Not too tired," I say.

"What do you want to do?"

I graze my palms up his body and think. My hands answer his question, wrapping around his cock, fondling and savoring the feeling of him, the weight as he grows. He rests back on his haunches between my legs to watch, running his hands along my calves.

"You're really beautiful," he says.

"Oh. Well, thank you."

He nods. "I always hoped everybody thought you were my girlfriend, back when you came to visit me."

I laugh, charmed by this announcement. "Sometimes I felt like I was… I wish they'd let you get food packages in there. I would have learned all sorts of new and impressive cookie recipes."

We stop talking, both watching my hands on Patrick's hard cock. I stroke him until I can see and smell how ready he is, until a clear bead forms at his reddened head. He looks restless, that wonderful strain tensing his features. I watch his throat as he swallows.

He slaps my hip, gentle. "Turn over."

I get onto my hands and knees for him, craning my neck to watch him get another condom ready. He slides in deep, smooth and confident as if we've been doing this for years. And in our minds, I guess we have.

A strong hand clasps the front of each of my thighs. He urges me to bring my legs together, my thighs adding the distance he needs to take me harder. "Oh, Robin."

It's just like my fantasies, feeling all his weight behind me, his voice punctuating the impact. The steady rhythm grows faster and rougher until he's pounding me. He kneads my ass, tugs my hips into his thrusts, loses his tempo as his pleasure turns frantic.

"Patrick."

"Yeah. Say it again."

I moan his name, feeling his cock stiffen with each repetition. "This is exactly what I wanted, all that time," I tell him. "You feel so amazing."

"I wanna make you come again," he says and I hear that beautiful desperation dripping from his words.

"Let me get on top."

He hammers me hard for a final minute and pulls out. He lies on his back and I swing my leg over his hips, angle my body so I can slide him in and find the right depth.

"Wow." I close my eyes and lean back on my knees, getting him exactly where I want him. I start to rock, rubbing my clit along the base of his shaft as my pussy fucks the remaining length. The thing about this that's so wonderful is Patrick himself, but I have to admit, his size is a massive turn-on. A shiver, warm and chaotic, trickles from the crown of my head down my back. "Wow. You're so fucking big."

My eyes open, finding Patrick's glued to my chest. He licks his lips and puts his hands on my waist. I grab his wrists and lead his palms to my breasts, where I know they want to be. I groan as his rough fingers tweak and tease and I ride him rougher. He sits up and I lean back a little so he can bring his mouth to my nipple. I drag my fingers through his hair and listen to the hungry noises as he suckles.

"You feel so amazing," I tell him again.

He meets my eyes as his mouth breaks away. "Fuck me," he says. "Use me."

I push at his chest until he lies back down. "Bring your knees up a little."

He does. It makes a seat for me, cradling my butt as I ride him. The pressure's mounting, spurred by the blazing-hot, wet friction between my clit and his dick. I fan my fingers over his chest and put my weight on him, knowing he can take it. My hips speed up, pussy aching for him.

"Fuck me, Robin. Use me. Use my cock."

"Patrick…" The heat builds in my body, tightening my cunt and making my motions messy and greedy.

"Come on my cock, Robin. Please."

"You are—so—fucking—thick." I slide my damp palms up his body and over his shoulders until they sink into the pillows. My nipples brush his chest, the teasing exquisite. I feel the pleasure tipping, spilling me into my climax.

"Yes," he hisses. "Good girl. Come on me."

The pleasure deepens and holds and crescendos until I collapse on him, limp.

"Oh fuck."

He lets me lie against his slippery chest and catch my breath for a couple minutes. I feel his dick, stiff and pulsing, ticking like an impatient clock. His fingers whisper over my damp back with fond, light caresses.

I get a hand on either side of his ribs and prop myself up. "Hoo… Okay. Now you. Whatever you want."

He reaches up to tuck my hair behind my ears and stroke my sweaty face. He licks his swollen lips and smiles at me, eyes darting between mine. Strong hands turn me onto my side, roll me onto my back. Patrick gets between my weak legs, stroking his slick cock. He guides himself back inside, slow and controlled. I groan my approval.

"Gimme your fist, sweetheart."

I ponder my new pet name as I wrap my fingers around him at my entrance. His force picks up, thrusts turning selfish. He moans and grunts in time with the impact, beautiful, disbelieving sounds.

"Patrick…"

"You feel so fucking good. You're so warm." His hips pump me deep, muscled arms flanking my soft ones. I wrap my legs around his waist and memorize his body. I touch his chest and neck with my free hand, feeling the fever humming in his damp skin.

"Fuck me," I say. "Show me everything you've been wanting."

He leans back and takes hold of each of my legs behind the knee. "You can let your hand go," he says. He closes my legs and hugs them against his chest, my ankles at his shoulder, feet by his ear. His cock slides between my inner thighs, testing the depth and finding its rhythm. I've never felt so controlled and possessed, so used in the most wonderful sense of the word.

"God, Patrick. You feel so good."

He speaks through gritted teeth. "Yeah?"

"Yeah. I can't wait for you to come."

He moans, eyes closing a moment.

"I've wanted to be with you for so long," I say.

His arms lock tighter around my legs as the fucking intensifies.

"I love your body, Patrick. I love your big cock."

"Yeah…"

"Let me see it when you come."

His voice rises an octave, reduced to shallow gasps. For another glorious minute Patrick Whelan fucks the sense out of me, until his hold turns shaky. He pulls my legs apart, reaches between us as he slides out to strip the condom and jerk himself with a frantic fist.

"Oh, Robin." The first spurt arrives, lashing my belly. I rub his come into my skin as he milks himself, gives me more, until his voice fades to panting and his stroking hand stills. His half-lidded eyes close and at that moment, staring at his face, I know I'm in love with him—that I have been since the second his arms wrapped around me when we sat on the hood of my car that horrible night six years ago.

I feel high for a long time. The room and the world hang surreal around me as Patrick gets up, finds me a towel, brings us a glass of water to share. We burrow under his covers. He lies on his back and

I curl against him, a palm plastered to his chest above his slowing heart.

I love you, I tell him telepathically. I won't say it out loud yet. The only language I care about right now is his breathing, his heartbeat, the gentle clench of his fingers in my sweaty hair. There'll be time enough for words some other night. Right now, everything's exactly as it's supposed to be.

CHAPTER TEN

I WAKE WHEN Patrick's alarm clock blares and I'm so sleep-addled it doesn't startle me at all. He reaches over me to click it off, rolls out of bed and disappears into the bathroom. I squint at the red digits—six fifteen. Turning onto my back, I feel his flannel sheets against my bare body and gaze up into the rafters that crisscross his bedroom ceiling.

I smile at all the new things I know about him now that I've spent the night.

Patrick sleeps like a hibernating creature. The steady rhythm of his quiet snoring never faltered, not even when I rolled myself into new positions or tossed an arm or leg over him. He's a bit of a covers hog, but I guess he's out of practice at sharing and anyhow I didn't wake him with any of my blanket-yanking.

I don't feel any morning-after anxiety with Patrick. I smile at him when he returns from the bathroom, not caring if my face is greasy or my mascara's smeared. He smiles back and I see leftover shaving cream by his ear.

"I hate to rush you, but I need to head out in a half hour," he says. "I'd let you lock up, but I don't have a spare key."

"That's fine." I fight my way out from under his heavy comforter and the cold fuses all my joints and muscles. We get dressed together, me in yesterday's clothes, him in fresh ones. Luckily I changed and showered when I went home for dinner, so Carrie won't be able to draw any conclusions from a fashion encore. I have plenty of time to go home again this morning, but I think I'll head into the shop early instead, maybe do all the Friday inventory before we open. Honestly, I don't want to go back to the house this morning and get my brain all muddied, pondering evidence of Jay, evidence of Jay-and-Robin.

"What do you want for breakfast?" Patrick pulls a sweater over his head. "I've got cornflakes and toast and oatmeal."

"Oatmeal," I say, rubbing my stiff hands together.

I get myself cleaned up in the bathroom, thinking I better pack an overnight bag if Patrick lets this become a regular thing. The only moisturizer I find is a tube of heavy-duty hand lotion, the kind fishermen endorse. I pat a thin layer over my face. He's left a new toothbrush out for me on the sink, still in its box. It's way too big, a freebie from the dentist's office, but I treasure it more than a dozen roses. I arrange it just so in the cup next to Patrick's and smile as I flip the light off.

I'm relieved to feel the heat coming from the woodstove when I join Patrick in his kitchen. He pours steaming water into two bowls of quick oats and stands a bottle of maple syrup on the table between them.

He sits opposite me, offering snatches of eye contact. "Did you sleep okay?"

"Yeah, wonderful."

"Good."

I stir my oatmeal and clear my throat. Patrick seems cagey.

"I'm really happy about last night," I say, before I can chicken out.

"Me too." Not cagey—shy. He measures a spoonful of syrup and mixes it into his bowl.

"I used some of your industrial-strength hand cream. I hope my face doesn't look all shiny."

He glances up. "Your face looks fine. You look pretty."

"Oh. Good."

"You can bring stuff over, though, if that's what you're getting at. I know I'm kind of…" He looks around the room, as though the right adjective might be sitting on one of his half-empty shelves. "You know."

"Tidy?"

He nods. "I wouldn't mind if you kept stuff here though." I catch him swallow and blush just the tiniest bit.

"Thanks. Maybe I will."

He nods again.

We eat in silence for a couple minutes then Patrick speaks.

"Sorry. I'm not great at knowing what to say. You know, after last night. I don't take people home very often."

"I suppose Dereham's not exactly a teaming hotbed of sexy single ladies."

He smiles into his bowl.

"Well, if you're worried about what to say, you can just let me be an obnoxious, pushy girl and I'll get way ahead of myself and start theorizing about our future together." I grin at him.

"Oh. Okay."

"Well," I say, "I'll start by trying to figure out a really emotionally charged Christmas present to get you. One that'll make you feel really uncomfortable and pressured. Like a piece of man jewelry. With a way-too-earnest engraving."

"You're cute, Robin, but I'm already in love with you. I know you're kidding, but you can't scare me off, even with jewelry."

"Cleavage tattoo?" I scrawl my finger across my décolletage, tracing his name in invisible script.

He smiles and scrapes the edges of his bowl clean.

"I guess if the last few weeks haven't been enough to strike terror in your heart, there's not much else I can do," I say.

He shakes his head.

"Then I'll go ahead and theorize for real… For starters, I'd miss you, when you're away in New Hampshire," I say. "Four months is a long time for a lady to go without her own personal lumberjack."

"It doesn't have to be that long," Patrick says. "I only do it for the money…" He trails off, some heavy thought weighing down the corners of his mouth.

"What?"

"My mom," he says. "I do it mainly because my mom's off her nut, and someday I'm going to have to move her into a home or something. A decent one."

I nod and reach across the table to touch his wrist under the cuff of his scratchy sweater.

"But I have plenty of savings," he says. "I don't have to do as much logging as I do."

"I wouldn't mind driving up to visit on weekends," I say.

"Maybe. Maybe we could throw a cap on the truck and go camping."

I laugh. "Wow, listen to us getting all ahead of ourselves. We're good at this."

He smiles, staring at the table before his brown eyes dart to the microwave clock. "We should get going."

I'm not ready to say goodbye to him. "Can I buy you a coffee, before you head to work?"

"Sure."

We get our shoes on and I follow Patrick into town. I park in the employee lot and jog gingerly down the icy sidewalk to meet him at the Dunkin' Donuts a half block from my shop. We get in line together, not talking, and order our coffees. We head outside and stand by a mailbox, warming our bare hands on our hot takeout cups. I toy with the little plastic latch on the lip, unsure of what I want to be saying to him.

"Maybe…" I begin.

He raises his dark eyebrows and takes a sip.

"Maybe you'd like to come by the shop this afternoon, during your lunch hour?" I ask. "We could grab something to eat at the place next door." I hold my breath, as if I'd asked him to the junior high school prom. Funny how it's so tough, even after all that nonsense over breakfast.

He nods, casual. "Yeah, I'd like that."

"And maybe some night next week I could bring over some food again, and we could watch a movie or something at your place."

"Sure."

Warmth forms in my middle, a little spark that swells to a permeating glow, spreading out until I feel flushed. This is everything that should have happened between us after he was released—frantic sex followed by a cautious courtship. I stare up at Patrick Whelan's face and I think, *This is my man.* My body's known it for years, screaming itself hoarse trying to get my idiot brain to accept it.

A million things won't be simple or easy in the next few weeks, but this, right now, feels the way it should. This, right now, is effortless. It's as easy to be with Patrick as it was impossible to stay away from him.

He clears his throat and looks at our feet. "I better head over there."

I nod and I tap my cup against his. "I'll see you in a few hours."

Patrick pauses a second then leans in and kisses my cheek. His own cheeks are pink when he straightens back up. "I'll see you."

I give him a little wave and watch him cross the street. I watch my man get into his truck and slam its door, and I watch him glance at me and raise a hand before he drives off. I watch my man until he turns down Brewster Street and disappears from sight and I think, *There goes my man.*

DIRTY THIRTY

CHAPTER ONE

EVAN HENNESSEY glanced at the clock on his computer screen for the thousandth time that hour, the day crawling, limping ever more slowly toward five.

He was turning thirty tomorrow, no big deal really…except tonight he was going to get his brains fucked out, one last hurrah before his twenties were officially over.

This evening's festivities were his wife's orchestration. Margie had planned the whole thing and done a damn fine job, just as she did with everything else she put her mind to.

Evan grabbed his phone and Margie picked up on the second ring.

"You're not chickening out, right?"

He laughed, kept his voice low so his officemates wouldn't overhear. "No way. Just obsessively checking the time. He said eight?"

"Yup, eight."

"And I don't need to pick anything up on my way home?"

"Nope. Your gorgeous charming wife has it all under control."

Evan toyed with the tin robot next to his computer, straightened the framed wedding photo beside it—Margie in torn white lace, tattoos, spiky pink hair, Evan in a tuxedo tee shirt, mohawk longer than it was these days and dyed deep red to match his silkscreened bowtie and carnation.

"I love you, Margie."

"Why wouldn't you?" He heard the smirk in her standard reply.

"I love you for doing this."

"I love that you asked," she said. "Listen, I've got to finish something for a six o'clock deadline. See you in an hour-ish?"

"Yup. See you soon."

He switched his phone off, drummed his fingers on his thighs. Four nineteen. Christ, this day was never going to end. Why did the laws of physics have to pick today to rewrite themselves? Didn't they understand Evan needed this, the slowest Friday in history, to be *over* already? Didn't they know tonight was the night Evan was finally going to get properly and thoroughly fucked by another man?

* * *

FIVE O'CLOCK DID EVENTUALLY ARRIVE and the second it did Evan was slinging his bag over his back and mounting his bike, his brain three hours ahead of his body. He cycled the twenty minutes from his office at one end of Portland toward his and Margie's little house on the other. Usually on a Friday as glorious as this one he'd be savoring the June breeze, appreciating the sunshine and the distant white peak of Mount Hood against a rare, nearly cloudless sky...but not tonight.

The events scheduled for this evening were four months in the making. It had started one drunken night in February after a friend's

Valentine's engagement party. Too much champagne, or perhaps exactly the right amount. At any rate, Evan and Margie had stumbled into the house giggling, kissing, tearing each other's clothes off as a good husband and wife should. At the height of Evan "performing his marital duty", as Margie liked to call it, she'd done that thing that drove him nuts—two fingers teasing his asshole as he drove into her, rough. No new feature, until Evan's drink-addled self-censorship filters had failed and the words came tumbling out.

"God, I want to get fucked by a guy."

She hadn't missed a beat, hadn't paused for the thinnest of seconds. "Oh yeah?"

"Yeah."

Her fingers had slowed, pressure building as she penetrated him. "For real, do you think?"

He'd held his tongue, body lost in the pleasure, brain cloudy. "Yeah. Just once. For real."

"Fuck, that's sexy."

And so that little confession grew, the topic making its way into their dirty talk, the thought working as a hit of some exciting new drug. A month after the initial drunken revelation, Margie had brought it up outside the bedroom—outside their house, even—over a picnic lunch.

"You know your dirty little secret?" she'd asked, spring sunshine lighting up her blue eyes, a chicken salad sandwich in her hands.

"Sure."

"Do you think you might ever want to go for it? Like, bring in a guy?"

Evan stared off toward the river, pondering the offer. His body sure as hell wanted it. His rational brain wasn't a hundred percent on board yet. Dirty talk was one thing, but this was their *relationship* she was offering to experiment on.

"I dunno. Maybe."

Margie took a big bite of her sandwich, licked mayonnaise off her thumb. "I'm down for it," she said, mid-chew.

He shrugged, hiding the hot jolt of curiosity zapping through him. "I wouldn't even know how to go about finding somebody." They ran with an eccentric, liberal crowd, but Evan didn't know about asking acquaintances for tips on finding some random gay guy to fuck his straight ass. Semi-straight. Heteroflexible.

"I think I already did find somebody," Margie said.

"What? Who?"

"Paul. Paul Seeto."

Evan blinked. "Paul our bouncer?"

She nodded. "Paul the Wall."

Evan pictured the doorman who worked at their favorite bar, the tall thug Margie called "that hot bitch", often within his earshot. Hot, yes. Bitch…Evan wasn't so sure.

"Is Paul even gay? He doesn't seem gay."

"He's close enough." She'd know better than Evan. Margie was a writer, covered gigs and events for the local paper, knew just about every bartender and band member in Portland.

"So what do you think? Is he the right sort of guy?"

"Well, sure, I mean Paul's hot and everything."

"If you want me to, I'll ask him. He's got a reputation. A good one, I mean. The good kind of slutty."

"What about you?" Evan asked. "How would you feel about inviting somebody else into our…you know. Inner sanctum or whatever?"

That adorable, evil grin. "How would I feel about watching our hot bouncer bang my hot husband? Is that a sacrifice I am holy enough to make?" She'd put a hand to her breast, faking martyrdom. "I think I can handle it."

Evan mulled it over for a long time, nearly three months, spent a few very distracted nights at the bar trying to not stare at Paul, to not imagine what it'd be like to get fucked by the guy. Spent quite a few nights fucking Margie, listening to her brilliant dirty talk on the subject.

And when Evan's thirtieth birthday approached he'd given in to the temptation, gave Margie the go-ahead to feel Paul out about the idea. She'd returned from the assignment glowing, reporting that Paul said he'd be pleased as punch to "fuck that scrawny little rocker boy for his birthday".

That's how Paul knew Evan. As Margie's husband and as the guy who brought his guitar to the bar's open mic nights and usually drank enough beers to get up on stage and perform his growly, dirge-y songs and earn himself a nice reception.

Evan glanced at his reflection as his bike flew past the glass façade of a car showroom. *Scrawny* was a bit mean, but yeah, he was slender. He'd always been like that, wiry and muscular, built like the cyclist he was, like the rock star he wasn't.

Margie called him a "scrapper", called Paul a "bruiser". Margie insisted she liked Evan skinny, enjoyed borrowing his jeans and said fitting into them kept her from letting herself go.

Evan turned onto their street, waved to their elderly neighbor. He coasted down to the end of the road, hopped off his bike at the top of their driveway and grabbed the mail.

Margie was hunched over the coffee table in the living room, hunting-and-pecking at breakneck speed on her laptop. She kept her eyes on the screen, held up her "just a sec" finger. Evan dumped his bag by the door, toed off his sneakers and unrolled his pant leg. He dropped onto the cushions beside her and tossed the mail on the table. He rubbed the nape of her neck, tousled her intentionally messy hair, bleached white-blonde. She had on a red-and-black-striped sweater, dark jeans, funny little tennis socks with pompons at the heels. Her cat-eye glasses were pushed up on top of her head, magnifying her dark roots.

He watched her screen, her spell-checker halting at such spurious entries as "fuckwitism" and "Caliguliberal". Evan wondered if that meant she'd gotten stuck covering a town meeting again.

God, he loved her. Still thought about her when he jerked off, just about every time, and not out of a sense of duty or respect, but because she still got him that hot, even after they'd been together five years, married for two. He probably wasn't the only one. Margie made everybody feel fascinating, because in her opinion, they were. Everything and everyone interested her and she wasn't afraid to show it. Evan thought it was a miracle he'd been the one she found fascinating enough to sleep with one very lucky St. Patrick's Day evening, then to date, then praise-be-to-God to *marry*.

Evan loved Margie so fully he couldn't imagine anyone *not* wanting her, so even if every last man in Portland fell asleep to thoughts of fucking her, he couldn't in good conscience hold it against them.

Margie finally sighed her relief, saved her document, opened her email and sent her story off to somebody, somewhere.

"Done." She leaned over and accepted Evan's kiss, smiled, went in for a second. "Excited for the weekend?" she asked, snapping her laptop shut and standing. "Can I start you off with a drink?"

"If I start drinking now I'll be wasted before we even get to the bar."

"Nervous?"

He followed her into the kitchen, watched her pour two iced teas. "Terrified. And excited."

"I think it's going to be awesome," Margie said in her infectiously confident way. She stirred a spoonful of sugar into his tea and handed it over.

Evan swirled his glass, watched the ice spin. "It's going to be way different than us just talking about it. There's going to be a living, breathing extra person in the bed with us."

"Well, I am *super* excited. I think this is going to be a blast."

"I need a shower," Evan said, downing half his tea. "I'm all stinky from my ride."

"I'll join you." She took his glass and set both on the counter. "I need to get to work loosening you up."

"How literally do you mean that?"

She laughed and grabbed his hand, led him to the bathroom and got the shower going. Evan watched her fold and set aside her glasses, peel off her sweater and shimmy out of her jeans. Cock already stiff, he objectified her pale skin and colorful tattoos as she unhooked her bra and kicked away her panties and socks.

"I can't believe you're my wife."

"You say that, like, every time I get naked." She stepped to him, unbuttoned his shirt. "Oh, what have we here?" She aimed her eyes downward and gave his erection a mean squeeze, opened his belt and slid it from his jeans. Half a pound of leather and metal studs clattered to the floor and Evan rolled his eyes as always, ruing the day Margie's cavalier attitude would finally crack the tile. He abandoned the scorn as she pushed his pants and boxer briefs down his legs, gave his ass a squeeze.

He slapped hers in retaliation. "Get in the shower, wife."

She got on tiptoe and kissed him, a nip of her teeth on his lower lip before she disappeared behind the curtain. Evan dropped his button-up off his shoulders and shed his undershirt and socks, joined her in the shower. He let the week wash away in the warm water, tried to send his nerves down the drain after it and half succeeded. Margie shampooed and rinsed and they traded places. She slicked conditioner through her short hair and Evan studied her face. He loved shower-Margie. Everybody else got Margie all-done-up, funky hair and bangs just so, crimson lipstick glistening like a rockabilly vampire. Evan got her bare—plain face, wet hair free of its gel shackles, and of course her slick pussy wrapped around his cock, all hail birth control.

She glanced down with a smirk as he stepped close, the underside of his dick brushing her belly as he lathered his hair.

"Subtle, Hennessey." She'd called him that on their first date, still called him that even two years after she'd adopted the name herself, along with the pearl ring on her left hand.

"Might be a good idea," Evan said, edging even closer. "You know, calm me down for later."

She shook her head, reached behind him for her razor. "No way. I want you as worked up as humanly possible. I want tonight to just *explode*. I want your brain completely and utterly blown."

He passed the soap, watched as she shaved her legs. "I don't want to explode *too* fast."

"We've got all night. I think you should explode as fast and frequent as you want, birthday boy. Just not before eight."

"Birthday eve," he corrected, rinsing his hair.

"Dirty thirty," she teased. "Enjoy your last night of youth, kiddo. The big three-oh really changes everything." Margie had been thirty for all of six months and hadn't changed a lick, aside from occasionally referring to Evan as "jailbait".

They swapped places and she washed the conditioner out of her hair, scrubbed her face. "I think tonight's going to be really fun," she declared, words muffled by the washcloth.

"Yeah, two dudes in your bed. Jackpot."

"That's your call and you know it."

"Fair's fair," Evan said. "He fucks me, he fucks you."

Margie rinsed her face. "He watches us fuck each other?"

"He fucks himself and we take pictures."

She laughed. "He gets us both drunk, ties us up and steals all our valuables?"

"Maybe." Evan shut the water off. "It'd certainly be memorable."

"Don't forget, if you chicken out at the last minute we can always bar-hop, take him to the Vern and split a pitcher. No pressure."

He climbed out and passed Margie a towel. "I know. And I don't plan on chickening out." But he did have to work to hide a pang of fresh anxiety as he dried himself.

He and Margie had done some crazy stuff in their time together, plenty of wacky things in the privacy of their own bedroom, but neither of them, not as a couple or in their previous sexual adventures, had had a threesome.

Margie liked to claim she earned the liberal West Coast slut prize, having dated both a girl *and* her own erstwhile pot dealer in college, but tonight was by far the skankiest thing either had done, and damn if Evan wasn't pretty fucking excited about it. He'd thought he won the lottery when Margie not only didn't bat an eye the night he got drunk and asked her to spank him, but had jumped at the chance and in time taken things farther than Evan had ever found the sac to come out and ask for himself. Intuition—that's what she had. Intuition and an almost pathological absence of fear when it came to looking foolish. It made her a fantastic reporter and an even better lay.

Evan crossed the floor, wrapped his arms around her middle and pulled her close so his ribs brushed her nipples with their tiny silver rings. "You have no clue how much I love you."

"I have *some* clue," she said and gave his hard cock a couple cruel pulls.

"No seriously. You have no idea."

Margie bit her lip, eyes rolling toward the ceiling as she thought. "What?"

She grinned, turned and shoved a few toiletries out of the way so she could hop her butt onto the edge of the cramped counter. She tugged at his arms. "C'mon."

"I thought you wanted me to explode."

"You will. But go ahead, let's get one out of you so you don't give yourself an aneurysm later. I want you to live to see thirty."

Evan pounced on the invitation. He stepped between her thighs and Margie draped her slender arms over his shoulders, both their sets of eyes trained on Evan's eager dick.

"Get me ready," she whispered.

He loved that order. There was lube in the medicine cabinet, handily within his reach, but he liked to earn his way in. He'd always had a hungry, insecure streak in him, a persisting need to prove himself even half a lifetime after he'd ceased to be the smallest and most picked-on kid in his neighborhood. Margie challenging him now got the junkyard dog in him growling, straining to show her what he had.

He brought their faces close as he pushed her legs wider, opened her up and cupped his palm over her pink folds to feel her heat. He let the pad of his hand brush her clit, listened to the soft sigh that warmed his temple.

"You excited about tonight?" Evan whispered. He trailed his fingertips along her lips.

"Of course I am. I'm dying to watch you with him."

"What about you?" he asked. "You want him too?"

He sensed her grin in his blurry periphery. "Maybe. Up to you."

"You've thought about it though, right?"

"Sure."

Evan rubbed her clit with one hand, angled his cock to her lips with the other. He teased her with his head, let his own pre-come ease the friction. "Tell me how you think he'd be. If you fucked him."

"If he fucked *me*," she corrected. "I don't think Paul's the type who *gets* fucked."

"Yeah. So tell me." Evan lowered his mouth, kissed her ear in that way that always made her shiver.

"He's big," she said. No lie—Paul had to be a foot taller than her and probably weighed as much as two Margies, maybe even a bit more. "I've thought about getting in his lap, feeling how strong he is as his hands bossed me around. Or just feeling how heavy he is on top of me."

Evan pictured it, his wife happily pinned beneath that looming body. The jealousy he felt didn't hurt—it just doused whiskey on his own desires, and the fire felt good. Over the past twenty years the chip on Evan's shoulder had morphed into a kink, and these days the thought of being bullied didn't make his blood boil so much as it made his dick stiff. Paul could fuck his wife if he liked, so long as Evan got to watch, knowing he was the one she fell asleep against every night.

He felt her getting wet, her skin growing hot and slippery against him.

Evan pushed the first inch inside her, gave her clit the light, grazing touch she loved with the backs of his knuckles and the edge of his thick silver wedding band. He listened to her sounds, got himself lost in the patterns swirling up her arm and shoulder, bright paisley-like stylized peacock feathers.

"Evan."

That familiar plea in her voice sent his pulse racing. He slid inside her, slow, easy, deep. They'd always fit this way, just perfect. Her body was small, Evan's cock a bit bigger than his frame suggested. She made him *feel* big too, as big and strong as Paul Seeto when he felt her pussy snug around him, wet and greedy.

Lately when they had sex, his dirty little fantasy was the star of the show. But right now his submissive desires took the backseat to his manhood. Tonight he'd get on his knees, turn his body over to Paul and be the one getting fucked, but for now he wanted to be the man. He held Margie's thigh tight, strummed her clit with his thumb and watched his cock sliding in and out, slick from what he could do to her.

"God, Evan."

"Feel good?"

"It feels amazing," she mumbled, eyes locked between their bodies. "You're so hot, baby. You're so good."

"Who're you thinking about?"

"Just you."

He smiled, held her tighter, pumped her deeper. "I want him to watch us together tonight."

"Whatever you want." She sounded distracted, attention focused on his driving cock.

"I'll make him watch *this*," Evan said, taking her even harder, enough to fill their tiny bathroom with the damp slaps of his hips against her thighs.

"Fuck me, Evan."

"Touch your clit."

She braced herself on one arm, reached her other hand between her legs to take over for him. He turned his attention to her breasts, leaning in to cup one and put his mouth to her nipple, closing his lips around its tiny ring. Her entire body shifted, her back arching so she could hold Evan's head as he suckled her, her fingers raking the damp stubble on the sides and the longer, dripping hair of his limp mohawk. Her legs hugged his waist and her butt wriggled on the counter's edge, hips trying to meet his thrusts. Her racing fingers teased his cock as she stroked her clit, fast and frantic.

Evan freed his mouth. "You gonna come for me, Margie?"

"Keep going."

"You gonna come?" He put his lips back to work, switching to her other breast. The fingernails on his scalp bit harder, gorgeous pain telling him how close she was. He spoke against her skin. "Come on my cock, baby."

"Evan."

The sound of his name got him close, his own orgasm mounting deep in his belly, a hot ache begging to be unleashed. "Come on."

Margie's voice dissolved to a guttural growl, as hungry and chaotic as the spasms Evan felt milking his dick. Her hands flew to his hips, riding his thrusts as her climax unwound.

Evan leaned back to take in her flushed, incredulous face. "Nice... Fuck, you feel so tight." He took hold of her thighs and sped in to the final stretch, a minute's selfish, graceless thrusting that banished all coherent thought from his head and left him panting for release.

Margie urged him on, eyes and hands roaming his chest and stomach. "Faster."

He obeyed, his need reaching its peak as he pounded her, merciless. For the smallest moment of clarity, Evan felt nothing but the steam, heard nothing but the whirring fan and the blood pounding in his ears, saw nothing aside from the blue of Margie's irises. As quick as the Zen came, it was gone. Pleasure crashed in, rearranged Evan's head and hijacked his body. He gave his cock what it wanted, a dozen violent thrusts as the orgasm wrung him out, left him reeling, slippery palms plastered to the counter, warm come trickling down his thigh.

"Oh, fuck."

Margie giggled, combed her fingers through the wet strip of his hair.

Evan gulped for air and let her kiss his neck and face, offered a weak smile when he caught his breath.

"There," she said, stroking his cheek. "Think that'll keep you from boiling over too quick tonight?"

He nodded, delirious. "Yeah. Yeah, that was good." Evan let his idiotic grin tell her what a massive understatement it was. He kissed her forehead, stepped back and got them each cleaned up. Margie hopped down from the counter and Evan went to work shaving his face. He stole glances at Margie in the mirror as she slicked lotion over her fantastic curves, shocked to find his own body already mustering arousal again. He rinsed his face, heard Margie laugh as she brushed a hand over his half-hard dick.

"How old are you turning tomorrow?" she teased. "Fifteen?"

"Blame yourself." He dried his face, left Margie to her moisturizing and escaped to the bedroom in search of clean clothes and self-control.

With his sudden rush of Neanderthal aggression gone, Evan settled back into the buzz of nervous excitement as he stood before his dresser. There was probably no "right" outfit for a guy's first time getting fucked by another guy. Evan decided to dress as he always did, jeans and a random shirt, his City Bikes tee winning fashion roulette as he pulled it out of a jumbled drawer. Margie passed by, rifled alongside him and hooked a polka-dot bra between her breasts, hiked matching panties up her legs and let them snap in place with a flourish. She walked to her closet, slipped a black dress over her head. Release valve or not, Evan still didn't know if he could make it until eight. He wanted her *again*, if only to express his absurd profusion of gratitude.

Instead he went back to the bathroom, squirted gel across his palm and tended to his hair. He coaxed it in to a short crest down the center of his head, the sides now overgrown stubble, black as his mohawk's roots. He twisted the bleached ends, a slim fraction of the effort he'd invested at twenty-five.

"Lookin' good, skunkie." Margie pinched his ass as she sneaked behind him for her makeup bag.

"Get out. I need to be a good little bottom and do the whole hygiene rigmarole."

She gave his butt a final squeeze and closed the door behind her. Evan stared at his reflection, offered himself a grin. "Kid, you are so fucked."

CHAPTER TWO

THEY SET OFF ON FOOT at twenty to eight, strolled in the cool June air to their second-favorite bar—taking Paul home from his place of employment was too weird, even for them. Even for this situation.

The Friday-night bustle heightened and eased Evan's nerves in choppy intervals. He spun his bottle on its coaster, tried to not watch the front door, failed. Margie was perched beside him on a tall chair at their tiny table, her knee pressed to his thigh.

At eight oh three the door swung in, Paul striding through so casual it ought to be illegal.

Evan's nerves jumped into overdrive, laced liberally with excitement. "Oh shit."

Margie squeezed his leg. "Magic time."

Paul spotted them and raised a hand, offered a smile. Margie slid off her seat and Paul stooped to hug her as he reached their table.

"Heya, sexy," she said and clapped him on his huge arm. The nickname didn't make Evan jealous—she called everybody that, even their neighbor's dog. Anyhow, in this case it was undeniably accurate.

"Hey." Paul's deep voice made Evan shiver. "You look awesome," he said, giving Margie in her little black vintage dress the once-over. "No surprise. And you're not too shabby either, Hennessey." He shot Evan a conspiratorial grin.

Evan raised his beer, unsure how men generally went about flirting with each other. He took a drink then got to his feet and accepted Paul's handshake. They'd done this a hundred times in the last few years, but this time Paul placed his other palm over the back of Evan's hand, an added signal that made his pulse jackhammer.

"Get you a beer?" Margie asked Paul.

"Sure, that'd be great."

Don't leave me alone with him, Evan entreated her back, but for once her intuition didn't hear him. He turned to Paul, feeling small...though not entirely in a bad way.

Paul was built and over six feet tall, Evan a wiry five-ten, not counting the hair. Paul's hair was shaved down to a shadow of stubble, dark brown as his eyebrows and irises. He crossed his arms over his chest looking every bit the bouncer. He looked different too, in the wrong bar for one thing, not wearing a black staff shirt for another. He cocked an eyebrow at Evan. "You nervous?"

Simply having the matter spread out in the open had Evan's shoulders loosening. "Yeah, I'd say so. You?"

Paul shrugged, eyes moving around the bar then up and down Evan's body. "Should I be?"

Evan laughed nervously and Margie saved him from the awkward moment by reappearing with three fresh bottles.

Paul accepted his beer and clanked it against Evan's. "Cheers."

"Yeah, cheers."

Ever the brilliant hostess, Margie waved her arm to invite Paul to have a seat at the table—high and small, perfect for close, hushed conversations. "Thanks again for coming," she said. "I know you usually work on Fridays."

"Tough invitation to pass up." Paul grinned, that half-wicked, half-flirtatious smile he'd been offering the Hennesseys since Margie had first approached him with this crazy plan. He set his elbows on the tabletop, leaned in.

Not ready for eye contact, Evan stared at Paul's tan, inked arms with their intricate tribal designs. The three of them must have looked like a meeting of the Portland Tattooed Bisexuals' Club.

"We're a little nervous," Margie said.

Paul shrugged. "Fine by me. Just let me know if I should be doing something to put you kids at ease."

Kids, Evan thought. Paul was probably only a couple years older than they were, but he had that air of gruff wisdom that Evan had forfeited in favor of a college degree.

"Have you done this before?" Margie asked.

"Be more specific," Paul said. "Been to this bar before? Gotten taken home by a couple before? Corrupted some innocent straight boy?"

"Any of those," she said.

"Sure. All of the above."

Margie flashed an impressed face at both men. "Good to know we're in experienced hands."

"It's cool to see a couple like you guys." Paul tilted his bottle to his lips. "Makes me think maybe marriage isn't the bullet to the head most people make it seem like. Good for you." He clinked his beer against each of theirs.

Evan cleared his throat. "We've already got a mortgage and grown-up jobs. We figured by tomorrow we'll both be in our thirties, on the fast-track to baby-land. This is our last big hurrah."

"*You're* our last big hurrah," Margie added.

Paul grinned, eyes on the table. "That's quite an honor."

Evan could feel his beer working, his body relaxing. "So are you... Who do you *usually* go home with?" he asked Paul.

He squinted up at the ceiling, doing some mental math. "I'd say I'm about three-quarters straight."

Evan nodded. "I think I'm like ninety-seven percent straight."

"That's a mighty tight margin," Paul said. "That gives me a bulls-eye's chance of blowing your mind and a whole lot of room to miss and completely traumatize you."

"I'm sure you've got good aim," Margie said, bobbing her eyebrows cheesily.

Paul drained his bottle and set it on the table, businesslike. "I have a couple questions for you two before we find ourselves naked in your bed."

Evan glanced around, searching for other drinkers within earshot...not entirely sure if he was disappointed or relieved to not find any. He turned to Paul. "Shoot."

"Firstly, when do you guys want me to leave? You want me gone as soon as the fantasy's done, or is this supposed to be some big cuddle-fest-plus-breakfast sextravaganza?"

Evan exchanged a blank look with Margie. "God," he said. "I hadn't really thought about it." He hadn't actually imagined this beyond the moment when Paul would pin his hips and ease his cock into Evan's ass. That point in the fantasy usually banished all logistical concerns.

Margie pursed her lips, holding in an opinion.

"What?" Evan asked her. "I don't really have an answer, so what's yours?"

"I don't think we'll know until afterward," she said. "Is that cool? Can we decide in the moment?"

Paul nodded. He grabbed Evan's beer, took a sip, slid it back over. "Sure. Just don't feel like I'll be hurt either way. Don't ask me to stay out of politeness then make me sit through awkward pancakes tomorrow morning."

She looked to Evan and he nodded his agreement.

"Great," Paul said. "And secondly, what are the boundaries tonight? Who am I allowed to touch? Am I the hired help taking orders or do you want me running this show?"

"Evan's in charge," Margie said. "We do whatever he says."

"Got it."

Evan blushed and hoped it didn't show.

"He said before, it's okay if you and me," she flicked a finger between herself and Paul, "you know. It's sort of anything-goes, but he gets to change his mind."

"Right," Paul said. "Sounds good." He leaned back, smiled at each of them in turn then gave Evan a hard clap on the back. "Let's get another drink in the birthday boy and see where this goes."

* * *

THREE BEERS proved to be the winning prescription and at a quarter to ten the threesome left the bar and walked the four blocks to Evan and Margie's neighborhood. The air had grown thick and damp, threatening rain. Margie felt giddy, beyond willing for this evening to go as planned—eager and excited just to see Evan so eager and excited.

"Look at you grown-ups," Paul said, waving a hand around their suburban block and its rows of little ranch houses. "What do you actually do, Hennessey?"

Margie smiled to herself, so oddly pleased to watch her bouncer flirting with her husband.

"It's mind-numbingly boring and involves computers," Evan said. "Let's leave it at that."

"Heh. I always assumed you were a bike messenger."

"Nope. Cube rat."

"They must have a pretty lax personal appearance policy." Paul grazed a hand over Evan's mohawk and Margie swore she could feel the thrill that must surely be echoing its way down Evan's spine.

"Yeah," he said, "the company founder's this computer genius stoner dude. The guy who runs it now is a business douche, but he's afraid to drive all us grungy nerds away by enforcing a dress code. It's pretty laissez-faire in there. You just can't wear shorts or tank tops or open-toed shoes."

"Probably for the best," Paul said.

They reached the house and Margie fished for keys in her purse, opened the door and clicked on the lights. She caught Evan casting a nervous glance back around the block, as though an errant, stirring neighbor might somehow be able to figure out exactly what they planned to get up to with their houseguest. Margie wished the whole world knew about it—she'd been dreaming about this night for months.

She dumped her bag on the coffee table and turned to smile at Paul as Evan locked up. "Welcome."

Paul looked around and nodded politely. "Very cozy."

Margie thought their house looked a lot like her and Evan's first apartment together, only on a larger scale—a jumble of houseplants and mismatched furniture and friends' weird art. But she wasn't ready to shop for matching dining room sets just yet. That level of adulthood could wait another couple years.

"Mind if I use the little boys' room?" Paul asked.

She pointed him in the right direction then walked to where Evan stood drinking a glass of water by the kitchen sink. She put a hand on his shoulder.

"How you feeling?"

He swallowed, nodding. "Good. Excited. Bit nervous."

She smiled at him, admired him. So handsome in that way she liked best…a recovering punk on the outside, responsible adult lurking on the inside, behind the studded belt and the thick silver hoops in his ears, the tattoos on his neck and arms. Pale skin, black ink, blue eyes. *Evan Hennessey, you have no clue how sexy you are.*

The bathroom fan and light clicked off around the corner and she gave him a quick kiss on the jaw—as far up as she could reach.

Paul appeared in the kitchen threshold, an entirely different breed of sexy. The kind of sexy that made girls nervous, prematurely jealous from the knowledge that he could have his pick of the women who paraded past him every night at the bar. Six-two, easily. Built like who-knew-what, built to fight and fuck and drink all night, in any order you pleased. Margie knew his dad was from someplace in Polynesia and that's where Paul got his dark eyes and tan skin, that faintly exotic quality to his features. If they were going to invite somebody into their bed to alter the fine print on their wedding vows, they'd be hard-pressed for a better candidate.

"So," he said, his voice as hot and dark as espresso. "We a go for this?"

She looked to Evan.

He nodded, eyes aimed bravely at Paul. "Yeah."

"Great. Why don't you guys show me where you get up to your nasty marital activities."

Margie rolled her eyes, put her hand on Paul's firm arm and led him to their bedroom. She reached around the doorway and eased the dimmer up. Studying his face, she remembered the look of hungry surprise there when she'd waltzed up to him at the bar, come right out and asked, "Paul, do you think you might be interested in fucking the shit out of my husband?"

"Nice and roomy," he said, nodding at their queen-sized bed.

"I promise we didn't pick it with this in mind."

She crossed the room to close the blinds just as rain began drumming the panes, pulled a box of matches from the bedside table drawer and went to work lighting the candles that lined the shelf above their headboard. She heard the familiar, soft thumps of Evan's sneakers hitting the floor. Louder, nonstandard thumps—Paul's boots. She swallowed, lit the last candle and waved the match out as flame licked her fingertips. Margie turned when Evan eased the lights down and she took in the two men in her bedroom.

It was tough to believe this wasn't *her* selfish birthday wish come true.

CHAPTER THREE

EVAN CAUGHT MARGIE'S SMILE, a polite little smirk that told him the ball was officially in his court. She pushed her flats to the floor and sat on their bed, leaned back and crossed her legs, looking as she did on the Fourth of July—lounging on the grass, ready for the fireworks.

Evan glanced at where Paul stood dead center in the room, arms folded over his chest. He seemed like a man who wasn't used to being patient and passive, a ringmaster waiting for the lights to come up…a lion tamer waiting to be handed his whip. His eyes narrowed in Evan's direction, smile coming slow and a touch ominous. Evan got his balls together and took a couple steps toward him. Paul's sheer size gave him a pang, nerves or excitement or intimidation… Evan allowed the chemicals to rush in and didn't try to resist what he felt, good or bad. He just let the high carry him. Almost without him willing it to, his hand rose to touch Paul's arm, taking in the heat of him, the hard muscle, the soft cotton of his tee shirt sleeve. Evan studied the still life, the chipped black polish on his own fingernails, his white hand on Paul's tan skin.

"You ever kissed a guy?" Paul asked, voice low.

"No." Evan reveled in the vulnerable thrill of needing to look up to meet this man's eyes.

"Interested?"

Evan nodded once. Margie rose from the bed in the candlelit background.

Their guest took the cue, took the lead. Evan's breath caught when Paul's strong hand slid across his throat and ear to cup the back of his head. Paul leaned in, put his mouth to Evan's, just lips at first. So many things about it were off—the man's height, his stubble, the sound of his breath so unmistakably masculine. Evan wanted to taste him and find out if that was off too. *Off* was hotter than hell and he wanted more. He parted his lips and angled his jaw, invited Paul inside. Two sensations warmed him at once—Paul's hot, wet tongue slipping between his lips and Margie's hands on his arm and back.

Paul tasted right, different in all the ways Evan was hungry for. With Margie by his side, watching and anticipating, he felt like prey—like the center of a feast, honored and doomed at the same time. Paul took the kiss deeper, tongue sliding against Evan's, mouth aggressive and bossy, just perfect. Evan's cock was already stiff, curious and impatient about the places he was being led.

Paul pulled away but kept his face close. He licked his bottom lip and stared right into Evan's eyes. "Good?"

"Yeah, real good."

"Can I touch you?"

Evan's dick coursed with excitement even as he worked to keep his voice casual. "Yeah, fine."

Paul grinned, leaned back in. As his tongue explored Evan's mouth, his broad palms roamed his shoulders, his arms, his back. He kneaded Evan's hips, drew him forward just enough for their groins to brush, just enough to push Evan off the cliff into free fall. He suppressed a moan, the sound slipping through his nose as a sigh. Paul slid one hand up to Evan's jaw as the other cupped his ass. He pressed them together, two straining cocks not quite level, two greedy mouths wrestling.

Evan opened his eyes a fraction, saw Margie's hand on Paul's arm, fingers under his sleeve. Jealousy didn't factor—he wouldn't begrudge her this exploration any more than he would a good payday or a delicious meal. He loved what was happening and he wanted her to share it, didn't mind if he was less exciting to her than the stranger in their bedroom.

Paul's hips shifted from side to side, rubbed the two ridges of their erections together. The taunting friction dashed Evan's composure and he moaned, put his hands to Paul's arms and pressed in to him harder. He felt and heard a tiny laugh escape Paul's throat. The hand on Evan's ass made a slow path around his hip and cupped his cock.

He broke his mouth from Paul's, needing air. "Oh, fuck."

Paul smirked, gave Evan's pounding dick a mean squeeze and triggered another moan.

"You feel big," Paul whispered, running his hand up and down. The compliment heated Evan from the inside out and made his head swim.

"He is," Margie said. Her voice warmed and brightened the room like a fire. Evan felt her hand join Paul's in the stroking and teasing. "He's got an amazing cock."

Evan wanted to die now before he could come down from the high of physical worship.

"Maybe you two should show me what you do," Paul said.

He stepped away to let Margie take over. Evan felt the chemical shift as he turned to face her and became the bigger body, the man. He touched her breasts beneath the slippery fabric of her dress, wanting to connect with all her softness and femininity after the hard domination of their guest. He lowered his face and kissed her the fierce way they had when they were new to each other and stupid with infatuation, the way they still did when one of them returned from a long absence, sorely missed.

Between kisses Margie muttered, "Is this still what you want?"

"God yeah."

She purred out a smug little laugh. "Oh good." She bit his lower lip. "It's so hot, watching you with him."

Evan caught her eyes dart over his shoulder, seconds before Paul's hands took hold of his hips. He lost the ability to breathe when Paul came close, offering the unmistakable push of his erection against Evan's ass. One big hand slid up his back, warm fingers curling around his shirt collar, tugging it down so Paul's mouth could find Evan's skin…wet kisses with a faint drag of teeth, rough to balance out the softness of Margie. Paul's other hand grasped Evan's belt, thumb slipping beneath his waistband. He held him in place and thrust, the gentle but insistent press of his cock taunting through two pairs of jeans.

Evan's heart thumped, blood pounding in his temples, fingertips, lips, cock. The room swayed as he fought to adjust to this blurry new reality. The hand on Evan's collar slid to his ribs, swept across his stomach in hungry strokes, slipped lower, lower, fingertips dipping just inside the waist of his jeans, so close, so far.

"Let's go to the bed," Margie whispered.

Evan nodded, letting himself be led by the hand. They lay down and his body knew these memorized movements by heart. Not a dull routine, merely a well-established one, their foreplay like a song both loved and knew down to the very last chord and lyric and breath.

He kissed her, dirty and slow as she stroked his chest. He kissed his way down her neck to the tops of her breasts, peeled her dress from her shoulders and eased it lower to expose her bra. Her fingernails raked his scalp as his mouth found her nipple through the fabric. He shifted to kneel between her open thighs, one hand sliding under her back, the other free to fondle the breast not claimed by his mouth.

Then this song he knew note for note changed, remixed. He sensed heated masculine energy altering the atmosphere as Paul took a seat, his body shifting the mattress and rearranging everything familiar about this. Heightening everything hot about it. Margie changed too, her soft breaths speeding, fingers on the sides of Evan's head clawing just a bit rougher. He wondered what she could see, what promises were written across Paul's face.

Her hands moved to gently push at Evan's shoulder. He knelt back and she tugged at the hem of his shirt. "Take this off."

He peeled it up and over his head and tossed it to the floor. Margie reached down to return the show, eased her dress up and off her body. Evan lowered back to the bed with a smile—Margie had a funny little kink about him rubbing against her while he was still wearing his jeans and belt. Her legs wrapped around his waist, hands on his arms, body eager for the tease. Evan reached down to center his cock then gave her what she liked—slow, rough strokes against her panties.

"God, you feel good," she muttered. Her fingers dug into his shoulder blades, begging for more.

For the merest of seconds Evan thought it was just the two of them, then a heavy palm alighted on his ribs. Arousal gripped him, swift and intense. The thought that they had an audience was intoxicating. Evan's pulse sped and his body grew warm, hot from the sensation of Paul's eyes on him. Another kind of hot from knowing Paul's eyes were surely on Margie too, though the territoriality didn't hurt, only excited him more.

Her hands left his arms to fumble between them with his buckle. She'd opened this belt hundreds of time but there was impatience in her actions, mimicking the frantic buzz tensing Evan's body. He groaned at the sound and feeling of his buckle releasing, grunted as she opened his jeans and coaxed his zipper down. Paul's palm drifted to Evan's lower back and in a matter of seconds Evan's bare ass might be on display, the main course at this dinner party and Paul the guest of honor. Fresh fear, dark and electric, crackled through Evan as he thought about this big man's hands exploring him.

Margie tugged at his jeans, a familiar request. He adjusted his knees and they got them off together, Evan kicking the final leg away and sending them to the floor with a clatter of his heavy belt. Her hand was on his cock before he'd even gotten back in position above her, hungry touch stroking his stiff, pounding flesh through the cotton.

"God, Margie." He shut his eyes, torn between surrendering to how good this felt and blocking it out, keeping himself in control. He had to settle for the latter, not ready for the thrill of anticipation to be dampened. Margie had been right, earlier—Evan didn't want the edge taken off this experience too soon. The release he'd had a couple hours ago was long gone and his body once again brimmed with sweet impatience.

He mustered self-control, reaching between them and gently taking her hand away, setting it at his hip.

"I don't want to lose it yet," he said.

"We've got all night."

Paul's voice cut in, darkened the room and raised its temperature by ten degrees. "Don't hold back, birthday boy. Lemme see what you two usually do before I turn your fucking world inside-out."

Evan shivered. He had to lower his face to Margie's shoulder for a moment and get a handle on himself. Her hands slid to his ass, kneading gently. He felt another hand, rougher and broader, running up and down the back of his thigh. The touch was hungry and appraising, as though Paul were sizing him up, already deciding his fate. The idea got Evan insanely hot and he pushed back to his knees, clumsy fingers shaking as he reached for the bra clasp between Margie's breasts. He slipped the hooks free and peeled the cups aside, exposed her milky-white flesh, perfect pink nipples with their tiny hoops. He braced himself on his elbows and took her with his mouth, lips tugging and teasing until she made those noises that drove him crazy, hot little needy grunts and sighs. He moved his attention to her other breast and she teased him in return, fingers tracing his ears then giving the thick rings in his lobes gentle pulls. He lowered his hips, centered his dick between her thighs and gave her light strokes, just a graze of his hard flesh against her soft folds through the fabric. He moaned right along with her.

"Take your panties off," he muttered. He wanted to feel the friction of her wet skin against his shorts, needed to smell her.

"Anything you want, tonight."

Evan moved back to kneeling, his shoulder bumping some unseen part of Paul, who was just behind him to the side. Margie got herself disentangled from her bra as Evan reached for her underwear.

He paused as Paul's weight left the bed. Evan turned to find him standing, watching, thumb toying with the buckle of his belt.

"Keep going," Paul said. Evan heard a new edge to his voice, evidence that his role went beyond mechanical to living, breathing, horny-as-hell real man in their bedroom.

Evan fought to refocus his attention on Margie as he peeled her underwear down and off her legs. He stole another glance to the side and saw their guest grinning. Paul reached for the bottom of his shirt and pulled it up and over his head.

Evan swallowed.

Margie muttered, "Damn."

Evan had expected Paul's body to impress, but this was more than he'd bothered hoping for. Paul's long torso looked powerful and sleek, the faintest spray of dark hair trailing from his chest to his chiseled navel, more ink decorating his pecs. If Evan weren't so ecstatic at the chance to get fucked by the guy, he'd have been dying of inadequacy. Paul unbuckled his belt, pushed his jeans to the floor. He had muscles Evan didn't know the names for, the kind swimmers had, the kind that drew your eyes from their ribs to their crotches like flashing neon arrows. The crotch in question was shrouded by Paul's boxer briefs but the erection filling them was impossible to camouflage.

Paul adjusted himself, fingers tracing his waistband. "You just do what you do," he said. "Gimme a nod when you're ready for me to join in."

Evan looked to Margie, still loath to do anything that might tip him over the edge. He wanted to savor the burning impatience in his body as long as humanly possible. "Let me taste you," he whispered.

She grinned and assumed the position, stretching out across their bed with her head on the pillows. Evan had done this a thousand times now, and as unfailingly hot as it got him, his mind wasn't on the task. He tasted Margie but he felt Paul. Saw him in his mind's eye, drawing close. He ached for that tilt in the mattress again, to feel Paul's thighs touch his as he knelt behind them. Strong hands on Evan's hips and ass, the cool air on his skin as Paul pulled his shorts down, deep noises of greedy approval. Hungry touches. Dirty ones, spreading Evan open, exploring him. Evan moaned against Margie's clit.

The fantasies in his head were messing with his sense of time and reality, but as Margie's thighs twitched against his ears, as her pussy went from damp to dripping against his tongue and lips and her flavor reached its lush, heady peak, he knew she was there ahead of schedule. Evan didn't blame her. Having Paul in the room with them amplified everything to deafening levels.

Margie dug her heel into Evan's back, her hips thrusting faintly to show him the rhythm and pressure she wanted, short nails raking his scalp. She made her soft noises—tiny, wounded, pleading moans.

"God, Evan." That's what she always muttered when she was done for, when Evan brought her to the edge and she was staring into the chasm below.

He held her thighs tight as she came, kept his lips sucking and his tongue flickering until her shaking body calmed. He lapped up her juices, groaned with cocky satisfaction as his mouth zapped her with aftershocks of pleasure. She gave him a couple whaps on the side of the head and he relented, sitting up and running his hands over her legs in happy triumph.

Margie smiled at him, eyes glazed. She stretched and sighed and they stared at each other as always, overcome for a few seconds by fondness.

Paul let them wallow in their flirtation a moment longer before he asserted himself. "He's good at that, isn't he?" he asked Margie.

She smiled broadly, dreamily. "The best."

"You're making me jealous," Paul said.

A shiver rippled over Evan's skin. He turned to face their guest, excited and terrified to see what threats might be waiting in those black eyes. What he found was curiosity, a gleam of wicked hunger that turned Evan's cock from stiff to steel in seconds flat.

Paul smirked. "How about it, Hennessey? You thirsty for more?"

Evan let the invitation work its magic, shut his eyes and enjoyed the waves of dirty anticipation washing over him for a couple beats before he answered. "Yeah."

He opened his eyes to find Paul still smiling, tongue tracing his lower lip. "Good. How about you come over here?"

Evan swung his legs to the floor and stood. He stepped to Paul, stopping with just a foot separating their bodies. He kept his eyes on the floor between their bare feet as he found his breath. He let his gaze drift up the landscape of Paul's intimidating frame, past his bulging shorts to the toned stomach rising and falling, his chest and arms and throat, all the way to Paul's shadowy face. Evan let Paul catch his eyes and hold him in thrall, awaiting instructions. Inviting orders.

"Touch me."

Evan obeyed, surveying Paul's hips, the dents at the tops of his thighs. He massaged the hard muscle there, imagined it flexing and pumping as Paul drove himself deep into Evan's willing body.

"You afraid?" Paul asked, taunting.

"No, just taking my time. I want to remember all of this." His eyes locked on Paul's cock, its broad ridge tenting the cotton only inches from Evan's own erection. It'd take the barest of steps to bring them together and feel the heat and power of Paul's dick against his.

Paul reached down and cupped himself, turning the tease into pure torture. His big fingers stroked up and down, up and down along the underside of his cock, his thumb on the top telling Evan how thick he must be.

"You wanna see?" Paul asked.

The motion of Paul's hand hypnotized Evan and he couldn't do anything aside from stare for a few seconds. He *did* want to see it. He wanted to see the dick he'd been promised, the one that would be fucking his ass before long if he went through with this fantasy. "Yeah," he whispered. "Show me."

Paul slid his thumbs behind his waistband and pushed his shorts down, slow, revealing his dark crown and inch after decadent inch of his powerful shaft. His cock was thick, thicker than Evan's and longer, but it felt like a gift, not a threat. His hair was trimmed, buzzed short and tidy as it was on his head. Evan placed his hand just above Paul's base and let the soft bristle graze his palm.

"How do you want me?" Paul asked. "How did you fantasize about it being? With a guy?"

"I want to be used. And you know…bossed around."

Paul licked his lips. "I can do that. Touch me."

Evan's face heated, warmed by the change in the man's tone. He traced his fingertips along Paul's length, weighed him in his hand. As he gripped him the skin felt as warm and smooth as his own, but so different. His eyes darted over Paul's body, desperate to memorize every detail of this experience.

"Get on your knees for me," Paul said. "Take a good look."

Evan had to close his eyes a moment, jolted by a tremor of fearful excitement. He made it to kneeling, the hard, cold floorboards beneath him the exact right breed of discomfort. Paul's cock stood at perfect chin level. Evan stroked him in one fist, brought his face close and kissed Paul's hipbone, kneaded his thigh with his free hand. His mouth watered, lips tingling.

"I like the way you look at me," Paul murmured.

Evan shivered from that voice. He looked up, eyes caught by Paul's dark ones staring down from so far above him. Evan must've looked like some enraptured disciple, wide-eyed and eager. Rounding out the picture, Paul laid an authoritative palm on the back of Evan's head, the other on his face.

"You want it?" Paul asked. His thumb stroked Evan's cheek, traced his lips. "Open up and you can have it."

Evan could see and smell Paul's excitement and his taste buds stung with curiosity. Finally he parted his lips, cast his gaze up to meet Paul's one more time.

"Nice." Paul reached down to grasp his cock and draw his head across Evan's lower lip, then the upper. Evan's tongue ventured out to taste the pre-come, to tease Paul's slit and trigger a groan that rumbled through the man's body. The hand on the back of Evan's head trembled and Paul's hips tensed, pushing the crown of his cock between Evan's lips.

"That's it. Take me in." Paul let go of his dick, took Evan's hand and wrapped it there in his place.

Evan's arm shook from the thrill of this moment. He bathed Paul with his tongue, sucked his head and did his best to keep his teeth out of the way.

"That's good. Keep that up."

Evan shivered. He imagined how Paul would sound as he fucked him, how harsh and mean he'd turn as he got closer and closer to coming. Evan moaned around Paul's dick as he fantasized about how they'd do it—face-to-face, or Evan on his hands and knees, aching to watch.

Paul's fist took over for Evan's and he eased himself out, ran his spit-slick cock across Evan's lips again.

"Lick me."

Evan obeyed, tendered worship with his tongue.

"That's so hot. Show me how much you love my cock. Show me how deep you can take me."

Evan opened his mouth, let Paul push in halfway, went to work sucking that length.

"Good. You want a little more?"

He pulled back enough to mutter, "Please."

Paul laughed softly. "Ooh, please. I like that."

Evan took him deeper. He didn't gag but he missed being able to *do* more. Paul's hand slid back and he pushed further, filled Evan's mouth and entered his throat, still no gagging.

"Fuck, you're good." Paul eased in the final inch, balls touching Evan's chin. He pulled back, slid out and fisted himself.

Evan took the cue, brought his mouth down to cover Paul's head. He wanted to spoil him, tease and suck until the man came apart.

Paul sounded smug. "You love that, don't you? You love sucking cock."

Evan slipped easily into his role. He freed his mouth to say, "Only yours."

The hand at the base of Evan's skull came forward, thumb brushing his cheek. Paul pushed between Evan's lips again, bossier than before. "You taste that?"

Evan moaned his reply.

"You know what that is? That's the cock that's gonna fuck your tight, virgin ass."

His entire body flashed hot. A tingle spread from Paul's warm, firm hand, oozed from Evan's neck down his spine, telegraphed out to his fingertips, his cock, his toes. He imagined it, that thick, hard length pushing inside him, so much more than Margie had ever given him with her talented fingers. He freed his mouth again.

"You have to go slow with me."

"Oh, I will. I'll make you remember every second. Every inch. Just wait 'til you feel what it's like to come with my cock up your ass. You're gonna lose your fucking mind."

Evan believed it. He never came harder than when Margie was inside him, two fingers rubbing and milking more pleasure from his body than he'd known possible a couple years ago. The thought made his mouth greedy and he took Paul deeper, craving the violation.

"That's right, straight boy. Suck that cock."

Evan moaned, gave himself over to his role. He found his rhythm, intoxicated by the feeling of Paul's hot length sliding between his lips, the soft bump of his dick against the back of Evan's throat. He didn't care what stigma this act carried, only wanted the perfect helplessness of the position balanced by the power he felt when he earned Paul's mean grunts and moans, tasted the evidence of his pleasure.

"You're making me wanna come," Paul muttered. "I wanna pull out and come right across those pretty lips and watch you drink it."

Fuck, Evan wanted that too. Wanted just what Paul described, and more. Wanted to kiss Margie just after that moment, share it with her, give Paul two worshipful lovers in one.

"God, you're good."

The words spurred Evan and inspired him to take more, suck harder. He wanted to be better than good—he wanted to be the best Paul ever had so this evening would be more than just a birthday favor. This fantasy was Evan's but it wasn't about him. It was about him serving someone else, someone as strong and bossy as the man looming above him.

"I wanna fuck your mouth," Paul muttered.

The words sent blood rushing to Evan's cheeks and neck, the thought unleashing a fever in his body. He stilled his head, braced himself obediently with a palm on each of Paul's thighs, waiting.

Paul's free hand stroked down Evan's messy crest of hair to cup the base of his head, the gesture dripping with ownership and approval. Paul's hips flexed, testing Evan's mouth. Evan took what Paul gave him, savoring the heat and the taste of the hard, thick cock slipping in and out between his lips. He wanted to reach down and stroke his own cock, soothe the impatience burning there...but the torture was red-hot.

Margie's voice drifted from the bed, soft and familiar. "You're so good, baby."

"He's fucking perfect," Paul said.

Evan had to work to keep from smiling at the compliment, exactly what he wanted to hear. He wallowed in his own muffled grunts and moans, the faint sensations of gagging that sent his adrenaline spiking as Paul pushed deeper.

"Fuck, you've got me close, Hennessey."

Evan braced himself for his prize, a hot mouthful of Paul that he prayed wouldn't equal the end of the evening's explorations. Instead he got a surprise. Paul stepped back and slid each inch of his cock from Evan's lips, leaving him dangling, thirsty for more.

Evan stared up at Paul's dark face in the candlelight, needing instruction. His own surely helpless expression was met with a slow, ominous grin.

"I think it's time we got to the main event."

CHAPTER FOUR

"GET ON THE BED," Paul ordered. "Lemme watch you two together."

Evan obeyed, his burning body needing more from this man and this experience. He made it to his feet, walked to the bed to lie down beside Margie. He accepted her eager kiss, shocked by how soft she was, how she tasted different after sampling Paul's mouth and cock.

She broke away, spoke low and private. "Did you like it?"

"I loved it."

She stroked his cheek then gave it a pat. "I could tell."

Evan propped himself on his elbow and stared at her body in the flickering light, creamy pale skin painted like stained glass.

Margie tugged on Evan's arm and he climbed on top, hyperaware of her soft thighs against him, her belly, her breasts. He kissed her, punctuating the delving of his tongue with the soft grazing of his cock against her mound. Her hands held his hips, urging him closer.

Just as Evan was melting into the moment, heavy footsteps crossing the floor tensed him. He kept his eyes locked to Margie's as a hot palm settled on his back, fingers tracing his spine and shoulder blades then inching downward.

"Let me see you," Paul said.

Evan brought his body up from Margie's and braced himself on his elbows, turned his head so he could watch their guest's expression. Paul's tongue wet his lip. He grabbed Evan's shorts at the waist and eased them down. The air on his bare ass felt cool, Paul's eyes scorching hot.

"Nice," Paul whispered. He pushed Evan's underwear down his thighs.

The exposure and anticipation, the thought of being so vulnerable to the whims of the rough man beside him set Evan's heart racing, his cock throbbing. He felt like a piece of meat to the beast in his bed, and it was pure heaven.

He moaned as Paul's hand slid up his thigh to brush over his ass with light, appraising touches.

"Now fuck her," Paul said. "Lemme see you work."

Evan struggled to get himself together, not ready to come yet. Which he suspected he very well could the second he pushed into Margie with Paul's hands still admiring his body. He took a deep breath and brought his cock to Margie's pussy, still slick from her orgasm. She groaned as he slid inside and her nails raked his arms.

"Fuck, you're so wet."

"You're so hard."

Evan pushed deep, felt Paul's palm following the action, taking in the flex of Evan's hip as he found his rhythm. A chemical high flooded him from the *ease* of everything—the intoxicating relief that his body was still on board, as excited for this in reality as it had been in theory. Paul's hand withdrew as his voice cut through the darkness to reignite Evan's senses.

"Show me what you two do. Fuck her."

Margie whispered close by his ear. "Fuck me, Evan. Show him how good you are."

He thrust deep, eased out slow. He kept his hips angled in the way that drew his wet cock along Margie's clit as he pulled out, repeated the motions until she was mimicking them, her body meeting his every move. He groaned as her hands slid down his sides to his hips, his ass. She kneaded him, spread him, slid one hand between his cheeks for a teasing stroke over his asshole.

"Faster," she said.

As their script dictated, Evan kept his pace even. Margie's corrective palm came down with a hard slap. He grunted at the pain and the thrill, from how naked and exposed he felt having a new witness to his kink. He let the sting fade to a warm tingle then dutifully sped up.

"Faster," she repeated.

The excitement blazed, driving away all rational thought. He stopped breathing as he waited for the next correction. When Margie's hand came down he yelped and shut his eyes, let the sensation linger.

Paul's voice cut through his reverie. "He likes that, huh?"

"Oh, yeah." She massaged Evan's tender skin. "He loves getting spanked."

An unfamiliar hand settled on Evan's hip, the gesture as thrilling as Paul's voice demanding, "That true, Hennessey?"

Evan ground nearly to a halt, inviting punishment. The anticipation had his body on edge and made it hard to answer. For a few seconds he just stared unsteadily at Margie's face with his mouth agape.

"I asked you a question."

Evan shut his eyes. "Yeah."

"Yeah, what?"

"I like getting spanked."

"Well." Paul's tone dripped with mean satisfaction. "This just keeps getting better and better." He kneaded Evan's flesh, a callous touch that made him feel small and objectified—exactly what he craved.

"Fuck her," Paul said.

Evan did as he was told, so focused on what was coming he barely felt his own dick in Margie's luscious pussy. He'd been imagining this for so long, it seemed inconceivable that it was actually happening.

"Faster." The order came from Paul this time.

If Evan were going to get punished, he'd damn well earn it. He kept his thrusts slow and steady, imagining how Paul's face might look, deeply pissed off.

"Faster." God, that voice—heavy and dark as molasses. As tar.

Margie now. "Faster, baby."

Evan finally did as he was told, wallowed in the mismatched hands palming his ass.

"You look good when you fuck, Hennessey."

Margie's hand came down, brought the noise and heat, freed a gasp from Evan's throat as she dragged her short nails across his savaged skin. Before the sensations faded Paul brought his palm down, harder and louder than Margie could ever hope to. Spots danced in front of Evan's eyes from the pain. He made his thrusts quicker, rougher, tried to not lose it from the slick warmth wrapped around his cock, the excitement of two strange, strong, broad hands exploring his body.

Another slap and Evan heard himself panting and groaning, felt his lips twitching with the urge to beg.

"You do love that, don't you?" Paul asked.

Evan nodded, too aroused to offer more than grunts.

Paul's hand came down mean and loud, scared Evan nearly as much as it thrilled him. "Tell me what else you love, Hennessey."

Unable to speak, Evan earned himself another spank before the first had even cooled.

"You like getting fucked?"

Evan managed to gasp, "Yeah."

"And you want me to fuck you tonight?"

Words abandoned him once more and another harsh slap shattered the silence.

"You know I will, if you want me to," Paul said. "That's all I've been able to think about since your pretty wife told me about your dirty little secret."

Pride bloomed in Evan's chest at the thought that Paul wanted him back. They were such different breeds of male, Evan found it tough to imagine this alpha specimen would find his so-called scrawny self attractive, let alone be kept up nights by the prospect. Plus Evan had only ever been on the men's side of the hunt in the dating jungle, always wishing he were taller or stronger or more charming, more of whatever women liked when they were being pursued. More like Paul. Now *Evan* was the one being pursued and damn if it didn't feel good for once to be the smaller man. The prey.

But just then it was Margie doing the dominating. Her small fingers slid between Evan's cheeks, massaging. "You want it?"

He met her eyes and nodded.

Margie reached for the little bottle on the side table, its cap snapping open then closed, tiny noises that had become potent arousal triggers for Evan over the past couple years, promises of the pleasure he was about to receive. He slid his cock from Margie's wet pussy and rested it on her belly as he moved his knees, straddling her thighs. He tried to picture what Paul saw—this filthy invitation.

Her fingers returned, cool and wet. Evan groaned as she traced his entrance and he angled his hips to give her the best access.

"He's so fucking hungry for it," Paul muttered, his grip on Evan's side tightening.

"Yeah." Margie's fingers drew an explicit circle. "He loves it. Don't you?"

Evan nodded again, frantic.

"You liked getting fucked?" Paul's hand slid to Evan's ass.

All Evan could do was moan, face pressed into Margie's neck.

His silence was met with a hard spank and a reprimand. "Tell me. Do you like getting fucked?"

"Yeah," was all he could get out before Margie's finger penetrated, reducing him to grunts.

"Yeah, you do," Paul muttered. "Take him deeper."

Margie followed the order, her slick finger easing past that tight ring of muscle, filling him to the brim with dark pleasure and anticipation.

He managed to gasp, "Fuck me."

"Fuck him," Paul said, his command echoing Evan's plea.

Margie's finger left and Evan groaned—from the sudden loss and also from what he knew was coming. Another snap-snap of the lube bottle, another thrilling, slippery glide of the gel over his skin. She pressed inside, deeper, thrust slowly until Evan was slick, his body relaxed and receptive.

He pushed up on to his elbows and stared into Margie's eyes. "More."

She smiled and Evan felt another finger pressing, entering, stretching him wider.

"Oh fuck."

"You're doing good," she whispered.

"Fuck me." He felt dizzy, brain clouded by static and fog at the sensation, from being penetrated, getting fucked and being watched. In an instant it intensified a hundredfold as Paul leaned across, grabbed the bottle from the nightstand. Snap, snap.

"You ready?" he asked.

Evan swallowed, mustered that syllable again. "Yeah."

Margie's palms moved to his waist. Then came the weight of Paul shifting the bed behind them, his thighs pushing Evan even wider, one dry hand on his ass cheek, spreading him open. More slick fingers, bigger and unfamiliar, rubbed that most intimate spot.

"*Yes.*"

He heard Paul laugh softly. "Yes, indeed." His fingertips teased, threatening penetration.

"Please. Do it."

"Say my name."

"Paul," Evan moaned as he felt the man pressing, demanding entrance.

"Oh, you're tight."

"More."

Evan got what he wanted, the slow, mean push of Paul's finger to the second knuckle.

"More?"

"Yeah," Evan said, panting. "More."

Another snap and the feeling of more cool gel between his cheeks. Paul slid the digit out, soaked it in lube, plunged it back inside. Evan grunted in time with the thrusts, hips flexing, begging for more. Paul gave it, pressed inside with two fingers.

"Yeah. Yeah."

"You like that, don't you, straight boy?"

"Yes."

"What're you thinking about?" Paul asked as he thrust, two fingers deep, deeper, to the base.

"Your cock," Evan gasped. "About you fucking me."

Paul spoke to Margie next. "He nice and hard still?"

Her small hands slid between them to grip his pounding cock. "You have no idea."

"Fuck your wife," Paul ordered.

With Paul's fingers still buried in him, Evan walked his body back, angled his cock to Margie's pussy, afraid he'd come the second he slid between her thighs and lips. He took a calming breath and thrust, tried to ignore how fucking astounding every inch of his body felt and just hold on so this experience wouldn't be over yet.

Paul's hand paused. "Fuck her."

Evan obeyed. Each push of his cock inside her became a loss of Paul's fingers, Evan's pumping hips getting him fucked in perfect harmony from both sides. The dirtiness of it made him hot, hotter than he'd ever dreamed.

"God, take me," he moaned. He hammered Margie, every quick withdrawal welcoming Paul's fingers back inside. Then he felt pressure, Paul pushing in farther, following Evan's thrusts and fucking him in time.

"You feel good, Hennessey." Paul's fingers twisted, bringing more pleasure plus a taste of pain.

"Fuck me," Evan begged.

"Fuck you how?"

He moaned as Paul's fingers slammed deep. "With your cock. Fuck my ass."

"Soon."

Another twist and Evan couldn't reply. His brain turned to mush and his voice faded to a raspy groan. He took what Paul gave him, managed to not come by some miracle of self-control. As he reached a plateau, he found he could fuck Margie without drifting too close to the edge. Her soft hands stroked his shoulders and chest, slow and soothing. Evan found his voice.

"Spank me."

Paul laughed, a small, low noise that made Evan shiver. "Look who's decided to start dishing out orders."

"Please," Evan gasped as Paul's fingers pushed in, eased out, hammered him for a beat. "God, please."

"Love it when you beg, Hennessey."

The smack landed with a harsh sound, an even harsher sting. Evan pumped Margie deep, knowing Paul's eyes were on him. He could feel them as surely as he felt the lingering burn in his skin. That thought got him more excited than the fucking or the spanking, pushing him headlong toward release. Self-control be damned, Evan pounded Margie hard, welcomed Paul's penetrating fingers with each withdrawal.

"Slow down," Paul said.

"I can't," Evan groaned as Paul's fingers left him, their absence a cruel punishment. "Please. I'm so close."

"Thought you wanted this to last all night."

"It feels too good." As bad as Evan wanted to come, he let Margie push him away, her hands guiding his hips until his cock slipped from her.

Evan pressed his sweaty forehead to hers. "Please."

"Paul knows what you need, baby. Trust him."

Trust wasn't the problem—the ache in Evan's cock was the problem. The sudden emptiness in his hurting body was the goddamn problem. Still, Evan relented. He let himself rest against Margie as he willed his body to relax, to breathe, to remember the anticipation was as sweet as the orgasm. The memories would be even sweeter if he could just keep it all going, to get to that ultimate act he'd dreamed about all these weeks. In time he felt control return to him.

"Okay," he said. "I'm okay."

"Ready for more?" Paul asked.

Evan nodded. "I'm ready." He moved back to his hands and knees above Margie, legs wide, cock resting on her belly. Two pairs of hands grazed his body.

"Good. Did you get nice and clean for me?"

"Yeah," Evan muttered.

There was more shifting behind him, then the cruel, slow slide of Paul's fingers penetrating, once, twice, then abandoning him again. Evan had a few moments to mourn before another sensation replaced it, filthier than he'd even thought to hope for—the rough stubble of Paul's cheek brushing Evan's crack, then the hot, firm, wet slide of his tongue.

"God, fuck." He buried his face in the pillow beside Margie's, grunted with helpless excitement as Paul coaxed his thighs wider, demanding more. He heard and felt Paul's harsh breaths as his tongue delved and tasted, the pure dirtiness of it shoving Evan right back to the edge, teetering. Paul's hand rubbed and squeezed, drew Evan's cheeks apart and introduced him to sensations he'd never bothered to imagine. His hips trembled as Paul's tongue pressed inside him, teasing for a final blazing moment. As Paul drew away, Evan remembered how to breathe.

"You ready? You wanna get fucked by a man?"

"Yes."

Paul's broad palms kneaded Evan's ass, thumbs between his cheeks, rubbing his asshole, spreading him open again. "God, you look good."

"Please."

Paul made a noise, a laugh or sigh, cocky with satisfaction. "All right. Since you asked nicely."

Margie reached for the side table, got the drawer open and passed Paul a condom and the lube. Plastic crinkled. The bottle snap-snapped.

After a couple seconds, a couple million of Evan's racing heartbeats, he felt the smooth, slippery warmth of Paul's sheathed cock head at his entrance. Chemicals exploded in his bloodstream—excitement and fear and anticipation blending to create a high that flooded Evan from his scalp to his toes and left him lightheaded. The pain that followed didn't hurt, only thrilled. He moaned as Paul pushed in, forced his head past Evan's tight hole and held there.

Evan jammed his arms beneath Margie and dug his fingers into her back.

"You're doing great," she whispered. She kissed his neck and reinforced the familiar, the safety amid all these intimidating new sensations.

"Relax," Paul said, his hands lightly rubbing Evan's hips, waiting. "Relax and let me in. Lemme give you what you want."

Evan gulped deep breaths, commanded the tension to leave his impatient body.

"Better. You ready for a little more?"

"Yeah, just go slow. It feels good, just go slow."

Paul's grip tightened and the pain returned—sweet pain, steeped more in taboo than actual discomfort. Evan grunted with each centimeter that edged inside.

Fuck, it was heaven—the dirty, scary, perfect paradise he'd fantasized about. "Yes. More."

"Oh, there's plenty still to come."

"Now. Please."

Paul pushed deeper, deeper than Margie's fingers had ever explored. Evan groaned and swore from the pain, from the blissful, fearful sensation of being filled this way. "God, slow. It feels so fucking good. You're so big."

"And you're tight, Hennessey. Tight and hot, just like I imagined." Paul edged in a bit more. "Good boy. Take that cock."

Evan leaned his head back enough to meet Margie's eyes. "I want you to watch."

"Sure."

Evan and Paul let her slide from beneath them to kneel beside Evan's hip and set her hand on his lower back.

"It looks so good, baby. He's so big and you're taking him."

"You want more?" Paul asked.

"Yeah," Evan said. "Slow."

"Good. Here I come." Paul's hands held Evan tighter as his hips forced his cock deeper, slow but insistent.

Evan could only groan and clench the bedspread in his fists. Paul was massaging him from the inside, sensations he'd only read about before, pleasure he hadn't understood until now. Pain too…though the sting of his body stretching to take this man's thick cock only made it hotter.

After a minute's steady, cautious progress, he felt Paul's balls touch his ass. He buried his face in the pillow, embracing how helpless he felt, pinned by this man.

"You ready to get fucked?"

Evan raised his head and nodded. "I'm ready."

Paul eased out a fraction, pushed back in deep. It felt so right Evan's legs went weak, shaking.

"Good?" Paul asked.

"Yeah. Amazing."

Paul's cock withdrew halfway, plunged back in faster than before.

"More."

Paul moaned and started to thrust.

"Make it about you," Evan said. "Use me."

"Fuck." Paul pulled out and returned a second later, cock slippery with more lube. "You're a fucking dream come true, Hennessey."

"Fuck me." Exactly the balance Evan needed—getting fucked, giving orders. He gasped as Paul entered him, caution abandoned. "God yeah, fuck me."

"Deeper," Margie said, reading Evan's mind.

He turned to catch her eye. "Touch me."

He saw her smirk before he cast his eyes down again, closed them. She laid her arm along his back, the other hand taking hold of his cock.

"Not too much," he warned. He wanted the pleasure, wanted to feel how intense it could be with Paul moving inside him, but he still wasn't ready for it to be done. He moaned as she stroked him, nice and light. His cock pulsed and the sensation tensed all his muscles, tightened his ass around Paul's dick.

"Oh, good boy." Paul pumped him harder, excitement underscoring his words and the force of his thrusts.

"Feels good," Evan grunted. "Fuck, don't stop. Use me."

"Jesus, you're hot." Paul's hand came down, spanking Evan so hard and he gasped, one elbow buckling beneath him. He made it back to all fours just as the second slap landed. Everything was right—too right.

"Stop," he said to Margie. "I'm close."

"You can come, Ev," she said, but took her hand away.

"Not yet. I want more."

Paul cut in. "You wanna watch?"

Evan groaned from the impact and the idea. "Yeah."

"Good. Turn over."

Evan felt Paul pull out. He flipped onto his back and Paul grabbed Evan's knees, spread his legs and walked his own body in close, his sheathed dick touching Evan's bare one. He grabbed the lube and slicked a measure down his length, angled himself to Evan's asshole. Evan held his breath, eyes glued to Paul's strong body in the warm, flickering light. He shut them when the pressure returned, that intimidating, intoxicating feeling as Paul eased the first inch inside.

"God, fuck."

"You look good." Paul's voice sounded as shallow and tight as Evan's felt, his throat clenched from the pleasure.

Margie scooted closer, curled her body beside Evan's and laid her palm on his chest. She put her lips right by his ear. "Is this still what you want?"

"Fuck, yes."

Eyes still shut, he heard her smile when she spoke. "He looks so good, baby. Don't miss out."

* * *

HE SWALLOWED and his eyes locked with Paul's the second they opened. He groaned as another inch pushed inside.

Paul eased himself deeper into Evan, nearly came from the sheer harshness of the man's moan. Fuck, he was sexy. It wasn't a new observation, either—Paul had been admiring Margie's husband since the first Friday Evan had mustered the Dutch courage to get up on stage with his guitar on open mic night. Bathed in red light, muscles twitching in his slender arms as he played, shadowed face, lips so fucking close to the microphone when he sang in that low, raspy voice... Paul had entertained a hundred fantasies about Evan in the past couple years, most of them shockingly close to their shared, present reality.

And now here Evan Hennessey was beneath him, bathed in candlelight, flat on his back with his thighs spread, attention nailed to Paul's chest and hips and cock. It took Paul's breath away—the tight heat wrapped around his dick, two pairs of ravenous eyes watching his body drive into Evan's. He slowed his thrusts and pulled out, leaned over to grab the bottle off the table.

"You're doing good." He flipped the cap open, smeared lube across his palm and held Evan's stare. "Is this what you'd hoped it'd be?"

"It's better," Evan whispered. His eyes dropped to where Paul's slick hand stroked his cock.

"Just wait 'til you come." With that, Paul brought his cock back to Evan's asshole, slid in quick and rough and was rewarded with a fresh, guttural, animal sound. He held Evan's thighs and drove into him with a greedy rhythm. "Use me," Evan had said. An answered prayer if Paul had ever heard one.

He let thoughts dull the edge of his pleasure, not ready for this evening to end. He'd expected a bit more ego from a man with crusty urban edges like Evan, but the guy was a natural-born submissive. Hungry, eager, the perfect balance of outward servitude and hidden greed.

Paul worked to find his pace without losing himself. He studied Evan's body...lean and raw, not an ounce of fat hiding a single tic of muscle or intake of breath. A bit of black hair decorated his chest, more framing the rock-hard, gorgeous cock between his pale thighs. His hands had drifted above his head to strangle the pillow, and the thick leather cuff on one of his crossed wrists filled Paul with other fantasies, ones involving rope and gags and threats.

But right now the man needed to get straight-up fucked. Paul would get his turn before long, but until then he had only one purpose—to blow Evan's mind clean out of his skull.

CHAPTER FIVE

EVAN WAS LOST, mesmerized by the impossibly perfect scene happening before him. To him. The pain was gone from his body, replaced with the purest pleasure he'd felt since he was about seventeen and discovering sex for the first time.

Paul's strong hands gripped his legs beneath each knee, held him wide open as that thick, merciless cock drove inside over and over. It was everything Evan had hoped it would be. More. Every time Paul pushed deep he filled Evan with intimidating pressure, the violation offset by ecstasy as his cock massaged Evan from the inside out, made his balls ache and his cock throb, made him bite back pleas to be touched.

Paul found his stride, grunting along with his plunging cock. "Fuck, take me, Hennessey. Watch me fucking you."

For seconds or minutes or hours Evan took what Paul gave him, moaned with the impact and committed every square inch of the man's body to memory. Evan had thought this might be too much—face-to-face as he got fucked—beyond intimate to scary. But he loved it. He loved Paul's expression with its mix of meanness and helpless arousal, and he loved *watching*. He loved Margie watching.

He gasped at a harsh thrust and noted with fear and excitement the smile spreading slowly across Paul's face. Paul moved his arms, caught Evan under each knee with the crooks of his elbows as he braced his palms on the bed, lowering his hips and forcing Evan's thighs wider.

"Oh, fuck." Evan tried to blink away tiny white sparks in his vision as Paul took him deeper. Then that body came down, Paul's hard stomach brushing Evan's cock, threatening to send him over the edge.

"Not yet."

"Not yet, what?" Paul's face was close, just inches from his.

"I don't want to come yet."

Paul brought his mouth to Evan's, kissed him deep and nasty and mean and leaned back with a grin curling his lips. "You'll come when I tell you to come." He looked to Margie, still kneeling, rapt. "You too. You'll both come when I tell you to. For now you let me watch." He nodded at Margie and Evan watched her reach between her legs to play with her clit. Paul kissed Evan again, bit his lip nearly hard enough to draw blood. "Eyes on me, Hennessey."

Paul sank back on his knees, hips pistoning as he fucked Evan, his hands drifting. He stroked Evan's stomach and chest, held his thighs as his cock hammered hard for an excruciating minute. Evan disobeyed and shut his eyes, overwhelmed by the sensations and the smells and sounds, by Paul's hungry face. His lids flew open with shock as Paul's hand wrapped around his cock.

"No. Not yet."

Paul grinned, gave Evan a pull that nearly sent him toppling headlong off the cliff.

"Not yet. Please."

"I said you'll come when I tell you to come." Paul's fist squeezed tighter as his hips slowed. He gave Evan's dick long strokes, his other hand clamping his balls.

"Oh fuck." The orgasm mounted, so intense and deep Evan stopped breathing. His body begged for more, hips clenching, trying to thrust and meet Paul's pulls, locking his ass like a fist around Paul's buried cock. Just as the pleasure came to a violent head, Paul pressed the pads of his free fingers hard into the flesh just below Evan's balls. The waves came, the most intense orgasm he'd ever experienced radiating from the inside and boiling through his cock, bolts of sensation making his entire body shudder and buck, endless moans and grunts streaming from his mouth.

Only he didn't come.

He fell down from the high hard as sin, cock still begging for release.

"Fuck. Now, please."

Beside him, Margie's panting breaths and whimpers told him she was close too. He met her half-open eyes, saw the hunger there then looked back to Paul. "Please."

"Please, what?" Paul asked.

"Make me come. God, please. It fucking hurts."

Paul held his tongue for a couple thrusts, staring Evan down. "Now? You sure?"

"God, yes. Please. Make me come."

"Okay then, birthday boy." Paul's act was good, but cracks were forming in his cool, mean veneer, and underneath shone the same desperate need eating away at Evan. Paul dug his knees wide under Evan's thighs, pounded him hard for a final minute before his fist tightened around Evan's dick.

Evan shut his eyes. "Yes, please."

The orgasm pooled in his belly, blood and heat and whirling energy draining from his face and fingertips and feet to burn in his cock, his ass, his balls. Paul drove himself deep, his dick adding another layer to Evan's climax as his body clenched around the stiff length. Evan reached out as the pleasure hit its violent peak, clawed at Paul's arms and shoulders. He felt Margie's palm on his damp chest, heard the groan of her losing it right along with him. Paul buried himself to the base and held there as Evan opened his eyes and watched his own come shoot across his navel, endless spurts drenching his fevered skin, wringing out his brain and body, leaving him a panting, pacified wreck.

His gaze jumped to Paul's face, that mouth parted and those dark eyes nearly closed—unmistakable satisfaction as he watched Evan drift down from the clouds and land back on the bed, quaking.

Evan blinked. "Jesus. Fuck."

Margie flopped down beside him and he turned his head, let her touch his sweaty face and neck and attack him with happy kisses. Then the slow withdrawal of Paul's swollen cock yanked him back into the ether for a few seconds of nearly too-intense pleasure.

Margie sat up as Paul knelt back. She reached to the table for the hand towel she'd left there, helped Evan get cleaned up. She leaned in and whispered, "Good?"

"Fucking amazing."

Margie turned to grin at Paul. He was still leaning back on his haunches, chest rising and falling deeply.

"I think it's your turn."

"Oh yeah?" His eyebrow rose and his gaze swiveled to Evan. "What's on the menu?"

Evan replied through a hitching breath. "Anything you w-want."

"Anything?"

"Any-fucking-thing."

Margie nodded her agreement.

179

"In that case, I want you both on your knees on the floor." To clarify what he meant, Paul swung his legs over the edge and spread them, stripped away the condom. Margie made it to her feet first, came around to the side of the bed and knelt before Paul. Evan was so spent he practically had to toss himself to the ground, but he made it too. Margie laid one hand on Paul's hip, one on his thigh and Evan did the same with his other leg. He exchanged an excited look with her before staring up at Paul's expectant face.

"Wait. Move back."

Evan and Margie shuffled backward on their knees and Paul stood, casting them in his shadow.

"Now. Show her how it's done," Paul said.

Evan lowered his gaze to Paul's cock and wrapped his hand around the base. He brought his mouth down, bathed him with his tongue, cleaning away the faint taste of latex and replacing it with the heady flavor of Paul's pre-come. He closed his lips over the head, sucked Paul and teased him, stroked him slow and tight. His cheeks burned with a dozen conflicting, perfect emotions as Margie watched.

"Good," Paul muttered. "Good. Now her."

Evan pulled away so Margie could take over. Evan watched, let the spark of insecurity he felt deepen the experience, enrich the taboo. Margie's eyes were glued to Paul's as she took his big cock in her small hand, dark skin against pale.

Paul moaned, barely audible. "Do it, sweetheart."

Evan's body warmed all over again as her tongue flicked out to taste Paul's head.

Paul's hand tangled in her messy hair. "Don't tease me, Margie."

"Do it," Evan said. "Take him."

She met Evan's eyes for a split second, lips twisting into a final smirk before they swallowed the first few inches of Paul's cock. Evan shuddered, knowing just how good she must feel—soft lips, the warm metal bead of her tongue stud tracing the ridge of Paul's dick.

Evan groaned along with him as Margie took more. He memorized the sight of his wife's mouth pleasuring their shared lover and couldn't figure out what made it so fucking hot—the current of jealousy running just beneath the thrill of voyeurism, or knowing this is how Evan must have looked too. Enraptured. *Thirsty.*

"Now him," Paul said.

Margie withdrew, licked her lips as Evan leaned in to take over. Paul made them trade off a half dozen times, clearly relishing ordering them around on their knees. Evan loved it too and he could see from the gleam in Margie's eyes that she made it unanimous.

Paul unraveled as Evan took his next turn. His hand pushed Evan's away and he pumped himself, rough.

"Who wants my come?" he demanded.

Evan let his mouth's actions speak in place of words.

"Both of us," Margie said.

"Both, huh?"

Evan groaned his accord. He let Paul's cock slide from his mouth, kept just his lips teasing and his tongue lapping as Margie joined in, mirroring the actions beside him.

Paul grunted in time with his quickening strokes. "Goddamn, you're fucking filthy. Both of you."

Margie took his head between her lips for a second then released him with a soft pop. "Come for us, Paul."

He was close—Evan could taste and smell it, see it in the whitened knuckles of his pumping fist. He added his own worship to the moment. "Please, Paul."

"Fuck…" Paul jacked himself hard, hand bumping each of their chins as they jockeyed to be the one who met his release. His moan built and crescendoed and Margie drew back, let Evan have the first taste. Hot come lashed his cheek and neck, then he caught the next spurt, let it run across his tongue and down his throat. Then Paul aimed himself at Margie, cream coating her lips and the pink tongue that came out to sample it. He switched between them until the spasms died and all that was left in the quiet, dim room were three panting, spent bodies and the heavy musk of sex.

Paul stepped back, flopped across the bed with a happy huff. Margie put her hand to Evan's face and shared a nasty, playful kiss with him. She grabbed the towel and they tidied themselves. They took a seat on either side of Paul, Margie patting his chest as he fought for breath. Evan watched but kept his hands to himself, unsure how their guest might want things to be, post-orgasm. Margie smoothed a hand over Paul's shaved head. He sat up, sighed deeply and looked to each of them in turn, eyes lingering on Evan.

"Happy, birthday boy?"

Evan blushed again and nodded. "Yeah. That was...perfect. That was everything I wanted. Plus a few things I hadn't thought of."

Paul grinned and glanced back at Margie.

"Perfect," she agreed.

"Excellent." He looked around the room, thinking. The rain had tapered to a faint drizzle against the panes. "Well, I think I'm gonna leave you kids to your wedded bliss, if that's okay with you."

Margie gave him a clap on the shoulder. "That's fine. Do you need us to call you a cab?"

"Nope, I'm good." Paul stood and gathered his clothes, not dawdling but not rushing either.

Evan hadn't known exactly how he'd feel at this moment, but he *did* want Paul to go. Not because he regretted any of what had gone on, simply because he wanted to be with Margie, alone. To be with the person who'd shared this fantasy with him from the very beginning, fostered it, now orchestrated it. He wanted to fall asleep with her body wrapped in his and listen to her familiar breathing, smell her familiar skin.

Margie slipped into a robe as Paul dressed and she walked him out of the room. Evan listened to them share a few words, a laugh, a pair of goodnights.

Evan exhaled as he heard the door close and the lock click. The hall light went out and Margie padded back into the room, replaced her robe on its hook. She smiled at Evan, touched his shoulder as she leaned over to blow out the candles above the headboard. The second she was on the mattress, he grabbed her around the waist and locked her in his arms, smothered her neck and ear and temple with grateful, messy kisses.

"Thank you," he whispered.

"Happy birthday." She looked to the glowing clock on the table beside her—a couple minutes past eleven. "Nearly."

Evan didn't have any further coherent thoughts to share and he felt sleep coming down on him like a cartoon anvil. He plastered his chest and stomach to Margie's back and held her tight, let his body tell her exactly how he felt as his mind went blissfully blank.

* * *

EVAN DIDN'T WAKE until at least eight, when the June sun finally breached the crack between the blinds and window frame and transformed Evan's sleepy world from black to pink. He squeezed his lids tighter and turned away from the glare, wrapped his arms around Margie on instinct just as the ache in his body launched him clear awake.

"Oh my God." He muttered it into Margie's rumpled hair as his eyes popped open.

Her body tensed and stretched then flopped back against his.

"You awake?" Evan asked.

"Yeah." She turned to meet his eyes. "Morning, birthday boy. How you feeling?"

"Sore."

She smiled, shut her eyes. "How about in your head?"

Evan thought about it, letting memories of the previous evening flash through his mind, light up his body. He squeezed Margie tighter. "I feel great about it. Thanks. What about you?"

She let loose a wistful, dramatic sigh. "Last night was like the shortest, most fabulous vacation ever. I only wish we'd taken slides."

Evan laughed into the pillow to spare Margie his breath. "You barely got to sample our tour guide."

"I still got exactly what I wanted, Ev."

He smiled, unseen, feeling warm and safe. Only the smallest trace of morning-after self-doubt clouded his mind, and even that felt right.

"Fair's fair," he said through a yawn. "Maybe for *your* next birthday we can ask him over again."

She craned her neck to fix him with a smirk. "I thought the whole idea was to get that out of your system before the big three-oh so we can begin our lives as responsible, boring, vanilla-sex-having grown-ups."

"I think my birthday was just an excuse to shit or get off the pot about the fantasy." He squeezed her around the middle. "If you want that sometime, just ask me."

"It's tempting… You know what I could really use, though?" She grinned, eyes crinkling. "A strap-on."

Evan blushed. They'd been talking about that for ages but he'd never quite managed to green-light it. Now, though… "Noted."

"For the moment," she said, "all I want is for you to limp your tender backside into the kitchen and make us some coffee."

Evan propped himself up on his elbow. "You're making me work on my birthday?"

She grinned, nose scrunching in that way that drove him nuts with affection. "If you had any inkling of the ways I plan on spoiling you today, you'd realize dumping grounds in a filter and flipping a switch is a pittance."

He leaned in and rested his forehead against hers, bad breath be damned. "What sorts of hideous treats am I in store for?"

She slapped his cheek lightly. "Make me some coffee and find out."

"Yes, ma'am." Evan got up, tugged his shorts and shirt on, turned as he reached the doorway to stare at his wife. "I love you, Margie."

"Happy birthday, Hennessey."

BRAZEN

CHAPTER ONE

HE WAS TROUBLE the moment Will hired him.

Now, to his credit, Will never once batted an eye in the four years he's been my assistant. And that includes the day I said, "Will, I need you to screen men for me. For a harem."

"A harem? Where are we going to fit a harem?" he asked, as if we were discussing the logistics of a dinner party.

"Right here in the brownstone," I said. "It's getting lonely around here."

That was a couple years ago and two years after my divorce. One year after I suspected I should be ready to start dating again but found the idea left me nauseous. And now this old house, for many months too empty to contemplate without risking self-pity, has come alive again, with the smells and the energy of eager young men. Not the sounds, however—silence is one of the requirements of the job.

Over coffee that morning I explained to Will—who enthusiastically shares my love of eager young men, in case you were curious—what exactly I envisioned. It was one of those idyllic, Boston spring days. I believe it was Easter, actually. A day for vibrant rebirth, for the resurrection of my sexuality.

"So," he said, tapping his pencil eraser on the tile of the breakfast bar. "We need a bunch of young men. Give me details. Give me specs." I should mention that Will is also my interior designer.

"Not *too* young," I said. "How about…twenty to twenty-eight. Tall, five-ten to six-two or thereabouts. Gorgeous, muscular but not too beefy—"

"What's too beefy? Is Ryan Reynolds too beefy?"

"I wouldn't kick him out of bed," I said. "But that's as beefy as I'd prefer."

"Who's your ideal body then?" Will's manicured hand hovered, poised to record my every whim. Bless him.

"Ideally," I said, thinking. "David Beckham?"

Will jotted this down. "So trim but built."

"Precisely. But not too slender. I'm thinking surfer-type bodies. Swimmers. Dancers but masculine, obviously. No wrestlers or linebackers." I had given myself permission to be choosy. If my husband taught me nothing else in our twelve mutually miserable years of marriage, he did drive home the importance of only paying for the best.

"Beckham body," Will said, making notes. "Whose face, Madam Photographer?"

"If the vision's *too* ideal we'll never find anyone. Just nice-looking men. Dark hair is best."

"Right. So, Caroline…" Will trailed off, eyes rolling thoughtfully up to stare at the ceiling.

"Yes?"

His gaze fell to mine. "What about…you know. Downstairs?"

"Sizeable."

"Cut?"

"I won't discriminate," I said, feeling gracious. "But they'll all need clean bills of health from within a week of the day they start, and they should be able to perform on command. This is a fantasy after all."

"Any shaving requirements?" Will asked studiously, scribbling.

"Down below? No. Just not messy. And no elaborate topiaries. And no one completely shaved," I added. "That's creepy. Ditto piercings."

"What about tattoos?"

"Use your discretion. Chest hair's fine, either way, but no back hair please. Facial hair's probably okay. Sideburns are a plus," I added. "Take headshots of everyone for me to approve."

"Good thinking," Will said. "Now how many, do you think?" He offered me the face he makes when we're both torn between the same two fabric swatches.

"I don't think I want more than four or five in the house at a time," I said. "And not twenty-four/seven, obviously. This is a hobby, not a lifestyle. I'll make up a calendar and we can fill it in each week. You're great with schedules, darling. I'm sure you can work it out."

"Right." He scanned his notes. "And what will they have to do for you? Or to you?"

"Actually, not that much." I'd been thinking about that, about what I desired from these young men. "I want them to sit around quietly, looking pretty, with their shirts off," I concluded. "And when I feel like it, I'll wave one over and do what I like to him."

"Do they need staying power?" Will asked, and his businesslike calm made me wonder if he'd ever worked as a casting agent in the adult movie industry.

"Not particularly. I don't plan on sleeping with any of them."

His eyebrows rose with surprise. Or disappointment. "No?"

I shook my head. "No. I think I just want to take advantage of them. I don't want a dozen feral young men manhandling me. Although if any of them are willing to manhandle each other for my entertainment, I'll pay them extra."

"Right. Anything else?"

"Yes, Will. Please fetch me another coffee."

* * *

AND SO THAT IS HOW I came to this moment, sitting primly on my overstuffed leather sofa, a glass of decent pinot on the coffee table and a fine young man in his briefs beside me, letting me fondle him.

I don't know this man's name, or any of the others'. This young man, who's probably twenty-four or so, tall-ish and built-ish, with brown hair and eyes whose color I haven't bothered to notice yet, he's not the one I called "trouble" earlier. This one, whimpering softly as I stroke his erection through the cotton, is exemplary. Quiet, obedient, responsive and passive. I'm half watching *Cool Hand Luke* on the television and half torturing him.

It's five in the afternoon on a rainy Thursday in September. Inside my old four-story townhouse on Beacon Street (with a fantastic view of Boston Common—what a legal coup *that* was) it is cozy and comforting and I am content. If my neighbors have the time to notice how many attractive young men come and go from my home in a given week, I think my excuse is solid; I've been a professional photographer for years. And even if they suspect the truth, I honestly couldn't care any less.

It's difficult to worry yourself about other people's opinions when a gorgeous man is sprawled beside you, thighs spread, dick rock-hard, face straining to try to hide how close he is to coming.

"You may moan," I say magnanimously when I know he's on the brink.

He takes me up on the offer and soon enough his grunts and groans drown out the movie.

"Push your shorts down," I say.

His fists are clenched beside his legs where they won't get in my way, and now he shoves his briefs impatiently down his thighs. The cock I've been stroking lazily for at least twenty minutes doesn't disappoint. Long and thick and dark.

Across the room, seated in my favorite reading chair, is the man I called "trouble". He is trouble because it's his first day here and he's already flouting my rules. One rule is that my boys don't wear shirts. It's a kind of anti-uniform. Jeans are fine or just underwear— although no billowy boxers, thank you—and bare feet. Pajama pants, after nine p.m., are also permissible. But no shirts.

This trouble-man, he's wearing a gray tee shirt. He looks good in it but he's a rule-breaker, nonetheless. I would say it's a first-timer's mistake, but something in his eyes tells me he doesn't make mistakes.

This trouble-man, he's beautiful. He may be the most stunning man I've ever seen, in person or anywhere. I bet he's in his later twenties. I bet he's six-feet even and I bet he's hung. That's what his eyes are telling me with cold confidence. Piercing eyes with a vague, charismatic sadness about them. Clear, bright blue like a chlorine pool. They make my own water, they're so intense. He doesn't blink. He doesn't watch my hand, busy in the other man's lap. He stares brazenly at my face. Staring is also against the rules. I will deal with him later.

I release the currently suffering young man's dick and slide the coffee table on its Oriental rug a few feet farther away from us across the hardwood. I move and I kneel, settling between his legs, sliding his underwear all the way off. I can tell from his twitching right hand that he wants to touch himself, that his neglected cock is paining him. I smile to myself, thinking of his suffering and push his knees a little wider.

"Scoot forward," I say, and he obeys.

His smell is as uniform and as unique as any of the others'. Personal yet universal. Potent and ten times as intoxicating as the wine. Summer is nearly over and his tan is just starting to fade. His thighs are pale and I like the contrast of his white skin against the rich brown leather. I like the contrast of the deep mauve of his cockhead and his blushing cock against the dark hair between his legs. I stroke his inner thighs as I think these things and I make him wait.

I can feel the trouble-man's eyes on my back. I touch the underside of the helpless man's dick, and he whimpers again. I wonder if the trouble-man is arrogant enough to be touching himself without permission. I pretend that he's the one at my mercy because these boys are interchangeable.

Or they're supposed to be.

"You look good," I say to the man spread wide before me. I stroke him until the pre-come glistens at his slit, until his groans become maniacal. Now he's ready. I'm ready. I hold him tight in my fist and lower my mouth to his head.

He tastes like he smells. Like desperation and youth.

I've tasted this man before, several times. He's been coming here for a few weeks and he's good. He has a perfectly suckable cock, not too big around, but enough to feel powerful in my mouth. He never disobeys the no-thrusting rule, never gives me cause to gag, never grabs my hair and tries to set the rhythm. He is an exceptional student. A star pupil. I hope the troublesome newcomer is taking notes.

I decide to reward the obedient man. I milk him with one rough hand and flick my tongue over his head rapidly, the way he seemed to love the last few times. His thighs tense and I see the knuckles of his fisted hands blanch.

I know, I know. This sounds so detached. What's in it for me? you might be wondering. Well, there's no accounting for kink. No link between what we want to want and what we actually do. And this is what *I* want. I haven't mentioned it yet, but I'm getting off on this. Somewhere beneath my tasteful, tailored housedress, I'm as wet as a lake. I was dutifully (read: grudgingly) on board with the whole monogamous sex thing for twelve years and my ex-husband, for all his faults, was a good-looking man and a good lover. A courteous and respectful lover, sometimes to a fault. But this, right now... Isn't this exactly what I thought about all those years when my eyes closed and he took me with his mouth or his cock? Some beautiful younger man, muscles strained as I pleasure him, the perfect marriage of dominance and submission. Giving and taking. I like balance. I'm very good at yoga.

And since you're probably interested, I'll be forty next month.

And yes, if I'd worked a bit harder at promiscuity at an earlier age, I suppose I could technically have been this boy's mother.

As lurid scandals go, I know mine is vanilla. But this is Beacon Hill, I'll remind you. My taboos are fittingly conservative, in keeping with the address and the decor.

Now back to the matter at hand. In hand.

As all of this is going on, as I'm teasing this handsome young man into hysterics, I'm wound tighter than a bedspring between my legs. I'm on fire. But I can't show it. I won't give away my arousal in front of these boys or touch myself or let them touch me. The stark utility of it is what gets me high. Again, contrast—cold control versus hot, quaking helplessness.

But in my mind, the rules are null and void. In my mind, the trouble-man surprises me. He sneaks up from behind as I suck his colleague, and I feel his steady hands ease my dress up over my hips. I can just about hear the clink of his unbuckling belt, the sound of a zipper sliding down over his straining cock. I ache, thinking of him tugging my panties to one side and the feeling of his head pushing into me. I'm so wet, he'd sink like a hot knife into butter. I haven't been penetrated since my husband, years ago now, and at this moment I want the trouble-man's hands clamped around my waist, and I want to feel every inch of him sliding in and out. I don't care which of us he's aiming to please. I only want the bump of his hips against my ass and the slap of his balls as he plunges all the way in.

That is what I'll think about tonight when I'm alone. For now the fantasy is cut short. The desperate man at my mercy gives in. I stroke him hard as he comes, wanting every drop he can give me. Not too sweet, not too bitter—just right. His body goes limp as his voice dies. I swallow and stand and wash him down with a sip of wine. I smile at his flushed face, his ragged breaths, and I lean over and tousle his hair.

"Very good," I say. "I hope to see you again this weekend. Talk to Will about schedules."

He nods deliriously.

I switch off the television and pick up my glass. I pass the man who spells trouble on my way out of the den and catch his eyes for a moment. He breaks another rule by holding the gaze and yet another by smiling. His grin is lopsided, much deeper at one corner and it gives him a dimple. He smiles like a man with something very clever to say, but he doesn't break that rule.

Not yet, anyway.

I smooth a lock of my just-starting-to-gray hair primly behind my ear, and I give the trouble-man a good looking-over. He's hard behind his fly, which I record mentally as a point for me. I'm going to keep this one waiting a long time.

CHAPTER TWO

IT'S SUNDAY EVENING. It's raining yet again, a heavy shower with the occasional clap of thunder. It's my favorite weather for staying home with four or five young, submissive men and enjoying the simple pleasures of domesticity.

If you're curious about what these men do when they're not actively being taken advantage of, it's quite low-key. Lounge, I'd say, is the best description. They sit on my comfortable furniture in the den or the sitting room or the sunroom and do very little aside from look inviting. They're allowed to read the paper or browse my artsy magazines, although if I walk into the room they have to put such distractions aside and await instructions. Unlike other sorts of pets, they're not allowed to stare or drool. They may cast me questioning, eager looks from time to time then glance away coyly, pretending to find the view out the window supremely engaging.

Tonight I am feeling atmospheric. I love thunderstorms, though it's unlikely that we'll lose power. Instead I flip off all the switches in the upstairs fuse box and light candles. It's worth having to reprogram the clocks the next morning. The lights from the Common leak in, but I pretend it's the nineteenth century and they're gas or however that worked. Sometimes a car drives past on the street below with its stereo blaring, but on the whole it's a convincing fantasy.

The trouble-man is here tonight. He arrived on time with the others, trickling in around seven, admitted by Will, playing the part of my stoical, diplomatic doorman.

Now if you will refer back three paragraphs and remind yourself what it is my boys are expected and allowed to do while they're on the clock, I will tell you now that the trouble-man is doing few of those things. He doesn't sit still or act particularly coy. He meanders. He leans against doorframes, an aristocratic cowboy, hip cocked, eyes fixed on me like a compass needle drawn north.

I will tell you more about him, though I'm not a writer by trade and a photograph would surely do him far more justice. He's tall and sculpted, as the requirements dictate. He's still violating the harem's rules by wearing a tee shirt, but I can tell from the way the cotton stretches over the two crests of his abdomen and the contours of his chest that he's got a body custom-made to keep me up nights. His arms look strong with pronounced triceps, matching veins at the crook of each elbow that make me think of pumping blood and the smell of male exertion.

He's blocking the threshold between the hall and the sunroom, and I want him to move so I can sit by the windows in the latter and wait for the next round of lightning and thunder. I have a fat candle in my hand as I approach him, and the flame lights up his face, his straight, noble nose and full lips. Even in the relative darkness, his eyes are bright. He's got his arms crossed over his chest, but as I come close he drops one and raises the other, taking hold of the top frame of the door, casual. He makes no move to quit blocking my way, but to scold him too openly would dilute my authority in front of the others.

"No shirts," I tell him in an even, bored voice.

His lips tighten in the smallest possible twitch of a smile, and he obediently reaches down and peels his tee up and over his head. Two feet away now stands a body even finer than the theoretical one I've been fantasizing about since the night he first appeared. Not an ounce of fat. Every shape and shadow of him is honed to conform to an imaginary manual of specifications shelved somewhere in my reptile brain. I want to sink my teeth into the rounded swells of his shoulders. I want to lap Scotch out of the hollows above his collarbones. And I want him to get the hell out of my way.

"Follow me," I say.

He steps aside the tiniest bit and I slip by, feeling his energy as if I were breaching a force field. I take a seat on the sofa, below the bay window, beside a young man who politely sets aside a newspaper he'd been perusing in the candlelight. He's European-looking with stylish, long-ish dark hair and an angular jaw. Black tattoos all up his arms, some kind of tasteful, intricate design. I beckon him to straddle me and to the trouble-man I say, "Sit down," and pat the empty cushion to my right. "You could use a tutorial."

The tattooed man relocates, pushing his knees into the upholstery on either side of my legs. He's wearing black boxer briefs, and I run my hands over his backside, hard as some impressive cliché. I stroke my palms up his stomach and chest, surveying the thin trail of dark hair that runs down from his navel to disappear behind his waistband. He's stiff already, and I admire the long curve of his erection where it strains to one side against his underwear.

The trouble-man sinks into the couch, looking relaxed.

"Take your jeans off," I order him.

He says, "Sure," in a voice I never asked to hear.

"No talking."

He stands and unfastens a thick leather belt, unzips his fly and lets his pants fall to the floor with a clunk of the heavy buckle. He too wears boxer briefs, gray ones. His hips make a V that draws my eyes straight down to his bulge. He steps out of his pants and sits back on the sofa.

I catch the eye of another man—the one I made suffer the other night during *Cool Hand Luke*. He's watching from a chair on the other side of the narrow room. I beckon him over to occupy the remaining empty cushion. He knows what to do, and I think he'll set a good example for his worrisome new peer.

I begin to stroke the tattooed man in my lap as my star pupil does the same to himself at my side. I pull down my man's briefs enough to free him and my pupil follows suit. The trouble-man just leans back, one arm draped along the back of the couch, and watches with a little self-satisfied grin tweaking his lips. He's distracting in his inactivity. I will probably have to fire him after tonight. Which is a pity, I think, glancing to where his dick weighs heavily against the cotton of his shorts.

"Touch yourself," I say to him coldly.

His lips part a fraction but he doesn't speak. He nods instead and runs a lazy hand down his belly, settling it over his cock. He's in no hurry.

To my left, my star pupil's strokes match the ones I'm using to torture the man in my lap. He adjusts, kneeling to face me so both their exposed cocks are pointed at my belly. The two obedient men exchange a look and then they each reach a hand out to cup the back of the other's head and they kiss—a bonus I happily pay extra for. They kiss deeply, faces angled, eyes closed. I take one of the tattooed man's hands and wrap it around the other's cock.

The troublesome man to my right is unscandalized and infuriatingly controlled. His two colleagues are unraveling rapidly, but he's fondling himself with a look of such obnoxious placidity that I want to slap him. Perhaps I will in a little while.

"You may moan," I inform the other two, and they waste no time in following my order. Both are glistening now, and I rub the fluid up and down the length of the tattooed man's long shaft. Unseen to them, my own body is priming too, putting his to shame.

As I play with him I think of the trouble-man again. Again, I imagine him coming up from behind, those hands on my hips. Again, no regard for the rules and the order of things in my little kingdom. That voice, loud and rough, cutting through the peace, barking orders of his own. His cock, cutting straight into my core.

In reality he's still sitting beside me, still stroking his hidden erection with a slow hand. He's not watching the other two—his eyes are on me. I can feel them. When I sneak a glance to confirm this, he runs his tongue over his bottom lip, looking hungry.

The two obedient men lose the coordination needed to continue kissing each other. I admire their flushed faces, lidded eyes. I guide my star pupil's hand and let it take over for my own on the man in my lap. I watch them jerk each other until they're panting and hoarse.

The man in my lap comes first, his cream spurting over the other's knuckles and wrist. His colleague follows suit seconds later, and their dicks touch as he releases with a deep moan.

Politely, they each stand and gather their garments and exit the room with all the dignity possible in such a situation. In their wake, the air is practically quivering with the heat and smell of sex. I will tip them very generously.

I'm alone now with the trouble-man.

I turn to face him, and he snatches the breath from my lungs with those piercing eyes. I try to ignore them. I focus on his hair—brown, glowing gold around the edges in the candlelight. A model's cheekbones. I wonder absently if that's his day job. Then I think of my complementary day job, and of laying him across my bed and photographing his strong, young body, naked and aroused. Gritty, high-contrast black and white, so I won't have to remember how blue his eyes are.

"Should I keep going?" he asks, and I realize with some surprise that he's English. Not posh—somewhere working-class. Manchester, or Liverpool?

"Don't speak," I tell him. "And yes." I watch his hand, the tendons in his forearm. He's casual and cool, but I can tell from the dark patch on the gray cotton that he's ready. He reaches a hand out to my shoulder and I slap it away.

"Don't touch me."

The trouble-man smiles and he says, "My name is Sean."

"I don't care what your name is," I say, narrowing my eyes. "Don't touch me, and don't talk to me. And don't make me tell you again."

"Let me taste you," he says, leaning closer and I stand.

"Follow me," I say.

I grab a candle and march through the fourth floor and down a flight of stairs. I hear the man whose name I'd prefer I didn't know behind me a few paces. I lead him to my room and point to the queen-sized bed. "Lie down," I say, and slam the door shut behind us.

He sits at the edge of the mattress, looking smug.

"I said 'lie'."

He stretches out across my claret-colored comforter.

I dig two pairs of nylons out of my hosiery drawer and walk to the far end of the bed. I yank his hands through the slats of the oak headboard and bind his wrists together.

"There's one rule corrected," I say. "Open your mouth."

He does and I gag him with the second pair of stockings, tying them tight at the base of his skull.

"Better," I say. "Now turn over."

I have no clue what the trouble-man's game is because he seems eager to follow directions, suddenly. Perhaps he just craves attention. He flips over onto his stomach, bound arms crossing, and I leave for a minute to fetch myself a glass of wine and a couple more candles. Outside there's a flash and a delayed peal of thunder and I jump, nerves crackling.

Mr. Troublesome is as he should be when I return. I set the candles on the vanity and close the door and perch at the edge of the bed. I sip my wine and admire his back muscles and shoulder blades in the jerking light. He has his head propped to one side on his arm, eyes on me, waiting. It's hard to tell with the gag, but I think he's smiling.

I take a deep drink and set the glass aside. "I'm firing you after tonight. You're extremely disappointing."

He watches as I crawl to the middle of the bedspread. I slide my feet then ankles then legs beneath his hips, until he's lying across my lap. I feel his hard dick against my thighs as I run my palm over his ass. He's excited, and his skin is damp and warm as I pull his shorts down his hips. I reach my hand between his legs to fondle his balls, teasing him with rough pulls. The weight of his bare cock makes me ache for something I swore never to do with any of my beautiful boys.

I hear his deep, nasal breaths and muffled grunts. I think of how flagrantly he disregarded the rules of this house—*my* house—and I make him feel every ounce of my anger when I slap him. The sound or the surprise of it jolts his body.

I spank him until I can see his skin branded red even in the dim light, until his back is shining with a fine layer of sweat and his ribs expand and contract fast and deep. He finally shows me some helplessness, and I relent. I'm not a powerful woman. I'm average height and of graceful build if I may say so myself. I was a dancer before I took up photography. I'm fit but not built for dominance by any stretch of the imagination, though at this moment I feel magnificent and cruel and masterful.

Our collective skin is warm and sticky as I maneuver my bare legs from under him, smoothing my silk skirt back down my thighs. He watches, still.

"Turn over again," I say, and I hear a new weight in my voice.

His smell is potent as he settles on his back. I explore him with my eyes, from his sweat-matted hair and furrowed brow, down his strained, muscular body to his long, thick cock. Longer and thicker than I'd prefer for my usual purposes. A very nice size for other activities, however. I pull his underwear all the way off then stalk up the mattress and jerk the gag from his mouth, letting it lie limp around his throat. Below his stubbly chin, just to one side of his neck, there's a mark—a reddish bruise like a hickey. I catch his eyes and I shuffle to the headboard and reach for his hands. I don't release them, but instead I feel his rough fingertips, the calluses on his left hand. I sit back down on the covers and study his face.

"You're a violinist."

"Would you like me to play for you?" he asks, and his voice is as deep and haunting and melancholy as his chosen instrument.

"Definitely not," I say. "I don't do romance."

His eyes dart condemningly to the candles, my wine, to the panes where the rain is pelting. One window is open halfway and we can both smell the earthy autumn air blowing in.

"Let me please you," he says, and the words come out thick and needy, his first real show of desperation. I need more proof like this. He humiliated me with his confidence earlier, and I want to hear him beg for forgiveness. I study his tight stomach, his deepening breathing.

I'm firing this man as soon as I'm done with him, but I think perhaps the time has come to take things to another level. He'd never work out as a safe, disposable toy in my harem, but he might make a fine whore for one night. And I'm goddamn overdue.

"Fine." I slip off the bed and unbutton my cardigan and unzip my skirt and stand before him in my camisole and panties. Nothing fancy—I hadn't planned on anyone seeing me so near to naked. Still, my bra and underwear match, a nice cream-colored satin set. Too good for this man but no matter.

I catch him licking his lips again.

"Untie me," he begs, pulling against the headboard.

"Why?" I ask, snotty. "What do you want to do?"

"I'll fuck you," he promises, tugging hard. "With my fingers while I eat you out. I'll make you come as many times as you want." A very pretty threat I must admit.

"I'll bet your fingers are very talented," I allow. "But I doubt your mouth has much to offer. So far it's given me nothing but grief."

"Let me show you. Untie me."

"Earn it," I say. I climb onto the bed and crawl to him, crawl over him, making my way up his body, letting his erection rub against my belly. The friction tightens my pussy like a greedy fist. I hold the headboard and hook one calf under his shoulder, then the other until I'm locked tight against his face. I feel his hot breath warming me then his tongue tracing the crotch of my panties. I moan. It's been so fucking long.

I make him work through the fabric, and he finds the swollen nub of my clit easily. The satin grows wet, feeling as though it's dissolving. His tongue teases and his lips suckle until I'm drenched from both of us. It feels so good it hurts, the pleasure a tight, hard streak running through my body, buzzing and impatient. Every stroke of his tongue sends waves of desire pulsating up from my core. I need more.

Reaching down, I yank my panties to one side and then he's there. His caresses are slippery and hot and firm. Hungry. I adjust myself and let him taste what he's coaxing from me. He laps up the juices with harsh little grunts, and as his tongue begins to spear me I make a terrible mistake.

"Sean," I moan. His tongue thrusts deep and the tip of his nose grazes my clit. I say it again, and it feels like the most forbidden syllable in the history of sex.

His mouth pulls away as much as it's able. "Untie me," he pleads. The words heat my tender skin.

I hesitate, and he laps at me. "Please," he says, and licks me again. "Please. You won't regret it."

I already do, but I reach over and claw at the knot in the nylons. All his tugging has made it impossibly tight, but I don't have the patience to leave his mouth and search for a pair of scissors. He senses how frantic and useless my efforts are, and he tugs harder. He pulls and fidgets until the material stretches to let one hand slip out then the other. He's on me in a flash. I'm flipped on to my back without preamble and he's above me, our heads suddenly at the foot of the bed. His hips push my thighs wide and his cock presses along the length of my lips, a flimsy strip of drenched satin and cotton my pussy's last defense.

"Don't," I say, even as I feel him reaching down. He adjusts his dick so he's pressing into my entrance, straining against the fabric.

"How long has it been?" he asks.

"Fuck you."

"Tell me," he whispers against my neck, and he kisses me there. No one has kissed me in a very long time. His hips thrust him into me over and over and I want to cry out, the desire is so violent, the need for his penetration like withdrawal from the cruelest drug. His roped arms are locked at my sides, his chest pinning me to the mattress. "Tell me," he murmurs again.

"Almost five years," I admit.

"Do you want me?"

"I hate you."

"I'll make you scream for me," he promises, and he pulls away. All at once the aggression is over. He steps to my bedside table and brings me my glass.

I sit cross-legged and sip the wine and watch as he picks up the tall cheval mirror from beside the closet and carries it to the middle of the room, centering the bed in its reflection. He takes my glass away. When he comes back, he pulls me by the ankles to the edge of the mattress. He sinks to his knees on the floor.

"You better be good." I scratch my nails across his scalp and grasp a fistful of his short hair.

I feel his fingers at my hips, and he tugs my panties off. His rough palms push my thighs wide and hold them there. As his head lowers I feel the heat of his breath on my skin. Five years…

I study his body in the mirror, his muscles lit warmly by the candlelight. Powerful arms, hands holding me open, that gorgeous, ripe ass, toned back and shoulders. I want to know him, suddenly. I want to know why he's here and who he is and what he likes and how his body came to be so perfect. I want to see his face as he comes. I want to see him cry and hold him tight. Most of all, I want my sanity to return.

"Tell me your name," he says softly. His eyes dart across my wide-open center.

"Go to hell."

"I want to say it when I take you later," he murmurs, and a hundred fantasies flash across my mind. Sean closes his eyes and brushes his stubbly cheek against my inner thigh, looking transcendent. He seems to understand the balance I crave, that impossibly narrow tightrope stretched between dominance and submission.

"Why did you come here?" I ask.

His eyes open and meet mine. "I wanted to know who you are. What sort of woman demands to have her selfish fantasies fulfilled so openly. By strangers. I wanted to meet you. And now that I have, I want you to use me. Even more than the others."

I like Sean's answer more than I will ever admit to him.

"Let me give you what they can't," he says, gaze dropping back down.

"They'll give me whatever I ask for," I remind him. "You're the one who can't follow orders."

"I won't take the money."

"Good," I say. "You haven't earned it."

"Caroline," he says in a low rumble, mouth millimeters from my lips.

I freeze. "How did you know that?" It's not a difficult fact to sleuth out, but I still want answers.

"You're a photographer," he says. "I saw your equipment downstairs. The framed prints on the walls are signed. Caroline Thom—"

"That's not my name anymore."

After a pause, Sean asks, "What was he like?" His tongue flicks me lightly, making my breath hitch.

"He's old enough to be your father," I say, hiding the arousal in my voice. "And he was *exactly* the right age to be my university professor."

"How did you find it, being the student?" Sean asks in his lower-class accent, and I realize now that he is *everything* my ex-husband was not. Rude and pushy, sensual and beautiful. Warm and available.

"Lucrative," I finally say.

"Do you wish he could see you now?" he asks, and the conservative in me feels as though I should slap him out of protocol.

I don't answer because at that moment Sean's tongue strokes my clit and my legs seize around his ears. The sensation pulses up my belly like a current—a violent electrical current, not a gentle, poetical stream. He pushes my thighs back open and holds them with his strong hands. He licks again, slower, so exquisite it hurts, the pleasure mounting.

I watch his reflection and I watch my fingers grasping his hair. In the mirror, I wear a wedding band. It's not actually a wedding band, just a fancy woven ring I wear on my right hand, but I pretend it's a screen, not a mirror, and I pretend that I'm still married. I pretend I'm my husband, walking in and finding me spread at the edge of our bed, a raw, tight young man on his knees pleasuring me. The guilt feels as hot and real as Sean's mouth.

"You taste amazing," he mumbles.

"And you never shut up."

He swirls his tongue around my clit until I groan against my will. One hand slides up my thigh. His left hand with its violinist's calluses. He runs two rough fingertips up and down my swollen lips, bathes my clit in the wetness. He covers that spot with his mouth, suckling, and his fingers tease my entrance.

"Say please," he whispers. "Say please and I'll do it."

"Fuck you."

"Five years, Caroline. Let me be the first."

"*You* say please, then."

"Please," he murmurs, and laps at me again. "Please."

I'm dying to grant him permission. At this moment I can't imagine my cunt was created for any purpose other than to take pleasure from this man. Those two threatening fingertips trace a shallow line up and down, up and down. I want to be his instrument. I want to be mastered.

"Please…"

"Fuck me," I say.

One finger at first, slow thrusts. His mouth is still on my clit, tongue flickering. He groans as though he's the one being served.

"More," I demand.

He makes his hand into a gun and gives me the barrel, slow and deep. I clench his hair tighter. In the mirror, his hips thrust at the same tempo as his fingers.

"Touch yourself," I say, and I watch the hand still holding my thigh slide obediently down between his legs. His groans turn hoarse as he shares my pleasure, joins the rhythm. I wish I could see his cock, see him stroking it in a tight fist, milking himself until he glistens. I picture him alone, in his overpriced, shit-hole Allston apartment or wherever he lives, on his back in his rumpled bed with its mismatched sheets. That lean, strong, young body, spread naked, the come lashing his clenched belly as he shoots. As he thinks of me.

His fingers make me feel empty as I remember how thick and stiff he was when I spanked him. If and when he takes me, it will hurt. At least at first. I want to know if he'll ram it in hard, or ease it in gently. If I were on top, I'd slide him in slow and steady, as if I were sinking into a Jacuzzi, dizzy from the steam.

I watch his pumping hips, needing him so badly it feels like mania. How easy it would be for him to stand up, to push his hips between my legs and make the longing go away.

"Take me, Sean."

He doesn't. His lips keep sucking me, his hands keep fucking both of us. I rake his scalp, demanding more. I feel his thrusting hand rotate, feel his fingers curling, his calluses tugging against that sinful spot deep inside me, beckoning, inviting me to come home. The pleasure is a flint, lighting me up with a spark each time his touch strikes. Molten heat seeps into my feet until my toes buzz, hot. My palms are sweaty and his hair is damp and our voices are one, the moans like a mantra, sanctifying the space we're sharing.

I jerk upright as the climax churns through me and my back arches and my eyes are fixed on Sean's body in the mirror. The heat rushes up from the flame he's ignited, burns through my cunt and my womb and my belly, through my breasts, up my spine until I feel it licking at each fingertip and pounding in my ears and tingling in my lips. He knows how to make it last. His fingers and lips and tongue slow, the touch deliberate and skillful, and he draws my orgasm out. It doesn't flash and fade. It builds, lingers, pummels me in fresh waves until I can feel the bedspread under my bare butt once more, smell us in the air, hear the rain on the glass.

I feel him lapping up the spoils of our intimate battle. He makes tiny, hungry, whimpering noises. When he finally looks up from between my legs, he's smiling like a wicked boy.

I shove his shoulders back with my knees. "Get out of my house."

His eyes widen but he stands.

I grab his underwear from the bed behind me and toss them unceremoniously at his chest. He watches me watching him as he pulls them up his thighs and over his raging hard-on. He runs his tongue over his swollen lower lip, and his expression is dark. I move away and slip my plain silk robe from the hook by the door and thread my arms into the sleeves. It feels like a straitjacket, just as his presence feels like an invitation to madness.

"I don't want to see you ever again," I say evenly, and it's true. If I have to look at him for one minute longer I'll want him in my sheets, his body curled around me. I'll want him seated across the table from me in the morning, drinking coffee and reading the paper, and that's not acceptable.

His mouth twitches, but he holds his tongue. His blue, blue eyes stare into mine for a long moment, and only the desperate motions of his ribs as he struggles for his breath give him away. He turns and he leaves me, leaves the bedroom door open behind him.

I sink down onto the mattress. Out in the hall, I hear the metallic squeak of a hinge. With a suddenness that makes me gasp, he snaps all the breakers back on, and my room and the hall glare bright and artificial. I feel naked and blind, and as I hear his footsteps fade down the staircase and the click of the front door closing, I feel more alone than I have in five years.

CHAPTER THREE

THE TROUBLE-MAN STAYED AWAY for an eternity. Well, four days. But trust me when I say it felt like years. I'd almost begun to believe he decided to respect my demands. I can't imagine what made me think he's the sort of man who would.

Will wanted an explanation when I announced first thing on Monday that Sean was to be struck from the roster, even as I could still practically feel his tongue sliding in and out of my pussy.

"I never want that man allowed here again," I said, buttering my toast. "The one with the short brown hair and the annoyingly blue eyes."

"*That* one?" Will sounded as if he were taking the news personally. "Are you serious? I was so excited to get him! He's perfect! His photo reminded me of Paul Newman, circa *Exodus*." Will shares my love of old movies, as well as eager young men.

"I should be so lucky," I said flippantly and sipped my coffee. Paul Newman should be so lucky.

"What did he do? Or not do?"

"He isn't housetrained," I said, and Will dropped the matter with a bitchy shrug and a sigh.

This evening, when Sean finally returns, he doesn't darken my door. He scales my fire escape, instead, and when he appears in my bedroom window I'm so startled I scream like a film star confronted by a mummy.

I recover quickly and glare at my would-be burglar. I stand before the tall window with my arms crossed sternly over my chest, and I can't decide right away if I should let him in. I'm dressed in my robe again, fresh from the shower. The scheduled boys aren't due to arrive for another hour.

I've come to equate Sean with the rain. In the past week I haven't had one without the other, and now that I think about it, both have the power to leave me wet.

He's framed in the window, face shining with drizzle, white dress shirt damp and clinging. It's dark out but he's lit by my bedroom lights. Very, very slowly, he smiles his lopsided smile.

I flip the latch and push the bottom pane up.

"Don't you dare get mud on my carpet." I turn my back on him and go to my vanity to finish brushing my hair out.

I hear the clang of his shoes as they drop onto the fire escape, and I feel his energy as he enters and approaches. He snatches the brush from my hand and takes over. I watch his eyes in the mirror, studying my shoulder-length hair as he runs the bristles through it, and I wonder if he's making an inventory of the grays. He looks melancholy tonight. Or guilty. And with good cause.

I push my stool back roughly and catch him in the knees. He takes it in stride and sets down the brush.

"I have to get dressed," I tell him, and then his arms are holding me. They snake around my waist from behind, enveloping me, pulling me against his wet shirt, his firm chest.

"I missed you." His hands slide up over my ribs and cup me. I feel his cock right through his jeans, pressing at the small of my back. He pulls the lapels of the robe open and palms my bare breasts, the pads of the fingers on the left scratchy, the right side less so. His hands are big and my breasts are small, but I feel more full and feminine and worthy of my sex than I have in twenty years. He pinches my nipples gently between his fingers and broad thumbs, arousing them with tiny pulls. He teases until I'm aching, until my face and chest are flushed and my attempts to appear cold are laughable.

"I told you not to come here again," I say, and I sound husky.

"You opened the window," he parries, and his voice is right at my ear. It's deep, a baritone, forever tarnished with that working man's accent. It's like a shot of lousy house whiskey, cheap and strong, and it goes down stinging, upsets my stomach and swims in my blood.

"The others will be here soon." I twist my arm around so I can cup the front of his pants behind me and feel his excitement.

"Good," he says. "They can watch."

I imagine such a thing for a moment—four or five young men standing in a circle around us, pleasuring themselves as they watch me get fucked by Sean. Watching me suck him off, on my knees as he barks orders, his hand on the back of my head. Watching what they're denied.

"No," I say. A fine fantasy, but no one can know about this. If Sean gets his way, it'll be our secret. And he shouldn't get his way. He's brought me nothing but trouble.

I step out of his embrace and rewrap myself. I turn to study the length of his torso plastered in translucent white cotton. "You have a hell of a nerve showing up here."

"So punish me."

I squint at him and nod. I grab the brush off the vanity and motion for him to go to the bed. "All fours," I say. "Hold the headboard."

He kneels and lowers down to his elbows, grabbing the slats. I settle in behind him and reach around, unbuckling his belt, tugging open his damp jeans, sliding them and his briefs down to expose that perfect, firm ass. I hold each cheek, my fingers curled into claws. He cranes his neck to meet my eyes and anger flashes in my chest.

I pick up the hairbrush. It's a paddle brush, pine with a wide, flat back. As it strikes him it makes a sound so fierce I almost feel guilty.

I work in slow, uneven intervals and his body bucks with fresh surprise at each spank and his breathing grows labored and raw.

I toss the brush aside and scrape my nails over his reddened skin. He flinches, muscles tensing.

"Up," I say, getting off the bed.

He hikes his jeans up with a wince and stands dutifully before me.

"Go upstairs and wait. Leave your shirt."

He slips each button free with a cruel slowness. He lets it drop to the floor before he exits, making me watch the muscles of his back writhe with each graceful step.

I dress in a cashmere turtleneck and a layered crepe skirt and flats, and I wander upstairs at my leisure. I pour two glasses of wine and find him in the den, the television droning softly, reading lamps glowing. He's watching an old movie on TV, probably just the last channel I left it tuned to. I hand him the glass.

"Join me," he says, as if this were his home.

I glare at him again but I sit and we drink, and we watch the movie for a few minutes. I know what's going to happen between us and it frightens me, so I drink more. He takes the glasses after a little while and sets them on the coffee table, ignoring the coasters. I fix this transgression and then he pulls me back into the cushions and kisses me.

It's been forever since I've kissed anyone. Since well before the divorce, and even before the sex dried up in my marriage. My husband and I still fucked long after we quit bothering to be affectionate toward one another. The last time I did this, it turned my stomach. This time, it's wondrous.

Behind the wine, I can taste him. The faintest trace of salt and some elemental human flavor. His hands cradle my jaw, and he's in charge. He starts with nips, little bites on my lower lip. Then suckling. His tongue traces the seam of my mouth then penetrates—just as it did to my pussy four nights ago, except this moment is a hundred times more intimate and personal and raw.

I study his handsome face with my hands, feeling his cheekbones and his temples, pressing my thumb against the shallow cleft in his chin, brushing my fingertips over his closed eyelids.

I pull my mouth away and ask, "How old are you?"

"How old do you want me to be?"

"Between twenty and twenty-eight." I'm nervous now, hoping he'll lie if need be. I study him harder. He has little signs of wear, a hundred tiny things that combine to create something the other boys don't possess. Dignity. Experience. Substance and wisdom.

"I'm going to disappoint you again," he says.

"My assistant is going to get a stern talking-to. Didn't he check your ID?"

"He did," Sean says. He kisses me. "Then he said something about an exodus and said you'd forgive him."

"So how old *are* you?"

"Thirty-two," he says, and I feel something cold drop into my stomach—danger. He's young, but not young enough. It has nothing to do with the fetish, the taboo, the harem, the rules. It has everything to do with reality. In reality, I could never be with a man who's fifteen or twenty years younger than me. It's an impossibility and a relief. That Sean is only seven years my junior is scary. That I could be seen with him out to dinner at a restaurant and not be judged is terrifying.

"This isn't going to work." I pull away from him and I feel chilly.

"I wasn't suggesting it would."

"What do you want from me? From this?" I wave my hand to mean the room, the house, the scenario. Us.

"What do *you* want from this?"

"I think it's pretty obvious."

"Let me stay for the evening," he says, "and I'll show you what it is you really want. Just let me stay, and watch you with the others and you'll see."

"You watch and *I'll* see?"

He nods.

"You're a cocky little shit," I say, and I smile at him, amused. "Let me pour you another glass."

* * *

BY NINE THIRTY, the boys are all here. Lots of them change into pajamas when they arrive, and soon the fourth floor is full of young men in low-slung flannel bottoms, like a fraternity sleepover with funeral parlor etiquette.

Troublemaking Sean is acting suspiciously well-behaved. He slid out of his jeans as the festivities began, and he's sprawled in his boxer briefs in my favorite reading chair again, looking as if he's in on some secret. And he must be. How else could he be here, looking so smug, drinking my wine, watching me with such disobedient fervor?

His eyes follow everything. Each time I sink into a new seat beside a new boy, he watches. There's a first-timer here tonight—Sean's replacement. He's young and tan and hung like Christmas has come early, and I make sure his legs are spread wide in Sean's direction as my hands unwrap the presents. When I order him to stand so I can kneel and take him in my mouth, I make sure Sean gets our profiles. I call another boy over and I take turns sampling them. It's hot, as hot as it's ever been, but they have nothing to do with it. Sean's eyes on me are ten times more erotic than either of their hard dicks in my mouth.

When I finish them they're dismissed, and I aim myself toward the sunroom for the next course.

Sean catches my sleeve as I pass by his seat, and he whispers, "Save room for dessert." I yank my wrist away coldly.

Five boys came tonight and soon enough, five boys have come. I work my way through the men on offer until only the uninvited one remains. Sean followed me into the sunroom, and as the last hired man exits in delirium, he draws my eye from his perch in the bay window. I wonder what the people in the park make of his near-naked silhouette from four stories down.

"Follow me," I say, and he's gotten very good at taking this one order. I lead him downstairs three flights to the center room with no windows, its corners piled with my photography equipment. I drag a chair in from the parlor and push it against the bare wall and toss a black drop cloth over it.

"Sit." I set up a camera and lights and an umbrella until he's bathed in the drama his bone structure demands.

"Sit the way you do in my den," I say. "Like you're judging me."

Sean reclines a bit, casual, and I begin snapping overexposed pictures.

Tonight is the last time I plan to see him, but I want to possess his body long after he's banished from my house. He follows my directions through dozens of shots, maybe hundreds. I capture his face in every emotion, his eyes boring into the lens, cast down, glancing to the side, closed. He touches himself when I ask, his hand over his shrouded erection at first, then dipping beneath the cotton. He holds the waistband down to show the camera then sheds them completely. The photos will document all of his details—the tendons that stand out along his throat when he moans, the crease in his brow when he's so hard and close it must hurt. I record his beautiful back muscles and the shadows of his shoulder blades, the still-glowing mark on his ass from his penitence earlier.

"Why do you think you're here?" I ask him as I near the end of my project. His eyes burn into mine through the viewfinder.

"Because I'm special," he informs me, and he laughs a little and smiles, and I photograph it.

"You think you're special?"

"More than the others," he says. "None of them have tasted you or kissed you. None of them will ever fuck you the way I'm going to. And you won't be able to forget about me like you can with them."

"What makes you so sure?" I ask, and I click the camera off.

"I don't know, but I think you feel it too."

I collapse the tripod and lights and shoo Sean from the chair so I can fold the drop cloth. I carry the chair back to the parlor and he follows.

"Where?" he asks when we reach the second-floor landing.

"My bedroom." We climb another flight.

"How?" he asks as I close the door behind us.

"Rough. Be mean and rough."

He nods once and then it's on.

He grabs my wrist and pulls me with him to the bed. I'm tugged hard onto his lap, face-to-face, and my skirt rides up as he wraps my legs around his waist. He's still naked, still hard as iron, and his strong hands make me ride the thick length of him. I wish my panties would just catch fire and disintegrate already, so we could be fucking right this instant.

"Keep that up," he tells me, and his hands take my face. His kiss is deep and explicit, same as the noises that escape him. I ride him and fantasize that he's inside me.

"Good," he moans against my lips, and for a brief moment I'm in charge.

"You better fuck me right."

"You won't be able to walk," he promises.

He pushes my sweater up and yanks it over my head. His lips find my nipple through the lace, sucking until it's a hard peak then doing the same to the other. His warm hands squeeze my breasts together and he buries his face between them, taking in the perfume and the sweat and whatever else he's after. I reach back and unhook my bra, dying for his wet tongue on my bare skin. He laps and suckles, greedy, and the pleasure mounts between my thighs, breaching the dam. My panties are so wet that I'm bathing his bare cock with them. It's too much. Too hot. Too right. I start to come, moaning low and harsh. His hands grasp my ass and keep me riding, keep me coming until he decides I'm done. Until I'm limp and reeling.

"How do you want me?" he demands, all but sneering.

"I don't care. Just hard."

He helps me to standing, such a selectively courteous gentleman. "I need to get something."

"No, you don't. I have a note from your doctor."

"You're on something?" he asks, stepping close.

"Since the dawn of time."

"All right, then." His face looms above mine, chest pushing into me. He's staring me down, forcing me to walk backward. "Get on your knees."

I obey.

"Give me what you gave the others."

"I don't *give* them anything," I say haughtily. "I take—"

"Just suck my bloody cock," he says, apparently disinterested in my semantics.

He's hot and thick and throbbing when I wrap my fingers around him. His smell makes the glands in my mouth pucker and sting, anticipating.

"Suck me."

I lick him first. I bathe the smooth, taut skin of his head with my tongue and I taste him. Heaven. I look up to find his hooded eyes staring down at me.

"More."

I do as he says. The first inch then another. I take half of his long dick in my mouth and stroke the other half, hard, from the base. He's big—bigger than the others—and I revel in the intimidation that tingles its way down my spine. I listen to his moans and swears, let him pump his hips gently, and I take what he gives me. He seems so close to the edge, but then he stops. I'm drunk from him and it feels wrong when he pulls away.

"Turn around."

I shuffle in place until I'm facing the cheval mirror. He angles it just so, and I watch his reflection fall to its knees. He pushes my skirt up over my hips, yanks the crotch of my panties to one side. Two fingers plunge deep, finding me still dripping and swollen from my climax. So ready. I watch his face in the mirror, the tremble in his lips and the narrowing of his eyes, as though he's in disbelief.

"Please," I say.

"Please what?"

"Fuck me," I beg him. "Now. Hard."

His fingers thrust deep. "Say my name."

"Please, Sean."

"Again."

"Fuck me, Sean. Please."

He finds the tiny zipper and jerks my skirt and panties down my thighs and off my calves. I watch us in the mirror, just two naked strangers, both dying for the same thing. Alone together in this empty house on a rainy, lonely night.

He guides his cock between my legs and runs it cruelly up and down my wet lips. I study the muscle and bone flexing in his hips as he moves, the tight ridges of his abdomen, the hard shapes of his arms as his hands clamp around my waist. Strong. Young, but not like the others. More real. Far more dangerous.

I catch his eyes in the mirror. "I want you."

"I know."

"Enjoy yourself," I say. "You're never getting this again."

I feel his head at my entrance, teasing.

"You're so wet," he murmurs, and it sounds suddenly like worship.

"Take me."

"I only get this once, you said. I'll do it how I want." I feel him easing in, slow as an hour hand.

"Come on."

He groans, giving me a little more. There's pressure. He's thick, and I'm tight with the craving. I want him to split me clean open.

"Don't be gentle."

"Fuck gentle," he says, laughing. "This is torture, sweetheart."

I push my hips back and force him deeper.

He gasps, against his better judgment, I suspect. "Cheater."

"So punish me."

I think this battle of wills is still raging, but I'm wrong. Sean's hands grasp me hard at the hips, and he slams his cock all the way in, until he fills me like I never knew a man could. One or both of us grunts, but I couldn't tell you who.

"Yeah." He holds me tight against him for several long breaths. I can feel his pelvis pressed against my ass, feel every inch of him pulsing inside me. "Remember me," he says, and the words rend the air between us like a razor.

It's time. He slides out, slow, then back in. Over and over. And over. It's a lesson, one I'm meant never to forget.

"Mine," he says, and his hips pump faster. His long, tight body in the mirror is the single hottest sight I have ever seen. Now that I know how old he is, I can't find the younger men attractive anymore. The *boys*. He's going to ruin me.

"Harder," I say. I want him to be rough and distract me from the pressure mounting in my tear ducts.

Sean fucks me like an animal—like he's in heat—and I watch his face turn flushed and strained and ferocious. His hands knead my backside, and I gasp when he slaps me.

"Say my name," he orders.

I do.

"Tell me how I feel."

"Power-ful." My voice jerks from the impact. "Hard—and thick—and long."

"And you're deep," he tells me. "I can give it all to you." He hammers me hard and I wish I could see his ass working.

"You want to come?" he asks.

"If you'll let me."

"I'll make you," he promises. He pulls out and flips me over and turns us in profile to the mirror. His knees spread wide and he pulls my thighs over his, sliding his wet cock all the way home.

"Sean—"

"I love when you say it." He pounds into me, ruthless, hands braced on my legs, torso long and proud and undulating with his gifted hips. He slips a thumb into his mouth and puts it to my clit. He traces a tight, cruel circle. I do the same to my nipples, wanting to feel this heat across every square inch of my skin. I turn my head, and in the mirror I watch the beautiful little knitted muscles below his ribs, the dent at his hip, the rounded swell of his pumping ass. I watch him fucking me, and it hurts as much as it thrills.

"Tell me you'll miss me," he says, reading my troubling thoughts.

My voice doesn't tell him this, but my body's no good at keeping secrets. His thumb teases me faster.

"I hope you'll think about me," he says.

I moan from the pressure mounting between my quaking thighs.

"I hope when you pass me on the street sometime, you remember this moment."

"Sean—"

"I hope you come to the symphony some evening with your fancy Beacon Hill mates. And when you watch me play, I hope all you can think about is the way I fucked you tonight."

He stops lecturing me and lets himself come undone. His lids grow heavy, his mouth slackens and I can feel him chasing me in my race toward release. Sensations rush down my belly, pooling in my cunt. I watch wide-eyed where his cock surges in and out, fast and steady, obscured only by his skillful hand. His balls slap me each time he thrusts deep and his voice is reduced to harsh grunts. His shoulders hunch forward, and the first droplets of sweat drip from his chest to mine. His teeth are bared, eyes clenched shut.

When I come, I watch his face. His blue eyes open as my pussy grips him, and it's like falling into a warm, chaotic sea. The pleasure tugs at me, pulls me, draws me into him even as he's sunk deep inside my body. It's slow motion, each twitch of his muscles, each bead of perspiration that slips down his skin. Heat breaches my core and radiates out through my veins and nerves, humming, until reality intrudes and I find myself shaking beneath him on the carpet. I hear my voice, small and quavering.

"Beautiful," he says. His ribs tell me how hard his lungs are working, how fast his heart must be pounding.

"Now you," I say.

He nods. My nerves are sensitized almost to the point of pain, but I need to see this—surely it's the only thing I was put on this earth for. He begins pumping me again, slow and deep. His body lowers and he braces himself on his forearms. His belly grazes mine as he thrusts. I let him kiss me for as long as his composure allows then his mouth finds a home against my neck as his hands slide beneath me, cupping my shoulders.

"Caroline."

I suck in my breath.

"Caroline." He says it again, and again. His body turns selfish losing control. I grab his ass and urge him on.

"Come for me," I say in his ear.

"Where?" he asks.

I think about it. "My mouth."

"Yeah," he grunts. "You want to taste me."

He thrusts a few more beats then pulls back. He crawls, legs flanking my ribs, until he's straddling my chest. He's stroking himself rough and fast but my eyes are on his face.

"Give it to me," I say.

He leans down and slides his palm beneath my neck. He cradles my head gently, lovingly, as if I were ill and he were about to spoon-feed me. His cock is at my lips, and I run my tongue over his slit, tasting the little droplet of pre-come, tasting myself. His fist pumps harder, and I memorize it for when I fantasize about what he'll look like, fucking himself, missing me.

"Caroline—"

"Come, Sean."

He groans so deep in his chest, I know he's done. I open my mouth wide, and he pushes past my parted lips, shooting his hot cream across my tongue. Five long lashes, five marrow-deep moans that shake me to the core. He tastes exactly how I knew he would, how I imagined. Savory. Familiar.

* * *

225

I DON'T KNOW who managed to disentangle us from our limp, sweaty heap on the rug and made it to standing first. I only vaguely remember stumbling to the bed, pulling back the covers and feeling a man envelop me for the first time in a long, long while.

When I woke, he was gone. Now I'm lying here, alone, staring up at the ceiling.

It's dawn, and the sparrows are chorusing outside, and the sun is breaching the half-open blinds.

Sean is gone with the night and the rain. There is no note. There is no sign of him. Only the mirror out of place and my clothes piled in an imitation of tidiness on my vanity tell me he was real. And the raw ache between my legs. When it fades, I'll miss it.

When the clouds roll in, my hopes will rise.

The next time it rains, I'll tell the other boys, "Not tonight."

DON'T CALL HER ANGEL

CHAPTER ONE

AT SIX O'CLOCK, Emily looked up as the rumble of the garage door announced her husband's punctual return.

She glanced around the kitchen as she passed through and deemed it tidy, a pleasant place for a man to come home to.

Emily's momma would have rolled her eyes at such a thought. Such a "wifey" thought—her never-married mother's favorite derogatory adjective. Emily didn't care. She loved that it still felt like the moments before a first date when her husband drove up, and that he still excited her as he had three years ago when they'd first laid eyes on each other.

She smoothed her hair, freshly brushed, her makeup just retouched, though her husband likely wouldn't notice either effort.

Yet he couldn't be faulted. More often than not, he came home with a head full of worries Emily couldn't begin to imagine, plus it wasn't as though he didn't look at her, or indeed enjoy looking at her.

Besides, Emily hadn't married Rasul for his ability to spot whether or not she'd gotten highlights done or changed her perfume. She'd married him for how he made her feel, and the way he looked at her, a stare so intense it probably melted all her foundation off anyhow. She'd married him for his strong hands, rough voice, his kind heart and the way she felt around him, a wondrous mix of secure and electrified.

The garage door rattled shut and Emily held her breath as boots mounted the steps, as the knob turned and the door swung in. Her blood pumped quicker and a grin overtook her face. Goddamn, how was this possibly her husband?

He smiled as he stepped inside and Emily waited. Certain things must be done before she could greet him properly. He toed his boots off on the mat and ditched his briefcase on the counter. He offered Emily a kiss—a quick kiss, firm and possessive, chased by another smile.

"Hey, you."

"Hey, yourself. You want a drink?" she asked.

Rasul nodded. He walked back to close the door, lingering there, waiting for Emily to turn away.

She grabbed him a beer from the fridge, listening as he went through his private ritual, turning the locks just so, jiggling the knob, tugging, starting it all over. He must have had a relatively calm Monday at work, as he only relocked the door four times before deciding it was sufficient.

As he took a seat at the dining room table with a sigh, Emily poured herself a glass of white wine and cut it with orange juice.

"My little lightweight," he teased in his warm, dark accent, and they tapped their drinks together.

She gave him a looking-over, curious as always about what went on inside that private head, though realizing she'd probably rather not know. "How was work?"

Rasul shrugged, as much information as he ever offered about his job. He worked for the federal government just a few miles from their home in Virginia, as an interrogator. Born for it. Back in the Middle East, he'd served in his homeland's army all through his twenties, and though he was five-eleven, something in his posture or expression made him look about seven-foot-three. Black eyes and brows and permanent five o'clock shadow, shaved head, a body that made a delicate Georgia flower such as Emily fan herself to fight off a swoon.

She imagined he spent his days slamming his fists on desks under the glare of bright, hoodless bulbs, scaring pertinent intelligence out of bad men, yelling until spittle peppered their faces. His bosses treated Rasul like a Rottweiler, only really caring what he did once they gave the order to sic, and as such he refused to adhere to the agency's dress code. Jeans and a black tee shirt were his uniform for every occasion save weddings and funerals. If his regular bonuses were any indication, he did his job damn well, and no one seemed to mind if he was occasionally mistaken for a security guard. In fact sometimes, here at home, he resembled that role a bit too closely for Emily's taste.

"How has everything been around here?" He often came home hoarse, but not tonight. Tonight his deep voice with that strangely elegant lilt sounded rich and mysterious. Commanding.

She glanced around the kitchen. "Fine. Quiet."

The house was too big for them, too new to her still after only eight weeks. She missed their old apartment, but she'd grow to love this home. Add a dog and a couple of kids someday and it'd be the perfect size.

"You look nice," he said.

Emily smiled, glad of this hint that he was relaxed enough to have spotted her effort. "Thanks. Thought I'd grill steaks tonight, since it's finally feelin' like spring. Made a casserole for you for tomorrow. Chicken and spinach and some other things."

His gaze jumped instinctively to the stove. He didn't rise to check the burner knobs though, another sign he was feeling calm today. "Sounds lovely. Though not as lovely as you being home."

She smiled tightly, annoyed he'd hit their one raw nerve. Rasul wished she'd stay home, as if her working were an insult to him and his earning potential, his manhood. Emily had tried playing housewife full-time for a month after they'd married, but it made her feel isolated and idle and paranoid. She was a fidgety person, and work kept her brain busy. "It's only two shifts a week."

"Two *night* shifts."

She smiled and shook her head. "You met me at that bar. Plus nobody's gonna jump out of the bushes and knife me in Reston."

His nostrils flared and he sipped his beer.

Neanderthal, her mother's voice said. Her momma had fashioned herself a breed of preachy feminism later in life, and had never approved of Rasul. She'd sat through their small backyard ceremony looking as though she were smelling something foul. His race and lapsed religion had nothing to do with it—not directly, anyhow. She simply thought her son-in-law was pushy and cold, and didn't care to listen to justifications about cultural rifts. Emily liked those things about him though. Plus he'd never outright forbid her to work if that's what she wanted.

"It's only for a few more months," she reminded him. When she'd moved here with her dusty GED she'd worked as a cashier at Target. She'd swapped it for a job tending bar, which she'd held on to for nearly four years, and now here she was, signed up to start a nursing course in the fall. That might as well be a fast-food gig in this affluent area, but for a girl who grew up in a single-wide, Emily felt poised for greatness.

"When September rolls around I can finally start feeling like a grown-up," she said.

"I'm very proud." Anyone aside from Emily might have been unconvinced by Rasul's dry tone, but she knew him. She knew from the shapes of his cheeks when he smiled and the way his eyes softened that he was indeed proud. He spent his days screaming threats to get the truth out of people, but Emily could read his emotions like a polygraph, every tiny, silent hint he offered.

He set his beer on the table and spread his legs, patting one. Emily relocated, straddling his thigh to rest her back along his arm and hard chest, relaxing instantly. An unlikely match, the ruthless former soldier and his small, blonde Southern bride.

Emily had spent most of her life being called "slow" or "simple", overhearing her aunts saying things like, "Thank goodness she's pretty. If she don't get herself in no trouble with the local boys she might just stand a chance at marrying well someday. God knows she ain't the brightest penny in the fountain." But Rasul never made her feel that way. He liked that she could sit in front of C-SPAN for three days straight with her eyes taped open and still not retain a single word of it. He liked that she knew the lyrics to every Patsy Cline song but stared blankly at people when they asked her opinion about this or that politician.

"But you live right outside D.C.!" people would say. In those moments Emily just shrugged her apology. Politics, foreign policy, current events…it all went over her head like Rasul's phone calls home. Like the voice of the teacher in those old Peanuts cartoons. *Yes, ma'am.*

"You feel nice," she murmured, taking in his warmth and the reassuring comfort of his size.

"So do you." A man of few words, but the ones murmured against her neck spoke volumes. "I'll miss you tomorrow."

"You too," she said.

"Miss your body in our bed."

Emily shivered, already slipping into her role, the quiet, obedient one. Strong hands palmed her bare arms and goose bumps rose across her skin.

When Emily had finally mustered the courage to tell her mother she planned to marry Rasul, they'd both been a little tipsy. Her momma had met Rasul twice and already deemed him an unfixable, backward-thinking chauvinist ogre.

"I'm telling you, you'll regret it. Welcome to the rest of your life, Em," she'd said, waving her hands as though gesturing at a movie screen showcasing Emily's bleak future. *"Welcome to forty years of selfish, boring missionary monotony with that man. You're just a blow-up doll to a patriarchal thug like him. A blow-up doll who can cook and nod and make babies and look pretty while she's at it. If he's doing anything to impress you in the bedroom now, honey, well, you can kiss that goodbye the second he closes the sale. That's all you are to him, baby girl. Another piece of property. Mark my words, kiss your own pleasure sayonara."*

Emily smiled at the thought.

Momma, if you only knew.

CHAPTER TWO

RASUL GAVE EMILY'S THIGH a light smack. "Up you get."

She stood. "You hungry now?" she asked, praying she could guess the answer.

"Not for dinner."

She smiled and headed for the stairs, to the second floor and their bedroom. She did like this about their fancy new house—carpeted steps meant she couldn't hear him on her heels, could only imagine his body behind hers.

She walked into the bedroom and headed for the picture window. Like the rest of the house, this room was too large. She slid the blinds closed to make it feel intimate, and to keep her mind off how badly she needed to order more furniture. She turned to find Rasul in the threshold, silhouetted by the light from the hall. He changed at moments such as these, turning into a version of his brutal, professional self, she imagined. Tough guy or not, he'd never raised his voice to Emily or handled her roughly the entire time she'd known him. Not outside this room, at least. And inside…inside he could do whatever he pleased.

"On your knees."

A shiver trickled through her, cooling her skin and heating her pussy. She took her place in the center of the bedroom's carpeted floor. Rasul stepped to her, slowly. For a minute he merely stood above her, touching her hair, smoothing it back from her face and running his fingers through it. Thoughts were surely racing through his mind, items from a menu flashing past as he deliberated over his selection.

"Strip," he finally said.

Emily tugged her shirt off and shimmied out of her shorts and underwear to kneel expectantly at his feet. He stripped away his own shirt, kicked his jeans and socks aside, standing before her in only his briefs.

Fuck, this body. Rasul was OCD about certain things—his lock- and stove-checking rituals, demanding about how close or how far they were seated from windows in restaurants. But for all the ways it drove Emily up the wall, she had to forgive him, because the thing he was most obsessive about was his workout. Up at quarter to five every morning, jogging to the park to perform some sadistic training circuit from his military days. At thirty-four he was as cut and lean as he'd been in pictures snapped over a decade earlier, reflexes like something out of an action movie.

My man. She cupped the bulge in his briefs and he was already stiff. Not a huge cock, but thick, as hard as his muscles and only getting harder as she rubbed the ridge of his erection. His hands held her head, gentle. Gentle for now.

She fondled his balls through the cotton, as taunting for her as it must feel to him. She took his shrouded shaft in both hands and squeezed, loving his size and smell, loving that she could tease him for an hour and he'd still have the wherewithal to fuck her senseless to her heart's content, no risk of him beating her to the punch. She slid one hand to his ass and objectified the dip of muscle at his hip— her favorite. When they used a mirror, this was the part of him she most loved to watch. Those hips pistoning as he gave her what she wanted.

She raised her chin to meet his gaze, the protocol. He nodded, her permission to take the next step. As she eased his briefs down his thighs, his scent grew stronger.

"Stroke it."

A taunting graze of her fingers to start. A light touch as she measured him from base to head, as their excitement and anticipation grew in tandem.

"Stroke. It."

She swallowed. Wrapping her fist firmly around his flesh, she obeyed. She felt him take hold of her hair, rough enough to intimidate but not to hurt. Rasul in sexual mode was a magical contradiction. Behind the orders and his seeming selfishness, this fantasy was purely Emily's. *His* fantasy was all about controlling her pleasure, granting her wishes. He had the intuition to know what those wishes were and the physical gifts to realize them…and the stamina to keep it all up until she dropped. This powerful man was hers to command in their secret, silent language of glances and touches.

"Talk to me," he muttered.

"You're hard." She stroked him with tight pulls, easing back the skin to expose his flushed head. "Hard and thick. Tell me what you want from me."

"Suck me."

She held back a smile, glancing up at his shadowed face, letting her expression turn hesitant.

A yank at her hair. "Suck me."

Emily lowered her eyes, then her mouth. She traced her lower lip with the smooth, hot tip of his cock until a bossy push at the back of her head forced him inside. She slid her free palm to his hip to feel the muscle flex as he pushed deeper. *Strong.* The sensation made the blood course fast and hot in her veins.

"Good. More."

As if she had a choice. She took what he gave her—steady, incremental thrusts until he filled her mouth, until his head touched the back of her throat. She moaned around him, a fearful noise.

"Good." His breathing came in sharp, nasal inhalations. She could picture the expression she couldn't see, the glint in his narrowed eyes and the stern set of his jaw.

For a minute she let him fuck her mouth, liking the degradation of it but craving a bit of control of her own. She pushed at his hip and he let her lean back to focus on his head. The way a man tasted had always been something she'd put up with before her husband, but with Rasul, she savored it. She teased his slit with the tip of her tongue, worshipping his spit-slick shaft with her hand.

A moan rewarded her. A moan was a rare thing to coax from this man, whose ability to perform like a detached, trained animal was unmatched. A tug at her hair slid her mouth from his cock and she looked expectantly to his face, taking in those bedroom eyes, as she'd heard them described. His hooded lids were at half-mast, heavy with lust. "On the bed. Hands and knees."

Emily obeyed. She'd told him a king mattress was too big for anyone, but how wrong she'd been. They didn't waste a square of inch of this surface. She got on all fours facing her dresser, perfect positioning to watch him in the vanity mirror. As he climbed onto the bed behind her, she shut her eyes. She felt the brush of his hard thighs against the backs of her soft ones and felt his stiff, warm cock on her ass. Opening her eyes, she found his reflection watching hers, his expression hungry, exactly what she desired.

He palmed her ass and thigh with one hand then guided his cock between her legs with the other. Sometimes they played games, taking on roles—pretending this was her first time, pretending they were strangers, pretending she didn't want this. Not tonight though. Tonight needed no fiction.

He pushed inside her, as deep as her pussy would allow at the moment. She was horny but she wasn't as wet as she could be. Rasul liked that, that little suggestion of resistance. That hint of a fight. He pushed harder and farther and, as he slid out, his cock spread her wetness from deeper in her cunt, easing the friction.

"Good girl."

His rhythm started slow, thrusts measured and precise. He fucked her like a machine so that when the shift came, the contrast would be starker. All the more thrilling.

He nudged her knees wider and she watched him in the mirror, those dark shadows of his muscles, dark chest hair, darker expression on his dangerous face. A heavy, possessive hand alighted on her lower back and she felt the warm metal of his wedding band. She bit back a smile.

"Are you thinking about him?" Rasul asked.

"I'm only thinking about you." True, though now that he'd brought up the subject, Emily couldn't help but imagine another body, here on this bed with them. Watching.

"Soon though," he murmured.

"Yeah."

The "him" Rasul spoke of was their faceless, unseen third. Emily's darkest wish, hers to enjoy but Rasul's to command. Rasul's to boss around for her pleasure. He was harsh with her. God knew how he'd treat another man brought in to fuck her. And only God knew if they'd ever find one who could handle it.

"Now you're thinking about him?"

"Yeah," she said again. No face to picture yet, as the selection wasn't official, just an anonymous, gorgeous body. Her husband's voice, perhaps his hands, commanding the man to do things to her, commanding him to watch, to take orders and instructions, Emily relegated to a mix of worship-object and slave. Perfection.

She stared at her husband's body in the mirror, pretending it was another man behind her, Rasul watching with instructions ready to bark. His hands on some other man's neck, pushing his face against her pussy, perhaps those hands on the man's hips or his ass, forcing him to fuck her faster.

Behind her, Rasul changed. His thrusts turned slow, making her feel each inch as it sank deep, the press of his damp, warm skin against her butt. He eased out, leaving her completely so she felt his penetration anew when he pushed back inside.

"I'll make him watch first," he said. "Make him wait while I fuck you like this. Make him understand you're mine."

She nodded. Though she'd been trying not to get her hopes up about an actual man, she did have one in mind. She let herself picture his face, just for a breath…that easy smile gone, replaced by a look of pained concentration. Desperation, as he worked to please her.

"You're mine, aren't you?" Rasul asked.

"I'm yours."

"For me to do whatever I want with," he murmured.

"Anything you want." Meaning anything *she* wanted. Her husband…many a man's terrifying nightmare, but her slave behind the domineering façade.

He slid out and slapped her hip, hard enough to sting. "On your back."

Emily reclined against the cool bedspread and welcomed the weight of him as he pushed her thighs wide with his. He sank deep. Muscular arms bracketing her chest, body intimidating, looming above hers. He pumped her roughly, filling the room with the sounds of their breathing and the smell of their sin. She felt drunk, this man's harsh energy as intoxicating as ten bottles of wine. She stroked his chest and dug her fingernails into his shoulders. Spurs, telling him to make it rougher.

He obeyed, spreading her wide enough to trigger a twinge in her hip. She paid him back with a rake of nails across his ribs. She stroked his fearsome arms, feeling the thin scratch she'd left there a few days ago. She smiled to herself, relishing such a mark. A territorial warning to other women to stay away, in case the ring wasn't enough.

Faster and rougher still, he took her.

She murmured a lie. "It hurts."

"Good." He fucked her so hard the oak headboard rattled against the wall. "The more it hurts the better it feels to me."

"Slower. Please."

He said nothing but his body bellowed a resounding *no*.

She shoved at his chest with both hands, and the instinctual frustration she felt—knowing her mightiest effort couldn't move him an inch—unleashed fresh, ugly sensations in her body. Helpless. Weak. Those sensations came with adrenaline, and they lit her like a fuse. Any other context and she hated these feelings, but with Rasul they were a release. She gave up trying to push him and cupped his ass instead, feeling how hard he was working for her. Her touch and the breathy noises that puffed from her mouth with each impact were giving her away. Rasul braced himself on one arm and went in for the kill.

Emily gave up the resistance game as his thumb stroked her clit. The mere control he commanded was nearly enough to do her in. She watched his stomach and hips, muscles utterly masterful. Worth the loss of his warmth between the sheets in the small hours of the morning, if this body was the result she got to enjoy. She watched his cock in the low light, its width and sheen, the dark, trimmed hair that framed it at the base. She watched as he owned her, her brain going fuzzy.

"You love my cock."

Her breath hitched at that word. *Cock.* His accent made the syllable sound hard and pompous, a violent threat spat at her. "I do."

For a dozen thrusts he took her slowly.

"Rasul."

"Come on my cock."

His thumb taunted her in tight circles, just the right amount of pressure. All these little nuances he knew so well…one day he might issue orders or threats to another man, punishing him for not knowing Emily's body inside-out as he did.

"He'll never fuck you this good," Rasul said, reading her mind.

"No, never."

"I'll show him how it's done."

She imagined a stranger's eyes on them, doing this. The blue eyes of a not-quite stranger, if her top choice might ever agree to the proposition. A violation of her and Rasul's privacy, perhaps, but fuck if she didn't want to show off. "He'll never be as good as you." *He* wasn't supposed to be. *He* was merely a toy for Emily to enjoy and Rasul to operate.

She thought of all her husband's commands. *Suck me. Ride me. Beg me. Hit me.* She thought of them directed at a third party. *Taste her. Fuck her. Faster. Rougher.*

She imagined greedy things, two large bodies pressed to her smaller one, two groaning voices, two cocks. The smells and sounds and heat of two men, a fantasy she'd never have guessed her husband would approve of. She'd only admitted it during a bit of role-playing, looking to incite some affected anger. That the idea seemed to excite him as much as it did her had been the shock of a lifetime.

"I want him to see what I get every night," Rasul said. "I want him to see how perfect you are and realize he could never please you the way I can."

She dragged her nails across his scalp. "Show him how you make me come."

His thumb sped up against her clit, hips hammering fast. Goddamn, that got her hot, feeling his strength. There were times in her life when she'd hated and feared the idea of a strong man, but he made the sensation different. With trust underscoring each aggressive motion, fear became excitement. It became empowering. Those old feelings she hated, she could turn them into pleasure.

A big fat fuck-you to the men who'd hurt her.

She pushed away thoughts of the bad men and of the new, kind one she'd yet to invite into her bed, and turned her focus a hundred percent to the one above her.

His lips were parted with heavy breaths, a sure sign his own pleasure was becoming difficult to ignore. She watched his cock and the flex of his stomach, and the pleasure gathered into a tight ball in her lower belly, surging and flashing in time with his thrusts.

"Rasul."

"Hit me."

She slapped him, a good one with a sharp smack. A noise rumbled from deep in his chest, a gasp of awe and fury and need. She hit him again and his thrusts took on a new intensity.

She muttered, "Fuck," as the fever rushed into her brain, dulling everything but the pleasure he gave her.

"Come. Come on my cock."

She grabbed his biceps and squeezed as the climax arrived. They came in all different ways—quick, slow, harsh, subtle. This one was slow and intense, rising like a crescendo against his strumming thumb.

She heard her own voice. "Baby." Then the pleasure swallowed her for a few blissful, oblivious seconds, until she found herself back inside her body, beneath his. He slowed then stopped, looking down at her, rapt. Suddenly tender, he pushed her hair back from her face. She could feel the tiny beats of his cock inside her, the only sign giving away his body's impatience.

"Thanks," she whispered.

He leaned down and kissed her forehead. She wanted to take hold of his head and press his face to her neck, keep him there and fall asleep. But first it was his turn.

"What do you want tonight?" she asked.

"Want you to watch."

She nodded, bedspread rumpling her hair.

Rasul pulled away and let her relocate to her hands and knees, facing the corner of the bed. The best angle to watch him in their mirror. He knelt behind her and slid his cock between her thighs, taunting her sensitized clit with a dozen cruel sweeps before he drove inside.

"Watch," he ordered.

She locked her gaze on their reflection and, spent or not, her body roused all over again. She'd never seen a man in her life—not in person or on a screen or in print—as attractive as the one she called her husband. She liked to imagine his body and his training were solely for her, this perfection honed specifically to please her. Their eyes met in the reflection, black and hazel, cold and awed. He took her faster, hands clamping around her hipbones, tugging her into each thrust.

Rasul spoke, the words staggered by his motions. "This is what he'll see."

"Yeah." She watched them, imagining she was an outsider. Sweet little blonde Emily on her hands and knees, getting her living daylights fucked out by this gruff man, this mercenary. A rough sight for many, hopefully an exciting one for the man they might deem worthy of sharing this.

She imagined her frontrunner again, pretending he did indeed want this. Waiting his turn, body burning up with impatience. Two men *taking turns*. The thought filled her with dark emotions—guilt and shame and fear—but they felt good. Wrong felt good to her in bed. Doing wrong in bed got her hotter than rose petals and love poems could ever hope to.

She heard Rasul's breathing turn harsh and pulled herself out of her own head. Her husband, merciless and selfish on the outside, could no sooner come before given permission than he could leave the house without checking the locks. Emily prompted the script he needed to fulfill before he could claim his release.

"Slower," she muttered.

He hammered her faster.

"It's too rough."

That earned her a sharp smack on the ass, harsher tugs to pull her into his impact.

"Stop."

She felt his body shift against hers as he snaked a hand around her waist, two fingers finding her clit. She watched him in the mirror, every muscle in his body coordinated to make this look effortless. She balanced on one arm and put her freed hand over his. She didn't have to pretend she couldn't pry it away—she couldn't. As she tugged at his wrist, his fingertips stroked her clit, bringing heat and pressure and pleasure, all of it multiplied by the fact that she couldn't stop him.

As the second orgasm rose inside her, it was his face in the mirror that unleashed it. Cold eyes, hard expression, but those parted lips giving him away. She fell apart once more against his fingertips, feeling him push deep and hold her tight against him as her spasms came and went. Her arms trembled as she came down from the high. She turned to look at his face.

"Did you…?"

He shook his head. "Want your hands on me."

She nodded and he slid out. He sat on the edge of the mattress and Emily mustered the coordination to make it to the floor, to kneel between his spread thighs and await instruction.

"Touch me."

She wrapped her hand around his cock—swollen and slick and blazing hot. "You need something?" she asked sweetly.

"Stroke me. Tight."

She did as commanded, earning a series of those too-rare moans.

"Talk to me," he muttered.

"Love your cock." She measured it with her eyes and hand. "Hard and thick. All mine."

Another moan. "Show him how much you love it."

A shiver rippled through her, not only from having her fantasy indulged, but from knowing the idea had Rasul hot as well. She worshipped him with aggressive pulls, making him wait a full minute before she lowered her lips to his head.

"Yes."

She lapped at him then looked up. "You want him to watch this?"

"Yes. Show him."

She closed her lips over his crown and stroked him tightly from the base. He pushed her hair back from her face, tucking it behind her ears as though giving their unseen guest a better view. She felt him wind a length of it around his hand then a gentle push forced her mouth farther down his cock.

"Good."

After a minute he pulled her hair, coaxing her back. He slid his cock out and nudged her hand from him, taking hold of his shaft. He ran the tip across her lips.

"Watch me."

She nodded and sat on her haunches, hands folded obediently atop her thighs. She gave him her full attention as he masturbated—his cock and fist and the flexing muscles of his arm and stomach. His face, most of all. His gaze flicked all over her body in return, and as his hand sped up she knew he was close.

"Lemme see," she murmured.

"See what?"

"Lemme see you come."

A moan gave him away once more. He reached out for her, grasping her shoulder with his free hand and drawing her close.

"Emily."

She felt the heat of his release lash her neck and collarbone and she shut her eyes, lost in the sounds of his pleasure, audio glimpses at the most elusive of animals—the strongest man she'd ever known, utterly helpless.

Breathing slowed and bodies cooled. Emily padded back to the bathroom to tidy herself then joined Rasul in bed. There was still dinner to be made and eaten, but that could wait a few minutes longer.

Wrapping his arm around her waist, he pulled her close, her back to his chest. He pressed kisses to her neck and ear, fond and sleepy. These quiet moments in the wake of sex were as intimate as the act itself. More so, perhaps. The only occasions when Rasul could be described as tender, borderline vulnerable. Hand him a newborn baby—nothing. A puppy, nothing. A crying child, nothing. Attentive perhaps, but unmoved. He approached all situations with one of two attitudes—controlled detachment or ferocious aggression.

Except this moment. This moment was how she imagined he might react in the presence of their own child one day. Calm, affectionate, accessible. Free of the memories and rituals and duties that haunted him. Or might that greatest of all responsibilities only intensify his paranoia? A worry for another time.

She felt him nod off behind her, his powerful arm going slack across her ribs. She slid from his embrace and dressed, pleased to leave him to nap while she started the grill. She'd fill her lungs with the brisk spring air and the smell of spices, knowing he was upstairs, asleep. Asleep and free from himself for a blissful half-hour, a fleeting gift she felt honored beyond words to be able to give to him.

CHAPTER THREE

RASUL PULLED UP TO THE BAR at nine, two hours into Emily's Tuesday shift. He slammed the car door and hit the lock button on his key fob. No need to obsess, as the only things of value inside were material.

An old feeling, a streak of excitement, warmed his body. He'd made this small journey—the walk from his car to the bar's entrance—hundreds of times. A few years ago this place had been his colleagues' favorite after-work drinking spot, and he'd gone along largely to socialize and unwind, though he wasn't adept at either activity.

As time went on, he'd paid less and less attention to the conversations and more and more to the sweet, honey-voiced woman who worked behind the bar. It had taken him a month to even ask her name. Two months to ask her out. Six months to propose and another year of living together before she'd say yes. Now he rarely visited Emily at work, knowing it constituted her small, autonomous social life outside their home. He'd selfishly prefer to be her *entire* life, but she didn't work that way. Most Western women didn't, and he could find that agreeable on an intellectual level, even if the caveman in him begged to protest.

He pushed in the door to the bar, the smell hitting him with nostalgia. It wasn't quite a restaurant, though they served a decent menu of pub food. Like everything in Reston, it was clean and pleasant, if slightly impersonal as a result. He'd never been a drinker back in the Middle East. In fact, he'd not been a drinker when he first started coming to this bar. Emily had poured him his first beer, first ever in his stubborn, control-freak life, and he'd come to associate that taste with her. And that feeling of ease. He probably never would have found the sac to ask her out if not for beer.

She was behind the bar, the overhead lights making her blonde hair glow white, like an angel, so fitting and yet so deceptive. She laughed at something a patron said and grabbed empty glasses as the other bartender replaced them with fresh drinks.

Had they been at home, Rasul would have smiled at her as he approached. He didn't smile much in public. He'd spent too many years being ordered to hide his emotions to feel comfortable changing that now. Plus, tonight he was undercover.

He caught her eye and returned her subtle wave, just another customer greeting his bartender. He scouted the backs of the people sitting at the bar, unsure. Then Emily gave a tiny, covert nod at the man seated at the corner.

There weren't any free stools at the moment, so Rasul ordered a beer from Emily's coworker and loitered on the floor, pretending to watch the basketball game playing on the TV behind the bar. After five minutes a pair of women left and he slid onto the seat beside his target.

Emily swept over to toss a coaster in front of Rasul. "Evenin'."

"Good evening." He had to bite down to hide his smile this time. This woman was far too fun to role-play with. He set his beer on the coaster and drew it close.

Emily turned to the marked man. "Another for you, Jeremy?"

"Please."

Jeremy. Rasul glanced to his side. The man's smile was warm, easy but not drunken. Sizing men up was in Rasul's job description. Emily's as well, in a sense. This was the man she'd selected for them, and he was relieved. Thirty, he guessed. Solid but lean, fit for a marathon, perhaps, but not a fistfight. His brown hair was shaggy, clothes as casual as Rasul's but with sneakers in place of boots. He had blue eyes and looked…friendly. Looked American, as approachable as Rasul surely seemed icy and foreign and gruff. This was a man most outsiders would have paired Rasul's sweet-tempered, charming wife with, if forced to guess.

Emily headed to the other end of the bar to ring up tabs. Rasul kept his eyes on her as he spoke quietly to Jeremy. "She's cute."

Those calm blue eyes met Rasul's dark ones. "She's married."

Doesn't stop you from flirting with her twice a week, Rasul thought, but Emily had assured him it was harmless. The kind of organic flirtation created when two people found one another both likable and attractive, with no intention or expectation from either side.

"That's a shame," he finally said.

"Shame for all of mankind," Jeremy said. "With the exception of one lucky man someplace."

"Very lucky. She works here a lot?"

"Couple nights a week. I don't even really like this bar," Jeremy said. "But she's a great girl. I come here to unwind and she does a better job than the beer, probably."

"Nice ass," Rasul added, baiting.

Something passed over Jeremy's face and his expression cooled. "I consider her my friend, so I'm probably not the man to say that to."

"Apologies."

"You're right though. She's as sweet on the outside as the inside."

Rasul let that sink in, a bit shocked by this man. He worked with two distinct types of American males—bossy, no-nonsense professionals, and criminals of both the sickening and cowering varieties. This man was neither. He seemed humble. Thoughtful. He appeared to care about Emily as more than a sexy body and a pretty face, a bringer of drinks.

"She seems very…" Rasul searched for the word as he watched his wife joking with customers, her smile and laughter so ready and genuine. "Genuine."

Jeremy nodded. "I thought for sure at first that Georgia-peach thing she has going was an act to get more tips, but it's for real." He took a sip of his beer then set it down, wiped his palm and held it out. "I'm Jeremy."

Rasul shook it, reading the gesture. Confident but not cocky. "Rasul."

Jeremy took his hand away and his eyes narrowed with a thought. They darted to Emily, to Rasul, back and forth a half-dozen times. "You're Emily's husband."

He nodded.

Jeremy laughed uneasily. "Sorry. I hope I didn't offend you."

Rasul mustered a smile and shook his head, knowing he seemed like the type to say, "Let's go outside and have a *talk*," in a situation such as this. Or the situation this surely looked like. Instead he raised a hand to draw Emily over.

She strung her bar towel through her belt loop and smiled at the men. "What'll it be?"

"Whatever he wants." Rasul nodded to Jeremy.

"You two acquainted then?" she asked, that Southern accent so sweet it sounded like an affectation.

Rasul nodded again. Jeremy still looked nervous, glancing between them.

"Don't you worry, my husband won't bite," Emily said. "Shot of Maker's for you?"

With a final look at Rasul, Jeremy said, "Sure. Thanks."

"You boys talking about me?" she asked over her shoulder as she measured Jeremy's bourbon.

"I may have just made an ass of myself in front of your husband," Jeremy said. "Gushing about you."

Her dimples appeared as she grinned. "You're sweet. And don't worry—he looks scarier than he is." She delivered his shot.

Jeremy cleared his throat and raised the glass toward each of them in thanks. He took a sip and set it down. "I, um, I get my ear chewed off about you all the time," he said to Rasul. "I was starting to think she'd made you up, to keep guys like me off her back."

"Nope, he's real," Emily said proudly. "All the stories are true. Or they would be if he told me anything exciting that happens at his work."

Rasul smirked and focused on his beer.

"Oh right," Jeremy said. "She mentioned you work for…you know." He jerked his head in an easterly direction to mean the agency so many of the residents of Reston called their employer.

"Very hush-hush," Emily said with mock conspiracy. A customer approached and drew her away to mix a drink.

Jeremy kept his voice low. "Again, I hope I didn't offend you. Honestly."

"On the contrary. Nice to know there's a man here when she's working who treats her with respect. Very comforting." Not as comforting as having her home every night, but still, a consolation.

"I should probably head out." Jeremy stood and fetched his jacket from a coatrack. He seemed slightly cagey, but not too much. A healthy amount, given the situation. He offered his hand for a final, brief shake. "Nice meeting the famous Rasul."

"Perhaps I'll see you on Thursday."

"Maybe. And like I said, you're a very lucky man."

"I am." *And you could be too.*

CHAPTER FOUR

ON THURSDAY NIGHT, Jeremy walked to and from his car, to and from his car, took his jacket off and put it back on four times, trying to decide whether or not going to the bar was wise.

He went there twice a week to see Emily. Not to be a creep. Not to watch her working and imagine what she looked like naked— barring the occasional slip of his imagination—or to harass her, or tip her outrageously with some insane hope she might one day let him take her home. He simply liked her. He didn't really like that bar, but he liked *her*.

His life was at a crossroads, as he hoped and expected to quit his job when his lease was up in August, and travel for a year. Maybe longer. As long as it took to figure out what he wanted from the next stage of his life. As such, he wasn't looking for a relationship at the moment, and flirting with Emily helped fill the romantic void. Sure, he hadn't had a crush this bad since junior high, but he wasn't deluded about it.

Especially not now that he'd met her husband. She talked about Rasul a lot at work, and the man lived up to the legend. Surpassed it. He looked like one of those men who could grab an enemy from behind, take hold of his chin and skull and snap his neck with a crack, leave him for dead with no remorse. He didn't match Emily—even their accents clashed. But Jeremy hoped the man deserved her. He also hoped he wouldn't run into the guy tonight and discover Tuesday had been a warning. Hell, maybe Emily had asked Rasul to scare Jeremy away…maybe he came off as a panting pervert without even realizing it.

But he didn't think so. He grabbed his keys for the fifth time and shrugged into his jacket. His heart thumped as he drove the fifteen minutes to the bar.

It'd be an overstatement to say seeing Emily was the highlight of his week, but she certainly relaxed him. He considered her a friend, and a much-needed breath of fresh air. Jeremy was a personal trainer, and his clients were nearly all highly strung, tightly wound, affluent women. Women who *wanted it all*, everything but happiness. Emily was a nice break from that. Kind and unassuming, calm. Soft, feminine. Quiet ambition, not grasping. That voice so sweet it sounded like an act, except that it matched her laugh so precisely. Hanging out with her reset Jeremy, reminding him that there was a world outside Reston and D.C., even within its bounds, a place a bit more like small-town Texas, where he'd grown up.

He parked and resisted the urge to check his reflection in the rearview. That habit was lame to start with, and obscene now that he'd met her husband.

The usual Thursday din greeted him as he stepped inside the bar and caught sight of Emily's hair under the lights. His heart gave its usual flutter and he scanned the seats, finding no Rasul. His chest loosened.

His favorite seat was free tonight, at the center of the bar near the taps, where he'd have plenty of chances to chat with her. If that wasn't ruined now. He watched her face as she approached and she looked as welcoming as always.

"Hey, regular," she said with a smile. "Guinness?"

"Please. How's it going tonight?"

She shrugged and did the first half of his pour. "Same old. The business crowd should be getting in soon. Starting their weekends a day early as usual."

He nodded.

Emily went to help another customer then returned and completed Jeremy's pour. As she set a coaster before him and delivered his pint, he thought there *was* something different about her. A shyness. He made a decision to not be overly friendly tonight. Maybe not ever again. His mood darkened and he felt foolish. Six months he'd been flirting with this woman, harmlessly, he'd thought, when maybe that entire time she'd thought he was a creeper. He saw those guys all the time, desperate and corny, grasping for the illusion of familiarity with a pretty girl. It scrambled his brain to suddenly worry he might be one.

"You okay?" she asked, mopping around his glass with a damp towel.

"Yeah. Sorry. Do I look un-okay?"

She made a thoughtful face. "I don't know about that, but you look a little worried."

"Just tired, probably."

"I'm a little anxious tonight," she said with a small smile.

"Oh? How come?"

She pursed her full lips and her permanently blushing cheeks flushed deeper pink. "Just nervous about something."

"You can tell me—" Jeremy stopped short as Emily's expression and attention shifted beyond him. He looked over his shoulder in time to see Rasul push in the door. Jeremy faced forward, feeling oddly complicit. Feeling suddenly obscene, as though he'd been *caught* here. Caught having an illicit drink with a married woman.

Just as he feared, Rasul took the seat to his left. "Evening."

"Good evening yourself, stranger," Emily said to her husband. "Beer?"

He nodded and she poured him a Stella. An arriving group of blue-shirted young businessmen called Emily to the end of the bar to fill orders and Jeremy mustered the courage to make eye contact with Rasul.

"How's it going?"

Rasul turned on his stool slowly, fixing Jeremy with a cool, calculating, searching look. He took a deep drink of his beer, then set it down and said, "Well."

Jeremy's heart began to hammer. "Well, what?"

"It's going well."

His pulse slowed slightly. "Oh, right. Glad to hear it." Jesus, even if he didn't *look* jumpy and guilty, he sure as hell felt it now. Strange. He was an inch or two taller than this guy, yet he felt dwarfed. Rasul's tee shirt hugged his thick biceps and made Jeremy feel diminished. He felt beat at his own profession. Emily passed by them without a glance to tend to something at the other end of the bar.

Jeremy took a steadying breath and decided to embrace this confrontation. If he was going to get his ass kicked, he'd step up and take it like a man, knowing why. "I can't help but think you're upset with me," he said, as calmly as he could fake.

Rasul's dark eyebrows rose. "Oh?"

"I want you to know, I've never been anything but polite to your wife. If she said she feels otherwise, I apologize. To both of you. I never intended to make her uncomfortable."

"That's why you think I'm here?"

Jeremy stared at the man. Emily had mentioned he worked as some kind of interrogator, and Jeremy felt distinctly like the next man in line to get roughed up. "I don't know why you're here, but I'm pretty sure it's about me." *Please don't break my fingers.*

"My wife is probably going to ask you something later tonight," Rasul said, breaking eye contact to stare at the woman in question. "I need you to know that I want the same thing she does. It's not a trick, or a trap. Don't feel pressured to answer any way except honestly. Don't even feel pressured to answer tonight. But I need you to know that I'm behind her a hundred percent in the request."

Jeremy blinked, torn between relief that he wasn't going to have his ass handed to him and confusion. "Okay. Understood. What exactly—"

"Emily will explain it far better than I could, I'm sure." Rasul stood and drained his glass, nodding curtly at Jeremy as he left. He didn't say goodbye to Emily, and come to think of it, she'd kept her attention away from the two men for the entire conversation.

Jeremy drummed his fingers on the bar. He sipped his stout, brain flying around in a hundred directions. He formulated a few ideas of what this supposed proposal might be about… They needed a sperm donor. That's what he had his money on. Something serious and personal, judging from Rasul's stony expression.

Emily approached. "Another?"

"Sure." He watched her prepare his drink and unlike usual, she didn't use the lag time between pours to make small talk. She was nervous. As nervous as Jeremy. When she set it before him, she said, "Cheers," and her smile looked forced.

"Did you need to talk to me about something?" he asked, hating seeing her so anxious.

She laughed and nodded, meeting his gaze. "Um, yeah. I think so. I'm gonna ask my manager for a break in a little while, and maybe we could go out back and talk?"

"Sure. Or I can give you my number, if you'd rather do it over the phone some other time."

She dismissed the suggestion with a wave. "Nah, thank you. I better do it tonight before I lose my nerve."

"Okay. Well, whenever you're ready."

"Here." She slid his drink closer. "You enjoy that and we'll talk after."

She walked to the phone beside the register and held the receiver to her ear, punching two numbers into the keypad. "It's Emily. No, it's fine over here. But I was wondering if maybe you'd be able to cover me for a break in a little bit, for maybe fifteen minutes? I hate to ask but there's some drama back home with my mother. I'd feel better if I could just call her...? Oh, you're a sweetheart. Whenever you're free. Thanks so much, Barb. I appreciate it." She replaced the receiver and Jeremy had to grin. So the girl could tell a lie.

She walked back over to him. "God forgive me," she muttered and touched a hand to the tiny silver cross suspended in the vee of her tee shirt collar. "My manager's going to cover for me in a little bit." She spoke quietly. "After I leave, come around to the employee parking lot and meet me at my car, if you're willing. It's a little white Mini."

He nodded, scared all over again. Bad things happened in quiet, dark, back parking lots.

He'd just finished his drink when Emily's manager arrived, wishing her good luck with her phone call home and ushering her out the rear door.

Jeremy stalled a fearful minute before standing. He tugged his coat on as he exited, feeling chilly and jumpy as he rounded the building and walked through the wide, well-lit alley to the employee lot. He spotted Emily's car easily, and as he approached a new sensation arrived to temper the fear. Excitement. He was having a clandestine meeting with his unattainable, pie-in-the-sky crush. She *needed* him for something. What, he had no clue, but she needed *him*.

She was sitting in the driver's seat and he knocked on her window. She gestured to the passenger side and he heard it unlock as he rounded the tiny car. He sat beside her and shut the door, and it was like a different universe. Quiet, dark, just the two of them in her private space. He could smell her perfume, something subtle and vaguely fruity. Or perhaps that was just a mixer she'd spilled.

"Thanks for coming," she said, sounding sheepish, gaze trained on the dark instrument panel.

"You're welcome. So what's up?"

She took a deep breath and blew it out, unmistakably flustered. "Forgive me if I don't look at you while I say most of this. I'm awful nervous."

"Me too. A half-hour ago I was pretty sure your husband was going to take me out here and bury me in a shallow grave."

She turned to stare at him, mouth open with shock or amusement. "Really?"

"Well, yeah. I thought maybe... I thought maybe you were uncomfortable with... I dunno. How friendly we've gotten. I thought maybe you asked him to come in and scare me straight."

She reached over to touch his hand, just a brief pat of his knuckles. "Oh my goodness, no. I love when you come in. It's such a nice change from all the usual folks."

His ego surged and his nerves retreated a pace or two. "Oh. Good."

"Lemme ask you somethin'," she began, looking down at the steering wheel and wrapping her hands around it.

"Go ahead."

"Do you like me?"

Jeremy smiled. "Yeah, of course I do. And I do have a crush on you, if that's what you're asking."

She nodded thoughtfully.

"But I'd never hit on you," he went on. "I respect that you're married. Even if your husband didn't scare the shit out of me, I'd never want to do anything that…you know, crapped all over your vows."

"That's sweet. You're a very sweet man."

He sighed, feeling lightheaded from all the uncertainty. "What's this about, Emily? Do you guys need a sperm donor or something?"

She looked over and blinked at him, then laughed. "Oh my gosh, is that what you thought? Sorry, I shouldn't make fun. The real reason's way crazier."

"What's the real reason?"

It was Emily's turn to sigh. "We, um… Oh gosh. We're wondering—and totally *do not* hesitate to tell me I'm a psycho—but we were wondering if you might want to join us sometime. Like, join us in bed."

Jeremy felt as though he'd been punched, a sharp jab that bypassed his skull and reordered his brain.

"Say somethin'."

"Uh… So like, a threesome?"

She nodded, expression earnest. Her brows were pinched together in a way that said she was terrified of getting turned down.

"Well. Wow. That is not what I was expecting. At all."

"Sorry if I've completely freaked you out."

He fell silent and Emily let him process the request. Jeremy wasn't a stranger to bold—often downright sleazy—propositions. In his four-plus years as an upscale personal trainer he'd been solicited by at least twenty female clients, surely a dozen of them married. Bedding a younger man, a hired professional, a *service* provider, seemed to be a common kink for high-powered women. He'd politely declined every offer—even from his single clients—knowing they'd likely never hire him again and probably talk badly of him to their peers. Fine. Good riddance. If he wanted that kind of degrading treatment he'd take up tanning and find a job as a pool boy.

But being solicited by Emily—sweet, married, God-fearing Emily—that was just weird. Her ears weren't even pierced. How could she be after a three-way with two guys?

And why wasn't Jeremy already sprinting for his car, or jolting awake in a cold sweat, back in his bed?

"I guess I need more details," he finally said. "I mean, I'll be honest, I am a little freaked out. But tell me what you were thinking of so I can try to wrap my head around it."

"Right. Well, it's sort of a fantasy of mine. That's so cliché," she said with a self-deprecating laugh.

"It's not cliché coming from you," Jeremy said.

"Anyhow. We were interested in invitin' a man to join us for a night. You wouldn't be doing anything with my husband. Nothing directly, if you catch my drift. It'd just be you and me." She waved her hand to encapsulate the two of them, and Jeremy's body warmed against his rational brain's wishes.

"But he'd watch, or…?"

She nodded. "He'd watch, and you'd watch us, and he'd boss you around. He's very possessive of, um…giving me pleasure," she mumbled. "You'd be there to take his orders, so like, I get what I want—two men—and he gets to feel in control of my experience. But he is very rough, I'll warn you about that up front."

He believed it. Rasul was more intimidating than any of the ex-military boot camp fitness instructors Jeremy knew from his professional circles. "Rough how?"

"Like he'd bark orders at you. He might rough you up a bit, physically, but not violent or anything."

The fever in Jeremy's body cooled. "But hands-on?"

"I expect so."

"Huh."

"I decided to ask you, because I thought you might like me," she said, sounding shy.

"Yeah, I do."

"And I like you too. I mean, you must know that, since we've been flirtin' for the last few months."

He shrugged. "I wasn't sure. I thought maybe you were that friendly with everybody."

"Nah, I have a little crush on you."

The fever redoubled.

"I, um, I think you're awful sexy. And you've never once treated me poorly, and I've never seen you drunk, which is very impressive, seeing as how I only know you from a bar. Anyhow, you've charmed me. You're my first—and at the moment my *only*—choice for this, um, project."

"Wow. Well, I'm flattered. I don't have an answer for you though."

"I wouldn't expect you to." She pulled out her phone and checked the time. "I ought to get back behind that bar. And you probably want to head out, and maybe spend a few days decidin' how crazy you think I am."

He smiled. "Yeah. Probably."

"Well, whatever you choose, and whenever you choose it, I hope I haven't ruined the bar for you. You're always welcome, no matter what you decide."

"Thanks. And no matter what I decide, I promise this conversation doesn't leave this car. I won't tell anyone that you…"

"Solicited you?" she supplied, a smile in her voice. "I know you won't. You've met my husband." It wasn't a threat, he didn't think. Merely a tease directed at herself and Rasul. Nice she had a clear appreciation of how frightening her beloved was.

"Not just because of that," Jeremy said. "Because I wouldn't ever mess with you that way."

She touched his arm, spreading more warmth through him. "I know you wouldn't. That's why I picked you."

She'd *picked* him. Another ego-gasm. "Right. Well. I better get home and give this some thought. I'll try and have an answer for you on Tuesday."

"There's no deadline," she said. "You don't even have to give me an answer. But if you decide you're interested, you just let me know, and we'll figure out the particulars."

He nodded.

"I promise I won't ask. Unless and until you bring it up again, this conversation didn't happen. We're just friends, bartender and customer, like always."

"Right," he said again. *Like always.* As if he'd be able to look at her the same way ever again. He pushed his door open a crack. "Um, enjoy the rest of your night. Don't let the business tools give you any grief."

"I'll try. You drive safe."

He offered her the calmest smile he had in him and stepped out of the car, smiling again as he slammed the door. As he crossed the parking lot to the alley, he wondered what he was to her, if she was watching him. What she wanted out of him, and how he felt himself. A guest, a victim, maybe a lottery winner, suddenly offered a chance to sleep with the woman he liked most in the world, even if there'd be some very sizable strings attached.

Jeremy got into his car and started the engine, flipped on his lights. He stared at the illuminated gauges for a minute or two before he backed out.

As he drove home, his brain felt cloudy, no fault of the alcohol. He tried to imagine being with her. He'd imagined it before. Jeremy had two fully scripted fantasies about Emily and both were probably pretty condemning. One began with a tragic car crash that left her a vulnerable widow in need of a thoughtful man's comfort. The other started with her announcement that her divorce had gone through, and ended in Jeremy stepping in to satisfy her in all the ways her ex-husband had refused to.

Egomaniacal or not, those dream scenarios were sweet and gentle by most men's standards, Jeremy's included. Pure as the movies liked to make romance out to be, candles and slow sex. What women were told their fantasies ought to look like. Funny how Emily's fantasy looked a lot different. Insane that Jeremy managed to figure into it... As a prop, perhaps? A toy?

She hadn't denied that his role was to get used. As much as it bothered him—being so unlike the script he'd composed in his head, should he ever get a chance with her—it also turned him on. That she had a secret kinky side turned him on, at any rate. The idea of getting bossed around by her brute of a husband was sobering, to say the least.

But one thing was certain. There'd be two men in the room, one she loved, one she liked. One who got to keep her, and one who got dismissed at the end of the festivities. He didn't yet know if this was a watered-down wish made real, or the death of his favorite pipe dream.

He had a fuck of a lot of thinking to do before Tuesday.

CHAPTER FIVE

ON NIGHTS WHEN EMILY WORKED, Rasul normally got into bed around ten and read until she was safely home. Tonight was different.

It was past midnight and he'd been nursing a beer in the kitchen for an hour, idly researching contractors online. Emily wanted a deck put in that summer. Rasul couldn't go upstairs without checking the doors twenty or more times and compulsively touching each burner knob just so, performing the tasks perfectly not to feel secure, but to simply feel a *lack* of terror. No way in hell he'd ever be able to hand over a set of keys to strange men and let them come and go all day while he was at work. If he had the job done by pros, he'd take that week off and watch them like a hawk, then replace all the locks as soon as the project was done, whether they'd been given keys or not.

Fuck that. He'd just have to teach himself carpentry.

Terrible things had happened to Emily as a child when she'd been left alone with strangers. Back in the camps where Rasul had grown up, terrible things had happened to his sister and their mother after his father died when Rasul was eight. Terrible men did terrible things when opportunities arose—that was the way of the world, the nature of human beings. But if anything terrible ever happened to Emily on Rasul's watch, he'd get sent away for cold-blooded murder, no doubt in his mind, and then there would be no one around to keep her safe.

He shut his laptop. No contractors. No fucking way. He got another beer from the fridge and sat at the table, staring out the window into the dark backyard for a long time.

So odd that he could be on board with inviting a man directly into their bed. That was the difference. An invitation was under his control. An invasion wasn't. A guest he could issue orders to. Emily's kinkiness was strange, but not surprising. Rasul didn't care to overanalyze it. She'd been hurt when she was helpless, now she craved that illusion with him for whatever reason. She trusted him, and trusted that she was really the one in control of the brutality, and he thought that helped her in some way. It got him off to please her, so he wasn't about to complain.

Headlights splashed across the adjacent den and he stood. The lights flipped off and a door slammed, and soon Emily's key sounded in the lock. He met her at the front door.

"Hey, you," she said. Same tired smile as always. Perhaps she hadn't had that talk after all.

He kissed her. "Welcome home."

She pushed her flats off by the door and walked to the kitchen, setting her purse on the counter. She turned and opened her arms. "Hug me. I'm wiped."

He did as commanded, embracing her tightly. His eyes darted to the front door but he tried to keep his attention on her. On the present. He must have stiffened in some incriminating way, since Emily murmured, "Go on. Do your thing."

He released her and crossed the den, twisting the deadbolt six times before the tone of the click was to his satisfaction. He turned the knob's lock six times also. The numbers had to match. Then he doubted his count and started over, fifteen twists until the bolt snapped just so, fifteen turns of the lock. Doubt. Repeat. Eventually he was able to back away and trust that the door was secure, that he and Emily were secure, another two minutes of his life lost to those hateful impulses.

He met her at the bottom of the steps. "You too tired to talk?" he asked.

"Nope."

They went upstairs and brushed their teeth side by side in front of the wide bathroom mirror. This house and this life, this woman…it all still struck him as odd, even four years after he'd moved to Virginia, to the States. So tidy and organized, Emily so gentle after everything he'd seen in his old life. He watched her wash her face, scrubbing until her cheeks burned bright pink, the image of childlike wholesomeness. She left the bathroom.

The impulses were bad tonight, and he pressed his thumbs to the window locks forty-eight times—a tidy, highly divisible number—before flipping off the lights and following her to the bedroom. She'd changed into her pajama bottoms and a tank top, and she sat cross-legged on the bed and watched him strip. They climbed under the covers together and he held her, her clothed body a tease against his bare skin, as always.

"Tell me," he whispered, and kissed her neck.

"I talked to him. I told him what we're after."

"And how did he take it?"

"I couldn't tell, really. He didn't run away screamin', but he didn't jump all over the offer, either. Which seems rational, considering." She laughed. "He thought maybe we needed a sperm donor."

Rasul laughed too, though the thought chilled him. How selective his male ego was that he could make space for another man in his wife's sexual fantasies, but that innocent wrong guess felt like an invitation to duel.

"I told him, you take all the time you need to think about it, and if you decide you're interested, let me know. If not, we pretend I never even brought it up. Who knows? Maybe I'll never see him at the bar ever again."

"Good work. I'm proud of you."

Another laugh. "Proud of your wife for findin' the balls to solicit another man for a three-way."

"It was brave. I'm proud," he repeated.

Her voice turned quiet and small. "Thanks." She was as bad at receiving praise as her mother had always been at offering it. Rasul wanted to change that. He wanted her to believe she was strong and courageous and perfect, as surely as he knew these things.

He slid his hands lower and tugged at the drawstring of her pajamas.

"I'm awful tired."

"That's fine. You don't have to do a thing. I'll put you to sleep."

He heard a warm hum escape her lips, an annoyed but permissive noise. He slid her bottoms down her thighs, relocating his body and the covers as he eased the garment all the way off. Propping himself on his hip and elbow and laying her thigh across his shoulder, he brought his face close, breathing her in. As his tongue traced her pussy lips, he fisted his cock. A cool, smooth hand grazed his scalp. He slid his bracing arm beneath her butt and tasted her, lapping deeper as he stroked himself.

"That looks good," she murmured.

He propped his leg wider to let her see. Then he let the fantasy loose in his head, those thoughts that had preoccupied him so thoroughly the last couple of months. His beautiful wife on her back, welcoming another man into Rasul's rightful territory. But he wanted to spoil her so much worse than he wanted to own her. And he would. He'd tell and show this other man exactly how to fuck her. He'd give his wife what she desired in her darkest, most selfish fantasies—two cocks. Two sets of eyes on her wickedness, two impatient bodies desperate to use her in those ways she wanted so deeply. Anything she wanted, he'd be the one to make it happen.

Against his tongue he could taste her excitement growing. He freed his mouth. "He'll be different than me."

Her reply was spacey with distraction. "Probably."

Rasul returned his mouth to her pussy, changing everything about the way he gave head. He offered her deep, slow licks, the opposite of the rapid, aggressive assaults he'd been so ably trained to give her. How would this other man try to please her, he wondered? Their visitor? He made his caresses hesitant and exploratory, to remind her how exactly he knew her needs and how clumsy a stranger would feel. The hand on the back of his head clenched and released, nails scraping. That warm weight could be his own hand on the other man's head, rough and bossy.

"Want you," Emily said.

He took the order, giving her pussy a final lap before climbing on top of her, sinking in deep. "Fuck. Take your top off."

She peeled her camisole away and tossed it aside. "Talk to me," she whispered, code for *Talk to me in Arabic*.

He dutifully turned into what she wanted—some illusion of foreignness, a stranger. As he took her roughly, he spoke everything he was thinking, dirty and fond thoughts alike that to Emily must sound like the exotic threats she craved. He planted his knees wide to spread her open. In English he commanded, "Look at me."

She did as she was told, attention locked on his ramming cock. Soon there might be someone else's attention on such a sight. He imagined an audience and adrenaline shot through his body, a strange, pleasurable hatred for the man who might be deemed worthy to watch this.

She clawed his arms. He repaid her with more orders in his native tongue then punished her with redoubled aggression when she failed to follow them. He wished the mirror were at their side, so he could see all their contrasts. Hard and soft, dark and pale, mean and sweet.

She huffed, "Baby," breaking character. The hold she had on his arms went from false resistance to greedy appraisal.

He issued a final order, a snatch of Arabic she could translate—*touch yourself*. He watched as she obeyed, slipping a hand between their bellies to rub her clit. Would he let her come with another man inside her? Perhaps. But before or after Rasul made her groan and twitch this way? Uncertainty usually filled him with dread, but this was Emily's adventure, and he'd keep it free of his overwrought male politics.

"Think he'll be able to make you come the way I can?" he asked.

"Not the way you can," she whispered, eyes shut tight. Her fingers sped and Rasul could feel how close she was from the tightening fit of their bodies. He slowed, knowing just how to draw out her climax.

"Oh, God."

"Good." Slowly in, then back out, just as explicit, all the way so she'd feel the next penetration afresh. The nails of her free hand bit into his shoulder, the pain racing through him stronger and more intoxicating than liquor.

"Faster," she begged.

He obeyed only the tiniest bit.

"Faster, please."

But slow meant control. Slow meant she'd come for ages, that she'd come in the midst of aching desire, not a flash of frantic action. Slow meant plenty of time for her to watch him, feel him, realize what he could do to her. Him and no one else.

He thrust quickly, deeply, three times to witness what it did to her then back to the torture. Her eyes opened, gaze restless, moving all over his body.

"Look at me," he commanded.

She met his stare, her own eyes widening. When her attention faltered he repeated the command, louder.

"Look at me."

She held his gaze for half a minute, then he redirected. "Watch my cock."

They both obeyed that one. A glorious sight, his body owning hers, her fingers caressing her arousal. He spread her wider with his hips and leaned back, taking her upright with his hands on her knees. Her lips parted.

"Imagine he's watching," Rasul said. He sure as hell was. A selfish part of him might wish he was the only man Emily had ever been with, but that fantasy was easily replaced with another—to be the best she'd ever had, and for her to know that beyond the shadow of a doubt.

Before him, the evidence mounted. She was scorching hot around his pounding cock, and he imagined the shock another man would surely feel, experiencing that.

Her eyes shut and he wondered what movie was playing inside her head. Maybe none. Maybe just their reality.

A final soft, pained "baby" escaped her lips. The hand on her clit froze as she drove her hips hard against his. He felt the spasms as she came around his cock and the scrape of her nails on his shoulder. All at once he was speeding to release himself, body electric with the thrill of watching her. He waited endless seconds for her to still and relax before he took his turn.

Her eyes opened as he slid out. As he fisted his cock he gazed across her skin, pale and rosy, her belly, her cunt, her breasts and nipples. Hazel-green eyes on his surging hand, cheeks and lips burning pink with what he could do to her. So unlike the woman he might have guessed he'd one day call his wife, yet now there could be no other vision.

His excitement mounted, the sensations nearing pain, and he closed in on his climax. The movement of Emily's hand drew his eyes from her face to her pussy, as her fingers traced her dark, flushed lips. His own hand sped, coordination waning as release edged closer. A moan tumbled from his mouth and he saw her smirk—a wry little smile that pushed him clear over the cliff, plummeting into sweet, thoughtless pleasure.

He watched his come empty onto her belly, lost in a haze of power and possession and blissful, fleeting, perfect calm.

As the high faded he felt her hands on his thighs, a grazing touch that eased him gently back to reality. He got control of his muscles and flopped to the mattress beside her. Before she could leave him to tidy herself in the bathroom, he pulled her close, chest to chest, and kissed her. He stroked her cheek and marveled at the softness of her skin, her hair, her very presence.

She bit her lip. "You tricked me."

He pulled back to show her a pair of raised eyebrows.

"Makin' me think we weren't about to have sex."

He grinned and stole another kiss. "You're the one who ordered me to."

"Yeah. True."

"So you only have yourself to blame." He kissed her a final time and she left him alone in the bed, alone but surrounded by her smell and warmth and lingering energy.

He closed his eyes and rolled onto his back, sleep coming down so fast and easy it must have belonged to some other, simpler man.

* * *

THE WEEKEND ARRIVED and passed, an idyllic two days of April sunshine that Emily and Rasul spent painting the guest bedroom and assembling the most overly complicated dresser in creation. Another barbecue for two; a long, pleasant walk. So normal on the outside, both of them burning up from the uncertainty of what this new week might bring.

Emily always took care with her appearance, but on Tuesday she gave it a hundred-and-ten-percent. With her plan already launched, she was invested now. She wanted Jeremy to say yes worse than she'd ever admit out loud. And if he said no, she wanted to accept that answer graciously—while looking as sexy as possible. She selected a shirt with a deep vee-neck, snug jeans made snugger by the dryer. She tugged on her old, authentic Texas cowboy boots, a little tribute to Jeremy's roots, a good-luck charm.

Rasul arrived home from work minutes before she left, and neither spoke of what was surely weighing on both their minds. Would Jeremy show? Would he have an answer? Were they in agreement about which answer they wanted? She kissed her husband goodbye and headed to the bar.

Jeremy usually arrived around eight, which would make the first hour of Emily's shift the longest imaginable as she waited, watched the door, examined each entering patron's face. She sighed as she parked and did her best to push the thoughts away.

To her great surprise and relief, Jeremy's was the first smile to greet her as she stepped behind the bar from the back room.

"Hey, you," she said. "Looks like you beat me here for a change. Hope that doesn't mean you got fired today."

"Nope. Just eager to see a friendly face."

Their eye contact lingered for longer than was professional before Emily got hold of herself. Jeremy already had a beer in his hand so she excused herself to greet the other usuals and log in to the register and timecard system. She filled a few orders and glanced at Jeremy whenever possible, finding his gaze always aimed innocently at the TV. Dear God, why had she promised not to bring up their conversation? She wondered how long she could make it, waiting for him to clue her in to what he was thinking, what he may or may not have decided.

She monitored his glass and made sure to be the one who offered a refill when it got low.

"'Nother Guinness?" she asked.

"Please."

She started his pint, and though it violated her promise to pretend their talk hadn't happened, she smirked at him. To her delight, he returned the mischief before glancing away guiltily.

"So how was your day?" she asked as the stout settled. "You kick those hotshot rich ladies' butts in the gym?"

He nodded. "In the morning, yeah. The afternoon was a bit different. I'm helping this one client train for the Marine Corps Marathon this fall. Today was her first long run in about fifteen years. She beat breast cancer last year and it's on her bucket list."

"Wow."

"Yeah. She's sixty-one and retired from government work, real nice change of pace from the usual. Different sort of driven, you know?"

"I'll bet." She smiled as she finished his pour, inspired as always by other people's ambitions, wondering what her own ought to be. "That's so cool. I could never run a marathon."

"Sure you could."

"I dunno, I'm awful bowlegged. Plus my face turns bright red just jogging to catch a bus." She set Jeremy's beer at his elbow and took away his empty glass.

"I'd offer to train you, but I probably won't be around here after August."

Her middle jolted and she frowned. "Really? How come?"

"Just time to move on. I've saved up a bunch of money to travel, and I think it's time to finally pull the trigger. My life here's nice, don't get me wrong. But I don't want to wake up in ten years still doing what I am now."

"Gosh, me neither." She stared at his hands. "I just hope that decision… I just hope it doesn't have anything to do with Reston, you know? Anything somebody might've done or said that made you want to leave for good."

She looked to his face and found him smiling.

"No, of course not. I think it's just spring. Whatever it is in the air that makes you want to try something new. Start over. Plus I always thought I'd do the travel thing before I was thirty. And I'll be thirty-two this summer. Clock's ticking."

She nodded. "I hear you." He knew better than anybody that Emily was looking to try something new. *Throw me a bone, here.* "Well, I won't be lying when I say I'll miss seeing you around this place. And runnin' around town with your dog. Oh my goodness, what'll happen to your dog while you're away?"

"My sister's going to watch him for me, back in Texas."

She gave the bar a whap with her palm. "Darn. I was half hoping I could take him off your hands."

"Yeah?"

"Sure, I'd love a dog. It'd give me something to do all day. But Rasul said let's wait until we know what my schedule will look like, after I get my nursing degree. *If* I get my degree."

"You will."

"He says it's ridiculous how Americans decide they want puppies or babies, then have to hire somebody—some stranger—to look after them 'cause they're too busy to do it themselves. He's awful traditional. About some stuff."

"I'll bet… You start school in September, right?"

"That I do."

"Sounds like we've both got our sights on the next big thing."

Another customer interrupted their chat and Emily left to fill orders. Things stayed busy and she didn't have a chance to resume their conversation for a half hour or more. By then it felt silly to try to jump right in and bypass the small talk.

"Doin' all right here?" she asked, nodding at his half-full glass.

"Yeah."

She busied herself wiping down the counter in front of the taps, praying he'd give her some kind of sign. An acknowledgment of what her mother called "the invisible rabbit in the room", though Emily didn't think that phrase was quite right.

Jeremy cleared his throat. "So, um…"

She held her breath.

"What are you guys up to this weekend?"

She wiped the already perfectly clean wood. "Oh, I dunno yet. How about you?"

He shrugged. "Don't know yet either. If the forecast's accurate, it's supposed to be pretty lousy. Back to the low fifties and rainy."

"That's too bad. Just when I thought spring was here."

He rotated his glass on its coaster. "Good weather for staying inside, I guess."

Her heart sped, chest inflating with hope and fear. "Yeah, I suppose so."

Her coworker Danielle's voice burst in at the worst possible moment. "Em? I have to change a keg. Could you ring this party up?"

"Yeah, 'course. Pardon me." She gave Jeremy a nervous smile and left him to do her job. It was another ten minutes before things quieted down enough to sidle back up to him.

"Sorry about that. So you were saying something…about the weather being lousy this weekend?" She gave herself a mental eye roll. *Oh yes, very smooth.*

"That's what I heard, anyhow. Like they're ever right."

"Yeah…" The only word left in her vocabulary, it seemed. "Well. Um. I'm making maqluba on Saturday night."

"I have no idea what that is."

Emily smiled, having known he wouldn't, proud to feel attached to anything exotic. "It's this dish made with layers of rice and eggplant and meat, then served upside-down. Not the prettiest thing you ever saw, but it tastes delicious. When we got married, Rasul's mother mailed me this huge box of recipes."

"Ah."

"Half the ingredients in her recipes you can't even find around here. But luckily Rasul doesn't seem to care. I just do my best and if I screw it up, he's nice enough not to tell me." Emily laughed. "But if my mother-in-law ever comes to visit I'm totally screwed. It'll be like an *I Love Lucy* episode in that kitchen."

He smiled. "So, maqluba?"

"Yup. It's real good. I make it with ground lamb. You, um, you ought to come over some night and try it."

She waited an eternity as Jeremy sipped his beer. He stared at the glass and said, "That sounds lovely."

"Saturday night, if you're eager. 'Round six."

"I'm free then."

"Oh?"

He nodded.

She went blank momentarily, antsy warmth filling her from the floor up. "Well. Lovely. Here, let me scribble my number down." She grabbed a receipt and a pen and wrote the digits nice and neat for him. "Not that I won't see you on Thursday. You can always change your mind. But I'll be sure and make enough for three." *Three.*

He accepted the paper, folding it tidily.

Danielle butted in as she passed by, hands full of empty glasses. "Giving your number out to customers?" she asked, flashing them both a teasing smile and nodding at the receipt.

Jeremy laughed and exchanged a glance with Emily. "Get your mind out of the gutter," he told Danielle.

"Just be careful, Jeremy. Her husband's an assassin or something."

"Oh, trust me, I know."

"I was just inviting him to dinner sometime," Emily said. "Been chattin' this poor boy's ear off for six months now and he still comes back. Least I can do is have him over for a hot meal." A hot meal, among other offerings.

Danielle put on a patronizingly heavy Southern accent. "You sweet little slice of Georgia pecan pie, you."

"I know. But you city folks should try it. Y'all don't even know your neighbors' names, I bet."

"Sure we do," Danielle said, filling the dishwasher. "I've got Baldie to the left, and the Parking Nazi to my right, and Guy Who Doesn't Pick Up His Dog's Shit right across the street. Very cozy."

Emily shook her head. Danielle headed out to pick up more empties and Emily looked to Jeremy.

She blushed and cleared her throat, realizing with a start she was likely going to sleep with this man. "Well, how exciting."

Jeremy raised his eyebrows in agreement as he sipped his drink.

She felt awkwardness descending and shuffled away to organize the register. With a glance back at Jeremy, she decided that was a stupid impulse. This was something to be over the moon about, not scared of. She should be flirting her head off, not avoiding the boy. She poured a shot of bourbon and filled a tumbler with seltzer, setting the former in front of him. He picked up his shot and she clinked her glass against it.

"To trying new stuff," she announced. "Travel and school. And *maqluba*." She said the final word with a wiggle of her brows, feeling drunk on their conspiracy.

"Cheers." Jeremy sipped his drink and smiled.

She might see a different smile on that face in a few days' time. Other expressions too—anticipation and helplessness, uncertainty, maybe fear. But when she said goodbye to him on Saturday night or Sunday morning—goddamn, she'd make sure he was smiling then.

CHAPTER SIX

EMILY HAD TOLD RASUL ONCE that the abuse she'd gone through as a child had been the best thing that could have happened to her.

"Not that it was good that those things happened," she'd corrected herself. "It was awful. But if that hadn't happened, and if I hadn't acted out and turned into one of the 'bad girls' in high school... Gosh, it scares me to think it. I'd probably have ended up one of those perfect, freaky pageant girls. And those perfect girls, none of them ever made it out of my crappy little hometown. They all wound up pregnant by twenty-one and married to the only guy they ever let get a hand up their shirt. Jesus forgive me, but I'm so glad I turned out rotten."

Rasul was continually surprised by his wife's odd brand of wisdom. He couldn't ever agree that her being abused was a good thing, but he was flattered beyond words that she seemed to think it was a reasonable price to have paid to end up here, with him, in the life they were making together.

It was four o'clock on Saturday afternoon and Rasul was reading the news online in the den. He glanced over his laptop at Emily puttering in the kitchen, assembling ingredients to mangle one of his mother's recipes. Not that he minded her mangling it, particularly. He forgave Emily a thousand things he'd never have guessed he would. He'd been issued a very specific set of expectations for the woman he'd one day marry, and Emily was few of them. Kind and patient, surely destined to be a good mother…a good cook, if not of the cuisine he'd grown up with.

But innocent, obedient, deferring? Not in the slightest.

"Do you need any help?" he shouted.

"Nope. All set."

"Let me know if you change your mind."

"Will do."

He'd not been taught to make such offers—yet another unexpected modification of his manhood that he'd come to enjoy. He trusted the States had little to do with this spiritual makeover. It was all Emily. She'd corrupted him so effortlessly. Without a trace of manipulation, she seeped through every miniscule hole in his armor, and now he'd never get her out. He wouldn't ever want to.

If someone had told him as a twenty-something that his wife would have a sordid sexual past before he met her, he'd have hit them. Yet looking at Emily now, flesh and blood and untheoretical, he couldn't care less.

Where he was from, it was far too easy for a woman to find herself ruined. That was how his sister had seen herself, and perhaps still saw herself, though she had eventually succeeded in marrying. Rasul no longer valued such things as perceived female "goodness". He valued Emily, a woman made up of flaws as well as gifts. Some other man might call her damaged or soiled, but to him she was merely Emily, angelic on the outside, all her scar tissue hidden by her soft exterior. Stronger than she ever gave herself credit for. She'd forgiven people who'd hurt her beyond Rasul's comprehension. He could fuck a man up in a hundred brutal ways, but he couldn't ever do that—forgive someone. That made her more powerful than him by miles.

He looked to the clock on his screen. Two hours until their guest was due to arrive. The thought filled him with a mix of emotions. Dread and excitement, insecurity and superiority. This was the man his wife had deemed worthy of playing tourist in their bed.

From the moment she came into the world with no father to hold her, Emily had been learning that men took what they wanted. Rasul would reverse some of those lessons tonight. Two men. One invited, offering the excitement of his body and attention, the other giving her the most selfless gift a husband could, stepping back and allowing her to explore the things she craved. Until he'd met her, Rasul had never known this trait even existed inside him, this ability and desire to give. With her it had grown from a trickling tap to a river, and sometimes it felt as though it might burst through his skin if he didn't create outlets with his words and actions.

Dear God, what had she done to him?

She'd made him a man. That was precisely what she'd done.

* * *

AT FIVE O'CLOCK, the maqluba prepped and layered and ready to cook, Emily headed upstairs to get ready for the strangest dinner party of her life.

She scooped out the contents of her underwear drawer and dumped it on the bed, standing naked before the pile, uncertain. Tonight was her fantasy. Going over the top with her lingerie selection might make this too much about Jeremy…but it *was* about him, as well as her. Still, she didn't want Rasul to feel she'd made more effort for a stranger than she might for him. Her shoulders slumped at the dilemma. She padded to the top of the stairs.

"Baby?"

His shout came from the den. "Yes?"

"Need your help up here, if you have a second."

She went back to staring at her underthings and he joined her shortly.

"I haven't got the faintest clue how sexy I'm supposed to look tonight."

"Look however you like."

She pursed her lips and looked up at his impassive face. "I don't want you thinkin' I'm trying harder for him, you know?"

He cracked a faint smile. "He's our guest. Go ahead and spoil him, if that's what you want."

She picked through a rainbow of panties. "Maybe."

"He's not here to fix the plumbing. You treat him like what he is—a very lucky man. You deemed him worthy of this, and I'm behind you. So wear whatever you like."

She nodded, an idea clicking into place. All the contrast of her and Rasul…she should drive that home. "Thank you, sir. You're dismissed."

He patted her arm and let her be. Rasul was the scary one, so she'd be the sweet one. Not creepy, little-girl-innocence sweet. Womanly sweet. She selected a pair of silk, red-and-pink plaid bikini briefs and dug the matching bra out of its tangled drawer. She studied herself in the mirror and thought that was about right. Like Valentine's Day. A gift and a seduction. She pulled a garnet jersey dress over her head then headed to the bathroom to sit on the rim of the tub and paint her toenails to match.

At twenty to six she headed downstairs and found Rasul crouched before the fridge, stocking the crisper with cans of Guinness.

"Aren't you a thoughtful host? Though I bet we'll all need a sip of something stronger to make this evening happen."

He stood and surveyed her body in its clingy sheath. "Well."

"You've seen this before."

He moved closer and pulled her to him by the waist, speaking against her temple. "Forgive me if you seem a bit different tonight."

"Am I acting different?"

"No. You're shockingly calm, in fact. But I'm seeing you differently. I feel like I'm seeing you through his eyes, maybe."

The thought warmed her. "How's your breakdown?" she asked, meaning the mix of scared and excited they'd each been feeling and monitoring since Jeremy accepted her invitation. "Fifty-fifty?"

"I'm barely nervous at all," he said, and stepped back to shut the crisper and fridge.

"Really?"

He offered her a rare grin. "Really. I'm excited for you. It feels like your birthday, and I've bought you the best present you could ask for."

"Well, don't you sound just a teensy bit smug?"

His smile deepened. "Better smug than insecure."

"Very true." She brought the maqluba to a boil then reduced it to simmering. Just as she set the lid on the saucepan, the doorbell sounded. "Oh my. He's very punctual."

One glance at Rasul and he left to greet their guest. Just to appear busy, she grabbed a stack of plates from the cupboard, watching the front door as Rasul opened it. The men exchanged a neutral greeting and Emily abandoned her hostess charade and nerves to cross the den.

"Hey, you," she said.

Jeremy smiled, looking just as handsome in her threshold as he did on a barstool. "Hey."

"Come on in." She beckoned him inside and took his jacket, hanging it in the closet. She turned to show him exactly how she was feeling, letting a goofy, grateful grin spread across her face. "Golly, we've never even hugged, have we?"

Jeremy opened his arms and she gave him a squeeze, enjoying how different he felt from Rasul, taller and leaner, an alternative flavor of man.

"That's better," she said, stepping back. "Glad you beat the rain."

"Yeah, but not by much." They both glanced out the picture window at the gray sky, dark from heavy clouds and impending dusk.

"Can I get you a drink?" Rasul asked Jeremy. "Beer, wine, scotch?"

Emily glowed, so grateful for all of this.

"Sure. A beer—but only if you guys are having something."

Emily laughed. "Oh, you better believe it."

"We've got cold pilsner or warm stout," Rasul said, heading for the fridge.

"Cold is good."

Rasul grabbed two bottles while Emily poured herself half a glass of chardonnay. "Cheers," she said, and the three toasted, no one ballsy enough to proclaim what the occasion was.

"Dinner will be another hour or so." Holy shit, what were they going to find to talk about for that long? Still, she shouldn't panic. This was just like having any other friend over…until the plates were deposited in the dishwasher and they all headed upstairs together.

"Here, let's get comfy." She led the men to the den, where she and Rasul sat on the couch, their guest on the love seat.

"Your home's really nice," Jeremy said, looking around. He bore the tight posture of a man sitting in a parlor with his date's overbearing father. "You just moved in, right?"

She nodded. "Two months ago. I still need to buy half the furniture. It's overwhelming. I know it's modest for this area, but compared to the shoebox I grew up in… I've got no idea how to decorate a place this big. What brought you to Reston, anyway?"

Jeremy sipped his drink. "Well, I went to college on a soccer scholarship—"

"A soccer scholarship? From Texas?"

He grinned. "I know. I was too small for football when everybody else was getting in to it. Late bloomer."

She smiled at that, the idea that her acquaintance had ever been anything other than tall and athletic.

"Anyhow, a friend of mine from college started a kids' training camp here a few years ago and invited me to coach. So I did that for a summer then I switched to personal training. The money was good and I ended up meeting a lot of cool new people, then I blink and it's almost five years later. What about you guys?" He finally made eye contact with Rasul.

Emily knew her husband would prefer she answer for him, but she kept her mouth shut and forced him to engage.

"I came here for my job," he said simply.

Jeremy nodded and turned to Emily.

"Well, when I was little, one of my best friends was a girl from Illinois who came to our town every summer to stay with her grandparents. We kept in touch, and when she moved here for grad school, she called me out of the blue and asked if I'd like to be her roommate. All I ever talked about when I was growing up was how I was going to get out of my hometown, and have an apartment, and do this and that. So I finally just went for it. I worked as a cashier for about six months before I realized I couldn't pay my rent *and* eat. Been at the bar ever since."

"Wow."

She shrugged and took a drink of her wine, feeling her cheeks heat. Odd to be flanked on either side by a successful man, each of them attracted to her, invested deeply enough in her pleasure to be in this room together, inventing a strange new breed of diplomacy.

"I wouldn't give it a 'wow', but thanks. Anyhow, can't believe I'm here." She nodded to indicate the room, this beautiful house and town, but to herself she meant here between these men, in this situation.

Jeremy turned to Rasul again. "So, if I can ask, were you recruited for your job?"

He nodded curtly.

Jeremy looked stymied.

"Rasul's useless at talking about himself," Emily supplied, patting her husband's shoulder. "But let's see. He's thirty-four, he grew up outside Jerusalem, served in the army for ten years and got recruited by the UN as a translator. He took his current job so he could send money home to his family." She looked him over. "That's about all I've ever gotten out of him," she said, smiling at Jeremy.

Rasul finally warmed up. He kept his eyes on the carpet as he said, "And when I moved here I swore I would never marry an American woman and settle in."

Jeremy laughed. "Where'd you two meet?"

"Same as you," Rasul said. He pointed his bottle at Emily. "She served me my very first beer, ever in my life."

"No way."

Rasul nodded. "Partly cultural. Plus I'm very…particular about certain things. About controlling things." He cleared his throat and a fever settled over Emily's skin, making her glow with appreciation for how out of character it was for him to share such thoughts.

"Before I came here," he said, "I loathed the idea of alcohol, and drunkenness. I thought it did nothing but make people lose their sense and self-control. Then I saw this woman, and she asked me what I'd like to drink."

Emily jumped in. "And he said, 'I don't know.' And I said, 'A beer?' And he nodded so I said, 'Okay, what kind?' and oh my goodness, the look on his face."

Rasul smiled, eyes still aimed at the floor. "I was practically drunk already, from her."

Emily flushed with pride at that. As poetic as her husband ever got.

"So she chose for me, and I changed my tune."

"He said if it wasn't for beer, he'd never have found the balls to ask me out."

Jeremy nodded. "Liquid courage."

"I, um… I have a lot going on, up here." Rasul waved a hand to mean his brain. "Not a lot of brilliant thoughts, though. A lot of noise. A drink helps turn the volume down, I find." His head finally rose, and he looked to Jeremy as he sipped his beer.

"I bet there are a million couples out there who'd never have gotten together if not for alcohol," Jeremy said.

"And probably a million more who *shouldn't* have got together," Emily teased. "I see them leave the bar together every week."

"Can I ask what you guys did on your first date?"

She smiled at the memory. "Rasul told me right off the bat, he had no clue what American women enjoyed except shopping. But I suspected I liked him so I grabbed those reins and said, you're gonna pick me up at this time, at this place, and we're eating lunch at such-and-such restaurant and if that goes well, we're going on a walk in the park. And that's what we did."

"Guess you're not controlling about dates then," Jeremy said.

Rasul took a drink and considered it. "I am not very controlling about anything she wants." He cast her a fond glance. "Maybe that's why I like her so much. She's the only thing I know that's perfect, just how it is."

Emily rolled her eyes but her burning complexion was surely giving away her pleasure. "You just know I'd never stand for gettin' bossed around." She paused a second before the wine led her to add, "At least not in most situations." She held her breath, wondering if that innuendo would cool the men's rapport.

Jeremy drained his bottle. "So you said."

"What else has she told you?" Rasul asked. He knew perfectly well from Emily everything they'd talked about, but clearly wanted to get a handle on Jeremy's perception of the situation. Emily rose to check on dinner, listening raptly and watching from the corner of her eye.

"She said... Lots of stuff, really. But nothing explicit. She said she likes how you are, you know. In bed. 'Bossy', I think was the word she used."

Rasul nodded.

"And she said that tonight, you guys inviting me and everything, that I'd pretty much be doing whatever you tell me to."

Emily refreshed her glass and brought two more beers back to the den, thinking they'd need them before long.

Rasul accepted his, attention glued to Jeremy. "Did she say it could get rough?"

"Yeah, she did."

Rasul nodded again, his face turning thoughtful. Emily didn't think she'd ever seen him look this way in front of a fellow male. "My wife," he began, and trailed off for a moment. "She has given me more pleasure than I knew was possible. In life, I mean, not sexually. I'm not good at a lot of things...being emotional or interpreting her emotions. But for all the ways I fail as a husband—"

Emily began to protest but he held up a hand to silence her.

"For all those ways I'm not so perfect," he corrected, still addressing Jeremy, "I want her to feel like I can give her anything she asks for. And you're one of those things. She wants you. She does not need you, but she does desire you. Another man, who she trusts and is fond of, alongside me. In bed," he tacked on, voice turning blunt once more.

Jeremy's face was hard to read. "To say I'm flattered is the biggest understatement ever."

"And I think you like my wife," Rasul said. "As a person."

"I do. I think she may be the sweetest human on the planet."

Rasul's lips twitched, expression softening. "Yes, she is." He held his bottle out and Jeremy realized after a second it was an invitation to toast. The bottles clinked and both men turned to her.

"Golly, if I wasn't blushing already, I am now."

"Before whatever happens tonight," Rasul said to Jeremy. "I have something else to demand of you."

Emily's eyebrows rose along with their guest's.

"Okay," Jeremy said.

"She and I are letting you inside our marriage," Rasul said.

Jeremy nodded.

"I trust you can appreciate how immense an invitation that is. And an honor." He shot Emily a look of aggressive, blinding pride.

"Of course," Jeremy said.

"I never would have guessed I'd ever let such a thing happen, but here I am. And I need something from you in exchange. Your word."

"My word about…?"

"I want your word that for the time you and Emily have left as friends, before you move away, that you will look out for her at the bar for me."

Jeremy's posture relaxed. "Of course. I'd like to think I do that already."

"I also want you to promise me that if anything happens to me, you'll be there for her."

He tensed again. "How do you mean?"

"If you are away, you will come back and help her in whatever way she needs."

291

Emily looked to her husband. "Baby, my family can do that."

He returned her glance with a telling one, reminding her that no, her family probably wasn't capable of supporting her all that well, in any sense of the word.

"He's just our guest," she said.

"It's okay," Jeremy said, catching her eye. "I'd be honored to do that. I'm sure it won't ever come up, but if you ever need me for something, I'll always make sure you've got my number or my e-mail."

Emily nibbled her lip, thrown by the serious edge the discussion had taken on. But that was Rasul's way. Or his price. A pittance to her, considering the gift he was offering, and apparently a price also reasonable to Jeremy.

Jeremy reached out a hand and Rasul shook it, his face looking grim once more, but calm. Such a fascinating, perplexing man, her husband. Such a charming enigma, her friend from the bar.

They chatted about less heavy topics for another twenty or thirty minutes, until the smell of dinner pulled Emily out of the conversation.

She stood. "You two stay where you are." She'd given this some thought and had decided to go casual—everyone eating off their laps in the den. The thought of them sitting down to a formal meal at the table felt awkward and stodgy, a mood-killer. As the dish cooled she fetched water glasses and napkins and freshened drinks. She flipped the maqluba upside-down onto a plate and doled out three helpings, delivering them then settling back on the couch, cross-legged. "Dig in."

Forks squeaked on plates and compliments were offered and accepted, but Emily was too distracted to really take in what either man was saying. These two bodies were hers to enjoy tonight. *Decadent*, she thought. Spoiled. Outrageously spoiled, but it would be a colossal waste of all their time if she allowed herself any second thoughts or guilt or hesitation about the evening. Her duty was to give herself up and wallow in this indulgence. This was a party, she realized.

"So Jeremy," she said between bites. "Do y'all have like, client confidentiality, or can you tell us about some of the most over-the-top women you work with?"

He laughed and wiped his mouth. "Sure...there's a lot to choose from though. The worst are the ones who treat me like some coin-operated machine. The ones who'll take every single call or text that comes in during a session, like they aren't paying me a ridiculous amount of money to be there with them. Makes me feel like a workout DVD they put on pause."

"Any really crazy ones though?"

"Everyone around here's a little crazy." He paused, glancing at Rasul.

"I couldn't agree more."

Jeremy went on. "There's a certain group that make me nuts. The power wives who don't have nine-to-five jobs themselves, so they turn their kids or their homes or their charities into their careers. I had a woman who brought her eight-year-old daughter in to work out, once. Wanted me to assess her and offered to hire me to train her. I was like, no fucking way I'm taking part in that level of psychosis. That's what I said in my head anyway. Out loud I think I said, 'I'm not sure it's appropriate for a child that age to undertake a training regimen.'"

"Diplomacy," Emily sighed.

"No kidding."

Rasul smiled, looking amused. "So glad I have one of a very few jobs in this town that pays me to be impolite."

Jeremy laughed. "I would love to send some of my bratty clients to your office for an hour. If what you do is anything like what I picture."

Rasul shrugged.

"I don't think we're cut out to do one another's jobs," Jeremy said. "Do you yell as much as I imagine?"

"Often. Do you kiss rich women's asses as much as I imagine?"

"More."

Emily laughed. "Where do you want to travel to, when you call it quits here?"

"All over," Jeremy said. "Spain, Italy, Brazil... Anyplace where they don't speak English, with amazing food and cheap hotels."

"You could backpack," she said.

He made a skeptical face. "Maybe ten years ago I could. Think I might look a bit tragic staying at hostels now that I'm in my thirties. Tragic or creepy."

"Plus you couldn't bring a girl back to your bunk bed," Emily added. She made her voice flirtatious, ready to shift the mood of the evening.

"I don't know how many girls I'll be luring anyplace."

"Oh, come on. Handsome, single foreigner? You'll have them linin' up. Plus, you know as well as I do a Southern accent is a powerful thing once you leave Georgia or Texas. I swear people look at me and I can see them wanting to like, pat my head and call me 'precious'."

"You *are* sort of precious."

"On the outside maybe. Ask the folks back home and they'll give you a different story. I'm like the Jezebel of Boyettsville, Georgia, the way they make it out." She shook her head.

"I can't imagine that."

"My two aunts, my momma's sisters... When I was growing up they'd warn me. 'Em, don't you ever take no wrong steps. Town like this, stains don't ever wash out, and everybody's dyin' to make it known their linens are whiter than yours.' I thought they were just being old-fashioned, but oh my goodness, did I ever find out they were right." She shook her head. After a sip of wine she added, "But you know what? Fuck them."

Jeremy blinked then laughed into his napkin. "Sorry."

"No, really, fuck them," she said. "All those folks. You laugh 'cause you've never heard me swear, and believe me, I didn't utter a cuss word 'til I was twenty. Went to church every Sunday, polite to everybody and meant it. But you kiss one too many boys in high school and suddenly you're packin' for hell. Well, they're all still right where I left them, in the slow lane to no place. And I'll bet you hell's a lot more fun."

"Fuck 'em," Jeremy concluded.

"Yes, indeed." She looked to Rasul and a familiar fantasy crossed her mind—the stir they'd cause if she ever brought him home. But it wasn't worth the slurs she feared she might overhear, plus she didn't need to prove anything to those ignorant busybodies. Might be satisfying, though, showing off her husband. A very selfish bit of her would love to see him goaded into a bar fight.

As they ate and chatted and refreshed their drinks, Emily relaxed into the evening far deeper than she'd expected or even hoped to. She was about to commit a pretty heinous sin with these two men. She'd decided awhile back that there wasn't actually any such thing as hell. There was heaven, for when you'd learned everything you needed to on Earth, and then there were do-overs. Do badly on Earth and you had to start over, repeat the whole thing until you got it right. If God wasn't pleased about what she planned to do in her bed tonight with these men...well, screw it, she'd make up for it the next time around. For what she was getting, she'd happily join a convent in her next lifetime.

CHAPTER SEVEN

JEREMY GLANCED AT THE CLOCK as Emily cleared the plates away. Eight thirty, damn. The thought relaxed him. He'd been making small talk with his hosts for over two hours, and it hadn't felt like that long. He watched Rasul helping his wife, accepting orders for where things went in the kitchen. Surely he'd be the one dishing out the orders soon enough. The idea still gave Jeremy an apprehensive jolt, though not as potent as before this evening. Emily had changed a little, for him—she had more depth. As sweet as before, but with a tougher past than Jeremy would have guessed.

Rasul had gone from ominous shadow to flesh and blood, a dramatic transformation indeed. He was more than a concept—brutish husband—and Jeremy respected him. He was an odd person. In some ways excruciatingly traditional, but in others, such as the premise of this entire evening, downright liberal.

Once they finished organizing the kitchen, the couple approached. Suspecting it was showtime, Jeremy drained the last of his after-dinner scotch and stood from the couch. All at once, his body shifted. As Emily neared, the friend and hostess he'd been chatting to all night dissolved, replaced for a second by the face and body that occasionally distracted him so unwholesomely on Tuesday and Thursday evenings.

"That was the best dinner I've had in ages," he offered.

Emily did a curtsy with the hem of her dress.

"Go and get ready for bed," Rasul said to her.

She smiled at each of them and disappeared up the stairs.

Jeremy looked to Rasul, heart suddenly pounding. Suddenly praying he was about to be dismissed, the evening called off, his test failed.

"Let's talk about what's going to happen." Rasul put a warm, bold hand on Jeremy, right where his shoulder met his neck, thumb on his jugular. Not a seduction. Jeremy's pulse sped and he allowed himself to be steered to the dinner table, his butt deposited on a chair with a firm push.

He sat up straight, trying to look agreeable and businesslike and only half as nervous as he suddenly felt.

Rasul took a seat across from him, leaning forward with his bossy hands clasped between his knees. "Tonight is all about what Emily wants."

Jeremy nodded.

"And I know what that is," Rasul went on, "so you'll be doing whatever I tell you to."

"Okay."

"Unless it's something you refuse to do, of course."

Jeremy's throat felt constricted. "I don't know exactly what she's into, but if it's really rough, no, I won't do that. I wouldn't be able to... I don't know, hit her. Or yell at her."

"Nothing quite that harsh, but not far off." Rasul looked thoughtful a moment. "Anything especially rough, I will be in charge of. You give her pleasure, I'll handle any corrections that need to be made."

Corrections? "Right. Good."

"You and I are partners tonight, in giving my wife this experience."

Jeremy nodded again.

"Her fantasies have much to do with getting bossed around. Sometimes with being held down, treated harshly, being controlled."

"Okay."

"Not always. But often. Other times she simply wants to do as she's told. I can read her like a book, so I hope you'll trust me as much as she does, and believe that whatever I tell you to do, it's what she wants."

"I think I can do that."

"Good. She's also a complicated person, with a complicated past. She was hurt when she was young, by men. It's made her how she is now, sexually, but that doesn't mean she's over it. Not completely. If you do anything without my word that upsets her, I too will be very upset."

Jeremy suppressed an urge to swallow, not wanting to give away his nerves. "I understand."

"And if at any point you want to run down the stairs and out into the night, do so. We don't want you to feel like a whore."

He laughed. "I don't. I feel honored, really." He nearly added "sir" then bit his tongue. "Like you said, I'm here to make Emily happy."

Rasul nodded. "Good."

"Any, um…any tips?" Jeremy asked.

A sly smile softened his host's stern expression. "I suppose… She likes noises. I'm not very noisy, so you will be a treat for her, if you are."

"I can do that."

"Don't call her 'angel'. It's a nasty trigger."

Jeremy conjured the vague, shadowy faces of those men Rasul had mentioned and made a mental note, underlining it twice.

"Also, you're coming last tonight," Rasul added.

Jeremy didn't have the first clue if the reality of the evening's events would have him red-hot or wilting with intimidation, so he merely nodded.

After a moment's hesitation, he asked, "Would you ever ask her to do this for you? Bring another woman in..." He trailed off as Rasul grasped him once again by the shoulder, thumb pressed uncomfortably close to his throat.

Rasul blinked and stared past Jeremy's face, seeming thoughtful for several seconds before speaking. His words were slow and cold. "I would sooner die than allow my wife to wonder for a single moment if another woman could stir in me any fraction of the desire she does."

Jeremy swallowed, the action feeling choked. Rasul let him go and Jeremy resisted the urge to rub his neck.

Rasul's voice returned to its relatively civil tone. "So no. No I would not."

"Understood."

Rasul leaned back in his chair. "Time to head upstairs, I think. I need to lock up first. Use the bathroom if you like." He nodded toward a door between the kitchen and den. "The bedroom is across from the top of the stairs, when you're ready."

Jeremy accepted the offer, wishing he'd thought to bring a toothbrush. He splashed water on his face and tried to tidy his messy hair, breathing deeply until the adrenaline ebbed. He thought of Emily, her curves in that slinky dress, and his cock grew warm and heavy. That in itself was a relief. He couldn't honestly own sleeping with another man's wife as a kink, but his body wanted this. He wanted Emily, and now he was being offered her, with no guilty, adulterous strings attached. And holy shit, she wanted him right back.

He finished in the bathroom and the second he shut the door behind him, his heart was hammering.

He glanced at the front door, the emergency exit, but before he knew it he was padding up the silent steps to the second floor. Their bedroom was the only source of light. Dim light, so that when he pushed the door in, he felt distinctly like an intruder.

Emily was sitting on the big bed still in her dress, barefoot. She'd let her hair down and when she smiled, Jeremy had to remind himself firmly of that name he couldn't call her. Rasul was standing at the foot of the bed, also barefoot, but looking just as Jeremy had imagined—like a drill sergeant. His huge arms were locked across his chest and his black eyes were glued on Jeremy.

Wanting to fit the protocol, Jeremy toed off his sneakers and socks and left them by the door.

"You two have thought about this for a while now," Rasul said.

Jeremy glanced nervously to Emily.

"Maybe not this, exactly," Emily said.

"What about you?" Rasul asked Jeremy. "What things have you thought about my wife?"

He nodded, mustering the courage to meet that cold stare. "I've thought about her. Being with her."

"Fucking her?" There it was, that harshness he'd been anticipating.

"Yeah," Jeremy admitted. "I've thought about that." He looked to Emily. She wore a small smirk, bashful or scheming, possibly both.

"I know you've thought about him," Rasul said to her.

"Only when you tell me to."

Jeremy's cock relinquished enough blood to allow him to blush at such a thought—that he'd already been a part of their sex life. That Emily may have been thinking of him when she'd been fucking

Rasul, thinking about Jeremy as she'd come, maybe. Maybe coming because of her thoughts of him. His blood headed south again.

"You want to kiss him?" Rasul asked.

Emily nodded. Rasul uncrossed his arms and waved to Jeremy. She stood from the bed and approached.

She was average height, Jeremy on the tall side. So often she was standing and he was sitting, and she seemed very small here, in this unfamiliar space. She stared up at him and he realized she was just about the prettiest girl he'd ever seen. Not glamorous, not crazy-sexy, but pretty. Soft in all those places his clients worked so hard to make firm. Cute, but with full lips and melancholy eyes that took the girlishness away, gave her the slightest edge. Damn, those lips. She ran her tongue over them now, and panic kicked Jeremy in the butt. Was she waiting for his move, or were they both waiting for Rasul's command? He glanced to his left.

Rasul gave the most minuscule nod—a dip of his chin and a narrowing of his hooded eyes.

Jeremy looked back down at Emily's face. Cautiously, he reached up to touch her neck. The most skin-on-skin contact they'd ever shared. And only the beginning, tonight. She returned the gesture, putting her palm to his chest. He could feel her warmth through his tee shirt and imagined other warmth… His cock stiffened further.

"Go on," she whispered.

Kissing. Right. He banished dirtier acts from his mind and leaned in.

Her lips were soft, and they felt just exactly as he'd guessed. Thoughts of how they might feel wrapped around his dick tugged at him, but he fought and kept his attention on the present. She parted those perfect lips and he took the invitation, deepening the kiss. As his tongue swept against hers, he slid his fingers into her hair. It felt like high school, like his first time ever making out with a girl. He doubted his skills but at the same time, couldn't give much of a damn. Emily kissed back. The palm on his chest slid up to cup his jaw and she angled her head, taking them from deep to dirty. More than anything else in the world, Jeremy wanted to press their bodies together and make her feel how hard he was for her.

Waiting for permission was torture.

Torture, however, was a small price to pay.

Rasul's voice broke through the haze. "Enough."

They stepped apart and Jeremy caught Emily's gaze jump to his crotch for a split second.

"Let her see you," Rasul said.

Jeremy looked to the man uncertainly.

"Strip."

Right. No mistaking that order.

"You too," Rasul said to Emily. "To your underwear."

Jeremy tugged his shirt off and tossed it toward his shoes. He unbuckled his belt and dropped his jeans, kicking them away. Emily carefully removed her necklace and set it on the dresser. She peeled her clingy dress over her head in one slow, smooth motion, static making her long hair dance. Her panties and bra were pink and red and Jeremy took back his earlier assessment. Not merely pretty. Crazy-sexy, after all.

"Are you happy?" Rasul asked her.

She smiled as she swept her gaze up and down Jeremy's body, lingering on his abdomen or the erection straining at his boxer briefs.

"Very happy."

Jeremy was all at once grateful for his job. He never could have guessed she'd study him this way, so hungrily, but he felt proud that his body seemed to please her. It redoubled his lust, making him want to please her in any way she could think of. Exactly the mission he'd been recruited for.

She stepped forward, her eyes darting to her husband for some veiled permission before she touched him, running a hand lightly over his belly.

"Wow," she murmured.

He was tempted to laugh. He might have a couple inches on the man, but Rasul was built like a Marine. Jeremy looked more like what he was—a distance runner who happened to know his way around weight machines. Lean and toned but not jacked. But as her hands stroked his chest, his shoulders, his arms...he felt big.

She lingered at his stomach, and her touch made his breath hitch, made his muscles clench and release beneath her palms.

"I like your body," she murmured.

"I like yours." He prayed for an invitation to touch her, but none arrived. Not yet.

Her hands explored his hips, thumbs stroking tauntingly close to his cock.

"It's been years since I've touched someone new," she said. "Or even seen anyone naked." She slipped her fingertips inside his waistband and drew them across his belly, not quite peeking.

Jeremy didn't downplay the labored breath that rattled from his chest. She liked sounds, Rasul had said, and he'd let her hear every last gasp and whimper she inspired.

"You've been on my mind, lately," Emily said. "When he and I..." She nodded to her husband.

"Oh?"

She smiled down at her busy, torturing hands. "Mm hmm."

"What about me?" Jeremy asked.

"About you watching us. Since I don't know what you're like in bed. Yet."

Yet. He let that word tumble around his skull as the pleasure simmering between his legs surged to a boil.

"What *are* you like?" she asked. "Or what *do* you like?"

"I'm here to please you," he said with a glance to his left.

"Well, tell me this," Emily drawled. Goddamn, she knew how to abuse a man with that accent. "When you've thought about tonight, what did you imagine?" Finally, she traced the side of his erection with her fingertip.

Jeremy twitched and fought to compose himself. "I, um... I thought about being on top, I guess. And I thought about your mouth. On me."

The mouth in question quirked into an evil smile. "Oh?"

He nodded. "I thought about that. I wondered if he'd allow it, and if he did, what you'd be like."

"Guess it's up to him to decide whether or not that stays a mystery," Emily teased.

"Yeah."

A cool command cut through the haze of flirtation. "Let him go."

Emily dropped her hands and obediently stepped back a pace.

The tone of the scene changed for Jeremy as Rasul walked to Emily. The way the man held her jaw as he leaned in to kiss her...an act of possession like he'd never seen. He kissed with an aggression and a confidence that cooled Jeremy's excitement and reminded him who he was—a guest, but perhaps not the guest of honor. He realized then this was the first time he'd seen the couple touch, but watching their bodies and faces, mismatched as they were, there was no mistaking that these two lusted for each other.

As he watched Emily being consumed by her husband, Jeremy felt put in his place. Accessory. Plaything. He didn't mind though. These two were insanely right together and he wanted to be a part of that, nearly as much as he might selfishly want her all to himself, in some alternate reality.

After a minute of filthy kissing, Rasul pushed Emily away to arm's length. He yanked his tee shirt up his torso and tossed it aside. Jeremy suddenly felt very small and pale and hairless. But Emily wanted him too. She'd invited him to come here, against whatever her wedding vows might dictate.

They must have been working from a well-practiced script, as Emily dropped to her knees the second Rasul's hands went to his belt buckle. Jeremy's cock hardened further, from both apprehension and excitement. He was being offered a show, a better one than he could ever find on the internet some lonely evening. Sounds and scents and sights, live and vivid, three-dimensional. All for him. Or at least all for Emily. His body was begging but he held back the hand dying to cup his crotch, knowing that too required permission.

Rasul kicked his jeans away, standing before his kneeling wife in black briefs tented by his erection. Reaching down, he stroked Emily's hair and cheek, seeming to make her wait. With his other hand he touched the bulge in his underwear, fondling for half a minute before he pushed the band down and freed his cock.

A petty bit of Jeremy relaxed to see this man's dick wasn't as larger-than-life as his fearsome charisma.

Jeremy and Emily watched passively as Rasul stroked himself, a slow taunt testing Jeremy's threadbare patience. But something shifted as he waited, or clicked into place.

He and this intimidating man were a team tonight. United in a mission to blow Emily's mind. With that realization grounding him, Jeremy let go of any intimidation or jealousy or insecurity, quit measuring their dicks and chose to see Rasul as a partner, not a rival.

A murmured word from Emily drew Jeremy out of his head.

"Please."

Rasul replied with a faint and patronizing, "Shhhh."

She licked her lips and Jeremy's cock surged, eager to volunteer if her husband continued to deny her what she wanted.

Rasul looked to Jeremy. "You may sit."

He obeyed, taking a seat at the edge of the bed. Rasul stroked himself with a few more slow pulls, then his arm flexed, the hand on

Emily's head urging her closer. She shuffled forward on her knees, turning ever so slightly to give Jeremy a better view. Rasul pushed her hair back then gave the order.

"Taste me."

She brought her face close, seeming to breathe him in. He held himself still as her lower lip grazed his tip. Jeremy's cock screamed its impatience. Rasul drew his head across her lips several times then pushed inside as her mouth opened.

"Good," he muttered. Then he issued another order, words in a harsh tongue Jeremy couldn't translate. Clearly Emily could, however. She took her husband's cock deeper. Jeremy studied her hollowed cheeks and fantasized how it would feel if it were him she was sucking.

Then something ten thousand times more exciting happened—her eyes flashed to his.

He moaned without even meaning to. Could she be imagining the same act as him? Wondering what he'd taste like and how he'd feel? He kneaded his thighs, aching to masturbate. Aching for an order.

Before him, the scene grew harsher. Rasul's hand on Emily's head seemed to transform from guiding to commanding. Another inch of his thick cock disappeared between her lips, then another. Her breaths turned strained and nasal as her mouth met his belly. His arm tensed, as though he were holding her in place, and his hips began to pump. Jeremy supplied the sounds his host was so masterfully repressing—groans and grunts of disbelief and longing. He wanted Emily's hands on him as he pushed inside her mouth. Always such a contradiction, her misleading sweetness made him ache to defile her. *That's what she wants. That's what gets her off.*

"That's good," Rasul muttered. He released her, watching with smug approval as he slid from her flushed lips. His gaze snapped to Jeremy but he addressed his wife. "Do you want to see him now?"

She looked from man to man. "Yeah."

"Come here," Rasul ordered Jeremy.

He stood and stepped closer, pulse rushing with dark, primitive aggression as he and this other man loomed above her kneeling body. The pleasure of imagining such a scenario would normally have been diminished by the thought that, in real life, no rational woman would want to be treated so like a lesser person, a servant. A victim, even.

"Let her see."

Finally, Jeremy was allowed to touch himself. Now in the role of menacing male, he suppressed his moans as he rubbed a palm over his shrouded erection. Emily's gaze on his hand only deepened the pounding pressure between his legs.

"Show her."

The air of the room felt dry and cool as he pushed his shorts down. His head was already beading with pre-come, and his scent must be potent to her, heady with impatience and undermining his imitation of callous detachment. Out of necessity, Jeremy shifted his thoughts to the mundane—the color of the walls and carpet. He focused on those details as he began to masturbate; if he thought of what was happening he'd lose himself in a single stroke.

Rasul directed his wife's mouth back to his own cock, dragging Jeremy from the safety of pondering the decor. He slowed his hand but the need to come was excruciating.

"Let her hear you."

He let them both hear everything, including how near he was to breaking his promise to climax last. His gasps were rough and desperate, breaths raspy. "Fuck. I'm too close."

"Let go." Rasul's order was sharp and its meaning plain.

Jeremy released his cock, resigned to the screaming need pulsing up and down his body. He tugged his shorts up and over his erection, the light touch of the cotton nearly enough to wreck him.

"Sit."

Jeremy went back to the bed, trying hard to focus only on his breathing. All was silent. Emily released Rasul from her mouth and sat patiently on her heels as both men recuperated. After two minutes or more, Rasul broke the peace.

"Let's show him what you like."

CHAPTER EIGHT

EMILY WAS BURNING ALIVE inside her skin.

This evening was more than she'd expected it would be, and more than she'd even hoped for. Standing before her, her controlled and controlling husband—arousal given away only by his hard cock. To her side, Jeremy—more worked up than she'd known a man could get. Just about *suffering*, and from her. The high was intoxicating and it had everything to do with power, but she hid that feeling, always the way with Rasul. One was in charge, the other their slave, and as usual, their true roles didn't match appearances.

"Get up," he ordered.

She stood and was immediately drawn into his kisses. His mouth was always bossy, but tonight its aggression had a new edge, unmistakable. New eyes were on them, and on the stiff dick pressed to her soft belly, surely. Well, they'd show their guest that, and much more.

Rasul pulled away and slapped her hip. "Let him undress you."

She feared Jeremy might explode if she did as Rasul commanded, but she took the order nonetheless. She walked over and stood before him, leaving him room to stand. As he got to his feet, his tallness felt new again, as did his lighter skin, smooth chest, blue eyes. But his lack of self-possession was the biggest turn-on of all. She saw his hands shaking as he reached around her, felt his fingers trembling as he found the clasp of her bra. He got it open with only a few seconds' fumbling. Warm palms slid to her shoulders, pushing the straps down her arms. Emily let the garment fall between them, standing motionless as he studied her bare chest.

"Wow," he murmured.

She smiled at that. She liked her breasts. They weren't especially big, but they were a nice shape. She liked them even more as she watched Jeremy's lips part, corroborating his spoken awe.

She expected him to touch her, and doubtless earn an angry bark from Rasul for doing so without permission. But Jeremy was good, a natural at this role. His eyes drank their fill but his hands obediently moved on to complete their assignment. Sliding his thumbs into the straps at the sides of her bikini briefs, he eased them over her hips, their faces coming close as he bent to push them down her thighs. He straightened and they held each other's gaze, Jeremy surely dying of curiosity over the next order, just as she was. Then her attention jumped to the mirror, her make-believe third. Unneeded tonight. Their witness was the real deal, and she prayed he'd be allowed to do more than merely watch.

Rasul moved, walking to the vanity and pulling out its chair. He set it beside the corner of the mattress and nodded curtly. Jeremy took the directive, sitting.

"On the bed," Rasul said to Emily. "The edge."

She sat, keeping her legs together. Rasul corrected that swiftly. He stepped close and pushed her thighs wide with his knees. She eyed his cock, half veiled behind his underwear, but he surprised her. He dropped to his knees before the bed and clamped a strong hand beneath each of her thighs. She draped them over his shoulders, studying his stern, handsome face as his mouth came close.

This was a rare moment when the two of them appeared on the outside as they truly were—spoiled wife, husband so eager to please. She stroked the faint stubble of his shaved head, and traced his ears with her fingertips as he took in her scent. She glanced at Jeremy, mere feet away, their eyes locking a split second before Rasul's tongue lapped her clit and she lost her mind.

"Baby." Her eyes closed and she concentrated on those first few slippery caresses, quenching after the crazy-making teases of the past ten minutes. When she opened them again she found Jeremy's gaze glued to her face. She stroked her husband's head as she stared at their guest, hoping her look said what she wished she could tell him telepathically. *I want this to be you, before the night's over.* She wanted many things. The cock he'd shown her, for one. His eyes, his mouth, his excitement. His voice. She replayed the sounds of his moans in her head, praying she'd hear them again as he slid inside her.

As Rasul brought the pleasure, fantasies flashed across her mind. Both men at once, perhaps Rasul taking her from behind, Jeremy in her mouth. Perhaps something more ambitious still, some ingenious order Rasul had at the ready, one she'd never have thought up herself. She let the guessing go and melted against the motions of his tongue, leaning back, luxuriating.

Rasul changed his technique. He brought one hand around her thigh and placed his palm on her mound, thumb stroking her slick clit. His mouth slipped lower, tongue delving deep.

She hummed her approval, and for a moment she imagined this foreign caress was Jeremy's. In her mind, she swapped Rasul's black eyes for blue ones, switching which man was serving her and which was watching. She longed to hear what orders her husband might issue. Maybe the practiced fingers strumming her clit would before long be tangled in Jeremy's hair, forcing his face closer against her pussy.

The fantasy hijacked her mouth. "Want to feel what he's like," she muttered.

Rasul let her legs go without hesitation, as though he'd been waiting for just such a request. He bade her to stand and took a seat on the bed himself before drawing her back down to sit between his spread legs. She felt his rock-hard erection at the small of her back and glanced at Jeremy's bulge.

"Give her what she wants," Rasul said coldly.

Jeremy made it slowly to the carpet before Emily. She propped one thigh over Rasul's to open herself wider. As Jeremy studied her, she reached down to touch his hair, his sideburn, his eyebrow. All so different, as different as his mouth would feel, surely.

"Please," she murmured.

"Taste her."

Jeremy answered both the plea and the demand with a soft press of his lips to her clit. His stubble was surely just a couple of days' worth, but after years with Rasul and his daily straight-razor shaves, the scruff above Jeremy's lip felt foreign and thrilling. It prickled against her sensitive skin as he tasted her folds. She fisted his hair. Rasul's hand came around to rest atop hers, pushing it and Jeremy's mouth closer.

"Deeper," he ordered.

She sighed as Jeremy's tongue slid inside her. He did indeed feel different. Unsure but eager.

Rasul's voice in her ear was low and rough. "Tell me what you want tonight."

"I want him. More than just his mouth."

"He gets nothing until he's watched me enjoy it."

She nodded. "Of course."

"I'll show him how it's done. I'll remind you how well I know you, before you let some clumsy stranger inside my territory."

Shit, that one sent blood pounding all over her body—cheeks, lips, pussy, toes. *Stranger. Territory.*

"He's not as big as me," Rasul said. It was a new game, this rude and blatant objectification of their guest. She liked it, and she could tell from the intensifying strokes of Jeremy's tongue that he wasn't opposed.

"I like his cock," Emily countered.

"He won't fuck you as well as I can."

"He doesn't have to. He only has to fuck me as well as *he* can."

Rasul's hand moved to fist Jeremy's hair. "You hear that? My wife wants you to fuck her tonight."

A muffled sound came as Jeremy's answer, a noise full of excitement that brought a fever to Emily's skin.

Rasul gave Jeremy's head a tiny shake. "You'll do as she wants, and you'll do it the way I tell you to. Answer me." He tugged Jeremy's hair, drawing his face back an inch.

"Yes."

"Yes what? What will you do?"

"I'll fuck her however you tell me to."

"Good." Rasul released Jeremy's hair, and their guest's mouth returned to its duties, more hesitant than before.

Emily shivered as Rasul's broad hands slid beneath her arms and stroked her breasts. He grazed his palms over her nipples, the pleasure pulsing between her legs flashing hot through the rest of her body, connecting her.

"Baby."

Warm, hard flesh against her back, wet, firm tongue against her clit…sinful or not, this was what heaven ought to be. An errant thought crossed her mind, the disapproving faces of everyone who'd gotten down on her for her reputation as a teenager. *If they could see me now.* If her mother could—all that nonsense about kissing her sexual pleasure goodbye when she married Rasul.

Then she shoved the intruders from her consciousness and focused on reality. This experience might come but once in her lifetime, and she shouldn't lose another second to such wasteful thoughts.

"He's good?" Rasul asked, mouth just behind her ear.

"He is. He's different," she added, and stroked Jeremy's hair.

He *was* different. When Rasul did this to her, his mouth was controlled and precise, every caress designed to edge her toward orgasm. Jeremy was needier…thirstier. It felt as though he were getting as much pleasure from this as she was, and unlike Rasul, his pleasure was tied up in the act itself, not its power dynamics. Everything about him was softer. His hair and expression and approach and voice, the motions of his tongue against her pussy. All at once, she longed to reward him.

"I want to come," she murmured, unsure what reply to expect.

Rasul kneaded her breasts for a few moments before he spoke. "You think he can make you come better than I can?"

"Not better. Just different."

"He can't have that. Not yet."

Her body cooled only the slightest bit.

"He can't have that unless he shares it with me," Rasul added. One of the hands stroking her breasts slid down her belly, his first two fingers finding her clit, forcing Jeremy's mouth lower.

Emily gave a soundless gasp, at the pleasure as well as the thought. Rasul's free arm locked around Emily's torso, locking her own arms in place. The sensation filled her with a familiar, scary, beautiful sensation—helplessness. Rasul rubbed her the way he was so trained at. Jeremy gave her folds deep strokes with his tongue and she could see his nose glance Rasul's knuckles, such an odd little bit of contact for these men to share. She studied his expression, wishing she could reach down and touch his face or hair. His eyes were closed, brows pinched tight in excitement or agony or apprehension.

"You enjoyin' yourself?" she asked him quietly. "Jeremy?"

He freed his mouth and opened his eyes. Forming a reply seemed a challenge. "Yes," he said simply.

She smiled down at him. "Good. You feel wonderful."

He put his mouth back to her pussy but his eyes opened every once in a while, flashing that unfamiliar blue up at her. She imagined him on top of her, their faces close, his eyes and breath and noises as his body worked to give both of them pleasure. She prayed he'd be allowed to climax inside her so she could watch his face as he came. She'd memorize whatever his expression would be, and imagine it on quiet nights when he sat across the bar from her at work. The contrast—Jeremy her acquaintance and Jeremy her lover—brought the experience to a new level. She could feel the orgasm building against his mouth and Rasul's fingers.

"You're close," Rasul said. He always knew. Something in the pitch of her breathing, the twitching of her thighs.

"I am."

His fingers rubbed her in a small circle. He released her pinned arms to fist Jeremy's hair once again. "Let her hear you."

Muffled groans rose from between her legs as Jeremy gave voice to his excitement. At the small of her back she felt Rasul's hips faintly stroking his cock against her. Two strong men, frantic with need, all her doing and hers to enjoy. The idea tipped her over into release.

The orgasm was sharp and deep, blinding but brief, and Jeremy's moans amplified the sensations. She held his face close, clasped her other hand around Rasul's wrist, begging him to stop as the pleasure became too intense. Her body dropped from rigid to slack and she leaned into him as the frenzy of pleasure trickled away, contentedness settling in its place.

"Wow," she mumbled. When Jeremy leaned back she moved her leg off Rasul's, flexing her toes. Brimming with gratitude, she combed her fingers through Jeremy's hair and offered him a warm and likely goofy grin. "Thank you."

His own smile wasn't so goofy—genuine but tight with what must now be a painful need to come.

"Let me up?" she asked.

Jeremy stood and she made it to her feet, pleased by the clumsiness the orgasm had left in her limbs. "I'm gonna grab a glass of water," she announced, and padded to the bathroom, leaving the men to whatever strange energy they were surely sharing. She filled a tumbler and brought it back. After a long drink she offered it to the men. Rasul declined but Jeremy accepted, seeming eager for a distraction of any sort. Emily studied his briefs and the outline of his erection as he drank. The gray cotton bore a dark, damp spot, more evidence that his pleasure was real. And likely maddening. She couldn't make him suffer this way for the rest of the evening. She looked to Rasul.

"I think our guest may need some relief. If we intend tonight's fun to go on for some time." Which she most certainly did.

Rasul's face was stony, but not mean. "I told him he comes last."

She pursed her lips and looked to Jeremy, still addressing her husband. "I think that may be cruel. Maybe he could be the last to…you know. Come inside me." She was dying herself for a notion of whether such a thing was on the table.

Rasul looked thoughtful. "What do you wish to offer him now?"

"That's up to you. But the poor boy's about to have a heart attack. Am I right?" she asked Jeremy.

He nodded, eyes glazed. "Yeah, kind of."

"And we can't have that," she said, turning back to Rasul. "What kind of hostess would that make me?"

Rasul stared at Jeremy a long time before he tendered his decision. "Fine. Get back in that chair."

CHAPTER NINE

JEREMY DID AS HE WAS TOLD, cock screaming for attention. His breathing was shallow and raspy, head cloudy. He hadn't been this wound up from lust in ages, and it felt like insanity descending. He could taste Emily on his lips, smell her on his skin. Rasul's voice snapped him into reality.

"You may touch yourself."

Jeremy didn't obey right away, unsure how he felt having the two of them watching. But as it turned out, he wasn't the show—he was the audience.

With a pointed glance at his wife, Rasul nodded to the center of the bed. This must have meant something to Emily, and she scooted back, lying in profile to Jeremy. Rasul stood only long enough to shove his underwear down his legs then he climbed onto the bed, spreading his knees wide between Emily's.

Jeremy had never watched a couple fuck, live and in person, but holy hell it was a thousand times sexier than the hottest porn he'd ever seen. Rasul braced his arms on either side of Emily's chest and lowered his hips. He looked impossibly tan and big and brutal atop her soft paleness. She reached her hand between them to guide his cock to her pussy. Both pairs of eyes shut as he pushed inside.

Jeremy licked his lips, knowing exactly how wet and warm she must feel. He watched them for a minute or more, the slow, methodical thrusts of Rasul's hips, the bounce of Emily's breasts. The insanity descended once again and Jeremy surrendered, shoving his shorts down to free his cock.

As he clasped himself, the pleasure was a five-hundred-volt shock. His groan drew Emily's eyes open, drew her gaze to his face then his dick. He wanted very suddenly to please her, and that meant lasting longer than three strokes. Fucking hell, she was right about his impending heart attack. He blew out a long breath, mustering control. After a few more steadying exhalations he ran his fist up, then back down, glacially slow to keep from losing it.

Emily's hands rose to Rasul's ribs and Jeremy could tell from the way her fingertips pressed into his flesh that it was no gentle caress. Yet another unspoken signal, as Rasul's body sped, thrusts as precise as before but faster and rougher. Still, it was Jeremy's cock that held Emily's gaze.

He stood just enough to push his shorts down his legs, then spread his thighs wider as he fisted himself. The way her lips parted and her cheeks flushed told Jeremy her attention—her pleasure—was centered a hundred percent on him. The thought had his hand tightening as he stroked himself. He couldn't put the orgasm off much longer. He watched Rasul's pounding hips and matched the tempo with his hand, imagining it was him fucking her. He paused to spit in his palm, adding the wetness, intensifying the fantasy. He imagined her face so close to his and her skin against him. A groan rose and rattled from his chest and he let her hear it.

Rasul finally turned to look at Jeremy, his hard, dark stare dialing back the pleasure.

"I get this any night I want it," he said, eyes narrowing.

Jeremy nodded.

"Perhaps later tonight, I'll let you have it too. Just this once."

Jeremy grunted his desperate approval and the pleasure surged back to its peak once more. He imagined if he were allowed such a thing, would it only be after Rasul had come inside her? The fact that such a nasty caveat only deepened his arousal left Jeremy panting. Dishonored guest, that's what he was. Allowed to watch this other man enjoy a feast while he prayed for scraps. Dishonor felt good though. It felt dirty and dark and perfect, considering he was really only spared the label of "intruder" by the thinnest shell of semantics and kink.

Rasul moved, grasping Emily's hips and turning them both over. She leaned back to straddle him upright. She watched Jeremy's hand for several breaths before she began to move, undulating her body atop her husband's. Rasul put his hands to her thighs, kneading, his gaze on her inattentive face.

"Fuck me how you wish to fuck him," he ordered.

Emily's eyes closed and she faced forward. Jeremy watched her butt and hips as she rode Rasul, knowing for sure this time she was imagining something else. Imagining *him*. Pretending that was his cock moving inside her, stroking her clit, his flesh exciting her. His release was edging close, and fast. The hot tension bubbled deep in his belly, pleasure streaking up his shaft as he jerked himself tightly. He pressed hard with his thumb, how he imagined it would feel were it her pussy stroking him, drawing him in then easing away, again and again.

"Oh." He shut his eyes, giving in.

Emily's sweet voice drew him ever closer to the brink. "Good."

He fantasized he had what Rasul did—his bare cock inside her. It had been ages since he'd enjoyed that with any woman and he craved that selfish, possessive privilege, to release inside her.

As though watching the same explicit, private footage he was, Emily said, "Come for me."

He obeyed that order like none other. His fist sped for a final flurry of beats and he lost it. He opened his eyes only wide enough to stare at her face as he came, and he let every last horny, undignified thing he felt tumble from his mouth in grunts and moans and rasping breaths. Warmth met his stomach and knuckles and he stroked still, not stopping until he was sure he'd shown her everything he had to give.

* * *

AFTER JEREMY LOST HIS MIND, Emily and Rasul slowed then stopped their lovemaking. She knew Rasul must be aching to keep going, but as always you couldn't tell by looking at him. Only the sheen on his flushed faced gave away his exertion and desire.

But who knew what Jeremy might feel in the wake of his release. It might be unnerving to regain one's sanity to find your hosts still fucking. Emily wasn't done with their guest yet, and she hoped a gentle descent from whatever he was experiencing would mean he'd stay for an encore.

Rasul patted her thigh and she obeyed, climbing off him to lean against the headboard, crossing her legs at the ankle.

"I'll be back," Rasul said. He grabbed his underwear as he left the room, and though Emily had no idea where exactly he was headed, she knew why he'd left. She caught Jeremy's eye and patted the rumpled comforter beside her.

Jeremy cleaned himself with a couple of tissues from the nightstand and pulled his shorts up his legs, pretty dignified, considering. His chest still rose and fell with fast, deep breaths as he sat at the edge of the bed. Knowing her job was to make him feel included after the voyeurism—a participant again instead of a prop or audience—she stroked his arm and offered him a smile.

"Very nice," she said.

He'd been staring blankly at the far wall, but now his gaze shifted to her face. "Was it?"

She nodded. "Very. Not sure exactly what kind of pervert that makes me, but that was... Well, you're very sexy when you're all worked up."

"That was beyond worked up."

She laughed. "Here, sit by me." She patted the spot again.

Jeremy joined her in leaning against the headboard, legs stretched before him, and they both gazed ahead at their reflections in the vanity mirror. With Rasul gone, she imagined this was how it might feel if she and Jeremy had one day stumbled into each other's lives under less complicated circumstances. They looked nice together, on this bed. She reached a hand down and interlaced her fingers with his.

"Wonder if this might've happened, if I'd never met my husband," she said.

"Maybe."

They stared at themselves a bit longer, and Emily decided that even if they had wound up in a relationship, it wouldn't have lasted. She'd dated guys like Jeremy—perfectly nice, attractive, charming men—but they weren't her type. She hadn't known her type until the moment Rasul had kissed her, until she'd felt that powerful body pressed to hers and been utterly enveloped in the safety it offered. So no. Jeremy would've been a fun fling, lasting as long as it took him to realize their ambitions clashed or for her to accept she simply wasn't one of those girls who wanted to marry their best friend.

"Where'd he go?" Jeremy asked.

"I'm not sure. But I think he wanted to give you some space to come down from everything. You know, to decide if you want to stick around for round two, without the pressure of having him in the room. And to recover."

Jeremy nodded.

"What do you think?" She nudged him gently with her elbow and squeezed his hand. "You up for more?"

"Is that what you want?"

"Of course it's what *I* want. But you have to want it too."

"I'm still here to give you your dream evening with two guys." Jeremy gave a small laugh. "Actually, I messed up already, losing it before I was allowed to. Sorry."

She thumped their hands against his thigh. "Don't be silly. Or sorry. You're human. We didn't invite you here to be a robot. Only Rasul can perform like that. I wouldn't expect anyone else to have that much self-control."

"He, um... He's a really surprising person," Jeremy said, lowering his voice as though the man in question might be standing just outside the door. "I don't know a ton about where he's from, but from what I understand, he doesn't fit the stereotypes."

She stared at their feet. "No, he doesn't... He said I changed all that, but I don't know. It's not like I ever made a project of stripping away all those years he spent over there, surrounded by all the patriarchy and everything else the culture dictates. I mean, he's got uncles with multiple wives." She smiled, realizing anew exactly how much of a rebel her husband was. She was surrounded by evidence of that right now—the scent and heat of two male bodies. "Rasul sort of—no, not sort of. He hates men. He doesn't talk about it much, but he definitely does. I think that makes him feel like women must be the opposite of that, and he wants to protect and please women. He's very close with his mother and sister."

"If he hates men in general, what's he going to do to *me* when this night is all over?"

"He hates pushy, selfish men. Men like the one he was probably destined to become if he'd stayed where he grew up. I won't go into it, but his dad died when he was pretty young, and some bad stuff happened to his mom and sister after. Bad stuff happens to lots of the women there. I think he sort of hates his dad, in a way, for 'leaving' them. And he hates the other men for obvious reasons. Probably hates himself for not being able to do much, but he was only a little kid."

"Is that why he's so tough now?"

"Partly. But also, the army did some of that to him. A lot, probably."

"Did his mom and sister come over after him?"

She shook her head. "He still wants to bring them here, but his sister's married and his mom won't leave, because she has grandchildren there now. Everything's there, except Rasul. And me, the daughter-in-law I'm sure she doesn't approve of."

Jeremy looked thoughtful for a while before asking, "So what about you?"

"What about me?"

He studied her in their reflection and she returned the curiosity.

Jeremy gave her foot a couple of playful pushes with his ankle. "Well, I know why your husband let me come here tonight," he said. "Because he wants to be the one who can give you whatever you want. But what about you? I'm sure you're not the only woman who fantasizes about two guys, but you're definitely the only one I've met who actually made it a reality."

She frowned. "Gosh, I'm not sure. I bet it has something to do with never having met my dad. That's what a shrink would say, right?

I never had a male role model—not a nice one, anyhow—and now I've gone all greedy, wanting more than one man in my bed. Or some bull like that. But I dunno. I just like the idea, and now the reality of it. I'm sure it's selfish, but I like the idea of two men wanting me. Using me, I guess. I like that feeling with Rasul, and having another guy just multiplies everything sort of... *bad* about it. I got a really lousy reputation when I was a teenager, for going with boys. I'm done feeling ashamed. Like, so much that I want to embrace it, you know? Does that make sense?"

"Sure. Makes as much sense as however a shrink might explain it."

She grinned. "People around here make such a hobby out of analyzing themselves. I listen to them every night at the bar, telling each other about how mysterious and complex their brains are. Their psychiatrists said they can't commit because their mother didn't hug them when they fell off their bike." She shook her head. "I guess it makes them feel better, making up some story to explain their problems. I just figure, we've all got issues. It's better to try to accept them and work at being a better person, instead of makin' yourself into a religion."

"I'm with you there. My clients do that too, compartmentalizing every last aspect of themselves, like it'll make them feel less...less of whatever they feel. If they just do X, Y and Z and assign blame for their shortcomings, they'll be happy. But most of them don't seem all that happy."

"Are you happy?" Emily asked, meeting Jeremy's gaze at her side, not in the mirror for a change.

"Um, here and there. And now that I'm about to start traveling, I'm excited, which I haven't honestly felt in a long time. I don't think anybody's ever really, truly happy all the time. But having something to look forward to definitely keeps me positive." His mouth opened and closed for a few seconds before he committed to adding,

"Looking forward to hanging out with you at the bar certainly puts me in a decent mood on Tuesdays and Thursdays."

She blushed at that and gave his hand another squeeze.

"Are *you* happy?" he asked.

"Oh gosh, yeah."

"Figures," he teased. "You're easily the sunshiniest person I've ever met."

"Well, some of that's an act. I was taught not to show it when I'm feeling sad or angry. But yeah, I've always been pretty optimistic. Not sure why, since I didn't have the greatest childhood. But since I moved here especially, I'm happy most of the time."

"That's a pretty rare admission."

"I know I haven't done much of anything except cross three state lines and get married, but I really like my life, more and more as I get older. I haven't figured it all out yet, but every year or so, there's something exciting happening. Rasul, or a new home, or nursing school, or kids, eventually... There's enough good changes happening to me that life seems pretty great. I don't think you have to be some huge somebody to be a success. You only have to keep getting better as life goes on."

"Is it ever tough, reminding yourself of that when you live in a place like this, where everyone's such an outrageously high achiever?"

"Um, no. I'll never be like them—I'm not built for that kind of life. They're some other species. I'm okay just being me."

Jeremy smiled at that and they fell silent for a minute or more.

"He'll probably be up soon," Emily murmured. "You think you're comfortable sticking around for more?"

Their eyes locked in the reflection again and he nodded. "Sure. Weirdest fucking date I've ever been on, but yeah. Sign me up for round two."

CHAPTER TEN

AFTER PERHAPS TWENTY MINUTES, Rasul decided Jeremy's departure wasn't forthcoming and he abandoned the dark quiet of the den. As he passed the front door, he wondered why the deadbolt wasn't calling to him. Why on earth would tonight of all nights not fill him with unmanageable insecurity? How could the thought of a contractor entering their home cripple him, yet an acquaintance alone with Emily in their bed somehow be acceptable? Even calming?

He went back, touching the knob, testing himself. Nothing.

Then the difference struck him.

A contractor or plumber or police officer coming to the house meant Rasul had to admit he needed another man—that there was a job that needed doing he couldn't do himself. Weirdly enough, inviting Jeremy here was more akin to renting a floor sander. Rasul was still the man in charge, getting the job done. He smirked at this self-analytical epiphany and shook his head, knowing another chunk of his old culture had just been gobbled up by his ever-growing Westernism. He let the doorknob be. Time to head upstairs and resume responsibility for Emily's pleasure, a worthy project only he could supervise.

As he pushed the bedroom door in, he felt a jealous twinge to find his wife hand in hand with her guest on their bed. It would've been unnatural not to feel such a pang, so he merely acknowledged it and let it go.

"You're staying?" he asked Jeremy.

The man nodded.

Emily released his hand and shifted to sit on her heels, attentive. Surely just what she wanted…two willing men partially clothed, her naked, the room abuzz with the promise of yet-to-be-articulated scenarios and orders.

Rasul's body had thoroughly cooled during his absence, but desire stirred at the hungry glimmer in his wife's eyes. She might hold this other man's hand for a few minutes, but it was Rasul who held her body tight to his each night. It was he who'd given this fantasy to her. Another man with his background might think it repugnant even to stoop to pleasuring one's wife with one's mouth. To allow her to openly lust for another man and to invite that man here to enjoy her body… Rasul ought to be stoned. Except he cared nothing now for the values he'd been taught. He cared only about this woman and making sure she wanted for nothing, every wish granted by his hand. *Control freak.*

He looked to Jeremy. *Floor sander.*

He addressed the man, keeping his voice hard, accusing. "You liked watching?"

A dip of Jeremy's chin and a quiet, "Yes."

Rasul turned to Emily. "You still want him?"

"Yeah."

"Spread your legs," he said to Jeremy.

With a nervous glance at Emily, Jeremy obeyed.

"Kneel in front of him," Rasul told her.

Emily nodded, slipping into obedience mode. She settled between Jeremy's calves and Rasul walked to the side of the bed.

"You want to touch him?"

She nodded again.

Rasul aimed a directive gaze at Jeremy and she scooted closer. She touched his belly first, then his chest. She stroked his thighs and hips, then slowly slid a hand between his legs to cup him. Their guest's expression shifted, from hesitance to surrender.

"Enjoy him." *Wallow*, Rasul thought. *Take this opportunity to be what everyone accused you of when you were young, and revel in it.* It warmed him with both lust and a tiny sliver of anger. He knew better than anyone the past couldn't be fixed, not even through vengeance and restitution, but he'd dedicate the rest of his life to making sure this woman collected as few new regrets as possible.

As Emily made her slow exploration, the muscles in Jeremy's arms flexed, his hands fisting the bedspread. His cock stiffened, filling his shorts, surely begging to be touched with more than the gentle caresses Emily was giving. Fine. Let him suffer.

Rasul stepped close to stroke his wife's hair. "What do you want with him?"

She glanced up, biting her lip as she pondered the question. "I want whatever you want."

He liked that answer, knowing much of her pleasure stemmed from his taking charge. He turned to Jeremy. "Show her."

Obediently, he pushed his shorts down enough to free his erection. Emily continued to fondle his balls through the cotton, hungry eyes on the cock she'd been gifted for this extraordinary evening.

"Let her watch you," Rasul said.

Jeremy stroked himself, slow and light, surely afraid of disobeying yet again that directive he'd been issued.

"And don't forget, you come last," Rasul added, just to be sadistic. He cupped a hand over his own cock, rubbing until the chaotic emotions coursing through his body coalesced, turning wholly to lust. Emily's gaze jumped between the two men's hands, and her lips were flushed and parted, always a giveaway.

"You want to taste him."

"Yeah," she said softly.

"Do you want that too?" he asked Jeremy.

The man's eyes flickered shut. "Yeah."

"You give your guest what he wants."

Emily nodded then leaned in close, resting on one elbow as her other hand wrapped around this near-stranger's cock. Rasul moved closer as well, touching her soft hair once more as he stroked himself through his briefs.

"Does he smell different than me?"

She nodded.

"Does he taste different?"

A loaded, breathy hum escaped her lips, just before she brought them down to graze Jeremy's head.

Such a strange sight... The lust wavered and Rasul felt disembodied, fumbling for a handful of breaths to recognize her or this room or himself, letting this happen. An unfamiliar man's groans rising from their bed. Wrong but somehow fascinating. He was tossed in a sea of conflicting instincts. Jealousy and fear hovered at the surface, but they were shallow. Deeper and more intense were less expected feelings, desire and surprise, but deepest of all, pride. This woman, with her needs and wants and courage, was his, and this scary thing she wanted so much, he was offering it to her. The cock she was sucking might as well be his. He'd given her this.

"You like this gift I've let you enjoy?" he murmured.

She eased her mouth from Jeremy to meet Rasul's eyes. "Very much."

"Good. You deserve it."

He wanted her to have no doubt that she was allowed to enjoy all of this, but enough tenderness, he decided.

He shoved his underwear down and got to his knees behind her on the mattress. Sliding two fingers inside her pussy, he suppressed a groan of his own. He wished he knew better how *not* to suppress such things, but she'd trained so many other habits out of him, surely that one would follow, one day. For now, she could enjoy the sounds of Jeremy's suffering.

He held her hip tightly and guided himself to her lips with the other hand. Fuck, so warm. Still wet from what had gone on before, from two men. He slid inside deep and fast, but held her still so as not to disrupt what she was doing to Jeremy. The time for reassurance and awe had past. Now he'd be the maestro and make this man into Emily's every fantasy.

* * *

"HOLD HER HAIR."

Before Jeremy even obeyed, Rasul's order had Emily's desire spiking. She felt uncertain fingers tangle in her long hair.

"Rough."

She gasped around Jeremy's cock as he did as commanded, that callous tug shifting everything that was happening. Rasul held her in place with an iron grip, not allowing her hips to jolt even as his thrusts turned aggressive. A hot haze fell over her, a lust that felt like drunkenness.

"Guide her."

The pleasure spiked again as Jeremy urged her to take him deeper. He moaned, the needy sound giving Emily chills. She imagined his view, if he had his eyes open. Surely an intimidating sight, watching Rasul fuck while he was in barbarian mode, but Jeremy stayed hard as sin in her mouth. She hadn't done this with a new man since…well, since Rasul had been new. Back when he'd been all hesitance with her, viewing every mildly creative sex act as degrading to one or both of them. Thank goodness she'd converted him on all those notions. She was no angel and she didn't want to be treated like one.

Jeremy tasted different. Slightly sweeter, she thought—very fitting. He was easier to suck, not as thick as her husband. Circumcised as well, and just generally more…American-feeling. Curiously nostalgic and wholesome. His uncertainty made her recall the misadventures of her youth, fumbling around on couches and in backseats, figuring out what sex was supposed to feel like. The sensation made her long for the mirror, to see Rasul with all his differences again, dark eyes and skin, self-control. She pulled her head back and Jeremy released her hair. She freed her mouth and turned to Rasul to mutter, "I want to see you."

"Do you?" came the cold reply. Rasul took her hard and fast for a dozen beats, rough enough for his skin to smack hers with each thrust. "It's not enough I let you have two men, you want to see us both as well?"

"Yeah," she huffed, voice stilted by the impact.

"Spoiled." Mean or not, there was a fondest in his tone. "Very well. In fact, I'll give you more than that."

He pulled out and slapped her hip, a signal she knew well. She turned over, heart thumping with curiosity, just a taste of apprehension.

Rasul moved to the end of the bed and grabbed her ankles, pulling her to the edge and letting her legs dangle over the side. Being yanked across the covers made her back burn from the friction, her breath knocked out from the surprise. As she sat up, he seemed tall and dark and new to her, exactly as she'd hoped. She ached for an order to touch his hovering cock, still glistening from her.

"You," he barked at Jeremy. "Get a condom on." He nodded to where Emily knew the box to be waiting on the bedside table. She felt Jeremy's weight shifting the mattress behind her and the room went dim for a few moments as his body blocked the low lamp light. Her breath turned short at the thought that she was about to get her most selfish wish—the two of them. Taking turns, maybe, watching her from so close by, both looming above, making her feel small. She looked at Rasul's face, his eyes on whatever Jeremy was up to behind her.

"Come here," Rasul said.

The light returned as Jeremy rounded the bed, standing before Emily. She admired his bare body beside Rasul's more familiar one, a shiver rushing through her and making the room feel cold.

"Stroke," Rasul ordered.

Both men took their cocks in hand and another shiver chilled Emily. Unless she craned her neck to look at their faces, there was an anonymity to these bodies. Two ominous, strong men, biding their time, hungry to use her. This was her fantasy, this very moment. Rasul reached out his free hand to palm her breast, spreading warmth through her middle.

He stepped between her legs, knocking them wider with his knees. Their bed was high and he barely had to stoop to bring his erection level with her pussy. Pleasure zapped her as he stroked her lips and clit with the head of his cock. Again, that drunken feeling, leaving her breathless and dim-witted. She raised her chin to gaze at Jeremy, finding his mouth open, eyes lust-glazed.

The forceful push of Rasul's cock drew her attention between them. She loved this view, his dark length disappearing inside her, stomach muscles flexing. She touched his abdomen as he went deeper.

"Come closer," he ordered Jeremy.

He did as he was told, the men's hips nearly touching—a wall of masculine energy that intimidated and aroused her equally.

"Keep stroking."

Jeremy's hand intensified from slow, grazing caresses to rougher pulls. The smell of latex reinforced the unlikely nostalgia of the atmosphere, and all the differences between who these two men were to her.

"Let her hear you," Rasul murmured, sounding uncharacteristically distracted. Emily glanced up to catch his eye and there it was, that look. A glimmer of helplessness like she saw there just before he came. Somehow, that hint of vulnerability thrilled her more than the perfection of his usual tough-guy act.

Jeremy did as he was told, and the soft groans and sighs he made in time with his strokes raised the heat and tension in Emily's body.

"You want her?" Rasul asked, the bite back in his voice.

"Yes."

After a dozen rough thrusts, Rasul pulled away. He stepped just next to Emily's knee and Jeremy took the hint, moving into position between her thighs. She gasped softly as Rasul put his hand to the back of Jeremy's neck, as one might hold a dog while commanding it to stay. Jeremy froze.

Don't rush, she wanted to beg. This might be the only chance she'd get to feel another man push inside her, and she wanted to savor it.

"Slowly," Rasul ordered, giving voice to her unspoken plea.

Jeremy was beyond obedient. He stared down at her a long time, masturbating once more, breathing deeply. It was impossible to know if this was the tease of a cruel lover or the hesitance of a man on the verge of throwing himself from a cliff. Finally, Jeremy bent his knees and brought his cock close, close enough to trace her swollen lips with his sheathed head.

"Jeremy."

A tiny groan, then, "Emily."

With the gentlest flex of his hips, he pushed inside, if barely. Her hands flew to his ribs and his warm palms cupped her shoulders. Another thrust and she welcomed him deeper, another inch, another thrust, until he was all the way in, so close their bellies touched. She looked up, and the sight of her husband's hand still clamped to Jeremy's neck made her dizzy.

"Tell me how to be," he whispered.

When Rasul didn't reply, Emily realized the question was hers to answer. "You've thought about me before? Being with me this way?"

"Yes."

"Then be however you imagined. Be whatever way you are in your fantasies."

Above her, in her periphery, she sensed Jeremy looking to Rasul. The latter man's hand fell away and whatever exchange their faces made gave Jeremy the permission to say, "Lie back on the bed."

He pulled out and Emily scooted back to lie down with her head against the pillows. Jeremy followed, crawling until his body was above hers and his thighs pushed hers wide.

He took her in a way she hadn't anticipated—fast and confident.

Their faces were level once more and he kissed her, messy and needy and wonderful. For a minute or two she got lost in him, and in this taste of an alternate dimension where he could perhaps have been her husband, or a man like him. Perhaps merely a fond one-night stand. She reveled in his newness, the fascinating imperfection of their union after years with a man who had her every nuance memorized and mastered.

A shadow passed over them as Rasul moved to the bedside, tight fist stroking his dark cock. The sight jolted her.

"Him," she said to Jeremy.

With a groan, he withdrew, moving to her side to let Rasul take over. Both men were humming with an energy that matched the exact pitch ringing through her own body. Rasul fucked her hard, lacking much of his usual self-possession. Above her, he let loose a deep, rumbling moan, the sexiest sound she'd ever heard him make. It seemed to signal danger, a nearing of his release. After only a minute—milliseconds for a man who could normally screw hard for an hour without tiring—he withdrew to kneel at her side.

"Fuck her," he said to Jeremy. His drill sergeant voice was back, but as shallow as she'd ever heard it.

Jeremy took over again, only given a moment to find his pace before Rasul shifted the tone once more. "Fuck her," he repeated. He put a hand on Jeremy's lower back, and all at once the man transformed.

Jeremy's grunts were harsh and his thrusts sped to match them— probably speeding to match whatever directives Rasul's hand was issuing. Emily hugged her thighs tight to his hips, welcoming him deeper. She stroked his sides to feel those muscles working.

"Good?" Rasul asked her.

She studied the smug look on her husband's face, loving it. "Good," she agreed.

Rasul moved his hand to Jeremy's head in a flash, grasping his hair. "You hear that? What my wife thinks of your fucking?"

"Good," Jeremy muttered, voice diminished by intimidation or arousal.

Rasul gave him a shake. "You think that's good enough for my wife?"

He shut his eyes. "No."

"I invite you here, let you enjoy her body, and all you can do is 'good'?"

"Sorry."

"Useless." Finally, he let go of Jeremy's head. "On your back."

Emily could hear in Jeremy's shallow breathing that he was nervous. Still, his cock stayed hard, and she mourned its loss as he pulled away to lie on his back as ordered.

"Fuck him."

Her limbs were shaking as she straddled Jeremy's hips, but he slid inside easily, nearly familiar. She leaned forward, bracing her hands beside his shoulders and adjusting the angle. The difference between his body and Rasul's felt starker in this position…narrower in the waist and trunk, smoother and cooler to the touch. But different was exciting. Different was the entire point of this evening.

"You feel nice," she told him quietly.

"I want to please you," he said, clearly meant for both of them to hear.

"Lemme find what I like then you follow my lead."

Jeremy shut his eyes and she realized, intimidated or not, he was as hard as he'd been before, who knew how close to the edge.

"Take him," Rasul said. "Use him."

She shivered at that. Normally she liked the idea of being the one who was used, but she could explore the reverse. She took his cock deep then drew herself off slowly. Jeremy sucked a pained breath through his nose. She felt the warm, familiar weight of Rasul's palm on her back, encouraging.

"You like your gift?"

"Yeah." She savored the slow sensation of Jeremy's penetration as she moved her hips. He began to mirror her movements, small thrusts punctuating the motions she dictated. Rasul's hands also followed the action, something sensual in the way he massaged her skin, something reverential. For two or more minutes Rasul let them find their way before asserting himself once again.

"Back up."

She eased herself from Jeremy's cock, walking her knees back an inch or two. Rasul relocated, pushing both her and Jeremy's legs wider as he knelt behind her. Clamping a hand to her shoulder, nearly hard enough to hurt, he rammed his cock inside. She gasped from the impact and the sudden change in their three-way dynamic. This aggression was something she'd not guessed Rasul might let their guest witness. He fucked her rough and fast, tugging at her shoulder to heighten the edge of fear this treatment always brought.

She looked down at Jeremy to find both his eyes and mouth open. His cock was still hard as steel, pressed against her navel. Her breasts glanced his smooth chest as Rasul's hand angled her lower, trapping her between two men, one bossy, one surely near to pleading. Her mouth and Jeremy's were mere inches apart, the distance feeling more intimate than a kiss. She wondered what he saw over her shoulder. A mercenary, or perhaps a cold, fearsome machine. Things she loved, and things she hoped Jeremy could bear to see. Still he stayed stiff.

"You see what she really likes?" As if to demonstrate, Rasul fucked her even rougher for a half-dozen thrusts.

"Yes."

"This is how she likes to be treated. You think you can do this?"

"I'm not—sure," Jeremy said between jolts, and Emily admired his honesty.

Rasul gripped her shoulder tight, his other hand taking hold of her waist and arching her back so she came upright again. She was dying to see her husband's face, but Jeremy's shocked expression was a fascinating replacement.

Then everything changed. Rasul pulled away, moving back on the bed and bringing Emily with him, dragging her until her legs were splayed before her, her butt against Rasul's knees and both of her upper arms locked in his grip.

"Fuck her."

Jeremy's eyes widened and moved to Emily's face. She craved to stay in victim mode, the role she liked best, but she broke character enough to nod at him, tendering the permission he clearly needed.

He moved close, edging his thighs beneath hers and pushing her butt up onto Rasul's knees. Jeremy angled his cock, and before he entered her he whispered, "You'll tell me if it's too much?"

"Of course." She offered him a little smile and watched his face relaxed. As he slid inside her the uncertainty disappeared, lust taking its place. She dissolved back into her fantasy, gasping as he pushed deep.

"Better," Rasul said, his dark voice behind her sounding so exquisitely like a stranger's.

Circuits seemed to connect inside her body, the ones that lit her up whenever Rasul indulged her darker desires. Her brain and body sizzled with white-hot excitement, adrenaline filling her with wicked pleasure.

"Harder," Rasul barked, her wishes spoken through him.

Jeremy obeyed and she could sense him getting into the part. The muscles in his arms and chest and stomach stood out as his entire body tensed, hips pumping hard. His face transformed enough for Emily to replace Jeremy her friend with a more selfish incarnation. But she held back the words she might say to Rasul—*don't, stop, please*—fearing that was too much to ask him to play along with. Instead she let him see how much pleasure she was taking from this, suppressing not a single sigh or gasp.

"Take her wrists," Rasul said.

Jeremy did as instructed, holding her hands tight to her thighs as he fucked. Rasul's palms slid down either side of her waist, stroking her belly before sliding up to her breasts. She felt his warm breath just behind her ear, then he moaned.

The noise was like a match struck deep inside her, growing to a blaze. He let her hear everything she ached for but rarely got from

him—groans and grunts and curses. He whispered low and scratchy
Arabic words, only bits and pieces she could translate. It didn't
matter what he was saying. It only mattered that her husband's voice
was the single sexiest thing there was, perfect, filthy evidence of the
pleasure he must be feeling.

She turned her head to whisper, "Baby."

"You like it?"

"Yeah."

"Good. Watch him fuck you."

She turned her attention back to Jeremy, his eyes barely open,
palms warm and slick now around her wrists. She looked between
them, to where his body was owning hers, and a feeling of deep,
warm, happy decadence filled her to the brim. She'd conjure this
moment when and if he next sat across the bar from her, their secret.

More foreign words caressed her ear, raspy and dark. She spoke in
turn to Jeremy, knowing how strange these two accents were
together. "You feel so good."

He broke character to pant, "I'm close."

Rasul's hand left her breast to pass over her belly, two fingers
grazing her clit, and surely Jeremy's driving shaft. The touch brought
focus to the pleasure whirling in her body, drawing it into a tight ball
of energy against her husband's fingertips.

She turned her head. "Talk to me."

Rasul leaned so close she felt his lips moving against her ear,
forming words whose meaning she could only guess at from his
ominous tone. For a minute she was held blissfully hostage between
Jeremy's demanding body, Rasul's practiced fingers and thrilling
voice. Then his lips left her ear to address their guest.

"Make her come."

More Emily's directive than Jeremy's. She nearly always waited for
Rasul's order before she climaxed, as he did hers. Now that she had
permission, the pleasure spread and grew, so pure it nearly hurt. She

watched Jeremy's cock, Rasul's fingers, listened to them both, smelled their skin and felt the warmth against her own. She tugged and Jeremy freed one of her hands. She clamped it to his hip to feel the racing thrusts, clawed his skin and groaned when he made the correct translation and took her harder.

"Jeremy."

She felt him coming apart, and that weakness was hotter than either man's impressive strength and stamina. Her climax came, owned equally by his cock and Rasul's caresses. Heat pooled and burst inside her, a spike of pleasure that lingered after it peaked, keeping her moaning and twitching between their bodies even once they each slowed. She felt proof of reality—Rasul's knees beneath her butt. Jeremy's cock inside her, one or both of them pulsing. She touched his face and offered a smile that was probably more cheesy than seductive, with her mind so thoroughly blown.

Rasul broke through her fog. "Come," he said to Jeremy.

Those blue eyes shifted beyond Emily's face. "Last, you told me—"

"Do as I say."

Jeremy released Emily's other hand and seemed to gather his wits before he began moving again. The post-release stupor left her as she watched his face, reading in his flushed lips and heavy lids how badly his cock must be aching for this.

"Inside me," she said.

He nodded.

She tried to guess what twisted aspects of this experience were surely darkening his pleasure—Rasul's eyes on him, their knees touching. The wrongness of enjoying another man's wife made acceptable by invitation.

"Fuck me," Emily whispered.

He took her harder and she hoped those two little words lodged in his brain, zapping him when their eyes locked across the bar.

Before her, against her, inside her, he came undone.

"Emily." Her name left him in a breathless huff as he grasped her waist, holding her immobile as he pumped his cock into her for the final time. He held her tightly through his release, shutting his eyes and not opening them again until his breathing slowed. She touched his face and ear, memorizing that shade of pink she'd brought to his skin.

"Perfect," she said.

Jeremy mustered a woozy smile and pulled away, sitting back on the covers. Rasul urged her from his lap and he too pulled away, though not to recover. He stood and beckoned her.

"Follow me," he said, already taking her wrist.

He led her down the carpeted hall to the guest bedroom. It still smelled faintly of paint, and of sawdust from the brand-new furniture. He closed the door quietly behind them, a gesture unmatched by his demanding body as he pushed her onto the bed. He was atop her in seconds, hips forcing her legs wide, cock sinking deep.

The room was dark and it felt unfamiliar, a perfect complement to Rasul's greedy thrusts. He hadn't fucked her like this in ages—not since they'd first begun exploring her kinks together, when the dynamic of that sex had driven him wild with its seeming wrongness. He took her fast, still letting her hear his sounds. She'd never known him to be this desperate for release, and it made her feel invincible. Running her palms up and down his back and sides, arms and ass, she soaked it up, this feeling of power.

"Come," she said.

He turned them onto their sides, moaning against her lips as he hammered into the homestretch and obeyed. Seizing her thigh, he held her hard against him as he came, the orgasm evidenced by his sudden silence and the three pangs as he ground his hips to hers.

"Good," she whispered.

His body relaxed, cock slipping from her as his arms circled her waist.

She realized then that of course he'd never let Jeremy see him come, or witness his post-climax haze. Surely no man had seen Rasul so unguarded and helpless since he was a child. Surely only Emily had been allowed that most intimate of things—evidence of his humanity. He relaxed against the never-before-slept-on bedspread, breaths growing longer and deeper.

She lay beside him and stroked his chest. "Beautiful."

"You go to him," he murmured.

"Are you staying in here?"

She saw him nod in the sliver of moonlight. "He's yours until the morning. No sex, but you may sleep with him if he wishes to stay. I'll be back from my workout no earlier than nine, but have him gone by then. Enjoy him before this is all over." There was no bitterness in these rules, only a presentation of facts.

"If you're sure."

He touched her hair, mussing it fondly. "I'm beyond sure. Go to him."

She kissed him first, lingering. "Thank you," she whispered. "For tonight."

"Thank you for every night, for the rest of my life."

CHAPTER ELEVEN

EMILY YELPED at a tap on her shoulder.

"Whoa, jumpy." It was only Danielle, wanting to pass behind her with an armload of empties.

Emily put a hand to her chest and laughed. "Sorry. Guess I'm a bit wound up." It was Tuesday once again, a good half-hour after she might normally expect to see Jeremy. And nearly three days after she'd hugged him goodbye on her front step, following a quiet breakfast for two while Rasul was out for his morning exercise.

"Good weekend?" Danielle asked, loading the dishwasher. "Do anything exciting while I was stuck here working?"

"Nothin' much." She touched her fingertips to her cross at the lie. Nothing special indeed. "You know Jeremy?" She nodded to the spot where he most often sat.

"Of course."

"He came over for dinner on Saturday, like we'd talked about. Sure hope he shows up tonight so I'll know I didn't give him food poisoning."

Danielle shook her head, smiling. "Southern hospitality. That's so cute."

Oh yes, adorable. Emily went out back to slice limes and replenish one of the ice buckets. When she returned, that familiar face smiled at her from right where it ought to be. Her heart leapt.

"Hey, regular." She dumped the lime wedges in their bin and rinsed her hands, giving Jeremy a covert smirk.

"Hey, yourself."

"What's new? Anything?" It was strange going back to the innocent banter, considering all of the intimate things she now knew about this man.

"Big news, actually."

"Oh?"

He nodded. "Called my landlord with the heads-up. Apartment's up for grabs as of September first."

"Wow." She felt a mix of things—happiness for her friend and his upcoming adventures, sadness that he'd no longer brighten her evenings here at the bar. Though shortly after his departure, she'd begin a new adventure of her own. "Well, congratulations. That must kinda make it real, huh?"

"Yeah. Next step is plane tickets."

"Where to first? Oh, sorry—Guinness for you?"

"Please. And I don't know," he said, watching her pour. "I'm a bit overwhelmed by choice. I think the frontrunners are Spain and Portugal, or South Africa."

"Golly, that's so exciting."

Danielle came by again. "Hey, Jeremy. Guess she didn't poison you after all."

Jeremy raised his eyebrows at Emily.

"Dinner on Saturday," she said.

"Oh, no. It was delicious, whatever the heck it was. Very exotic," he added, with a mischievous glance at Emily.

"Maqluba," she reminded him, hoping Danielle wouldn't notice her cheeks coloring.

"Right."

"If your travels take you to the Middle East, maybe you can find out what it's supposed to taste like."

"When are you leaving us?" Danielle asked.

"End of the summer." He accepted his beer. "Thanks."

Danielle shook her head melodramatically. "Too bad. You're the nicest guy we get in here. And very easy on the eyes…in fact you're the only guy who gets sexually harassed by us, and not the other way around."

"I've never harassed him," Emily said. Propositioned, perhaps.

Jeremy smiled. "I'm not complaining. But anyhow, I'll send postcards."

"Like you'll have time to," Danielle teased. "You'll be too busy cozying up to way more exciting, foreign barmaids than us."

"Impossible."

Danielle left them to greet a group of customers.

"That *is* awful exciting," Emily said quietly, pretending to organize the garnishes.

"Nursing school's exciting too."

She nodded. "Yeah, I guess it is."

Emily couldn't begin to diagnose the silence that fell between them…awkward, nervous, comfortable, lazy? She was itchy inside her skin, now so unsure how to feel toward her friend. It felt very slightly like a breakup, as she knew that there would never be a repeat of Saturday night. Such indulgences had to be one-time-only, or at least one-time-only with a given guest. Anything more went beyond a gift to a proper modification of the shape of her marriage, Emily felt, and she wasn't looking to do that. Plus if Christmas came more than once a year, surely its specialness would be cut in half.

"Everything all right?" Jeremy asked.

She met his gaze and smiled as casually as she could. "Oh, I'm fine. Bit tired is all."

He sipped his beer. "Nothing eating away at your soul or anything? Any regrets?" he added in a mumble.

She shook her head. "No, definitely not. Maybe just a little sad that the weekend's over. You ever get like, a Christmas hangover? Or on a birthday, when you were a kid, after all the excitement's done for another year?"

"Sure. I always get that after vacation, when life goes back to normal. But I hope… You know, I hope that everything's okay."

"Everything's fine. In fact everything's better… I got a gift I really wanted, and it's made me so grateful it kinda hurts, right here." She made a fist and rubbed her sternum with it. "I think maybe I feel a little undeserving."

"Don't feel like that. Giving people gifts that you know they really want feels even better to the giver, usually."

She considered that, recalling that, yes, Rasul had seemed notably self-satisfied the last three days, made more lively than normal with some quietly bubbling pride. Cocky, in his own understated way. "I suppose that's true."

"So enjoy it. It's okay to be spoiled once in a while. You deserve it, anyhow."

"Thanks."

Jeremy laughed then, and she knew he'd reached his limit with this cryptic discussion, given that he was the indulgence they were speaking of.

Emily grabbed a rocks glass and filled it with ginger ale. She held it over the bar between them. "To your upcoming tourism."

Jeremy withheld his participation in the toast. He spoke quietly. "Not sure where I could end up that'll be much more thrilling than Saturday's adventure."

She lowered her glass and offered a playful frown. "How about to tourism in general, then?"

"Let's just toast to your husband," he whispered.

She nodded. "Indeed."

Jeremy smiled and tapped her glass with a "cheers" and they drank. Two friends on the threshold of personal change, keepers of a shared secret and this small patch of shiny wood, a tiny scrap of this generic bar made intensely personal.

She turned away to attend to her job, full of warmth. She felt Jeremy's gaze on her, conspiring and familiar.

When she got back from work that night her husband's eyes would alight on her, seeing someone slightly different than they might have a few days ago, but miraculously loving that woman no less. She'd be home, in a house and a city neither of them was yet at ease in. Then she'd feel his hands, possessive and stern, and she'd know there was no place on the face of the earth made so exactly with her in mind.

READY AND WILLING

CHAPTER ONE

"WELL, YOUR PAPERWORK IS FANTASTIC. When are you available to have sex?"

The man opposite me smiles nervously. Our table is positioned beside the café's front window, and the silvery winter sunlight bounces off the brushed aluminum and lights up his eyes. They're pretty and complex, greenish gray with a hint of yellow. He spins his coffee cup around on its saucer, considering his schedule.

"I guess that's up to you," he says. "When are you...you know."

"Ovulating?"

He nods.

I study those eyes again. There's an intriguing dark ring around his irises. Shit, I'm not supposed to be noticing things like this. On paper he was a tidy inventory of genetic factors, and it'd be simplest if I could keep thinking about him that way. Then again, if I really wanted this to be simple, I'd have just gone to a sperm bank. I give myself a mental shake, pull my hair back, and twist it into a bun with the elastic from my wrist, as though this might magically imbue me with an aura of professionalism.

"Next week," I say. "And since you're being so open-minded about all this, I feel like I should let you in on something. In the interest of full disclosure."

He—Noah Aubrey is his name, I may as well mention—offers me a warm, kind smile. "You already showed me a letter from your gyno. What else is there to tell?"

"Well, have you ever heard that thing about executioners—"

Noah's laugh cuts me off. "Oh, wow, I can't wait to see where this is going."

I wave a hand to dispel his worries. "No, no. It might be an urban legend, but I heard once that when someone's being put to death by lethal injection, they administer it using a button. Like you push a button and it opens some valve, and the condemned gets poison through their IV or whatever."

He laughs. "Okay, now you're just scaring me, Abby."

"But there's two buttons and two guys who push them, except only one really releases the death serum. So neither man has to spend his life knowing for sure that he killed someone."

"You're telling me there's another guy."

I nod.

Noah nods as well, slow, not seeming bothered by the news. "Okay. Better than you telling me there's death serum involved. Oh wait—unless you're about to announce we'll be pushing our buttons at the same time."

I swat him with my folded-up copy of his medical history. Noah is easy to swat. It's easy to forget we're meeting to discuss fluid procurement and not for a first date. He feels very familiar. Not as if we've met before, but as though he's made up of pieces of a dozen friends I've known for years. Like a car I've driven a hundred times, just in a different color than I'm used to.

"Nothing that scandalous," I say. "So, that's okay with you?"

He shrugs. "Why wouldn't it be?"

"I dunno. Can you tell I've never done this before? I don't really know how the politics go." I study his face...kind and intelligent. I'd like an intelligent-looking baby who'll wind up with a fine, straight nose and black eyebrows like this man's. That easy smile. And tall doesn't hurt.

My fingers fuss with his paperwork, squaring up the corners with the edge of the tabletop, giving me something to stare at so I don't disturb Noah with all my scrutiny. "I have to ask...what did you think when you first saw the ad?" I'd placed it in the *Boston Globe* classifieds, not trusting my womb to Craigslist.

"My colleague found it, actually. At first, to be honest, I thought it was nuts."

"I'm guessing it's the money that piqued your interest?"

"No, not really." Noah's expression turns thoughtful, his fascinating eyes drifting to take in whatever's going on out in the street beyond my shoulder. "I've always tried to take interesting opportunities when they come to me. New experiences. This one was a lot scarier than spelunking, though, I have to tell you."

"Did I mention we have to spend the night in a haunted mansion first?"

Noah laughs, and it gives him a dimple. I wish I were in a position to develop a crush on him, but this conception arrangement is supposed to be no-strings-attached, and romantic feelings surely qualify as a string. A particularly thick and tangled one, no doubt.

He leans back as though he's given himself permission to finally relax in my twisted company. "So I have to ask why not a sperm bank?"

I shrug and take a sip of my coffee. "It never sat right with me, just picking a man out of a catalog. I wanted to meet you. You and the other guys I got in touch with. I wanted to make sure... I don't know." I twirl my hands around, searching for the right wording. "That your souls seem right, I guess. Sorry, that sounds so oovy-groovy."

"No, that makes sense."

"And it seems kind of fair that you'd meet me. In case you cared what kind of sperm-wrangling she-devil is planning on possibly having your child. If you care."

"I care," Noah says, nodding. He's so good-looking I want to suck on his fingers. Which is weird, because that thought has never occurred to me before with anyone, under any other circumstance. This man is saddling me with unforeseen fetishes.

"I wouldn't agree to this if you seemed like some kind of psycho," he says, and I decide never to mention my finger-sucking impulse in case it contradicts his conclusion.

"And also," I say, "I figured since I'm doing this the old-fashioned way..." In a moment of juvenility, I make a little in-out-in-out motion with my fingers. "I thought you'd want to see me, so you'd know if you could pull it off. Without beer goggles. Or with," I add with another shrug.

He smiles and looks at the table, pink flushing his cheeks, so damned cute. There was nothing about cuteness in his medical history. He glances up again. "Don't worry. You're... I think you're very pretty."

"Well, lucky you, I guess." I feel as though we should shake hands or toast. Or kiss. Wait, no, definitely not kiss. I push my cappuccino mug across the table until it clanks against his cup. "How about next Monday evening?"

"Yeah, I think that'll work. What time?"

"Whenever you're free. By the way, in case you were worried," I add, "I'm not going to be taking the temperature of my womb or anything and calling you up at four a.m. to come over and service me."

He laughs. "No pagers. Good."

"And you don't need to keep your balls in a hermetically sealed jar or anything. Just try and keep them safe, at least until after next week."

I catch Noah blushing faintly behind his smirk. "I've been doing that for thirty-four years now. I think I can handle it."

"That's all I ask of you. That and a waiver, you know, about relinquishing your rights and not suing me. I'll have it ready for Tuesday."

"I love foreplay," Noah says drily, but his smile is warm.

"Good. Oh, and you probably want to know about the money."

"I was curious."

"Well, here's what I thought up. I'll give you a hundred bucks for every...successful interaction," I say, embracing how stupid this sounds. "Plus the cost of the screenings, of course, if you bring me a copy of the bill. When and if I do get pregnant, I'll be paying you and the other guy each twenty-five hundred."

His handsome eyebrows rise. "Wow, pricey project. I wasn't...I wasn't expecting that much."

"Yeah, well, this kid's going to end up costing me way more than that over the course of its life. I'm willing to shell out for the best, genetically speaking. And to be honest, I think I'll like, um...working with you. Both of you. And to be even more frank, if this does take more than just the first try, it's my hope that you won't sleep with anyone else for the time being. You know, because of STDs and just general complicatedness. So I want to make this worth your time."

"Well, I hope I can return the favor," Noah says, his smile turning shy.

I take out my card and scribble my address on the back. I did a background check on him and the other man, Rob, and it's a calculated risk, bringing them into my home. No more risky than a date, I suppose. Probably less, since no one's heart is on the line.

I hand the card over. "So, I'll see you next Monday night. How's six thirty?"

He nods, tucking my card into his wallet. "Sounds perfect. I'll come straight from work."

"Oh." A pang of unforeseen panic tightens my chest.

"What?"

"Do you want... I can make us dinner if you want. Or we could meet up later. Is that too weird? Me making dinner?"

Noah laughs. "I'd love dinner. I'll bring wine, if you drink."

"Yeah, we'll probably need it. Okay, good. I'll make ziti or something. Something not gassy," I add, feeling oddly at home being silly with this man. After all, his threshold for my potential weirdness is already high, given the nature of our meeting. I know the guy's sperm count, for crying out loud.

He stands; I stand. We hesitate a moment then I put out my hand and we shake, such an innocuous bit of contact considering the deal we're signing off on. His touch matches his smile, warm and easy. When his hand releases mine it heads for his wallet, but I swat him again. I leave a few bills for our drinks and tip and let him hold the door for me. I walk him the half block to his car, an old black hatchback splattered with salty winter mud.

"Thanks again for meeting me," I say. "And all the doctor rigmarole."

"Sure."

"And just so you know, if Monday comes around and you decide I'm a psycho after all, don't feel like you need to call or make any excuses. If you don't show, I'll just have plenty of leftovers for dinner on Wednesday."

He smiles, and his teeth are as white as peppermint Chiclets. I want to run my tongue over them, discover what he tastes like. Probably just coffee, same as me.

"Thanks for the escape hatch," he says and unlocks his door.

"Thanks for the sperm," I say, and I laugh at my own ridiculousness.

"Yeah, no pressure." He makes a funny little theatrical stressed-out face and slides into his seat, then gives me a wave as I shut his door for him.

I can't believe this might actually work.

CHAPTER TWO

"HELLO THERE," I say to the sexiest man I think I've ever met. His name is Rob Fellows, and he's here to impregnate me on an otherwise unremarkable, overcast Sunday afternoon in December. He's punctual too. It's *exactly* two o'clock according to my cable box.

"Hi, Abby." He smiles, standing on the landing to my condo in a long herringbone tweed coat. The gesture crinkles his eyes at the corners and makes his fantastic bone structure all the more enticing. He's brought flowers: red gerbera daisies wrapped in cellophane.

"Aw, you didn't have to do that. Come in." I take the flowers and close the door behind him.

"It seemed too early to bring a bottle of wine. But it felt rude not bringing *something.*"

"Oh, you've brought plenty," I say, and in the grips of nervous, tactless jokiness, I aim a glance pointedly down at his crotch.

"Yeah, true."

I take the coat he drops from his shoulders and walk to the door to hang it up, relieved for a chance to get control over my shallow breathing. "And I don't know about you," I say as I turn back, "but *I'll* be having a drink. I don't do this every day." Just *most* days this week.

He follows me into the kitchen, and I trim the daisies and arrange them in a highball glass. I steal glances at him, trying to remember everything I learned from our e-mails and our coffee-shop meet-up. He's not as chatty as Noah and his company's not as relaxing, but he's *fucking* good-looking, and nothing about him sets my intuition on edge. I think he said he works in "development," though for the life of me I can't remember any details. It's hard to look at Rob Fellows and focus on anything beyond his perfect shell. I squint at his fitted black sweater, trying to guess what's waiting for me a couple of layers down.

"Great place," he says.

"Thanks."

"You rent?"

"Nope, condo."

"Nice," he says.

"Thank you." It's the top unit of a three-story house in Somerville, Cambridge's more affordable, less snotty sister. Nothing fancy, but I'd like to think I have decent taste. The space is funky with eaves, and it won't be fun hauling a fat baby up and down three flights when the other half of my two-person family arrives, but it's my first piece of property, and I love it.

I open a bottle of wine and pour two half glasses, and Rob follows me to my little living room. He takes a seat on my couch, and I perch on the arm, still anxious, not quite ready to plunk down beside him. Stupid, really, since we'll presumably be having sex within the hour. I clutch my glass like the hand of a comforting friend.

He smiles and takes a drink. "You look nervous."

"I am. I'm a little rusty. And to be honest, I've never paid for sex before."

Rob laughs. "What can I do to make you less nervous?"

Not much, I think, surveying him. Over six feet, and judging from the shapes beneath his sweater, built for performance. I know he kickboxes, because it was listed in his medical documentation under "exercise habits," and it intrigued me to no end. He has shaggy, wavy, dark brown hair. Noah has dark hair too, as do I. I'm glad it worked out that way, so I won't have to worry about popping out, say, a red-haired baby, and wrecking the arrangement's anonymity.

"I'll be fine," I say. "There's way less pleasant things to get nervous over. I think I just have performance anxiety. This is the first attempt."

"Is it creepy?" Rob asks after a long pause, one I fill with a big gulp of wine. "Sleeping with a guy who answered an ad? Like, *that* ad? A guy who'd volunteer to impregnate you for cash?"

I look out the window, drum my fingers on my glass. "Ooh, that's a brave question. No. I haven't given it too much thought, honestly. I'm just grateful you came. Er, bad word choice." I grin like a dope as I meet his eyes. "But no. Not creepy." Sexy, I think, looking him over. Out-of-my-league sexy, under more traditional circumstances. "Would you mind doing the waiver now?"

"Fine with me."

I fetch the paper, and he reads it, signs his rights away. I file it carefully and return to the couch.

I take another sip. My wine's starting to work, mercifully, or perhaps it's just this man's proximity. He's got a quality, as though he's giving off a signal to a sense science hasn't yet identified, his message as tangible as a scent or sound. "You know what made me want to pick you?" I ask.

He shakes his head.

"We have the same birthday. Not just the same day. The same year too."

His eyebrows bob up. "Wow, really?"

I nod. "I know—what are the chances? I read it in your medical history. I thought it was a good sign."

"Unless we're twins, separated at birth."

I laugh, take another drink. "Okay, *now* it's creepy. Anyhow, there was that neat coincidence plus, you know, your lack of congenital diseases and mental disorders," I add with a guilty grin. "So, are *you* nervous?"

He shakes his head. "Not really."

"Let me know if you need anything special. You know, porn or anything."

He shakes his head again. "I think we'll be okay. I'm pretty easy. Actually, can I be honest with you?"

"Please."

"I don't think I can get much skeezier than offering myself up for money, so I may as well admit this whole thing kind of turns my crank."

A warm flush of relief and curiosity moves through me. "Oh yeah?"

"Yeah. I've actually never had sex without a condom before."

I blink at him. "Never?"

"Never. And I've definitely never tried to get anyone pregnant, let alone a stranger. It's sort of…" He trails off, squinting as he searches for the right word.

"Taboo?"

He takes a sip of his wine. "Yeah, I guess. Or like, fake dangerous."

"Well, I don't think that's skeezy at all. I'm glad there's some fun in it for you."

Rob's eyes squinch up when he smiles, so frigging handsome I want to bite him, just to make sure he's real.

"You want to get started?" he asks.

"Oh," I say, suddenly feeling like a rude hostess. It cools my perking libido a bit, thinking I may be just another thing on his Sunday to-do list. *Go to laundromat, return library book, impregnate Abby Winchel, buy paper towels.*

"Sure. Whenever you want."

I spent some time picturing how this moment might play out once I'd let Rob into my home. Would we kiss? Would we talk about it? Or would I just lie down, and he'd do his thing? And what would his thing consist of?

He drains his glass and sets it on the coffee table. The clink sounds like a starter pistol in my brain. "You want to use your bed?" he asks.

"Yeah, I figured we'd go there." I down my last couple of gulps and stand, take the wineglasses to the kitchen, and leave them in the sink. Rob follows me into my bedroom. My heart's sudden pounding could be from fear or arousal or some combination of the two. I turn to face him, and he's pulling his sweater over his head. I stare at the sexy shapes behind his gray T-shirt. He has a tattoo on his arm, a thick band of black vines. I wonder absently if my future child might ever take up kickboxing or come home with a similar tattoo and blow my mind.

"Are there any ground rules?" he asks, looking around my room.

"No, not really. You should feel free to do whatever you need to…to accomplish your goal. You know, within reason." I laugh. "Don't smack me in the face or call me any mean names, please."

"Is it okay if I say stuff?" Rob has a sexy voice, a little deep, a little scratchy, an octave lower than it was a second ago if I'm not mistaken. His gaze moves up and down my body, and heat flashes between my legs.

"Sure. Just nothing derogatory. But you know, whatever it takes. Close your eyes and say someone else's name if you want to. It's nothing personal. And if you need me to do anything, let me know."

"Sounds good." He puts his hands on his hips, businesslike, and looks me in the face. "Can I watch you undress?"

"Sure." Predictable self-consciousness cools me for a second; then a glance at his eyes to confirm the desire burning there banishes my inhibitions.

I unbutton my cardigan and slip it off and toss it on the floor, sit on the edge of the bed to pull my socks off. I smile nervously up at Rob, who's watching with mischief on his face. He pulls his T-shirt up and off, and my breath catches. His skin is winter pale with a line of black hair running from his chest to his navel. My pulse hums. He's got the finest, tightest body I've ever been this close to, and I suddenly understand why someone might pay for recreational sex. My eyes drink in his long abdomen. I pray he likes doing it face-to-face so I'll be able to watch his muscles working as he fucks me.

I pull off my camisole and drop my jeans, stand before this insanely hot stranger in a matching set of silly polka-dot underwear. His expression's hard to read, but I think he's pleased. He unbuckles his belt and unzips his fly and pushes his jeans down just enough to reveal the bulge in his shorts. His chest muscles contract deliciously as he runs a hand over his erection. He looks predatory, but the intimidation I'm feeling is welcome, as welcome as the wine heating my skin.

I reach back and unhook my bra. I try to remove it nonchalantly enough that it doesn't seem as if I'm trying to seduce him but not so quick that it feels completely mechanical. I watch as he eases his underwear down and takes himself out.

His cock is long and heavy-looking, standing out proud from its nest of black curls. He wraps his hand around his base, gives himself slow pulls. I glance up to find his eyes locked on mine. Fear and guilt and excitement stand all my arm hairs on end and tense my nipples. I've never been to bed with someone I've known as briefly as Rob, and it's hot. I have a free pass to ignore my own standards, to enjoy the gorgeous, ready man right here before me and not feel sleazy or used when he leaves. The rule-breaking is an honest-to-God chemical high.

He licks his lips. "Keep going." His voice is low and hungry, and his command gives me another taste of that thrilling intimidation.

I push my panties down my hips and kick them off. I watch him stroke faster. I swallow and sit on the edge of the bed. "Should I lie down?"

He nods, his gaze darting all over my naked body.

I recline against the pillows and watch him. He's taking some private inventory of me, thinking of whatever it is I am to him—a conquest, a kink, a gig. I don't mind what. I only care that he's here, and he's hard, and he's going to give me what I'm after. And look great doing it. Bonus.

He pushes his underwear and jeans down his strong legs. The powerful shapes of his arms and sides and hips and thighs look like art in the cool December light struggling through the half-open blinds. In two paces he's at the edge of my bed, then kneeling at my side, dipping the mattress with his weight.

"Would you touch me?" he asks, demonstrating with his hand.

"I'll do anything you want. Just ask."

He straddles me, knees sinking into the bedspread on either side of my waist, hard dick looming above me. His hand moves away, and I reach out to take him. Warm. Goddamn hard, pulsing softly. He smells potent and ready and dirty in the best way possible. His eyes close, and little noises, tiny grunts, escape his throat as I stroke him.

"Tighter," he whispers. I clench my fist and give him rough pulls until he's moaning, rhythmic and steady. "Just like that."

I masturbate him until I'm light-headed with excitement and impatience, wishing he was touching me too, but thinking it's not my place to make demands. I stroke him until pre-come glistens at his slit and his hips are thrusting him into my hand, urgent.

His dark eyes open, staring down at me. "I'm ready," he says. "You have lube?"

"Yeah." I reach over with my free hand to open my bedside table drawer and find the little bottle and pass it to him. He moves back, taking his cock and his body heat away, taking my excitement away and replacing it with fresh nerves. I want him inside me now, shutting out reality and replacing it with pure animal selfishness.

He scoots his knees between my legs and squirts a dollop of glistening gel onto his first two fingers. When he touches me, the length of my spine curls and the pleasure drives the crown of my head into the pillows.

"Do you want this?" he asks softly as his fingers leave me.

I glance up, and he's rubbing the remaining lube over his big dick, looking a little flushed, a little dangerous, a lot horny.

"Yeah, I do."

"You want me to fuck you?" There's a new roughness to his voice, a harshness that catches me off guard and tightens my pussy.

"I'm dying for it," I say.

He lowers down, bracing his arms at my sides. I shudder as he runs his warm, slick cock between my legs, over my folds.

"I like it kind of rough," he says. "Is that okay?"

"Whatever you need."

"Just tell me if I need to back off," he murmurs, reaching between us to guide himself to my entrance. His movements are deliberate and slow as he teases me with his head.

"You've really never done it without a condom?" I ask. The idea thrills me, like a tiny scrap of virginity I'm about to take from him.

"Never," he says. I can practically smell his excitement. He pushes in with a groan. "Yeah."

"More," I whisper. I watch him disappear inside me an inch at a time, the sweet pressure of him redoubling my excitement, banishing the doubt.

"Shit, you're tight. And hot." His lips stay parted, his eyelids heavy. "Fuck, this feels amazing."

"Use me."

"Okay." He pushes in deep, almost all the way, then draws back. His expression transforms, looking mean in a good way, promising me greed and aggression, things I'd never ask for but long to see.

"More," I coax. "I want all of you." The dirty talk feels a little forced, but I'm determined to be a fantastic lay for this man.

He starts pumping, slow, faster, until he's surging deep. "Yeah. Fuck, yeah."

"Good."

"Say my name," he orders, a little taste of the roughness he promised.

"Rob."

Faster now, greedy. "Yeah. Tell me what I'm doing."

"You're fucking me, Rob. Deep and hard."

"That's right." He leans back, pushing his knees under my thighs so he's on his haunches, still pumping. I watch the way his belly contracts and swells with his breaths and thrusts, muscles tensing, and I'm so hungry for him I feel a growl rising in my throat. His cock is thick. Dark. I watch his wet skin slide in and out, in and out.

"Rob."

"Yeah. Yeah." His broad hands grasp my thighs, pushing me wide as his hips take me faster. His aggressive touch heats my blood like a drug. "Tell me you love it."

"I do. I love the way you fuck. I love your cock. It feels so good, your thick, bare cock. Fuck me."

"Yeah… Tell me I'm big."

"You're huge, Rob. Nobody's ever fucked me this deep."

I watch with satisfaction as his excitement mounts from my words. I feel raw and elemental and *grateful*. I want *him* to feel like the most powerful beast in creation. I wonder if I should fake an orgasm for him.

"Fuck me, Rob. I need your come."

He sucks in a rasping breath, as though I've uttered the magic words he's been waiting for. "Yeah, you need my cum." He takes me harder and faster still, the impact of his body echoing just how desperate I feel.

"I need it. I need you to shoot it inside me."

He groans. "Turn over."

I ache for the handful of seconds his cock leaves my pussy, leaves me feeling empty. I shift to my elbows and knees.

I feel his head teasing my lips. "Beg for me," he orders.

"Please, Rob. Fuck me, please. I want your cock."

He gives me half his length.

"More. Fuck me deep with your big cock. Please, Rob." It sounds so porny, but it's working for him, undeniably.

"Yeah." He pushes farther, feeling hot and thick and forbidden. "Yeah, you're so tight." He holds my waist roughly, a tug matching each of his thrusts, the damp skin of his hips slapping my ass. He pumps mean and fast, and I can feel his balls hit each time he rams deep. "I want to spank you."

"Okay." I hold my breath, anticipating the sound and the sting.

He slaps my ass lightly a couple times. Then harder. "Take my dick."

"Rob."

He slaps me again, harsh and loud, making my skin prickle and burn, making pain and pleasure tighten my core. But hotter than the spanking is Rob himself, the way it feels to be under his command.

"Say it."

"Rob." Another spank.

"I'm gonna come in your pussy," he promises—*threatens*—and I can hear him losing control.

"Do it," I say. "Shoot your come in me." His fingers knead my ass, and I gasp as he slaps me again. I like him rough, the messy contrast of it compared to his self-possessed facade. I want him to feel huge and strong and full of himself. I clench my pussy around him and join his rhythm with my body, meeting his plunges, feeding his pleasure. A talented pair of fingers teasing my clit would probably get me there too, but this is all about him. That's how I want it. That's how I want to remember him in case we never fuck again—the embodiment of pure animal greed.

"Yeah, take my dick."

"Rob." I arch my back. I moan for him.

"Yeah, you love it. You gonna come for me?"

"Yeah," I lie.

I feel him losing coordination; I feel the desperation in his body, the quaking in his hips. I squeeze him like a fist and grunt his name, pushing my ass into him.

"Yeah, yeah, yeah." He eats my performance right up, even eases his thrusts considerably for a few beats. "That's right. That's right."

I let out a theatrical "*Mmmmm.*"

"Now me."

"Come, Rob."

"I will." He takes me hard again—harder. "I'll shoot you full of my come."

I moan for real now, so fucking hot for this moment.

The headboard clatters against the wall, and he's groaning like a maniac. I wish the whole neighborhood could see me getting fucked by this gorgeous, aggressive man. I wish I were horrible enough to have hidden a video camera.

"Oh fuck. I-I'm gonna give you what you w-want," he stammers.

"Good."

He slaps my ass. "Say it," he orders.

"Rob. Come for me, Rob."

He slams inside me, pushing deep, mashing our bodies together, his hips pressed hard into my ass, fingers digging into my flesh. I feel him spasm two, three, four times. I feel him emptying himself for me, squeezing every drop into my thirsty cunt. His moan crescendos and fades in perfect time with the fantasy.

As soon as he slides out, I roll onto my back and hug my knees to my chest. I know it probably doesn't really help anything. But hell, it can't hurt, right?

Rob's kneeling beside me, catching his breath. He watches me, and as he comes down from his release, his expression turns uncertain. Cognizant. As if he just woke up in some stranger's bed after a drunken one-night stand, blinded by the glare of sobriety.

I sigh and purr luxuriously, telling him he did everything right. Because he did. He got the job done, and it was hot to boot, my ideal outcome. I can't wait for him to leave so I can masturbate, thinking about everything that's just happened, and satisfy the ache between my thighs. "Thank you."

"You're welcome," he says with a little laugh.

"I'm going to keep lying like this for a bit," I say. "Whenever you're ready to head out, there's an envelope on top of the microwave for you. But feel free to recover. Use the bathroom. Shower if you want."

He nods. I can tell he's relieved, glad to have been given permission to take off.

I offer a dorky smile, since that's all I can be expected to pull off given that I'm curled before him in a fertilizing ball on my bedspread.

"I thought that went really great. Can I e-mail you in a couple days? To maybe do it again?"

"Sure," he says, neutral.

"If you feel weird when I do, feel free to ignore me or say no. But seriously, this was just what I was looking for. I'd tip you if it didn't seem so lurid."

He laughs out of protocol, but I can tell he's a little uncomfortable. I hope if I drop off his radar until later in the week, he'll conclude that I'm not a nut and take this at face value and offer me a repeat performance.

Rob stands and picks up his clothes. He wanders out of my room, and eventually I hear the toilet flush, and he reappears in the doorway, dressed. Handsome.

I wave at him good-naturedly, still hugging my knees tight. "Find your envelope?"

"Yup." He looks unsure. He summons the nerve to walk over, and I'm surprised when he plants a warm, friendly kiss on my forehead.

"Drive safe," I say, sounding cheerful and ridiculous. "I'll be in touch."

"Sounds good. Bye, Abby." He gives me a wave as he leaves my bedroom. I lay still, listening to his far-off rustlings as he pulls on his shoes and coat, as the front door opens and closes, as the weight of him makes the house vibrate faintly when he descends the steps.

I decide to lie this way for ten more minutes; then I'll grab my vibrator and probably come quicker than I ever have in my entire life. I turn my head to look at the clock's red digits. Two thirty-six.

Nice. I can still catch *This American Life* with time to spare.

CHAPTER THREE

"OH, YOU'RE BLEEDING!" My smile fades as I open the door to the landing and find Noah Aubrey holding a bloody Dunkin' Donuts napkin to his knee.

"Hi, Abby," he says brightly, half bent over. He sets a paper shopping bag at his feet. "Sorry about this. I slipped on the sidewalk."

"Out front? Shit, I'm so sorry, I should have salted it again. Well, come in, anyhow."

He shuffles past me. "It was your neighbor's sidewalk."

"Let me get you a Band-Aid. Here, take your shoes off." I close the door and pick up his bag. I see a bottle of wine and a DVD case inside, and I steal a glance at him. Even injured and hunched over, he's more handsome than I remember, especially with snow still melting in his hair and an apple green scarf wound around his neck. His handsomeness doesn't punch you in the face like Rob's. It sort of sneaks up from behind and gives your shoulders a massage, makes you forget about how stressed you felt before he arrived. Having Noah here relaxes me. I take his sporty black coat and toss it over the loveseat. "Hang on a sec."

I jog to the kitchen and return with a wet hand towel and a big bandage. "You may as well take off your pants," I say, laughing.

He unbuckles his belt. "This wasn't exactly the icebreaker I'd envisioned." He drops his black slacks around his ankles and lets me wipe the blood off his skinned knee.

"Ooh, that looks painful," I say, and I hear him suck in a breath as I pat it dry. I keep my eyes politely away from his crotch.

"It's fine."

I smooth the bandage over his knee, stand and crumple the wrapper, and smile at him. "Wow, we're off to a great start! It's six thirty-three, and I've already gotten your trousers off."

"Thanks, Abby." He hikes his pants back up, pretty dignified, considering. He takes a step forward and catches me off guard, laying a hand on my shoulder and kissing my cheek. "It smells amazing in here."

"Ziti, as promised. With sausage."

This feels so much different than with Rob. I feel as if I know this man. And I'm not a hundred percent sure if that's okay. There's a reason I chose to not go the anonymous donor route, but there's also a reason I didn't scout for an open-minded male friend to do this job for me. I'm all for finding a human connection with the potential father of my future kid, but putting myself in a position to *miss* that man after the conception's over is another matter entirely.

"I brought a bottle of red," Noah says. "And a movie."

"A dirty movie?" I ask and waggle my eyebrows at him.

"Oh. No, actually. *Chinatown.*" He casts a glance at the bag, and from the scrunch of his eyebrows alone I can sense him questioning this entire crazy arrangement. "Sorry, is that wrong?"

I shrug. "Hell if I know. I'm making this up as I go."

"I thought maybe we were making a night of it. But if you were thinking of something more utilitarian...?"

"I honestly have no expectations." Or I hadn't until Rob set the initial tone. Now Noah's here with an entirely different approach, and I feel flattered that he wants to hang out for more than just the food and fucking. "I'd love to watch *Chinatown* with you."

"Oh good."

"Shall we bust open that wine?" I ask. He follows me into the kitchen where the red daisies stare at me accusingly from the counter. I find him a corkscrew, and Noah works on the bottle while I grab glasses, probably the same two from yesterday afternoon.

"Dinner will be ready in fifteen or so."

He pours us each a glass, and we toast. I have to squint at him to remind myself we're not already friends. Before my brain completely clouds over, I grab the waiver off of my computer desk. He signs it after a quick scan.

I put it away, business complete. "Did you work today?"

He nods. "Yeah, I'm a nine-to-fiver, roughly. I teach at Emerson."

"Oh, right. Professor Aubrey, is it?"

He smiles. "Dr. Aubrey."

"Wow." I'd only asked the candidates if they'd gotten a bachelor degree or higher, no specifics. "You have a PhD? In what?"

"Cinema Studies. NYU."

"Wow." I make an impressed face, jostle his shoulder with mine. "Well, Dr. Aubrey, I work like three blocks from you. A little past the movie theater on Tremont."

He laughs and shakes his head. "We better be careful. I could run into you in the park on a lunch break, bringing your baby in to show your coworkers."

"Oh shit, you're right." I decide to not let such a thought throw me off. "Small town."

"No kidding."

We're quiet for a moment, caught in our own internal dialogues.

"Abby," he says, sounding careful, staring at my counter, the flowers.

My heart sinks. "Too weird now?"

"Oh, no. I don't think so. Can I talk to you for second? About tonight?"

"Absolutely." I take a drink, then set my glass down, offering him my full attention.

"I'm crap at casual sex," Noah says. "Can we pretend this is a date?"

I smile at him and wonder if he can tell how relieved I am by that proposal. "We can treat it any way you want to. I just want you to feel comfortable."

"I'd like to sort of pretend this is just a first date that goes better than I expected."

I nod, thinking the idea over and coming up pleased. I'd been curious about another Rob-style performance but also a little unsettled by the prospect. After the hotness of our encounter with Rob had dissipated, I'd been dogged by a lingering seediness for the remainder of the afternoon. "Sure. Whatever works for you."

"Did you have other things you needed to get done tonight?" I detect a tiny note of panic in Noah's voice.

"No," I say, laughing. "You're the main attraction. Come on. Let's go sit down."

He smiles apprehensively, and we head to the living room.

"You have a decent day?" I ask as we plop onto the couch.

"Not bad. It's pretty quiet before Christmas. Just me in my office, reading papers, fielding panicky requests for finals extensions."

"Do you get a long break?"

He nods. "Not as long as the students, but a big chunk of January."

"Very cool."

I'm surprised when he leans close. His hand is warm and soft, and he puts it to my jaw. He kisses my lips—a lingering, sexy, closed-mouth kiss.

He looks shy as he pulls away. "Sorry. That was going to stress me out all night if I didn't get it out of the way."

"Glad to put you at ease." It's so the opposite—I'm relieved beyond measure to have the physical tone of my night with Noah set. Not just relieved now—curious too. I'm tempted to lean in and continue that kiss, but Noah speaks.

"I have to say, this whole thing... I feel really...honored. No, sorry, that sounds way too earnest. But I feel really *flattered*, you know, that you chose me."

I smile at this and pat his hand. "You should. I was prepared to not pick anybody, if no one felt like the right match. And believe me, a ton of them didn't. So...thank *you*. For showing up."

His gaze jumps between my eyes and my mouth and back again, and we both shift a bit, turn so our knees touch. The next time he leans in, I kiss back. Our mouths part, and we catch each other's lips in turn, softly, no tongues. I feel the ache return to my body, right where Rob left it. I couldn't tell you exactly what I'm wanting from Noah—his body and his warmth—for a baby or for my own selfish pleasure, I'm not sure. The feeling is nice but confusing, and I want a little reality check to help me understand where Noah's coming from.

"You're only doing stuff you want to, right?" I ask as our mouths separate. "That was nice, but don't feel like you *have* to do all the romantic stuff. If you don't want to," I reiterate, babbling.

"Does it bother you?"

"No, it was sexy."

"Okay. As long as you don't mind, I'd like to do things the cheesy traditional way," Noah says. "The illusion makes me feel less...sordid about the whole thing."

"Gentleman's choice." I hold my glass up, and he follows suit. We clink them together, then take a drink just as the oven timer buzzes.

In a few minutes we sit down with heaping bowls of ziti and start the movie. Once my wine kicks in and I've set my bowl aside, I scoot over a couple inches and rest my knee on Noah's thigh. He smiles, looking equal parts guilty and appreciative.

After another glass and another hour, his hand is on my leg, rubbing idly. I know neither of us is really watching the movie. I study his profile, the handsome details of his face lit by the TV in the relative dark. My body's been priming for him, growing warm and restless and curious in tiny ways he can't see but maybe he can sense. I want to feel his stubble when he kisses me deeply. I want to explore the parts of him I diplomatically averted my eyes from when his pants were around his ankles when he first arrived. I want to know what he sounds like and what sorts of things he might say. I bet he moans more than he talks during sex, and I bet he goes slow, right up until the very end... I feel like I know this man already, and I want all my suspicions about him confirmed.

He finishes his second glass and sets it on the coffee table. I let him do the same with mine, and he turns to me. My nerves reach a low simmer, and my stomach's gurgly—not the way it was with Rob, not from adrenaline and apprehension. More like first-date jitters.

Noah's warm, strong hands take my face, and our mouths reconnect. He's bolder than I expected. His tongue slips between my lips after only a few seconds' hesitation. The penetration is divine and dirty and sweet all at once. He kisses deep, wet sweeps of his tongue against mine, firm fingertips on my skin. His palms slide to my shoulders, and I can't wait. I swing a leg over his and straddle him. My knees sink between the cushions, so I end up pushed hard against him, my skirt pooled in our collective lap, more forward than I'd meant to be. Noah's only protest is a deep, accidental-sounding moan and a thrust of his hips. His erection grinds against my inner thigh, spreading heat up and down my legs and making my pussy clench.

I touch his arms through his soft sweater. They're strong. I wasn't expecting that. Curious, I tug at his hem, and he breaks away to peel his top off for me. Beneath he's got on a white button-up shirt, and I squeeze his biceps through the cotton as his mouth captures mine again. Damn. I squeeze him tighter, fascinated to discover his body is hard, breaking the promises made by his easy smile and his kind eyes, his slow, no-pressure approach.

I slide my lips to his neck, tasting the faint chemical flavor of his aftershave, running my tongue up his jugular vein. His hips pump softly as I stroke his chest, trace his collarbone through his shirt. His mouth is just above my ear when he moans. The sound and the heat of his breath splash gasoline all over my flames, flash a hundred dirty ideas through my mind, thoughts of Noah's weight on me, the look on his face when he comes. His hands take my thighs, guiding me to rub my pussy over his cock where it strains against his pants. I want him now now *now*.

"You feel so hard," I murmur.

"I am." He pushes my hips away enough to slide a hand between us. His touch is a shock, zapping through me. There's one flimsy layer between my aching cunt and his fingers, and he finds my hard clit through the damp cotton, stroking.

"You're wet." He whispers it like a beautiful accusation.

"I want you."

"Right here?"

"Please," I say.

His hands leave me to unbuckle his belt and unzip his fly. I lean back so I can watch him push his pants and shorts down enough to take himself out. Big. Not as long as Rob, but thicker, just as mouthwatering.

I reach down and wrap my fingers around him, and his hardness is shocking. I imagine it must hurt, being this hard. He even sounds pained, making little whimpering noises as I stroke him.

"I love it," I tell him, luxuriating in the feel of his skin sliding up and down his shaft, the harmony of his hips pushing to meet my strokes. He slips a hand between us, cupping his balls, fondling them and setting me on fire so instantly I feel light-headed.

"God, yeah." It's impossible to express how badly and completely my body needs his, how this strays beyond attraction into the desperate wilds of biology.

He kneads himself, a show for me. "I've got what you want," he whispers.

"I know you do."

His contracted brows and parted lips betray his cool, teasing façade. "You ready?"

"I'm aching for it," I say, God's honest truth.

He slips his fingers behind the crotch of my panties, runs his knuckles over my tender, slippery lips, and groans. "So wet."

"Take me, Noah."

He does, but with his fingers first. He thrusts deep, driving into my juices and my swollen, willing flesh, an excruciating tease. His thumb finds my clit.

"I want you. Please." My fist tightens around his cock.

"Soon."

"Now. Please."

"*Soon*," he repeats, and I can detect an evil smile in his tone, a taste of some secret side of this man. I guess I don't know him as implicitly as I'd suspected, but I'm not sad to be proven wrong, just curious and impatient, fascinated.

His fingers fuck me and my hand jerks him, and we masturbate each other for a long minute. Pre-come is beading at his tip, and I slick it over his head.

"Now," he says. He yanks my panties to one side and angles his cock. He plunges in deep in one thrust, pulling me down by the hips, burying himself.

"Oh, Abby." His eyes close. We sit motionless for a few breaths, just experiencing each other. Deep inside me, he's pulsing. I feel full and quenched…and yet still so thirsty. I have what I wanted, but my body's screaming for more. I know how he feels, but now I want to know how he moves and sounds and smells. Everything.

"You're so thick," I murmur in his ear. "And hard. Show me how you like to fuck."

His eyes open halfway, trained between our bodies. I lift my skirt up so he can see.

"Ride me," he says.

I start to move, pulling back and pushing forward, taking him slow and explicitly.

"God, Abby."

"You feel so good." To emphasize, I draw back at a sharp angle, milking his thick cock with my hungry body. I want to hear him unravel as he nears his release. I want to feel his hands grab my hips and control me when he reaches that gorgeous point of no return. I want him frantic and nasty and demanding.

"Want to make you come," he moans. "Tell me what you need."

I consider the demand. And why shouldn't I come, if he's offering? "Just let me fuck you," I say. "Slide forward a little."

He shimmies his ass closer to the front of the cushion.

I ride him slow, brushing his pubic bone with my clit. I want to remember all of this: the faint, repetitive scrape of his zipper against my thigh, the smell of his sweat, the look of need on his handsome face. His cock feels so right, so big. I want to use him for more than just his precious come.

"Touch my breasts," I beg.

He pushes my shirt up, and I yank it off. I undo my bra, and his hands on my bare skin are absolute heaven.

"God, you're hot," he says.

"And you're big. I wanna come on your cock."

"Abby." His fingers tweak my nipples, flashing pleasure between my breasts and my cunt, lighting me up. He pulls me close, and his lips draw me in, suckling.

"I'm fucking you, Noah. I'm fucking you." It's all I can think to say. My pussy is burning up, tight and frantic and needing not just *a* man, but *this* man. My clit burns white-hot. I ride him fast and rough and groan his name into his hair, insane with the feeling. My consciousness and every atom of my being is drawn down to my core, like the eye of a violent, swirling storm. For what feels like forever, I'm floating in the pleasure, suspended... Then the climax strikes, wringing my body out. The spasms flood me with heat and relief and beautiful, drunk happiness and hug me tight around his dick.

"Yes, yes, yes..." He's whispering against my skin as my pussy flutters and calms. I hear us breathing. I hear Jack Nicholson talking in the background. I smell ziti and feel Noah's soft, short hair between my fingers, feel his cock throbbing inside me. I smooth my hands over his head and lean back to study his face.

"Wow," I say stupidly.

He smiles broadly and cranes his neck to kiss my lips.

"I haven't come that hard in forever," I tell him, feeling dim-witted and grateful. "Your turn."

"Okay. Can you keep riding me, like before? When you're ready."

I nod, commanding my jelly legs to get their act together. I pump him, slow at first. His fly is soaked from my orgasm, the wet fabric rubbing the back of my thigh. I feel a little embarrassed, mostly proud. Noah's lost in his pleasure, looking hypnotized and handsome and just perfect.

"Yeah. Faster." His eyes shut tight, and he leans back into the couch.

My knees are raw from grinding into the upholstery but it feels good taking orders from him. His breathing turns rapid, a rhythmic string of grunts as he gives himself over.

"I want to make you come," I say.

"Yeah. Fuck me, Abby."

"Your dick is so big. I want to make it shoot for me."

I never found it so easy to talk nasty to a man before this one showed up. Noah makes things comfortable, his mere presence like a sip of liquor that dulls inhibitions and loosens lips.

"Fuck me. Fuck me." His hands grasp my ass, making the thrusts faster and rougher, taking charge, losing control. "Fuck my cock. Fuck it."

"Come on, Noah."

"Your pussy's so tight."

"It loves your cock. Give it what it wants, Noah."

He licks his lips, catches my eye for a split second. "Yeah, you want my come."

"Yeah, all of it. Give it to me. Shoot it for me. Nice and deep."

"Just fuck me. Fuck me." He's a goner.

I'm glad he can't see my smug grin as his possessive hands pull me hard against him. He drives deep with every last inch and releases. He groans like a madman, like a suffering animal. "*Abby. Abby.*"

"Good…"

He keeps me close as he stills, wraps his arms around my back.

"I have to lie down," I say, stroking his hair. He nods against my neck. His embrace loosens, and he lets me flop down along the couch so I can hug my knees. At least this time my panties and skirt offer a scrap of modesty.

I hear him clear his throat, regaining coherence.

"Thanks," I say.

A nervous laugh. "You're welcome… What are you doing, exactly? Is that a conception thing?" I feel him squeeze my toes.

"It's probably pointless," I admit. "But the theory is that you hold it all in, and gravity sort of helps the process."

"I guess it can't hurt."

"That's my thinking."

A silent minute passes before Noah speaks. "Um…should I go?"

"Up to you," I say, trying to sound casual and friendly and hurtproof.

"Could I stay a *little* while longer? I should drink some water and let the wine wear off before I drive."

"Of course. You stay as long as you like. I'll be done absorbing in five minutes or so. We can back the DVD up, or see what's on TV."

"Cool, thanks." His voice drips with relief.

"Hey, Noah?" I say to the ceiling.

"Yeah?"

"Thanks for coming tonight. In every sense of the word. But you know, thanks for showing up. This was really nice. Thanks for making me come too."

"Oh. Well, thanks for making me dinner."

I laugh. "This is like some base-desires meet-up. What do we have left? Should we build a fire and some shelter?"

He squeezes my foot again. "I think you've wrecked me for the rest of the night."

I suddenly think of poor Noah, venturing out into the fifteen-degree darkness, braving the lumpy, icy sidewalk again, starting up his cold, lonely car, and driving home to Jamaica Plain. It's hard to stop myself from telling him he can stay the night…but it's not fair to put him in a position to make that complex and nuanced a decision for us both. And I don't know if I'm ready to wake up beside him or in the next room from him, to negotiate the shower in the morning, to wind up commuting downtown with him or whatever else might happen if we're not vigilant.

Then again, we could have bonus sex in the morning.

Eventually Noah gets up, and I listen to him wander to the bathroom. I use the opportunity to put my bra and shirt back on. I can feel him leaking from me, like some precious prize escaping my grasp. I like it. It feels dirty and decadent, as though this sexy, sweet man has soiled me. I'm grinning when he reappears from the kitchen with a tumbler of water.

I speak without even knowing I had something to say. "Can I talk to you?"

"Sure." He sits on the coffee table right in front of me, attentive.

"I like you," I say. "You seem really nice and thoughtful, and I really enjoyed having sex with you."

"But?" he prompts.

"No, no buts. I…I can't help but feel like I should be telling you to feel free to crash here. But I don't want you to worry about what I really mean by that. I don't want you to think I've changed what this is all about. I'm worried I'll scare you off. Which is stupid, considering the psycho circumstances."

"I think I understand what you mean."

"So, what this is, it's still the same. You're here to impregnate me, for money. I'm not after a relationship. But we're going to know each other kind of intensely for this week and maybe next month. Is it okay if I say stuff like that? Invite you to stay over? It doesn't mean anything aside from, 'I'd like you to stay over, if you want that too.'"

"I think you should feel free to say whatever it is you want," Noah says, looking me in the eye. "And I promise to take you at face value and not read anything into it."

I release a trapped breath. "Thank you. That's what I was getting at."

"And we'll just both have to agree to not feel offended when the other person says no. I mean, there might be some night when I come over, and suddenly it's two a.m., and it's snowing, or we're a little drunk, and I really just want to crash here. But if you say, 'not tonight,' then I'll go home."

"After you sober up," I say and nudge his uninjured knee.

"Yeah…unless you feel like picking up my cab fare."

"You keep doing what you just did, and you can help yourself to a kidney."

CHAPTER FOUR

NOAH DID SLEEP OVER. In my bed. We finished our movie, then stayed up watching TV, and I fell asleep toward the end of one of the late shows. We slept side by side, cautious, neither of us ready or wanting to risk the intimacy of bringing up spooning. He woke up just after me, and we smiled at each other before we spoke. It felt nice and just the tiniest bit nerve-racking, opening my eyes and finding him there.

He's in the shower now. I hear the water turn off, and soon he emerges in the same clothes from yesterday.

I pour him a coffee and point at his torn pants. "Whatever will your fellow faculty members say?"

"If anybody asks, I'll tell them I slipped this morning… Thank God my students are on break. They would've been all over a suspicious wardrobe repeat like a rash."

"Can I pay for your pants? It's my fault you ruined them."

He smiles, filling me with warmth. "I'm a big boy, Abby. I can buy my own pants."

I slide along the counter until I'm close by him. "What time do we need to leave?" He already offered to drive us, a nice change for me from my icy trudge to the Porter Square subway stop and its endless escalator descent into the dim, grumpy realms of commuterdom.

"Half hour, probably, if you start work at nine," he says.

"I do… May I attempt to seduce you?"

He takes a deep drink of his coffee, eyes focused out the window. "You may."

Soon enough I'm on one of the barstools with my legs around his waist. His pants drop, and his boxer briefs join them, and I hold my panties aside for him. His cock looks great in the daylight as he strokes it to his fullest arousal. He could be a penis model for whatever it is penises might model. Condoms? Cock rings, maybe. Even weirder things I probably don't want to know about.

"You have a great dick," I say, not seeing why he shouldn't hear this from me.

"Thanks." He sounds distracted. He guides himself into me, pushing deep. "Abby."

"Be greedy." I'm lousy at coming first thing in the morning, plus we're on a schedule.

Noah holds my thighs and pounds me. He's as good at fucking as he is at getting ridden. At first his eyes are on the action; then he looks up, right at my face as he's moaning.

"You feel so good," I say. I make a circle with my thumb and index finger and position it at my entrance, giving his surging cock an extra tight treat.

"Your pussy's so wet," he groans.

"Yeah, for you. You have something for me?" I purr.

"Oh, yeah."

"What do you have for me?"

He grunts, hips slapping hard. "My come. I'll give you all my come."

"Good."

He moans my name again and again, and I know he's close.

"Noah," I say right back. I reach my hands around and grab his gorgeous ass. I wish there was a mirror behind him so I could watch it working, see those unexpected muscles tensing and thrusting at my command. I bring my palms around his waist and push his shirt and sweater up, just enough to catch a glimpse of a lean, muscular stomach I hadn't even thought to wish for.

"God, I'm gonna come." He presses his forehead hard into mine and groans. His hips hammer fast, then plunge deep, holding there, giving me what I need.

"Good boy," I mutter through a deep breath. I let his shirt drop and run my hands over his arms, his neck, his hair. He withdraws, delirious, and I toddle to the bathroom. I don't have time to lie around marinating so I slip in a tampon, hoping it might work like a cork, though I suspect it could easily do the opposite. Classy thing, conception.

Noah is tucking his shirt back into his pants when I reappear.

"We better head out," I say, glancing at the microwave clock. "Parking's on me, by the way."

"I've got a pass. No worries."

I laugh at his woozy expression. "And you're okay to drive, right?"

"Yeah, I'm good."

We head downstairs and climb into his car. It's a cold, bright day. I direct him to Broadway, and we're quiet for a half mile.

"So, how long are you ovulating for?" Noah catches my eyes at a red light, his question so casual, as though he's asking how long I'm in town.

"I don't know exactly. The window to conceive is maybe three or four days, with a day's wiggle room on either end. Right now is the peak, I'm pretty sure."

"Ah," he says.

"Why do you ask?"

"Would you... Are you free tonight?"

I smile at him. "Sure. I wasn't going to ask you to service me two nights in a row. I thought you might want a day or two to realize I'm a crackpot. But yeah, I'm free. You want to come over again?"

"Kind of."

"Then you should. Why don't you meet me after work? I have to go to the paper store to get Christmas cards. Want to meet me in the Public Garden at six? The corner across from the church?"

"Works for me."

I smile to myself. Rob's coming over tomorrow evening, or he said he would. Chances are looking good this week...though a small part of me selfishly thinks a repeat performance next month isn't so bad as consolation prizes go.

* * *

I SPOT NOAH walking toward me at six precisely. He waves, face lit by the white Christmas lights decorating the trees along the pond. A Macy's bag swings from his hand.

"Let me guess," I say as we meet. "New pants?"

He nods. He looks a little shy, a little devious. The expression of a man guaranteed to get laid.

"Good day?" I ask. "What do you teach, anyhow?"

"Film history, mostly. Some screenwriting."

"Wow, cool. What's your favorite era for movies, then?"

Noah's face lights up, not unlike the way I hope my future child's might one day. "Seventies, hands-down. *Taxi Driver, Dog Day Afternoon…*"

"*Chinatown.*"

He nods. He looks about ready to lean in and cheek kiss me, but we're interrupted.

"Abby?"

Oh, fuck me. It's Rob. He strides as much as one can over the ice heaves in our direction.

"Rob," I say, just as Noah says the same. Then I say, "Huh?"

"Noah, right?" Rob reaches us and extends a gloved hand. Noah nods and they shake.

"You guys know each other?" I ask, horrified. So much for discretion.

"We work out at the same studio," Noah says and aims a thumb down Boylston Street.

"You kickbox?" I ask him. Noah's medical history just had "cardio" down for his exercise habits.

"A little bit. Just for the workout, not for real." That explains the arms.

"How do you know Abby?" Rob asks Noah, and my stomach churns.

"We, um…" Noah trails off.

"He's trying to impregnate me," I say, then blush so hard I feel overheated, even in the numbing breeze.

Rob laughs, a loud bark, and Noah's eyes widen. He stares at me, horrified.

"It's okay," I say. "So's he."

"Holy *shit,*" Noah says.

"God, fucking Boston." I look around us, torn between wanting to laugh and die. Adrenaline leaves my body, making me feel drunk and hyper.

"That's a relief," Rob says. "I was afraid you were her secret infertile husband or something," he says to Noah. "Or that I'd gotten caught up in some really twisted infidelity scheme."

"It is twisted," I remind him. "But only in the capacity you guys already knew about."

Noah's smiling tightly at my side. I wonder if the whole plan is wrecked, if he's totally creeped out by putting a face to the genetic competition, or if a bright light has been shone on my spurious morals. I stare at the disgruntled ducks huddled by the edge of the frozen pond for a moment.

"Is this weird?" I ask, looking between my two donors.

They glance at each other for a few beats; then Noah shrugs. "No, I don't think so. Just a bit nuts that we know each other."

Rob shakes his head in an agreeable way.

"Oh, good," I say, though I still feel as though I've been caught doing something unseemly. I suppose I have. But the fact that I've come this far with my crazy scheme gives me hope that I'll survive this lapse in donor diplomacy. Provided Noah and Rob can shrug it off.

"We can compare notes in the locker room," Rob says. I'm fairly certain he's kidding, but Noah laughs nervously, and even in the streetlight I can see his cheeks pinken.

"I feel like such a slut," I say, unable to keep the words from tumbling out, and I start laughing so hard I double over, diaphragm convulsing until it hurts. When I recover I find them both smiling at me.

"Don't feel bad," Rob says. "We're the ones getting paid."

I put my hand on Noah's arm. "Right. Well, we better get back to the harem." I sound so obscenely cavalier I want to slap myself.

"Good luck," Rob says, hurdling right over the tactlessness bar I just set. He gives Noah a little wave. "I'll see you later, Abby."

"Have a good night." We watch him continue on toward Boylston and turn a corner.

"Wow," Noah says and rubs a hand over his face. "Weird."

"I'm so sorry. Did that wreck the whole evening?"

He looks me square in the eye and shakes his head. "I knew what the deal was." He's quiet for a while longer, and I watch the breath rising from his nostrils as he's thinking. He gives me plenty of time to guess what he's about to say, exactly how he'll word it when he tells me he needs some time to rethink this whole ridiculous arrangement. When he opens his mouth to speak again, I'm expecting something dramatic, possibly ruinous.

"Should we grab a pizza on the way back to your place?"

* * *

NOAH IS DIFFERENT NOW. Because he's met the competition, I assume, and maybe because the competition is someone he's possibly seen naked and maybe even gotten punched in the face by. In any case, he's on me as soon as I shut the door behind us. He tosses the pizza box on the floor, and I'm pushed up against the wall, his mouth claiming mine. I try to guess if he's hot over the wrongness of it all or if he's looking to prove something. As his tongue slips between my lips, I decide I don't give a shit.

We kiss hard, eager hands groping through clothes until the fabric feels hateful. We pull our coats and sweaters off, and Noah struggles with my bra clasp as I tear at his shirt buttons. Buckles clink, and zippers unzip. We kick our pants away, touching each other through our underwear. Noah's fingers rub my clit, and I lose coordination, pausing to admire his body as he pleasures me.

"Jesus," I mumble.

"What?"

"Your body, Professor Beefcake." I run teasing palms over the lean, defined muscles of his chest. He's smooth, just the faintest spray of soft brown hair as proof he doesn't wax to get this look. Good. Call me traditional, but the whole manscaping trend turns me right off. "I can't believe we've had sex twice, and I didn't even know what you look like under your clothes."

He laughs. "I'm always a little fatter in the winter," he says, laying a hand on his stomach. "Too icy to go running every morning."

"Oh yeah, you're a real tub." I tap the backs of my fingers against his supposed gut. "Look at this." I poke my own middle, persistently doughy no matter how often I talk myself into going to Pilates.

"Girls are supposed to be soft," Noah says. He runs his hands over my stomach, up to my breasts, spreading heat over my skin.

"Not according to *Maxim*."

"According to *Maxim*, every guy is a total asshat. That's why I read *Harper's*. According to *Harper's*, every guy's a liberal wingnut."

"I'll take wing nut over asshat."

"Lucky me," Noah says softly and pulls me close. "You know, pretty soon you'll be *hee*-uge." He cups my sides as if he's imagining my massively pregnant belly. Something about this innocent tease gets me so hot I feel crazed, burning and impatient, ready to tear at this man's skin and pull his hair and force his body inside me. I cup his head in my hands and yank his mouth down to mine, kiss him deep and rough and earn myself a few gorgeous moans from this gorgeous man.

He's hard already, the ridge of his cock pressing my pubic bone. I step back a few paces, and he follows. Next thing I know, we're on the floor, and he's yanking my panties off, shoving his legs between mine and grinding his stiff dick against me. I bring my knees up and hook a toe into either side of his waistband, push his shorts down to his ankles. I love his weight. I love how warm his skin is on mine, love the insistent push of his hips, his thick, ready cock finding my entrance.

"Jesus, Noah." I slide my hands to his ass, feel his muscles working as his thrusts tease me.

"You need lube?"

"I don't think so."

"You comfortable?"

My bare ass is on the hardwood, shoulders and head on the throw rug. I'll probably end up with both bruises and carpet burn, but right now I can't be bothered about it. "Just fuck me, Noah."

He reaches down, eases his dick inside my pussy, finds me wet after an inch of tight friction. He slides in and out until the fucking's smooth and easy. "Yeah," he murmurs. "Good girl."

"More."

"You're so wet." He repeats it a couple times, finding his rhythm. The room is dark except for the reading lamp by the door, but I can see everything I want—all the shapes and shadows of his fantastic body, the cut of his triceps, and the swell of his ass.

"Abby," he moans, and steadily his body slows until he's just braced above me, breathing hard. It makes me nervous, makes me worry he's thinking about the whole Rob thing, that it short-circuited his brain or his dick.

"What's wrong?" I ask, holding my breath.

"Nothing…"

"Are you sure?"

"Can I go down on you?"

"Oh," I say, as intrigued as I am relieved. "Sure."

He pulls out and sits back, his eyes glued to mine as he runs two fingers over my pussy lips.

"Sit on the couch," he says. I like the bossy edge to his voice.

I move to the edge of the cushions, and Noah pushes the table to the side, gets in front of me on the floor, takes hold of my hips, and brings his face in close. "You smell so good."

I hold my breath, waiting. I've missed this in the six months I've been single—seeing a man on his knees, mouth between my legs. Noah kisses my clit, and I groan, curl my whole body into the pleasure. Heat pools against his lapping tongue, and I rake my fingers through his short hair, wanting to possess him. His licks are firm and slick and explicit, tight little strokes thrumming my clit, complemented by the soft brush of his stubbly chin against my tender lips. I close my eyes and imagine him above me, coming. I imagine watching him come, not just his face but his cock, his hand as he strokes himself, loses control, and shoots across my stomach or breasts. The heat mounts, and my legs tremble, my feet feel tingly, and my clit is burning up.

"Don't stop."

He keeps his tongue working and moans, the sound vibrating through my body and magnifying all the sensations. One hand leaves my leg, and I feel his knuckles brush my pussy, tease my crease before he slides two fingers inside.

I keep one possessive hand on the back of his head, then palm my breast with the other. I study his strong arms and shoulders, the shapes of his eyebrows. "Yeah. Fuck me, Noah."

He moans again, deep, and it pushes me over the edge. My pleasure reaches its peak against his fluttering tongue, hot tremors tightening and bursting and wringing me out until his licks are too much, and I have to scoot back to escape the sensations. He moves his mouth lower, lapping the spoils with hungry, happy noises. I catch my breath while he feasts, stroke his hair, feel spent and grateful and spoiled.

"Thank you," I mumble as he leans back on his haunches.

He grins and squeezes my thighs. "Don't thank me for that." He gets up to sit beside me. "I fucking love eating pussy."

I take a final steadying breath. I glance at the big bandage on his knee, wonder if my hardwood has exacerbated the damage already done by my sidewalk. "You ready to give me something else now?"

He nods. There's an intensity to his eyes that thrills me. I recline as he gets a leg between mine, his other foot on the floor. I wrap my thighs around his waist as he sinks back inside with a curse.

"You're so. Fucking. Wet."

"Because of you." I tug on his hips, and he pushes deep. "You feel so good. You're so thick."

He makes a smug *Mmmmm* noise and starts to move. He locks an arm behind one of my knees and spreads me wide, hammering hard so his balls slap me with each thrust. The arm of the couch is awkward under my back, but I don't care. All that matters is Noah's hips pumping, Noah's cock surging, Noah's moan mounting as he gets closer and closer.

"God, Noah. Keep going. Give it to me."

"I'm gonna come in you. Fuck, Abby, I'm gonna come."

"I need it, Noah. I need your come. Give it all to me."

"Yeah. Yeah…"

He fucks so hard I can feel the couch moving across the wood, so hard he knocks a puff of my breath out with each impact.

"Yeah. Here it comes, Abby. Here it comes." Noah falls apart, rams himself deep deep deep, and freezes, stomach clenching with each spasm until he slumps, all his wonderful weight pinning me, his smell and his panting noises lighting up my senses like electricity. I feel his lips on my neck, kissing idly between deepening breaths. I rub his back and arms, comb my nails through his hair, and trace the curves of his ears. He pushes himself up, sinks into the center cushion. I make it to sitting, feeling high and filthy and full of myself. Full of both of us.

"Fuck *me*," I mutter. "Let's eat some pizza."

CHAPTER FIVE

"KNOCK, KNOCK."

I lean around the counter to smile at Rob as he steps through the front door. "Hey, there. Be right out." I finish the dish I'm scrubbing and dry my hands. Rob kisses my cheek as I come over to take his coat.

"Downstairs door was unlocked," he says.

"So I gathered. How are you?"

"Not bad." The way his eyes drop from my face to my chest, the way his smile turns from polite to wicked, tells me this night will be much like his first visit. It makes me miss Noah's sweet cautiousness, but I still want him. Rob's still the best-looking man I've ever been with, and I'd be lying if I said it wasn't a turn-on.

I dug out a stack of takeout menus when I got home, in case Rob was hungry, but food doesn't seem to be on his radar. He puts his hands to my waist, lips to my temple, brings our bodies close.

"I've got wine in the kitchen, if you want some."

"Maybe." He leans in and kisses my neck, cradling my jaw in his palms.

"Or we can just get down to it," I say.

Rob steers the conversation somewhere I hadn't expected. "I didn't make you come last time."

"Sure you did," I say, sounding way too surprised.

He grins at me. "It's cool, Abby. I know I didn't."

I gnaw on my lip, mortified. I guess Rob's better at faking gullibility than I am at faking orgasms.

"But I figured maybe that's all either of us wanted out of it," Rob says. "The illusion... But I have to say, my ego's a little bruised."

"Oh," I say, mustering flirtation. "We can't have that."

Rob kisses my mouth, easing in slower than last time. I assume that the three of us crossing paths yesterday has had the same game-upping effect on Rob as it did on Noah. And the fire burning in Rob's body as the kissing intensifies convinces me that he's up to the challenge. That he was practically born for it. If I can manage to quiet my racing thoughts and give myself over to what he's got planned, I'll be happy to oblige.

I lead us to the couch. Rob turns aggressive, leaning close, pushing me steadily back until I'm half-reclined, his strong, heavy body against mine, bringing all that same dirty excitement from Sunday and far less uncertainty. His promise scared me at first, made me worry what might happen if I *couldn't* come tonight, but now...now I want everything this gorgeous man can give me.

Rob's mouth moves to my neck, his hot tongue teasing my skin as his soft moans light me on fire.

"Tell me what you want," he murmurs.

"You know."

I hear him laugh softly against my throat; then he grabs my hand and puts it between his legs, presses it to where his cock's grown stiff behind his jeans. "You'll get my come, Abby. But what first? I wanna blow your fucking mind."

"God, I'm not—" I yelp at the blare of the door buzzer.

Rob laughs. "Ding-dong, pizza boy."

I glare at him. "Not funny. You have no idea how close to a porno my life's become this week." I'd ignore it, but I can already hear feet ascending the steps. Rob lets me up, and I smooth my palms over my skirt and hair and pad across the living room. I open the door halfway, not honestly surprised in the least by the face staring back at me.

"Noah." I slip out onto the small landing so maybe Rob won't overhear us.

"Hey," he says. "Your downstairs door was open."

"Yeah…I've got, um, company tonight. Of the impregnation variety." I make a face, one I hope conveys apology and tactful embarrassment and goofy well-adjustedness.

He purses his lips, pink blooming in his cheeks. His posture changes noticeably, shoulders rising but not in a self-assured way. "Oh. Sorry. You said this morning you were doing your Christmas cards tonight. I didn't know it was code-speak."

I shake my head and laugh. "It's not. I *am* planning on doing that. You know, when the other stuff is done with." I toy with adding, *he's not usually as thorough as you*, but think better of it.

"Sorry. I was just… Somerville Theatre's showing *Mean Streets* at eight. I just thought if you were free… Well anyway. I'm really sorry. This is awkward." He manages a smile, and I return it tenfold, wanting to alleviate anything bad he's feeling.

There's silence for a moment; then I sigh, frazzled. "It's—"

Rob's voice cuts in from behind me. "Let him in."

I glance at Noah, our eyes locking for a long, awkward pause. "Do you want to come in?"

He makes a charming, terrified face and shrugs.

Rob pulls the door wide open on us. "Hey."

"Hey," Noah says.

"Don't worry. I got here like five minutes ago. You didn't interrupt anything scandalous. Come in and have a glass of wine." There's something pointed and devious in Rob's expression, a quality that both excites and scares me—an invitation. I look at Noah, who just purses his lips, looking between us.

"C'mon," Rob says. He leaves us and crosses to the kitchen. I hear my cupboard doors opening and closing and glasses tinkling.

"I think he's propositioning you for an impromptu threesome," I whisper to Noah.

"Yeah, I sort of sensed that."

We trade more insecure eye contact.

"Do you want that?" he asks.

"Do you want to wake up tomorrow having *done* that?" I ask.

"I asked you first," he says.

I think about it and answer honestly. "Yeah, I sort of want that. But it's not really about what I want."

"You're kidding, right?" Noah crosses his arms over his chest. There's an edge to his discomfort, something tough to pinpoint but unmistakably male and possibly territorial. Like the hard body he hides behind his unassuming clothes, this quality both surprises and excites me. His eyes are bright and intense, that same primal, animal intensity I feel when I imagine conceiving his child.

"Both the guys in your apartment right now are here because of what you want," he says.

"Well, what I want, and what you guys want too. Don't pretend like there's not money and no-strings sex on offer, here."

Noah opens his mouth, closes it, grinds his jaw.

"What?"

"I don't know. I don't want you to think it's just about a hook-up or a paycheck with me. Trying to get someone pregnant isn't no-strings in my book."

"Well it is in *his*." I jerk my head in the direction of the kitchen.

He takes a step closer and whispers, "What about you?"

"You *know*, Noah. It's about me conceiving. The fact that you're a nice guy and I like spending time with you with my clothes on is a bonus, okay?"

"You kids want to quit whispering in the doorway?"

I turn at the sound of Rob's voice and find him clutching the wine bottle and three empty glasses.

"Just give us one sec."

He sets everything on the coffee table and wanders back to the kitchen. I lean in the threshold, a little pissed at Noah. "I feel like you think I've been leading you on or something."

He takes a deep breath, rolls his eyes in a relenting way. "I'm sorry. I just... This isn't what I pictured happening while I was driving over here."

I nod.

"I know what this is all about," he says, sounding suddenly resolved. "I just forgot, I guess. When I found out he was here."

"Well, I hope—"

Noah steps inside, throwing me for a complete loop. He pushes off his shoes, and I take his jacket and scarf and close the door, bewildered by this sudden U-turn in his attitude. His face is set and tough to read as he pours three generous glasses. Rob comes back to the living room.

My mind is swimmy. One of these men is oozing filthy mischief; the other hemorrhaging a breed of competitiveness I don't entirely trust. I take the glass Noah hands me, wondering who the fuck this man is. An image of the two of them coming to blows flashes across my brain. They're both trained in hand-to-hand combat, and I take an inventory of the breakable things in the room.

Rob clinks his glass against mine, as if he's toasting this bizarre turn of events. I swallow. I can't stand the sloppy ambiguity going down in my orderly home.

"You're trying to turn this into a three-way, aren't you?" I ask Rob. He laughs. "Aren't *you?*"

"I didn't invite Noah over," I say. Noah shakes his head in confirmation.

"Oh." Rob nods at Noah and takes a drink. "I kinda thought you planned it. Anyhow, I'm game if you guys are." He's so casual it shocks me. Impresses me too. I tend to overthink things, and I'm jealous of how simple Rob makes the whole decision seem, how easily he can roll with these punches.

Neither Noah nor I speak, so Rob goes on. "I don't mind sharing my night." He grins and steps close. I take a deep breath and watch his mouth as it lowers to mine. He kisses me, deep and slow, tasting of wine. I feel a hand on my arm, and I open my eyes to find Noah coaxing me to face him. He kisses me the same way Rob did, though it feels different, tastes different. Different, the way their skin smells, how their hands hold me, the sexual energy warming me on either side.

"Me and Abby were just talking," Rob says, "about how I ripped her off last time in the pleasure department. I guess this'll make up for it. You been with two guys before?" he asks me.

"No."

It's impressive how Rob controls the sexual atmosphere of a place, how easily he can waltz in as a paid guest, then take right over as ringmaster.

"You two seem close," he says, dark eyes darting between us. "Why don't you show me what she likes?" he asks Noah.

Rob steps back a pace, and Noah embraces the deference, musters an air of authority that thrills me. He kisses me deep, leads me to the couch, pulls me down into his lap. I press my pussy against him as his tongue plunders my mouth, and I rub until I feel his hard-on pressing back. I wrestle my lips from his and kiss his ear, taste his skin, feel his throat vibrate with a low moan. His hips shift beneath mine, begging for more friction.

"Yeah," he mumbles. "Ride me."

I feel the couch shift, and Rob's thigh brushes mine as he kneels beside me. Noah's hands are on my hips, and I feel another one smooth my hair from my face and touch my neck. It's a vulnerable feeling, but that's not a criticism. The only thing that truly worries me is the thought that Noah's here under duress, and the stiff cock thrusting against my pussy is telling me he's just fine.

His hands slide up to my breasts, and Rob's move down, his cool, smooth palm rubbing my thigh, inching up to knead my ass. I let him slide it beneath my panties, slip his fingers between my legs. I lift myself from Noah's lap, and Rob dips inside, testing.

"Fuck, yeah." He pushes in deeper, eases his fingers out, and slicks them over my clit. He takes his hand away, and I press back against Noah.

"I want you," I whisper.

Noah moans, pushing gently at my hips. I move to the side so he can open his belt and fly, push his pants down enough to take himself out. Rob cups my breasts from behind, and we watch Noah stroke his ready cock.

"Nice," Rob says, lips on my neck. One of his hands roams down, gathers my skirt, slides back inside my panties, and finds my clit. I moan at the touch and lean into him, attention jumping between Noah's dick and face. He's beyond horny: lids nearly closed, mouth open in a silent, continuous moan.

"Touch him," Rob whispers.

I knead Noah's thigh, watch his hand until it takes mine and wraps it around his hard flesh. He covers my fist with his and guides my pulls. Bossy. Rob's wet fingers strum my clit in taunting circles, slide into my lips now and again to offer a tease of penetration.

"You wanna suck him?" Rob asks. "You wanna suck him while I fuck you?"

I force my mouth to form the noise. "Yeah."

"Yeah," Noah echoes.

"Do it." Rob's fingers leave my pussy. He stands, pushes the coffee table away, and strips his shirt off, drops his jeans and shorts and kneels on the floor. I watch him pump himself until he's long and hard and flushed dark; then I join him, getting to my knees before the couch. Noah's eyes take it all in as Rob flips my skirt up, yanks my panties down my legs. He pushes my thighs wide with his. He teases his head over my clit, bathes it in my juices. "Fuck, she's so wet."

"Yeah." Noah stands and pulls his shirt off, kicks away his pants and underwear. He sits back down on the couch before me, naked and hard. He tugs gently at my shoulders, and I scoot forward, bracing my arms along his thighs. Rob comes forward as well, and his hips meet my ass, cock finding my pussy, sliding along my wet lips.

"Good," Rob mumbles. He sets a steady rhythm with his hips, and I match it with my hands, massaging Noah's thighs as I watch him stroke himself. Behind me is the most factually attractive man I've ever had the good fortune of seeing naked. Despite the talented motions of his dick teasing me, he barely registers. I'm so locked on Noah that the rest of the world is fading to gray around him.

"Ready?" Rob asks, cutting through my haze.

"Yeah."

He reaches between our bodies, angles his head to me. His cock presses hard, finds my entrance and slides in deep in one thrust.

"Yes," I moan, hot from so much more than just the thrill of him filling me. Hot from the whole dynamic, hot from Noah's eyes on us. He looks hungry and enthralled and a little afraid, just how I'm feeling. He's offering himself up to this filthy turn of events, and that gives me permission to do the same, to quit overanalyzing and just wallow in the moment.

Rob starts pumping, possessive hands on my waist. "Yeah, so tight."

"Harder," I say, shutting my eyes and just *feeling*. Listening. I want to hear his body slapping mine, his voice reduced to animalistic moans. I want every filthy thing about this moment multiplied until I can't even recognize myself.

Noah groans. I open my eyes to find him staring, hypnotized. "That's so fucking hot."

"Stroke him," Rob says.

I take Noah obediently in hand. He's rock-hard, throbbing. He pumps himself into my grip and watches Rob fuck me.

"Take her," he says.

Rob leans in close, a hand holding either side of my ribs, his hips pumping fast.

"Fuck her," Noah says. "Make her nice and wet for me."

A bolt of exquisite, nasty longing zaps through my body as Noah takes control, asserts himself as the one dishing out commands. Rob obeys, pounds me, fucks me with long, explicit strokes, makes me feel every inch of him.

"Yeah, yeah." He slaps my ass. "Suck him, Abby."

I look up at Noah's face, seeking permission, wanting to make it clear it's his orders I'm following, not Rob's. His mouth parts, and he licks his lips. "Do it."

I nod. Noah scoots closer, spreading his thighs wide. Rob slows as I lean in and tease Noah's head with my tongue.

"Yeah," Noah moans.

"Lick him," Rob says.

I lap his cock, tasting his skin, his pre-come.

The rough thrusts return. I let the impact rule, let Noah slip deeper into my mouth with each bump of Rob's hips.

"Suck him, Abby." Rob pounds me hard, spanks me. "He's nice and thick, isn't he?"

Noah groans as my lips tighten around him with affirmation. "She likes it."

"Don't let him come," Rob tells me.

I slow my mouth, concentrate on every tiny sensation as I give Noah light, teasing head. I flicker my tongue over his slit and fondle his balls, make him moan.

"More," he begs. His hands urge my head closer. I ease my lips down his cock, worshipping him, wanting him to feel big and powerful, all the things he is to me when we fuck alone. Another slap from Rob pulls me out of the hormonal clouds, lands me back on my knees on my living room rug. I'm torn between the undeniable hotness of what's happening and an urge to protect Noah, the sanctity of me and Noah. But the impulse is ridiculous, and it has no place in what's happening in this room or in my arrangement with either of these men. I push it away, let myself get lost in the taboo.

"She's so greedy," Rob says. "She wants us both."

I do. I'm filled by these men, but I want more. I want to drown in them, in their desires and sounds and smells, in their simultaneous pleasure and in mine. I moan around Noah's cock.

"You want us both?" he whispers, gathering my messy hair back from my face.

I moan again.

"What do you think?" he asks Rob.

"Let's give her what she wants." Rob pounds me hard for another minute before he withdraws. I let Noah's cock go as Rob helps me to my feet. He peels my shirt up as I feel Noah's hands on my skirt, easing the stretchy waistband down my hips. As Rob kisses me, Noah undoes my bra clasp, palms my freed breasts, and tweaks my nipples to hard peaks. I feel Noah's smooth chest and stomach against me, his cock at my lower back. He pulls my hair to one side and kisses my neck. I feel lost between their two bodies, my attention yanked between too many hands and mouths and rumbling voices, mind swimming. I feel drunk, as though my body's not my own: just a pleasurable vehicle taking my brain along for the ride, too fast to allow for questions or hesitation.

Rob leads me past the kitchen by the hand, Noah close behind. Rob lies on the bed, and I let him pull me down and press his sweat-slick chest along my back. I don't know exactly what he's got planned, but I won't deny him. Tonight I trust him with my pleasure the way I trust Noah with everything else.

"Bring your leg up," Rob murmurs in my ear. I swivel my hip, and he grabs my leg behind the knee, propping it up as his cock slides into my pussy from behind. "Yeah."

Noah watches from beside the bed, silhouetted by the light from the kitchen. He sits on the mattress and draws close, stretches out facing me, putting his hand to my waist as Rob sets his rhythm. He kisses me, deep and sweet. The contact feels so odd, one man's sensual tongue teasing mine, the other's cock pumping into me, rough.

"You feel good?" Noah asks. I sense his gaze boring into mine in the relative darkness.

"Yeah. I'm glad you're here."

His hand holds me tight, and his hips close in until his erection presses against my mons and belly. "Do you want me too?"

At the same time? "I think so."

"She wants us both," Rob moans, cock sliding in and out, so hot. So wrong. Still, we're the only witnesses to what's happening here in my bed, and my body's telling me the only way I'll regret this evening is if I back out now and miss my chance.

Noah kisses me again. He sucks me into him, into his desire, into this gift. I take hold of his dick between us, stroke him, measure his girth again with my hand, wonder if such a feat would be possible, let alone pleasurable.

"We can try," I say. "There's lube in the bedside table."

Noah pulls away and grabs the bottle from the drawer, squirts a measure into my palm. "Get me ready."

I rub the slippery liquid up and down his length until he's panting.

"She's so tight," Rob says over my shoulder. "Let's make it tighter."

Noah's mouth drops open, and I know he wants this too.

"Go on," I say. Then I lower my voice so only he can hear, put my lips to his ear. "It feels so empty without you."

"Come on," Rob grunts. "Let's spread her wide open."

Noah reaches down and takes his cock from me. I hold my breath as he guides himself close. He's watching—watching Rob already fucking me. Rob pulls out so just his head is penetrating.

"Do it."

Noah puts himself there, eases his head inside me alongside Rob's. The pleasure, the fear, the sheer *nastiness* of it is a drug.

"You ready, Abby?" Noah whispers against my lips.

"Yeah."

He pushes, forcing himself in, forcing me open. Rob pushes too, and as they sink deeper, I stretch, my body cautious.

"Slow, boys," I mutter.

"Just relax," Noah says, and I do, because it's him. His voice, a stranger's only days ago, calms me. He edges in another inch, surpassing Rob for a moment. It feels amazing, their cocks sliding against each other inside me.

"Yeah," Rob moans, and he pushes deeper. "This is so fucking tight."

"Yeah," Noah echoes.

"You're so big. Both of you."

"That's what you like, isn't it?" Rob teases, voice right in my ear. "Nice big dicks?"

"I love it."

"How does it feel, taking us both?" He starts to pump at a slow pace as Noah holds still.

"It feels...really fucking dirty."

Noah pumps too now, two pairs of hips pinning me, two hard dicks filling me, two men's strong legs tangled between mine. I squeeze Noah's shoulders and push my face against his throat, lost. "God, fuck me."

"Can you come?" Noah asks it quietly, a private whisper. The intimacy of his voice and question thrills me as much anything else happening to my body.

"I can try," I whisper back.

His hand leaves my waist, slipping down between our damp bodies. His two fingers find my clit amid the crush of hot flesh, and I groan at the touch. I lean back enough to meet Noah's half-closed eyes.

Rob pumps faster. Noah keeps his thrusts steady and predictable.

"We're fucking you," Noah tells me, and the words light a trail of fire from his fingers through my clit, up my belly to my breasts and cheeks. "We're fucking you, Abby."

"Yeah." The bossy self-assurance has left Rob's voice, replaced by desperate excitement. "Do you like it? You like two cocks?"

"I love it." And I do...though perhaps not for the reasons I let Rob assume. I love this for more than my own selfish pleasure, but as an exploration, something I'm sharing with the man whose sex-addled face is just an inch from mine.

Noah's fingertips tease me toward rapture.

"Maybe we'll both shoot together," Rob says. "Would you like that? Both of us? Filling you up with our come? Just like we're filling your pussy with our big cocks?"

Jesus, he's filthy. The words leave me reeling. "Yes."

"Yeah, you want that."

I only half understand what he's saying. I'm falling over the edge. Noah's expert fingers are dragging me down into the dark, beautiful oblivion of my pleasure. My feet twitch and kick, toes curling.

"Come on. Come on," Noah urges. For him, I will. I let go, falling away. For a few beautiful, suspended seconds, I feel nothing but our three bodies as one, our smells, our sounds, our shared desire, their cocks impossibly big inside my clenching cunt.

"Yeah, yeah, yeah." Rob joins me. I feel him, frantic and needy, hips slapping my ass. He pushes deep and holds, his body pressed rigid and damp against my back as he comes.

"Good," Noah murmurs, and he's saying it to me. He's still. As Rob slides out, he does too. He kisses me lightly, and I feel his cock—stiff, slick from me and from Rob—pressed against my belly.

Rob runs a hand down my side, and his voice is breathy behind my ear. "Beautiful."

I turn my head to smile at him. "Thank you."

As the haze burns away, Rob seems unsure of what to do, the dynamics between us three so different with the intoxication of the sex stripped away.

"I'll leave you two," Rob finally says. I assume he knows where to find the envelope. I don't want to say it out loud. Not now. Not in front of Noah.

For a couple minutes I listen to him gathering his clothes, using the bathroom, letting himself out. I feel Noah release a deep breath against my neck.

He pulls away and looks me in the eyes. "Would you come with me a minute?"

I get up and follow him to the bathroom. I feel Rob's come dripping down my thigh, as though he's still with us. Noah leans inside the shower and turns the taps, fusses until the temperature's to his liking.

He holds out a hand to say I should get in. He joins me in the steam and the warm water, kisses me lightly. He takes my soap from the caddy and lathers his hands. I let him run them over my shoulders, up and down my back, over my breasts, my hips, my butt. He kneels and soaps my legs, then turns the bar in his hands until they're coated in lather. He coaxes me to stand wider, and he washes me. His touch is gentle against my savaged, sensitized lips and clit, intimate as he soaps my curls.

I know what he's doing. I let him. I let him bathe me until he's convinced that Rob's gone, that he's the only man here with me. I study Noah on his knees, so reverential. We both know what he's doing is a violation of the entire point of recruiting two men for this job, but I don't stop him. I don't want to. I want this intimacy as badly as I thought I wanted anonymity.

As the bathing comes to an end, he stands. He rests his chin on my temple, sighs deeply, clears his throat as the water rinses the soap from our bodies. No words come, so I take over. I twist the taps shut and grab him a towel, and we dry off together in the silence left in the water's wake. When we're done I walk back to my bedroom, and he follows. I tug the bedspread flat, trying to erase the wrinkles and lumps from earlier, the evidence.

We lie on our sides on the covers, facing each other with our knees linked.

"Tonight was the most fucked-up thing I've done, sexwise," Noah whispers. "I didn't actually know I was capable of anything like that."

I study his chest with its faint spray of soft hair. "It's the dirtiest thing I've ever done too. Like, straight-up porno dirty. I hope you won't feel creepy about it. I hope you won't feel weird at your boxing studio now."

I glance up as Noah makes a face, a familiar glimmer of the man I've come to know. "I'm a grown-up."

I let him think a while longer, combing his wet hair with my fingers as I wait patiently for him to speak.

"I'm sorry about what I did," he says. "In the shower. That wasn't fair. I know that's not what we're all about."

I purse my lips, eyes glued to his chin as I mull it over. "I think you and me are probably equally guilty when it comes to fucking up the politics of this experiment. And to be honest, I thought it was sweet that you did that."

He angles his head and kisses me lightly, apologetically. The room still reeks of sex, the smell hanging potent around our clean bodies.

"You can still make it up to me, Noah." I hope the tease comes off as gentle and innocuous as I'm intending. I drag my lips along his jaw, kiss his ear, listen to his breathing. He tenses—first with caution, then excitement. His mouth takes mine, tongue as explicit and deep as the groans rumbling in his chest.

He rolls me onto my back, grabs the lube, and gets himself ready. He spreads me wide with his knees and slides in, just the faintest sting from the gel on my tender lips. Noah grunts and holds himself still, savoring something—maybe the fact that I'm all his now. That's what I'm feeling, at any rate. I want to spoil him, make him feel as if he's the only man on the face of the earth.

"I need you, Noah."

"Yeah?"

"I need you to fuck me. You're the only one I want."

He starts to thrust, going from controlled to frantic in less than a minute, arms locked tight around my back. I grin unseen over his shoulder, loving his strong body above mine, his deep grunts, the flex of his ass under my palms.

"Come on, Noah. Come for me. Nice and hard."

He answers with his hips, fucking me deep and graceless and greedy.

"Come on. Come on."

"Fuck, Abby."

"Shoot it deep."

He hammers me hard, then freezes, holds, pushes his hips into mine so hard I feel the bite of bone on bone. I rub his back as his body melts and his breathing returns. He slides out and lies beside me, curls against my side as I hug my knees. I feel his lips on my shoulder, kissing idly for a couple minutes; then he's out—asleep. I reach over and stroke his hair and cheek, smile at him.

Noah wakes just as I'm about to nod off. He makes an adorable noise, a soft, startled snore; then I see him blinking in the low light.

"Hey," he says.

"Hey."

We cuddle for ten minutes, exchange a few lazy kisses. Finally Noah clears his throat and breaks our silence.

"Hey, Abby…"

"Yeah?"

He kisses my shoulder, thinks for a moment. "How come you're doing all this the way you are? The conception? And I don't mean the sex."

"What, then?"

"I mean, why me and him? Why strangers? Why…single? I know this'll sound cheesy and probably a little patronizing, but I can't imagine you couldn't find a good guy and settle down and do this the…"

"Old-fashioned way?"

He shrugs and nods. "You're pretty and smart and interesting, and you've got your life together. I've met you under the strangest circumstances imaginable, and you still don't seem psycho at all."

I laugh. "Even after tonight?"

He nods again.

"Well, thanks. I guess I just don't want to wait. Even if I met the right guy tomorrow, I'd still need a long time to know if he's *really* right. Right enough to be my kid's father. And at the risk of sounding a bit desperate, I don't think I can wait another two or four or more years."

"Sure."

"I ended a serious relationship this summer," I say. "I'd been going out with my boyfriend for almost three years, and we weren't even living together yet. I know I loved him, but I know it would've taken me *another* three years to figure out if he was The One or whatever. The traditional way is just…too damn slow. For me, anyway, because I'm sort of cautious, believe it or not. But my body's still like, tick-tock, tick-tock," I say, tapping my middle. "Biological time bomb. But I knew I didn't want to settle down with the most convenient guy just because my ovaries started calling the shots. That probably makes me seem obnoxious and wishy-washy."

"It sounds like he probably just wasn't the right guy," Noah says, "if you still had all that room for doubt."

"That was my thinking in the end. But you know how it is when there's nothing actually *wrong* with someone but they still aren't quite right. It makes everything really confusing."

"Yeah," Noah says. "Those break-ups are the worst. When you don't have a good reason for why you're ending it."

I nod my passionate agreement. "So yeah. That's why I'm doing this the crazy way." It's strange, but I'm as certain that I want a child—and that I'm ready for it—as I was *un*certain about my ex.

Noah kisses my forehead, shifts his body. Something about the drag of his sweat-damp skin against mine ushers reality in, tightens me up as rational thought drives away the lazy tenderness.

"I think I have to ask you not to spend the night tonight." I say this to his ear since I can't seem to look him in the eye. "Just because this whole evening was sort of…"

"Insane?"

"I was going to say 'complicated,' but sure. That works too. I think I need to just be by myself, sit around in my pajamas, and you know, come down from it."

"Sure."

"But I promise I'm not upset you came over."

He kisses my temple again. "It's okay if you are. Don't worry about my feelings. I'm tough."

I nod, wishing it were that simple. Wishing it was anywhere *near* as simple as I'd envisioned.

Noah rolls away and gets up. I follow suit, and we get dressed, both wearing polite smiles, a vaguely uncomfortable energy strung heavily between us. My stomach growls as he's tying his shoes. I glance at the coffee table at the three identical half-drunk glasses of wine. I glance at the bare tree branches outside in the streetlight. I feel guilty sending Noah out into the dark and cold after everything that's gone on, but I know if he stays and spends the night, I'll wake up tomorrow not knowing what he is to me anymore.

I have a thought, jog to my tiny office space, and scribble him a check, a desperate little attempt to reassert the rules of this fucked-up arrangement.

I get back as he's shrugging his coat on. "Here," I say.

Noah winces, opens his mouth, closes it, stares down at the check with a blank expression. I worry I've insulted him, but I need something about this night to go according to the plan. He folds the paper neatly and slips it into his pocket. "Thanks."

"Sure. Enjoy the movie," I add.

"Yeah." That one dispirited syllable tells me Noah's not going to see *Mean Streets* tonight, maybe not ever again, now that it's tangled up in the memory of the psychotic threesome he deigned to have with a sperm-hungry harpy and her other willing donor.

"See you later, Abby."

I open the door and close it behind him, listen to him clomp down the steps. A car starts up outside, idles for a minute. I'm aching to go to the window and watch him drive away, but I don't want him to look up and catch me. I hear an engine rev and ice crunch, listen to Noah pull out, heading back to Jamaica Plain and away from all the confusion I surely brought into his life—maybe regret, if the memory of this night greets him tomorrow with a hard slap as he wakes.

I rub my face, feeling about a hundred years old. I click on the TV so I'll have more than just my cyclical internal monologue for company. I flip channels until I find a bad prime-time drama, consolidate the three glasses of wine into one, dig some leftovers out of the fridge and toss them in the microwave, embrace my spinsterhood. Flopping back down on the couch, I remind myself that this is about a baby, and that babies conceived during their selfish mothers' impromptu threesomes aren't any less deserving of love than ones from boring old happy marriages.

An ad for fabric softener comes on a while later, and I wad my napkin up and toss it at the perfect mother on the screen, swaddling her toddler in a fluffy towel. "She conceived you in a port-a-potty at the county fair," I tell the child. "Your dad was a carnie. They were very much in love, but he died in a tragic Tilt-a-Whirl accident."

The child ignores me, lost in the rapture of tumble-dried terrycloth. I zap the TV off and head to bed, praying I'll wake up a different person.

CHAPTER SIX

I NEVER KNEW how many kinds of pregnancy tests there are.

For ten minutes or more I stare at boxes in the crowded downtown drugstore near my work, blocking the family planning aisle with my fistfuls of Christmas shopping bags. Eventually I pick two: a cheaper one of the pink-line, blue-line variety, and a more expensive one with a digital read-out.

I grab a can of soup, knowing I'll be in no mental shape to cook anything decent when I get home, no matter the outcome. The woman in the next line over casts tactlessly nosy looks at my purchases as I pay. I stick out my tongue at her back as she leaves, and the cashier laughs.

As I'm skirting the snowy Common to get on the Red Line, I'm so lost in my thoughts I practically knock Noah Aubrey down before he gets my attention.

"Oh God. Sorry, Noah. I was worlds away."

He smiles his nervous smile. We haven't spoken since the night of the impromptu threesome, but I feel relieved by the simple fact that he intercepted me when he could just as easily have run off.

"How have you been?" he asks. "You excited for Christmas?" I know what he really wants to know—the exact same thing I do: am I knocked up yet?

"Yeah, I'm officially ready." I waggle my many bags. "You?"

He nods, chewing his lip. "Sorry. I didn't mean to make you uncomfortable. Just thought I'd say hello."

"You aren't making me uncomfortable. I'm just... I've got pregnancy tests in my purse," I say with a laugh. "They feel like nitroglycerin. I'm just eager to get home and...you know."

He nods again, for longer than I've ever seen a person nod before; then he finally asks, "Do you want a ride? That's a lot of bags to cram on the subway."

I think for a minute, not knowing what the right answer is. I haven't seen Noah in nearly three weeks, and if I'm completely honest, I've missed him, in spite of the strange way we parted. After a few seconds' deliberation, I realize what I'm doing is already a hot mess, so blurring our boundaries for another twenty minutes probably can't fuck things up much worse.

"Sure, Noah. I'd love that."

He takes a couple of my bags, and we reroute toward the underground garage. "Aren't you on break?" I ask.

"Technically. But I came in to view some student films. Hence the shabby clothes." He gestures to his jeans and sneakers.

"I hate to break it to you, but all the cool professors wear jeans to class."

He nods, smiling. "Maybe. But I'm still pretty new, so I have to trick my students into respecting me in whatever ways I can... What do *you* do, anyway? I can't believe I never bothered to ask you that."

"I work in the legal department of an architectural firm." I point in the direction of Chinatown, toward my office. "Zoning laws and permits. Very sexy stuff."

He holds open the door to the underground garage's vestibule. "You like it?"

"I do. I've always liked that kind of law. Especially in Boston. The antiquated, ridonkulous little colonial-throwback rules are fascinating." We take the elevator down two levels and head to his car.

"Are there law nerds the same way there's film nerds?" he asks.

"God yeah, nothing but. I bet any field with minutia to memorize attracts its fair share of know-it-alls."

Noah unlocks his little hatchback, and we shove my bags into his backseat. I strap myself in, and he starts the car. Unable to resist, I open my purse and take out the expensive test's box, unfold the instructions. I feel Noah's eyes on me as we get in line to exit the garage.

"I'm sorry," I say. "I'm probably crapping all over semi-anonymous sperm-recipient etiquette, doing this with you right there. But I'm really nervous. This is a really important night for me."

"I'll bet."

"I haven't felt like this since I was waiting to hear back about law school applications. Feel free to dump me at a T stop if it gets too weird for you." I scan the paper, feeling like maybe the looming result is encrypted in the directions.

"You're fine," Noah says, turning us onto Charles Street. "I hope it comes up however you want it to, Abby." He turns for a second to look at me when he says this.

I smile tightly and nod. "Thanks." I don't know what Noah feels for me, but I can appreciate the effort I suspect it's taking him to sound so casual.

"Are you late? Your period, I mean," he mumbles.

"By a day, which means nothing. And you're really not supposed to test this early—false negatives and all. But I can't help myself."

"Understandable. How's, um...how's your family taking this whole thing?"

"They don't know yet," I say. "Actually, you and..." I forget his name for a few seconds. As handsome as I know it is, I've almost completely forgotten his face in the last two weeks. "Rob. You and Rob are the only people who know about the plan. I figured I'd clue my family and friends in once I'm in too deep to get talked out of it."

"I could see that. Sounds kind of lonely, though. Not that I know the first thing about it, of course."

"It doesn't feel too lonely," I say. "It feels exciting, like I'm planning something in secret to surprise them. My parents trust my decisions. I mean, they have to since I'm thirty-two, but I don't think it'll freak them out. I think they'll be eighty percent excited, twenty percent worried for me."

"That's a healthy mix."

"I figured if it turned out to be really tough, getting pregnant, I didn't want to put anybody else through that stress. I want to bring them in right at the happy part and deal with any frustration on my own."

"They live close?"

I nod. "In Marblehead."

"Could be an exciting Christmas."

"They'll be in the Bahamas, actually." My heart deflates at the thought.

"Brothers or sisters?" Noah asks.

"I have a younger sister, but she's out in California. If I'm not preggers, I'll probably call on my Jewish friends to invite me over for Chinese food."

"And if you are?"

I make a thoughtful face. "Me and the embryo will probably hang out on our own…drinking sparkling cider. Watching Christmas specials."

We drive over the river just as light, harmless flakes begin to drift from the gray sky.

"Have you thought about names or anything?" Noah asks. "Unless you're not comfortable talking about that kind of stuff. With me."

"Trust me, I've thought about pretty much nothing but baby stuff for the last six months. You're the one I'm worried about traumatizing, talking about this."

"I don't mind. I think it's kind of fascinating. Could've been a cool documentary, if I'd thought of it sooner."

I smile. "Well, I guess I won't know for sure until I meet the baby, but for a girl's name, I like Audrey."

Noah laughs.

"What?"

"Sorry. I just thought, thank goodness this didn't happen in some alternate reality where you and I were actually a couple. Audrey Aubrey would be in for a lifetime of stolen lunch money."

I laugh too. "Abby Aubrey's not much better."

He snorts.

"But anyway, for a boy I like Lucas."

Noah nods, and we're quiet for a while.

When we get to my neighborhood, I feel suddenly scared of being alone with my tests in my empty condo. Still, no way in hell I'd ask this kind, thoughtful man to join me. Mostly because I suspect he'd say yes.

He eases up alongside the curb. "Well, good luck. I'll have my fingers crossed for you."

"Thanks. And thanks for the ride."

We sit in silence for a moment.

"Well," I say through a sigh. "I'll let you know what happens, so you'll know to expect a check or not."

Noah looks poised to say something; then his mouth closes and he just smiles.

I open my door, and Noah does the same. He grabs half my bags and walks me up the front steps.

"Thanks," I say again

"Have a good Christmas, Abby." Noah leans down and kisses me on the cheek, well choreographed to be more brotherly than romantic. He straightens and offers me a cheesy smile, holds up two sets of crossed fingers.

"Merry Christmas." I wave as he slams his car door and glances at me through the window. When he drives away he takes all the warmth in the world with him, takes all the sparkle out of the snow, and leaves nothing but icy air and salty brown slush.

CHAPTER SEVEN

TWO DAYS LATER ON CHRISTMAS MORNING, I find a letter in my mailbox from Noah. He must have dropped it off himself, since there's no stamp. The thought makes me feel warm even as the message hidden inside the business-sized envelope sets my nerves buzzing. I drop the thank-yous I'd brought downstairs into the box and carry the mystery letter back up, heart beating harder with every step.

I take a seat and a deep breath and rip the end open, pull out the letter. Three slips of paper flutter out as I unfold it: his checks for services rendered. Rob deposited his ages ago. I let them sit on the rug while I read Noah's small, tidy handwriting.

Merry Christmas, Abby. I hope everything is going well for you. I decided to return the checks. I don't feel wrong taking them, but I wanted to say I enjoyed everything I may have done to help you, and I don't really want any money for it. Consider it a Christmas present. If you got good news and you don't need my genetic materials anymore, please don't worry about the big check either. Use it to spoil your future baby. That's better than anything I would have thought to spend it on.

If you didn't get such good news yet, feel free to give me a call next time you're ovulating, if you want. I'd be happy to help again. But hopefully I'll run into you in the park again in a few months, and you'll be as round as a beach ball. I hope you'll forgive my indiscretion if I give you a thumbs-up as I pass.

All the best,

Noah

I fold the letter and slide it and the checks into the envelope, file it away neatly with the waivers. I head back to the living room, click on the TV, and skim through the channels, taking nothing in. I pick up my phone and turn it over and over in my hand, and soon enough I mute the television and dial Noah's number. I realize as it's ringing that it's Christmas morning, and Noah picks up just as I'm about to hit end.

"Hi, Abby." His voice is hushed, and I hear music and voices in the background.

"Hi. Sorry, I totally forgot it was Christmas. I can call later if you're busy."

"No, now's fine. I'm at my sister's house in Arlington. All the exciting stuff's already done with. My nephews had everybody up by six. I don't recommend having twins if you can help it."

"Oh, that sounds nice." I feel so suddenly lonely I could burst into tears. "Well, I called because I just found your letter. That was very sweet, thank you. And if you change your mind about the money, feel free to tell me so."

"I won't, but thanks."

There's an awkward silence, me wanting Noah to ask about the test, him surely wanting me to shit or get off the conversational pot.

"I um…I didn't take the test yet," I finally say. "I chickened out."

"Oh."

"I might just wait and see if my period turns up. Anyhow, no word on whether or not I'll need you next month."

"That's cool," Noah says. "If you do, my schedule's wide open till classes start on the twentieth."

"Okay. Great. Well, anyway. Merry Christmas."

"Merry Christmas, Abby."

I shut my phone off and rub my face, surely beet-red with embarrassment. At least Noah and I are equal in our utter uselessness about knowing when to call or turn up.

I spend a couple zombielike hours puttering, wondering if I should go hang out with friends tonight. I want the company, but I don't want anyone asking why I'm not drinking. I guess I could say I don't feel well... Just the thought of this excuse is a relief, and I realize that lonely or not, I don't want to go out.

I'm just settling in with a fresh stack of thank-yous and a DVD of *It's a Wonderful Life* when my doorbell rings. I frown at my pajama bottoms and flip-flops and camisole. I grab my robe off the back of the couch and launch myself down the stairwell, practically suffocating on hope.

My wish comes true, and there's Noah standing on the front steps, a Tupperware in one hand.

I work hard to keep my smile friendly, suppress the crazy grin that's itching to consume my face. I look between Noah and his car parked on my curb like an old friend.

"Hi."

"Hi, Abby. You um, sounded sort of down on the phone. So here I am."

My face crumples, and I start crying, as shocked by my reaction as Noah must be.

"Uh..."

I take a step down onto the stoop and toss myself into his arms, not caring if I frighten him away or not. I just need another human to hug me, and he's the one who showed up. He's the one my heart suspected would appear when I needed him most, and here he is. The best kind of predictable. Dependable. He squeezes me hard and keeps his strong arms tight until I pull back. I rub my sleeves over my face, glad I didn't have any makeup on to smear.

"Sorry," I say. "I was feeling really lonely. Christmas is a lousy time to not be able to talk to your family or friends about your crackpot conception scheme."

He nods. "I'll be your friend, if you want."

"You want to come up?" I ask through a laugh. If anything's going to scare a man away, it's got to be the hysterical neediness of the woman who solicited him for his sperm. But Noah doesn't look terrified, only kind.

"Sure." He follows me up the steps. "I brought you some cookies." He rattles the Tupperware. I take it so he can slide his coat from his shoulders and toe off his shoes. He leaves his apple green scarf on. His sweater is deep red, and he looks like six feet of much-needed Christmas standing in my living room.

I shut the droning TV off. "Sorry again about the phone call. I promise I wasn't *trying* to get you to come over like this."

"I don't mind if you were."

His answer scares me a little, the old fear of complication sneaking through as the relief endorphins dissipate. I nod.

"Can I do something? Make you some coffee?" he asks.

I pull my shit together. "No no no. I'll make *you* some coffee."

He follows me into the kitchen, and I arrange the sugar cookies on a plate. It's easy to spot the homely ones that were frosted by a child. They make me smile. I set the plate right where Rob's daisies had been. I tossed those weeks ago, before they were even officially wilted.

Once the kettle's on to boil, I excuse myself to get my face in order and pull my messy hair back—it curls up like nobody's business when I don't bother with the blow-dryer, and I hadn't been in the mood to bother with much of anything today. Noah's flipping through a book about pregnancy at my breakfast bar when I come back in, and I grin at him, feeling caught.

He closes it. "It's crazy what complicated stuff you ladies get up to, biologically. Makes me feel like nothing more than a DNA squirt gun."

"I like to think of myself more like an Easy-Bake Oven." I sit beside him, let him take hold of my knees and swivel me on the stool until my feet are dangling between his.

"You know," I say, "it's strange that I know your blood type and sperm count and what your grandparents died of, but I don't even know like...your favorite band."

Noah smiles. "Sonic Youth."

"You know what I mean... Sometimes I feel like I've known you for ages. Then other times I look at you and I think, 'who is this strange man in my kitchen?'"

"Which do you feel right now?"

"Right now I feel like we must've gone to kindergarten together. But then tomorrow it might take me a minute to even remember your last name."

Noah just nods, and we're silent for a few moments. I'm adrift in a sea of what-ifs. What if I'm pregnant? What if I'm not? What if I am and it's Rob's, not Noah's? Would I love it any less?

Noah interrupts my racing internal dialogue. "I'll stay with you. While you do the test. If you want."

"Things feel blurry between us," I say. "Do they feel blurry to you?"

He nods again. "I like you. You probably knew that."

"I wondered."

"I know that's really shitty of me. And it was probably shitty of me to come over today or give you back the checks or even stay the night those two times. I know I've broken a lot of unspoken rules. It's pretty unfair. I'm surprised you're not royally pissed off at me."

I shrug. "I let you do all those things. We broke the rules together."

"I guess."

"Can you tell me how you feel, exactly? About me? Like, what do you want to happen with us now?" I hold my breath, not sure what reply I want to hear. One answer could break my heart, but the other could turn my life upside-down and force me to rethink a decision I already accepted as best.

Noah stares at our knees. "It's hard to say. I mean, we really *don't* know each other. But I think you're just...fascinating. And part of it *is* the idea that you could be carrying my child. It's hard to just push that concept out of my head, you know?" He meets my eyes.

I nod, impressed by his honesty and self-awareness. "I'll bet."

"But I don't have any expectations. I signed your waiver, and I'm not going to try and renege on it. That said, I won't lie to you... This whole thing is a million times more complex than I ever expected. I don't know how I'll feel if I see you pushing a stroller in the park someday."

The kettle whistles and I fill the French press, eyes on Noah to tell him I'm listening.

"Part of me feels really desperately like I want us to be friends," he goes on, "so I'll be allowed to walk up to you and say hello and squeeze your baby's little hand without feeling like a creep. Or a...a nobody."

"That might be possible," I say. "Lots of people use their friends as surrogates and donors."

"Yeah."

"Maybe I should just do the test. So we don't go constructing elaborate scenarios when I might not even be pregnant."

"That might be a good idea."

I nod my head passionately, putting down my foot for the both of us. "Definitely." I leave Noah and do fearlessly what I haven't been able to for the past few days. I march into the bathroom and pee on a stick.

"Done," I say as I return to the kitchen. "Three minutes."

"What should we do for three minutes?" he asks.

"Blur some more lines."

I step to where he's sitting. Our eyes are level, my boring brown ones and his fascinating green-gray ones. As much as I still genuinely crave genetic anonymity, I secretly hope my baby will come out with those eyes.

I lean in and kiss Noah, then let him take over. I knew he would, just as I knew it was him at my door, as I subconsciously knew he'd come over when my fingers dialed his number. His cool, smooth palms cup my face as his hot tongue slips between my lips. Before I know it we're stumbling toward my room. I yank Noah's sweater up his chest and over his head, and he pushes my duster off my shoulders. His big fingers fumble with the bow of my pajamas' drawstring as my small ones struggle with his belt. After a minute's frantic pawing, we get each other undressed in such a desperate rush you'd think a trophy were riding on it.

"God, Abby." Noah pushes me onto my unmade bed, climbs on top of me. He's ready—so hard it's intimidating. He tries to push into me, but my body hasn't caught up with his yet. I reach for my bedside table drawer and get the lube. I prep Noah while he does the same for me, two slick fingers sliding inside me, the stiff, thick cock in my fist promising me everything I want at this moment.

"I need you," he mumbles, eyes unfocused as he guides his head to my pussy.

My hands scream their agreement, grasping his hips and tugging him close, driving that delicious, familiar length inside.

I hold him close for a moment, just savoring. "Fuck, you feel good."

Noah starts to thrust, his body pumping fast and greedy, everything about it hot and needy and desperate—everything I want too. His moans are the deepest, most animalistic and wondrous sound I've ever heard, and my hands grip his ass, keeping the strokes rough and the sex dirty.

He groans, eyes shut tight, then flips us over so I'm on top. "Use me," he begs. "Use my body."

I do. I draw him in deep, stroke my burning clit along the base of his shaft with each thrust, lean back on my haunches and stare down at him. He brings his knees up, cradling my butt and hips. I rock in his lap, the need so tight and hot between my legs I feel high.

"God, yeah. Use me, Abby. Come on." His strong hands urge my hips, keep the rhythm fast as I lose coordination. His aggression is twice as hot as the thick heat spearing my pussy, the mean, horny look on his face sexier than every last perfect detail of what's-his-name's body put together.

The pleasure hits its peak so suddenly I gasp. All the warmth and pressure and tension built up in my cunt shatters, floods my limbs and chest, and leaves me a panting, gasping mess, arms shoved under Noah's back as I fight for breath. He's moaning, hips thrusting softly between mine. He turns us over and starts pumping again, slower, steadier.

"Don't be gentle." I don't fear the tenderness as much as I simply crave the rougher stuff. This experiment is so intrinsically selfish, it's a relief and a thrill when Noah makes it seem as if he's the greedy one.

He locks his arms tight against my ribs, and I revel in his body, his raw, flexing muscles as he takes pleasure from me. I run my palms up and down his chest and stomach. "Good."

"Oh fuck. I'm gonna come."

"Good. Let me see it this time. Lemme see when you come, Noah."

He hammers me for half a minute, grunting and moaning, skin slick under my palms, cock flashing between our bodies with every racing thrust.

"Oh fuck." He pulls out, leans back, and jerks himself home, bathing my belly in that thing that's become so intensely sacred to me. He strokes until there's nothing left to give me; then he collapses at my side. He kisses me deep, and I feel his fingers rubbing the warm come into my skin, possessive. I put my hand over his and join him. He laughs—a tiny, smug noise that warms my lips.

We lie together until our collective sweat cools, until neither of our minds is on the sex anymore.

Noah clears his throat. "Coffee's probably ready."

I don't think for a second he's any more concerned about the coffee than I am. We slowly get cleaned up and dress, and neither of us speaks until we're back in the kitchen.

"You want me to stay in here, or…how do you want to do it?"

"Why don't you come stand in the doorway while I check."

He follows me to the bathroom. "Is it the two lines or a plus sign, or how does it work?"

"This one's digital. It'll just say 'pregnant' if it's positive."

"Ah."

I keep my eyes away from where the tester waits on the rim of my sink. Noah leans in the threshold, and I reach back and take hold of his hand.

"Okay," I say through a desperate, huffing sigh. "If it's negative, that means I still get to drink on New Year's."

Noah squeezes my fingers. "Go on, Abby."

I grab the smooth plastic wand and shut my eyes, bring it close. I open them.

"Oh my God." My arm starts shaking, followed by my entire body. I hold the tester over my shoulder to show Noah that one immensely loaded digital word.

"'Pregnant'," he reads. He looks bewildered, like it says 'banana' instead.

I shake harder, clench my fists around the wand and Noah's hand, and start to cry. I let Noah turn me around, and he hugs me so hard it knocks my wind out. I wrap my arms around his middle, bury my face against his warm, sweet-smelling neck. God, I hope it's his. I want it to be. I want this man's blood in my child's veins as surely as I want his warm, strong body against mine right now.

I speak against his throat. "I hope it's yours."

"It's *yours*," he whispers, melting me. He stands up a little straighter, pushes me away enough to establish unsteady eye contact. "Even if it's me who gave it to you, it's just *yours*. I'm just going to be the best friend I can be to you, for as long as you want me here. I don't know if it'll be anything near as simple as that, but that's what I'll try to do."

"Thank you."

We hug again, softer than before. I feel my nerves subsiding, and behind the adrenaline cloud, there's a wide, blue sky of pure joy.

"Merry Christmas, Abby."

I laugh and wipe my cheeks. "Thank you."

"Do you want to be alone now?"

"No. You can go if you want, but I'd like you to stay. Let me pour you an insanely strong cup of lukewarm coffee. You can enjoy caffeine for the both of us. Holy shit—for the three of us." I laugh, the sound caught somewhere between silly and maniacal.

"Sounds good."

I fill a mug for Noah, and we sit at the breakfast bar, knees locked like zipper teeth, tester beside us on the counter.

"Thanks again," I say, barely a whisper.

"You're welcome." Noah takes my hand and gives it a squeeze. "Congratulations. I'm really happy for you."

"We should get to know each other," I say, my subconscious hijacking my mouth, voicing what my gut wants even as my mind struggles to sabotage the impulse with its tiresome logic.

"Okay."

"Why don't you ask me over to Jamaica Plain some time? To your place. We can watch one of your favorite movies, and you can tell me nerdy film-buff things about it. Maybe go out for Thai or something. I can watch you drink."

"Like a date?"

I turn that idea over in my head a few times. "I don't know. Every ten minutes I seem to make a decision about you that complicates everything I thought I wanted to keep simple. I want to say, 'let's just be friends for a few months.' But I honestly don't trust my body to stay on that bandwagon."

Noah looks thoughtful, staring at our hands as he speaks. "We're both grown ups…and this situation's already woefully complex. We could try and just be friends, and if we fuck it up, we'll agree to not be psychos if things go totally Hindenburg."

I nod my agreement, but I don't really feel it. *Feel* it. If the past couple weeks—if the past half a year—taught me nothing else, it's that my feelings make better decisions than my head. My feelings ended a comfortable relationship that was leading me nowhere, and they brought me the little white wand with its fabulous headline.

"I already know we'll fuck it up," I tell Noah. "If we try to just be friends."

His face falls. "Oh."

"But that's okay. I want to fuck that up. With you."

He blinks, considering what I'm saying.

"I mean, we can pretend we're just going to be friends…"

"But you think we'll fail?" he asks.

I nod and smile. "Yeah. I want us to fail. I want to wake up in a few weeks with you and me as…as you and me. I don't care if it messes everything up that was supposed to be simple."

Noah's lips purse. At first I think he's hesitating; then I realize he's suppressing a smile. "I'd like that too."

I grin, reach out and squeeze his thigh. He straightens up, looking instantly confident.

"So, would you like to come to J.P. this Friday after work?" he asks.

"Okay."

"Cool. Meet me near the garage at five fifteen. I'll get us a copy of *Rosemary's Baby*."

I punch Noah gently on the sternum.

"*Firestarter*."

I hit him again.

"*Raging Bull*?"

"Better." I smile at him, feeling suddenly very shy. "Should I bring an overnight bag?"

Noah shakes his head with well-faked conviction. "No, we'll be good. I'll give you a ride home after."

"Okay." I'm a big girl. I can live without Noah's body for a night, maybe a few nights, if we decide to pay lip service to our half-assed attempt at staving off a romance. And if we do manage it, the fact that I could be carrying his child is physical intimacy enough for the immediate future. Plus I'll still have all the filthy-good sex memories to keep me going until we inevitably crack and wind up in bed together again. I give us about two weeks… But who am I kidding? I give us two *hours*.

I rub my thumbs over the backs of Noah's hands and let them go. "I'd like that."

"Me too." He drains his coffee, sets the mug beside the plastic wand for a second, then slides it farther down the counter, as if that spot is reserved for more significant objects. "Well, I should head back to Arlington. My sister's got more relatives due this afternoon. I've got my fingers crossed her in-laws might give my nephews *Garage Band* so I can totally commandeer it."

"Cool." I follow Noah to the living room and watch him get his coat and shoes back on. I follow him down the stairwell and out onto the front steps, savor a final study of his eyes in the silvery winter light. "What did you tell everyone when you disappeared to come over here?" I ask.

He grins. "I said a friend was having a tough time. That I'd be back when she was feeling better."

I return his warm smile, wrap my arms around him for a quick hug. "She is, thank you. I'm going to start composing my speech for when my parents get back from their trip—the big announcement and all." You're supposed to wait until twelve weeks to tell people, but I know myself too well.

"You should finish watching *It's a Wonderful Life*," he says. "I love that movie."

"Oh yeah. One of Scorsese's finest, I'm sure," I joke.

He puts his hand on my arm, gives it a little squeeze. "Merry Christmas, Abby."

"Merry Christmas. I'll see you Friday. Oh—that's New Year's Eve."

"I know. Is that okay?"

I think for a second about the symbolism of that evening, about new starts, the romantic adventure I suspect we're about to embark on together. I grin. "Yeah, that's just perfect."

He gives me a big smile and makes an *okay* ring with his thumb and finger. "I'll get you and the kid some sparkling cider."

The kid. I like that. "Thanks," I say. I scream it in my head, *thank you thank you thank you.*

He heads down the front walk and calls back, "We're going to be just fine, Abby."

"I know. Drive safe."

"I will. Keep the kid warm."

This time as I watch him drive away, it doesn't hurt. I watch his brake lights flash red as he reaches the corner, and warmth bursts in my chest. I run my hand over my stomach, poke it with my finger.

Your father's a very nice man, I tell my middle. He did a very nice thing for your crazy old mother, a nicer thing than anybody should be asked to.

I head upstairs out of the cold. I wash Noah's mug and set it in the rack, head back to the couch, and turn the movie back on. I watch it and I cry and I laugh. I smile as George Bailey runs screaming through the middle of Bedford Falls. I think about clothes—about tiny baby clothes and about what I might wear on New Year's Eve when I see Noah. I drum my fingers over my belly and look around my place, as content now as I was restless before. I decide I'll learn how to knit. I'll knit tiny socks and hats, maybe something homely but thoughtful for Noah, if that still seems advisable a month or more from now. Yes, I'll learn to knit very soon. But for now I have thank-yous to finish. I know whose to write next, but no clue what to say.

In the end I just write *Thanks* in the center of the card, slide it into its red envelope. I don't like the thought of it downstairs, waiting in the cold metal mailbox with the other notes, the ones saying thank you for earrings and gift cards and baked goods. No, I'll give it to him myself when I see him on Friday. I'll wave at him from across the park, and I won't know exactly who it is I'm looking at yet, but I'll suspect I'm looking at more than a friend, perhaps even more than the father of the child in my belly. Only time will tell, and that's exciting. Everything is exciting. Everything good and unexpected and scary that will happen to me this next year, everything I succeed at, and everything I royally fuck up, will be exciting.

And I will be just fine.

ABOUT THE AUTHOR

SINCE SHE BEGAN WRITING IN 2008, Cara McKenna has published nearly forty romances and erotic novels with a variety of publishers, sometimes under the pen names Meg Maguire and C.M. McKenna. Her stories have been acclaimed for their smart, modern voice and defiance of convention. She was a 2015 RITA Award finalist, a 2014 *RT* Reviewers' Choice Award winner, a 2012 and 2011 *RT* Reviewers' Choice Award nominee, and a 2010 Golden Heart Award finalist. She lives with her husband and son in the Pacific Northwest, though she'll always be a Boston girl at heart.

caramckenna.com
facebook.com/authorcaramckenna
twitter.com/caramckenna

ALSO BY CARA McKENNA

After Hours

Curio and the Curio Vignettes

Hard Time

Her Best Laid Plans

Shivaree: The Complete Series

Skin Game

Unbound

Willing Victim

THE SINS IN THE CITY SERIES

Crosstown Crush

Downtown Devil

THE DESERT DOGS SERIES

Lay It Down

Give It All

Drive It Deep

Burn It Up

AS C.M. McKENNA

Badger

AS MEG MAGUIRE

Caught on Camera

Headstrong

The Reluctant Nude

Thank You for Riding

Trespass

The Wedding Fling

Wild Holiday Nights

THE WILINSKI'S SERIES

All or Nothing

Going the Distance

Takedown